THE WOMAN
IN THE YARD

Also by Stephen E. Miller

Wastefall

THE WOMAN IN THE YARD

STEPHEN E. MILLER

PICADOR USA   NEW YORK

Picador® is a U.S. registered trademark and is used by St. Martin's Press under license from Pan Books Limited.

For information on Picador USA Reading Group Guides, as well as ordering, please contact the Trade Marketing department at St. Martin's Press. Phone: 1-800-221-7945 extension 763 Fax: 212-677-7456 E-mail: trademarketing@stmartins.com

Book Design: James Sinclair

Library of Congress Cataloging-in-Publication Data

Miller, Stephen E.
    The woman in the yard / by Stephen E. Miller.
       p.   cm.
    ISBN 0-312-19962-7 (hc)
    ISBN 0-312-26414-3 (pbk)
    I. Title.
PS3563.I42143W66   1999
813'.54—dc21   98-43849
                                                                              CIP

First Picador USA Paperback Edition: August 2000

10 9 8 7 6 5 4 3 2 1

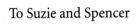

To Suzie and Spencer

My Lord calls me,
He calls me by thunder,
The trumpet sounds within my soul,
I ain't got long to stay here.

Steal away, steal away, steal away to Jesus.
Steal away, steal away, steal away home.

Green trees bending,
Poor sinner stands trembling,
The trumpet sounds within my soul,
I ain't got long to stay here.

—Traditional

THE WOMAN
IN THE YARD

ONE

She was a tramp.

Trash. That's all.

He could see it. See it in every movement that she made. Hear it in the ring of her voice. Feel it in the way other men turned their heads when she went by.

He watched her, too. That was his sin and he only noticed it too late. He tried not to think of her and he only thought about her more. He'd lie there in bed and think about nothing else. Miserable.

His own misery fascinated him. He never thought a human being could feel like this for another human being, that much pain. He'd just stare up at the ceiling, writhing away like a man in some fever until he exhausted himself and settled on the puzzle of trying to remember the first time he had seen her, really *seen her.*

And realized what she was. Why she was.

In a way, latching on to her like that made her his own. He was possessed by her long before he developed the ability to have her anytime he wanted. That's how much he was thinking about her that fall. Just lie back and bingo.

So what was stopping him? Finally, he decided that nothing was. Just go get her, he was thinking. Get her. Buy her? Why not? It was obvious that she didn't care who it was that came along.

He thought he might do that. Maybe he would. He thought about it, dreamed how it would go.

He'd get her, since it was either that or go crazy. And that way at least she'd be happy. She'd win that way.

And he would lie there and think about falling that low and how much it had cost him already.

He tried to stop. It wasn't that he didn't try.

But it had become an addiction by then. He had made a mistake once, he had seen another woman. Her, he thought, but when he got closer it was just another girl that looked like her. He just stood there laughing.

"What do you want?" she'd said to him, scared and angry, as he walked away.

He tried transferring it all to some other woman. It wasn't that they weren't available. But all he was doing was cutting off her head and putting on their bodies. That didn't work out so well.

He was lost, he finally decided. And he gave up for a while. He accepted that she'd won. She was going to be his first. He was an addict, helpless. She'd won already and at that moment he'd made up his mind.

He watched her. He might as well be invisible, she was so far off on her own. She didn't listen to anybody's rules at all.

She'd listen to him, he thought. She'd do that.

She liked men and music and money and power. All women liked that, he thought. No matter what they might say, they all went for it. He could see that clearly enough. It was like she was made of chrome and neon, like an advertisement. She was saying it, broadcasting it as loudly as possible. She admitted to what she was. Admitted it freely.

Okay. Okay, then, he thought.

Now he let himself think about her, let himself get hard thinking about the way her legs were, how her back curved, her breasts. He saw her smile at what she was doing to him. And he smiled back.

She still thought it was all a joke. She thought he was on her side. He might as well be invisible.

But she'd see him, he knew that now.

She'd smile like that again for him. He'd be her friend, someone she felt safe with, just another man for her to fool. That's what she'd think. If she thought about him at all.

She'd think of him. She'd think of him a lot. He'd fix it so that she thought of him just as much as he was thinking about her. She'd be amazed and dazzled by how much she found herself thinking about him.

She'd do things for him she'd never dreamed of.

TWO

Q.P. flinched. Curled back his arm suddenly and twisted around in his bed.

And then fell asleep again having got himself into an impossible pose, passed out from drinking too much New Year's eggnog. His head like a stone from the bourbon.

Not a drunk. Not falling down and slobbery. He didn't do that anymore, the price being too high, but yes, he could put it away. It was a real accomplishment, he sometimes thought. Late at night and all alone, still kicking himself over Marie, he'd put on a sweater and drink out on the porch and watch the stars and then he'd pass out in bed.

So that was Q.P., unconscious and dreaming, until the banging on his screen door finally woke him. Wind, he thought at first, but then he heard Nokes calling out for him to open up.

"'Scuse me, Sheriff, but you got to rise and shine . . ."

As the banging continued he managed some basic thoughts—was he awake or asleep? Who's that knocking on the screen? Is it a dream? And then he fell back into his war. It was Korea, but it could have been anywhere. He twisted into the covers, frightened. Scared in the dream-war and scared that when he woke people would say he was just another crazy veteran.

Shards of his past were mixed all through the dream. Flickerings of the woman he imagined becoming his wife not so long ago. Flickerings of his life stateside. And then the dream of Marie got mixed up with the gunfire and he jerked up in bed and snapped into reality as his deputy, Donald Nokes, jimmied the lock and let himself in.

"Goddamn, I sure hope you don't keep nothin' of value in here, Kewpie, I sure do . . . How come your phone's off the hook? Where *is* the phone?" Nokes was kicking his way through the place, re-arranging things with his boots, stumbling around in the dark. He would be bringing news, always bringing news. Always something important. Always something bad. The door kept banging. Just wind, he tried to believe.

"It's a woman they found. Washed up down at the radar base," Nokes said.

Q.P. managed to sit up on the bed and get himself dressed, grabbed his revolver, and took it with him to put on later. He took his time down the steps, still shaky and chilled from his bourbon nightmares.

"You gonna be all right, Kewpie?" Nokes reached out but was a little shy of actually helping him down the stairs.

"Yeah, I'm fine," Q.P. said firmly, meaning *Just shut up.* The wind was pounding against the side of the house, coming from the northeast. Nokes got him outside to the car. It was going to be a long drive across town and then all the way down to Fort Fisher.

Quentin Payne Waldeau, the "Acting Sheriff" of New Hanover County, North Carolina, wedged himself into the corner of the seat, put his temple against the cold metal of the Chevy's window, braced one shoe against the base of the radio, and tried to go back to sleep and get back to Marie.

Before Nokes got to the end of Orange Street, he made it as far as Korea. Endless frozen mud; endless cold. So cold that everything hurt, so cold his .45 froze solid once and to thaw it out he put it deep inside his jacket. He walked around like that, with this heavy freezing hunk of metal stuck in his belt. What good would it do him in there? Too cold to care about killing Commies.

Q.P. jounced in and out of consciousness as Nokes drove down the peninsula. He kept trying to float back to the place where Marie was dressed in blue. And laughing. No guilt, no resentment. And happy. Happy with him, happy with everything. Nokes turned on the radio. The only thing on was some kind of bluegrass. He'd turned it on on purpose and Q.P. sighed and straightened in the seat and blinked himself awake. Nokes looked over. "I think this is going to blow right over us, you know?"

"Yeah. Might do that," he said.

As far back as Q.P. could remember he'd wanted to be a cop. Not a flatfoot or a motorcycle cop but a detective. A detective in the hard-boiled sense. As a job he'd figured it would be exciting and he'd met a few cops by way of his aunt. So when he had a chance to decide, he thought getting into the military police would be a good start in this career direction. But it turned out that in Korea it was the officers who did all the detecting. Being a police-man in the army equated to two years of rounding up drunk servicemen out of the bars and whorehouses, and endless pa-trolling of rows of identical Quonset huts in a fruitless attempt to scare the looters away.

There had been no unusual crimes to solve, no intricate myster-ies. Nothing interesting to do when he was off duty, and as it turned out, nothing that qualified him for police work back in the States. All through the first year after he got back he tried to get into police departments; in Philadelphia, Baltimore, Richmond, and in Wash-ington, D.C. Nothing. It was simple. They liked him. On paper he was great, but there were no vacancies and the guys who had come back from Europe or the Pacific were already there ahead of him. He was one war too late, they said.

So he drifted around Baltimore, sponging off old friends, fell hard for Marie, and got shit for his trouble, then he got depressed and got to drinking too much. Heading for the skids, his aunt Yvonne said. Well, she would know, having been there herself.

He'd finally lucked into a place as a deputy to the sheriff of New Hanover County, North Carolina. The contact had been made for him by a cop on the Baltimore force, a friend of his aunt's who'd liked him and had helped him through the job-seeking labyrinth.

When it came Q.P. had to read the letter through a couple of times before he realized it was a real job offer. New Hanover County? North Carolina? He'd scrounged up a greasy road map of the Eastern seaboard and found New Hanover County down at the bottom corner of the state. Down on the beach. Shaped into a triangle with its point teased into a long sandbar tail by the con-verging forces of the Cape Fear and the Atlantic. County seat was

Wilmington, he read. From the size of the circle on the map, it was almost a city. Fifty thousand people.

"A job at the beach" was the first thing he thought. Why not?

They had given him two weeks to get down there, but he had left early after giving Marie a call that he really handled badly, saying too much. Words he couldn't ever take back. Well, she wasn't going to change any, was she?

He woke up as Nokes bumped over pavement that had buckled along the coast road. So here he was.

Hell with Marie, he thought.

"Why are we going down to the radar base anyway?" he called over to Nokes. His voice was hoarse, clogged up from sleeping. He coughed and rolled his head around trying to wake up.

"Well, Kewpie, you know that 'drifted down' is what they're going to say."

"Yeah . . . drifted down. Shit . . ." It was about what Q.P. had been thinking, too. Was the victim killed down on the base or somewhere upriver and then did the body float down onto federal property from the county? Jurisdiction. That's what being a sheriff was all about, he was beginning to realize, how to seize or avoid jurisdiction. Not so much power but the limits of power. Where your authority stopped and someone else's took over.

He hadn't realized any of these peculiar occupational intricacies when he had taken the train down to Wilmington and settled into being a deputy.

It turned out that Wilmington's population was around thirty-five thousand, having dropped more or less steadily since V-J day. But if it wasn't exactly bustling, it was still an active port city and it got its healthy share of crime. Right off he got along well with Sheriff Franklin, who had known the cop in Baltimore who had set him up. Mary Helen, the department secretary, knew a place up at the end of Orange Street that was for rent at something she figured he could afford. So he took it and installed himself out on the porch and sat there and watched the sunset and made up his mind to be careful about the bourbon and do a good job.

It didn't take long to realize that he was a member of a lackluster department. In Wilmington it was the police who were supposed to be the hard-boiled detectives. But over the next year, Franklin took him under his wing, introduced him to all the important people, and began delegating more and more responsibility his way. It was as if the old man knew what was coming. And when it did, when Franklin suffered a series of strokes, the county commissioners met and, complying with his wishes, voted Q.P. "Acting Sheriff." The job came with a thirty percent raise, a commitment to serving out Franklin's term, and the almost certain obligation of running for Franklin's position in the upcoming elections.

He reached over and adjusted the heat in the car and jammed his hands deeper into his jacket and tried to go back to sleep.

He should be counting his blessings, he thought.

He did actually manage to conk out until Nokes turned off the pavement and bumped onto the potholed Davis Beach Road, just inside the boundaries of the air force radar station.

"They don't hardly use this place anymore," Nokes said. "They used to have submarines down here. Submarine *pens,* yeah. Had 'em all down through here. Couldn't get up this road at all during the War. They had it locked up tight. We used to try to hunt down here and they'd get all over you . . ."

The road to Davis Beach had existed long before the radar base, of course. It was the kind of road that couples liked to drive down, with room at the end for two or three cars to park with enough space to ensure a certain amount of discretion. But the war had eliminated the popular parking spot; now the only people who stopped there were air force sentries to run an occasional fisherman off the beach. Nokes pulled off the side and parked. They walked down to the river past a row of light gray Jeeps and an air force ambulance, a large red cross painted on its side.

If anything, the wind was strengthening and he pulled his collar tighter around his neck. How could the South be so cold? he wondered as they walked down the ruts to the beach. There were about a dozen air force types standing around at the top of the little bluff that ended Davis Beach Road. They all looked around when Q.P. and Nokes walked up. Behind them he could see the long darkness of the Cape Fear as it surged toward the ocean. The rain had started again and the flyboys were breaking out their slickers. Down on the sand at their feet was something covered up with a canvas tarp.

It's not too bad was the first thing he thought . . .

In the early light of dawn she looked steel blue. Someone played a flashlight beam across her body and he saw that her arms were cruelly bound behind her back, pulled tight and tied in four places—shoulder, above and below the elbows, and at the wrists. Her legs had been pulled behind her and then her ankles knotted to her wrists. *Hog-tied,* they called it in the South. Now that the county cops were on the scene, the airmen were leaving in ones and twos. The rest stood around smoking and waiting for someone to decide what to do.

A flashbulb illuminated the body.

"She looks real young, to me," Nokes said quietly as they squatted there with the air force men standing around in a ring above them. "Just a little nigger girl . . ."

Of course, nobody knew her.

The two sentries explained how they'd pulled up at the foot of Davis Beach Road and one man went down the slope to take a leak and saw her caught up in the dead branches of a live oak that had fallen into the river there. They'd called it in and waited for the O.C. to come and tell them what to do. The officer-in-charge was a tired lieutenant who was eager to get his men and himself out of the weather in time for the changing of the guard. He was the one who had made sure she was carried up to the road where the current wouldn't pull her off the branches and sweep her down to the ocean. The way he put it, it was pretty obvious that the woman had been dumped somewhere north of Davis Beach. "Our post boundary is just through those woods there, see, just right up there, only about a hundred yards upriver," he explained.

For a few moments Q.P. held on to the hope that the body had somehow drifted *across* the river, from Brunswick County, but he'd gone out fishing in the Cape Fear enough times to know that something like that was a long shot. Stupid idea to even think of it.

The lieutenant was looking down at him a little strangely, frowning, like he didn't believe that someone as young as Q.P. was actually who he said he was. "I'll have a detail take her to the hospital or wherever else you want, Sheriff," he said.

"Well, all right, then," he said as he got up and walked down to the bank and looked out at the water. The river widened out here; it was almost a mile across to Brunswick County. In this weather the current was too fast to idle along fishing; if you didn't watch, you'd run aground on one of the bars that were constantly forming and reforming along the banks.

He realized that all the men up at the road were waiting on him.

"All right, then," he said loudly to make himself heard over the wind. She'd almost certainly been killed within his jurisdiction. His case.

"Get your boys to take her in to Beverly's," Nokes told the lieutenant, who had wrapped himself inside his slicker and was already walking back to his Jeep and his early breakfast. There was a whine and a growl as someone started the big ambulance motor, and the road was flooded by diesel fumes until the wind shifted.

He managed get to sleep again in the car going back, and this time he didn't dream at all.

THREE

"You don't look so good . . ." Mary Helen, the secretary, had come in his office on the pretext of replacing a vase of cut flowers that she'd started to freshen regularly, a way of having access to the inner sanctum, Q.P. realized.

"Yeah . . . I just, uh . . . dozed off there . . ." He grabbed reflexively at the papers on his blotter. Tried to look busy. The writing on the reports in front of him made absolutely no sense at all. Did he black out?

"Here you go, Sheriff." She had gone out and come back with a cup of coffee. He tried to take a sip but it was too hot.

"Well," she said, "while you've been immersed in your paperwork, all hell has broken loose again, I swear." It was his cue to ask her to fill him in.

"What?" he said as he attempted to sip a tiny amount of superheated coffee.

"Are you sure you want to know?" She went over and pulled open the venetian blinds. "That storm went right over top of us," she mused. To Q.P. the room suddenly flooded with light. He shut his eyes. "I'll tell you if you're sure you're ready for it . . ."

"Okay, okay," he mumbled.

"Overnight we had two admissions to the Fifth Floor. First was Lonnie Conners—"

"Drunk and assault . . ."

"So it's right back out to the farm for him, probably before the weekend, and then a woman—"

"Okay . . ."

"Colored gal, Mrs. Dolly Talcott. She put down that she's a maid over at the hotel. Got into a fight and fell down some stairs. They went and got Dr. Terry out of bed to see her—"

"Oh, God," Q.P. moaned. Terry was in with the NAACP and he'd raise as much shit as he was capable of if there was anything wrong with the woman.

"Who'd she get in a fight with?"

"The assistant manager and then some other woman that came out in the hall from somewhere, they *all* got into it, I guess. I don't know . . ."

"Okay, okay . . ."

"And then this morning first off Mr. Sanders phoned. Lamont Sanders? Sanders Construction?"

"Mmm . . ."

"Fit to be tied. Not the most polite man I've ever talked to on the phone. He's all het up 'cause he says there's a burglar casing his home."

"So what?" Q.P. knew Sanders. He was the patriarch of the largest construction firm in the southern part of the state and one of the richest men in town.

"So what? Kewpie, he says there's a *burglar casing his house*—"

"He lives in the city."

"That's what I told him, but he wants everybody to get to work on it. The Wilmington P.D. *and* the Department. He says it's a man in a Pontiac car hanging around out there at his business. He says if he sees him again he's going to shoot him."

"Jesus . . ." He shook his head in despair. It felt like there was a hot ball bearing rolling from one temple to the other. "Mary Helen, he lives in *Forest Hills*. We're not supposed to do anything about that. That's in the *city*, that's completely outside our jurisdiction," Q.P. heard himself starting to whine. He finally managed to sip a mouthful of incredibly bitter, near-poisonous coffee.

"Well, *I* know, but his business is out there on Sparger Road and *that's* in the county, and the city itself is in the county, too, so . . . I told him you'd look into it."

"Great, yeah . . . okay. Is there any aspirin?" He made a mental note to check out the report from Sanders, get a description of the car. It might be linked to a ring of safecrackers who had been plaguing businesses in Wilmington and the surrounding counties, but he couldn't believe they'd be so inept as to case out a target in the middle of the day.

He leaned back in Franklin's huge chair. It was the one extravagance in the tiny office that was otherwise devoted to filing cabinets and stacks of paper. Around the walls were framed awards and photographs of several generations of Franklins. It would be indecent to take them down so soon, Mary Helen had said quietly, even if it just made it more obvious that he was filling out Franklin's term until he somehow won an election on his own.

Mary Helen came back with two aspirins, which he immediately proceeded to drop on the floor. She stood there in silence watching him grub around on the floor under the desk.

"I guess y'all were out real late last night down at the radar base, weren't ya?" He had found one tablet but the other had disappeared into thin air.

"Real early is more like it."

"Kewpie, you don't have to go out on a call like that, if you don't want to. You can always delegate authority, you know? Especially on a holiday."

"Umm," he muttered, stirring up a little cloud of dust from under the desk.

"Assuming you're takin' the democratic process seriously, there's other, more important things you should be pursuin'," she said.

He found the other tablet hiding behind the corner leg of the desk, climbed up and put the surprisingly bitter pills on his tongue, and then tried to choke them down with the too-hot coffee.

Mary Helen watched him gag. "Oh, and they think there's a vampire over in Bladenboro . . ." He raised his neck and made a little gasping sound, trying to free the dried aspirin from his gullet.

"Well . . . I guess it's probably not a real *vampire,* but they've found about a dozen sheep over there that have been completely drained of blood, and some dogs have been all torn up. There's a write-up about it in the paper. See?" She pointed to a headline on the front page of the Wilmington *Morning Star:*

Bladenboro Beast Eludes Hunters

"Ahh . . . Jesus . . ." he muttered, finally choking the pills down.

"Y'all can read that at your leisure, Sheriff," she said and went out to fill the vase. Mary Helen had been working at the department since she was a teenager, sometime way back in the Coolidge administration. As far as Q.P. knew, she'd never missed a day of work, and although she never seemed to actually do anything, she was an unending source of information—much of it conflicting, yet at times uncannily accurate. For Mary Helen, life centered in the basement offices of the New Hanover County Sheriff's Department. Down under the courthouse she ran everything with an invisible iron hand, manipulating the careers and love lives of anyone employed or associated with the department. She was called the "Queen Bee" and the nickname was utterly accurate. She was proud of it, thinking it was a reference to the beehive embroidered on the shoulder patches of both the Wilmington police and the sheriff's department uniforms.

Mary Helen had never married, but it was alleged that over the years she had submitted to the occasional advances of law enforcement personnel in the backseats of various vehicles. And although there were no actual witnesses to any of these trysts, the stories were accepted as truth. It didn't seem to bother Mary Helen. If she liked you, and Q.P. guessed that she liked him, she was a provider of secrets and gossip. She knew people talked about her, because that's what all people did—they talked behind your back.

She came back with the mail and put it on his blotter with kind of an unusual look and then spun around and left.

Right on top was a manila envelope from the North Carolina State Bureau of Investigation. He fussed with the envelope, finally using Franklin's letter opener—an ivory hula dancer with bare breasts and rhinestone eyes. Inside was a long form letter explaining the qualifications for admission to the Bureau and an application.

In North Carolina the SBI functioned as a big-brother agency, supplying personnel and expertise to local police and sheriff's departments when needed. It also held jurisdiction over crimes committed on state property or against state employees. The SBI ran the only real crime lab in the state and attempted to coordinate efforts to track criminals who might have fled one jurisdiction for another within the state. SBI agents wore suits and ties just like their counterparts in the FBI and they were often brought in to solve cases that were beyond the depth of the locals.

An SBI agent needed a thorough knowledge of North Carolina criminal law and ideally should have laboratory or accounting skills. Field agents spent a lot of time on the road, but they were reimbursed for their expenses. Altogether Q.P. figured he'd be making more as a field agent than he was even on Franklin's salary, and in his imagination the job would be much more exciting. A ticket out of New Hanover County.

Q.P. folded the application back into the envelope and tucked it in the corner of the blotter. There was no point in keeping it secret, since Mary Helen probably knew all about it anyway, but he'd fill it out once he got back home, since it probably wouldn't wash too well with any of the county commissioners, should they chance to wander in, to catch him busy applying for another job while supposedly attending to his duties as sheriff.

Nokes came in and settled back in the chair and stretched his long legs. He rubbed his almost nonexistent red hair roughly. "I sure am tired. I think I got a goddamn cold," he said disgustedly and gave another exaggerated stretch. "How're you doing, Kewpie?"

"Mmm, that's right . . ." he muttered. He may have fallen asleep for a second or two; he wasn't sure.

"You look pretty dangerous," Nokes said and started laughing.

"I'm feeling kind of dangerous, you know?" He said to the deputy as severely as he could, looking straight at Nokes.

"It's Dr. Sykes on the phone, Sheriff," Mary Helen called to him from the door. Sykes was the coroner who would be examining the dead girl they'd found. "He says he'll see you at four. Is that good?" she asked.

Nokes looked up at him with a sour expression. "Shit . . ." he said under his breath.

"Yeah," Q.P. said, "that's just great."

FOUR

"Where the hell've you been, Mr. Waldeau?" Dr. Timothy Sykes straightened up from the porcelain sink he was leaning against. He was dressed in a fisherman's rubber apron and wore a pair of rubber gloves. "I gotta get going, goddamn it."

On the table in front of him the dead girl had been placed on her stomach, her hands and legs still tied behind her. The air force tarp had been thrown over in a corner of the room where Nathan Giddings, one of the Beverly cousins, waited quietly, almost invisibly.

"Sorry, Doc. We got held up out there a little," Q.P. said. Sykes was a gross, weedy little man but, because of some arcane law, as the county coroner, he was the only person who could officially fire a sheriff. The difficulty was, he knew it.

"Can I cut these goddamn things, yes?" He stuck out a finger and gave the rope that held the Negro girl's ankles to her wrists a twang. Q.P. shrugged.

"Sure," Nokes said. Sykes already had started. "Help me out," he said as he rolled the girl over. Nokes reached out and hesitated for a moment before grabbing her ankles.

"I have some equipment, if you need it, sir," said Giddings from the corner of the room.

"Goddamn it," Sykes said around his cigarette, "help me out, here, I gotta get *going*. I've gotta be at the goddamn church . . ."

Q.P. reached over and put his hand under the girl's cold shoulder and together the three of them rolled her over onto her back. "I can tell you right now what killed her," Sykes said, puffing a little. He made a quick incision down the center of her chest between her breasts and another long cut across the top of her stomach. Beside him Nokes let out a long sigh.

"Don't throw up on me, Deputy," Sykes warned him as he worked. "You throw up, go do it out the goddamn door. Y'all don't want him throwing up in here, do you, Mr. Giddings?"

"No, sir, we sure don't."

"Thank you," said Nokes quietly.

"All right, I can tell you right now: she was strangled and died of asphyxiation *before* whoever did it threw her in the water, and— Can I go ahead and cut this here?" His scalpel was poised at the ropes that were tied around her shoulders.

"Sure, sure . . ." Q.P. said quickly. He wanted to get out of there, too. Sykes's scalpel snicked out and the ropes fell away. He reached up and pulled the light down to inspect the girl's skin.

"All right, she was killed while she was tied up, and—" He moved his scalpel up to her neck and cut the double cords around it. There was a little wheezing sound from the girl's throat. Like a gasp.

"Oh, gee . . ." Nokes said, beside him.

"All right, she was strangled with these ropes. Whoever did it tried this'n here round her neck and probably stuck a stick or something back here and turned it up tight like a tourniquet. That's how come she didn't sink on you, Mr. Waldeau, okay?" Sykes poised there for a second.

"What about . . ." Q.P. said.

"I can't find any sperm in there, she's in the water too long. Shit . . ." He quickly moved to the foot of the table and stuck his finger in the girl's vagina. "Goddamn . . ." he said under his breath and reached up and pulled the light down so that it was shining directly on the girl's crotch. "Shit . . ." he said again and then reached over and grabbed something that looked like a circular pair of forceps from the tray beside the table. He twisted it into the girl's vagina and clamped the handles open, a stream of dirty water and blood dribbled out onto the white porcelain.

"'Scuse me . . ." Nokes said, heading for the door.

"All right, she's got scars and some bruising here, so I *do* think she was raped. I don't know why the hell anybody's going to go to all the trouble to kill somebody like this and not take advantage of the opportunity to get a little, you know?" He smiled up at Q.P. and laughed.

"And she's got some old scars. These're from VD. Probably a hooker, wouldn't you say?" he asked as he appraised the dead girl's body. "Probably did all right for herself there for a while. I don't know if you'd call this rape or not," Sykes laughed. "Probably a heart attack is what killed her. Hell, somebody took my clothes off and tied me up like that, I'd have a heart attack, too."

He took a final drag from his cigarette and brushed his fingers across the girl's thigh. There were some marks there, a design raised on her skin.

"What's that?" Q.P. asked. He reached up and moved the light to a lower angle so the marks showed up better. Standing close, he could smell the girl starting to decompose, Sykes's cologne, the tobacco on his breath. Giddings came over and looked in.

"Y'all know what that is, right there, Mr. Giddings?"

Giddings wrinkled up his face for a second and peered down at the girl's leg. "That looks to me like something bit her," he said.

"Like she got caught in something?" Q.P. was trying to see it. The marks looked like they might have a pattern.

Giddings reached out and stretched the skin on her thigh. "Some kind of voodoo marks, it looks like maybe," he said.

"Nah, hell, that's nothin'. Goddamn bruise . . ." Sykes put his thumb over the mark so they could see it was a bruise.

"We had her down as a juvenile," Q.P. said, looking at the girl again; hardly any breasts at all, thin with a peaceful little face. No makeup that he could see. She looked about twelve, he would've said.

"Juvenile, my ass. She's about twenty. That's old enough, ain't it, Nate?"

"If the Sheriff here say so, I guess it is," Giddings said from over in the corner, laughing.

"Goddamn right, she's old enough. Nice little ass. I bet she did all right. Okay, I gotta get out of here. My wife'll cut my balls off if I'm not at the church by five." He pulled the apron off and hung it over the edge of the sink.

"Time of death is maybe a maximum twenty-four hours ago. I did the prints already. Nate's got 'em, and I'll do the paperwork in

the morning if that's all right with you, Sheriff," Sykes said, meaning that he'd do it in the morning regardless if it was all right or not.
"You got a name on her?"

"Nope."

"All right then, 'Unidentified Nig—'" Sykes caught himself in
time. "'*Negro* female.' I got to get my ass out of here. See you, Nate,"
he said to Giddings as he headed out the back door to the parking
lot.

"Yes, sir. God bless you," Giddings said behind him as he went.

Q.P. walked over to the table. Sykes had left the expanding forceps inside her. He felt like taking it out but he didn't know how it
worked. Nokes came back inside and lit a cigarette over by the door.
Giddings moved to the head of the table and adjusted the light so it
fell on the girl's face from above her.

"You know, Sheriff," Giddings said quietly as he worked, "I think
I've seen this young lady around town, but I sure couldn't tell you
what her name was." When he was satisfied that he'd rearranged the
girl's features into something less horrible, he gave up trying to
bend her neck down to a normal angle and went to the cupboard
and came back with his camera and some flashbulbs.

"Where do you think you've seen her?"

Giddings stood there and thought about it for a second. "I don't
know, but it wasn't at church, I don't think."

"Maybe at a funeral?"

"Yes, sir . . . Maybe it was something like that." Giddings came
around the table and put the camera up to his eye.

"Well, if it comes to you, Mr. Giddings, just phone us up."

"I certainly will do that thing, I certainly will . . ." Giddings
spread his feet apart and lowered his body so that he was at table
level and then leaned over, held himself steady.

"That's nice right there," he said.

FIVE

Sitting by the window of his apartment over the weekend, Q.P. sipped bourbon, pondered his SBI application, and combed through a stack of missing persons' reports he had brought home with him.

The SBI application was a little problematic, he figured, in that he didn't exactly qualify for the Bureau and was going to have to fudge a little. Not tell any lies exactly, and carefully not dummy up anything the SBI could check up on, but simply accentuate the positive and definitely eliminate the negative.

He had his high school and he had his MP time in Korea, and it certainly wouldn't hurt being a county sheriff, except that there was a not so subtle discrimination against county law enforcement. Ironically any of his deputies would have a better chance getting into the SBI than he would. In North Carolina a sheriff was an elected position, and it was not uncommon to find county sheriffs who owed their jobs to their association with local bigwigs. To get the job you had to get nominated by the local Democratic Party, and what sometimes happened was that sheriffs were elected who had little or no prior police experience.

What the SBI was after was someone who was deliberately *not* connected locally. So, as he thought about how he'd phrase his letter of application, he realized he should emphasize that he had been *hired,* not elected, and was an "Acting Sheriff" because of Franklin's untimely passing. Some little detail like that might make the difference, he thought.

When the SBI problem got too frustrating, he sorted through the list of people who'd gone missing in New Hanover County over the last year. When he got done he'd come up with twenty-seven names of Negro women, but nobody had reported a Negro woman missing in the last few days. Nothing.

He tried a rough draft of the SBI letter, got as far as "I would like to be a member of the SBI because . . ." and then ended up sitting motionless looking out on the river for nearly an hour. Stuck. How could he explain that he just wanted to be a detective and solve crimes? And lurk in dark alleys, and lean on stoolies and puzzle out who was guilty or innocent from the flimsiest of clues? And wear a suit and a trench coat and a fedora, instead of his stupid sheriff's hat? If he even tried to put that on paper, it would sound stupid. It sounded stupid just thinking about it. The SBI probably didn't give a damn about how he *felt* about being an agent. They just wanted to see if he could write a reasonable letter. It was an application, not a piece of scripture. He made up his mind to go dig through the files at the department and paraphrase a letter somebody else had written applying for a deputy's job. Just use whatever reasons they might have been able to invent for wanting a career in law enforcement.

He decided he would cook something, made a sandwich instead, and then tried filling out the N.C. State Employee questionnaire with all his job experience and biographical information. He had to go back and count up what years he was in Baltimore and look up the addresses for his former residences. Some of it he had forgotten and would have to telephone Baltimore to get right. There was a space for the place of birth of his grandparents, and for his father's side he wrote in Lowell, Massachusetts, instead of Quebec, thinking that having some foreign blood, even that far back, might work against him.

On every page of the questionnaire was a warning that to knowingly falsify any information was punishable by a lengthy jail term and a fine. There was a long list of organizations that it was apparently illegal to belong to. Included was every possible variation of Communist or Socialist Parties; there was the "American Communist Party" and the "Communist Party of America," evidently two separate organizations. There were also several varieties of the Knights of the White Camellia and the Ku Klux Klan, since these organizations, for reasons probably diametrically opposed to those of the Communists, also advocated the overthrow of the U.S. government. There were various committees with ambiguous names that Q.P. honestly couldn't be sure he'd heard of or not. *Sons of American Heritage, Workers' Peace Committee for Freedom, League for* this, that, and the other . . .

It got dark and he ended up tossing the files and the application on the floor and spreading out on the couch and listening to Dick Haymes on the radio. He finished the rest of his allotment of bourbon and fell asleep and didn't dream of Marie or of Korea either for once.

Monday morning there was a fresh pile of paperwork and a *Morning Star* that Mary Helen had brought in and piled on the center of his blotter. About halfway down Monday morning's front-page was a dark headline:

Beast Kills Two More

Apparently a farmer had lost two of his best coon hounds to the Beast. The animals were ripped to shreds in the middle of the night. Before the man could get to his gun the Thing, whatever it was, had gone, leaving huge tracks, like a panther or an alligator, as it escaped across his yard. The article said that a group of nearly sixty farmers had gone out hunting that same night and found nothing. It wasn't surprising, since they had been combing an area way over on the other side of Bladenboro, miles away from the attack.

The phone rang and he found himself caught up in making sense out of a complaint that was being made on behalf of Dolly Talcott by D. L. Terry, of Utner, Whale & Terry, Wilmington's most successful black law firm. Terry was contending that the Talcott woman had been beaten while she was up on the Fifth Floor. Q.P. phoned up there as soon as he'd read through the complaint and got Mrs. Baker.

"So what the hell happened up there?" he asked her.

"Woke me up, I'll tell you that," she said. Mrs. Baker was deep in her fifties and weighed in at a solid two hundred.

"Well . . ."

"She was real drunk, Kewpie. Drunk out of her head."

"Did you have to subdue her, or—"

"She was beat up when she got here. That complaint is just hogwash."

"When did you call Dr. Terry?"

"When she started throwin' up. I thought it looked like she was throwin' up blood, but it might have been some wine or somethin'."

"And you didn't have to wrestle with her?"

"No, sir. She didn't want to get in the cell, but we didn't have to work her too hard."

"All right," he said and hung up. If something different had happened, she wasn't going to tell him right out. A few minutes later Spud Reid phoned down and told him not to worry about the complaint, that the county would handle it by dinnertime.

He got back to the paper again and fumed awhile over a long, glowing article about how Woody Forbes over in Brunswick County had broken a ring of thieves who had been robbing shrimp houses since August. They'd been stealing anything they could get. Money, cigarettes, shrimp. They even stole ice out of the bait locker. They had the combined forces of five or six counties looking for them. But now Forbes had rounded up all seven of the thieves, including two of their wives, in the early hours of New Year's Day. Right about the time he was standing in the rain down at Fort Fisher, he realized.

Q.P. tossed the paper in the waste can and walked out into the corridor and got himself a coffee from the urn. Forbes wouldn't have to worry about reelection this term, he thought, not with a write-up like that spread all over Brunswick County from Southport all the way to the Wilmington bridge.

Mary Helen put one hand over the receiver of her phone. "Guess what?" she said. There wasn't any way out of it. He'd have to guess.

"Okay, I give up."

"Wilmington City P.D. is inducting five new officers; one's colored and, get this, one's a *woman*." She smiled and rolled her eyes.

"Wow . . ." he said. "That is news."

He went back and hid out in the office and drank his coffee and then got embroiled on the phone with Bucky Nelson, who was deputy chief of police, about a plan that was being cooked up to catch the safecracking ring. It was a stupid plan from the beginning, he told Bucky, who didn't seem to be hearing him very well.

While he listened to Bucky's strategizing, he fished the paper out of the garbage and was reading about how a ten-year-old boy in Aulander had lived in a barn for five days with nothing to eat but pecans and crackers because he was scared his father would whip him, when Nokes popped in. He held up one of Giddings's eight-by-tens of the dead girl they'd fished out of the river.

"Got her" was all he said.

SIX

He and Nokes met the two neighbor women who had recognized the photograph at Beverly's. They were crying and wailing together with little wads of Kleenex balled up in their hands. It took a while to calm them down.

Her name was Cora Snow, they said. Barely in her twenties, born and raised right in Wilmington. She was a party girl, they said, but nice all the same. Her family was just about gone and she didn't have anybody to take care of her, so what choice did she have?

No, she wasn't married, but she had a boyfriend. Nokes had already got the name: William Scowen, a fisherman and a tough customer. "Red Billy," the women said he was called on account of his light-colored hair. He'd been living with Cora in a little house up on the corner of Eighth and Castle Streets. He was a mean man, they said. They'd kept late hours and it was a noisy house. Sometimes there were fights and music coming out of there, they said.

After they'd told him all about Scowen, the women had recovered enough so that Mr. Beverly figured they were ready to go into the back. Q.P. and Nokes followed along down the hall, through the swinging doors to the embalming room. Giddings had managed to straighten the girl's legs out somehow and she was covered with a sheet.

"Oh, Lord . . . oh, Lord," one of the women started moaning as soon as they'd come in. She approached the table with one arm out as if she were going to lay hands on the girl and try to bring her back to life.

Beverly got there ahead of her and the woman stopped, with her arm still outstretched, trembling like it was electrified. He reached over and pulled the top of the sheet down so she could see.

"Is this her, Miz Bess?" Beverly asked in his quietest voice. The other woman came up to the table and they both immediately erupted into a whole fresh set of tears and wailing. "Okay, okay, Miz Bess." Mr. Beverly escorted them out into the foyer, got them little paper cups of water, passed out more Kleenex.

There was another man there waiting for them. Tall and absolutely motionless. He stood lit from behind so that they couldn't see his face, but then he stepped forward into the light and Q.P. saw that he was a preacher.

Q.P. and Nokes watched while he had a quiet conversation with Beverly and Giddings, all of them looking very grim, and then he detached himself and came over to where the women were sitting rocking back and forth and crying. He knelt down on the carpet and held their hands and spoke with them for a few moments.

"Who's this bird?" Nokes whispered beside him.

"Got me" was all Q.P. said. They watched while the trio prayed together for a moment, and then the tall preacher got up, bracing himself with one hand on the bench as he raised himself on his long legs. He came right over to where Q.P. and Nokes were standing by an old-fashioned water cooler that Beverly had installed beside the entrance.

"Sheriff, I'm Reverend Gaylord Chaffee. I came over soon as I heard about poor Sister Cora."

Chaffee was a lean man, and tall, nearly half a foot taller than Q.P., who stood an even six feet in his socks. His face was creased and pockmarked so deeply that the first image that came to Q.P.'s mind was of a burned log. The eyes were so dark that Q.P. couldn't see the pupils, and when they shook hands, Q.P. felt the rough calluses and strong grip of a man who was still doing a lot of outside work even though he must have been going on toward sixty.

"I've come to lend my support any way I can. Cora was a good sweet child and she sure didn't deserve to be killed." He looked over to Beverly and Giddings, who were standing with their hands clasped in front of them, looking like undertakers.

"Did you know her very well?" Q.P. asked.

"Oh, yes. I knew her from when she was a little girl. And I know William, too. They both attend services from time to time, though he wouldn't have come unless she made him, I don't think." Chaffee smiled. It was only a small movement at the corners of his mouth.

"Do you know where this Scowen boy is now?" Nokes asked. Chaffee gave him a long look.

"No, sir. I don't. Brother William gets around. He could be fishing, might be at a baseball game or getting drunk someplace. He could be just about anywhere, I reckon."

Chaffee was one of the holy men who ministered to Negro Wilmington; his church was over on the north side of town in the neighborhood called Brooklyn. Chaffee's parish was populated mostly by illiterate workers, drifters and unemployed fishermen, prostitutes and their handlers, and an occasional genius. It was the territory of Negroes trying to escape the cotton and tobacco fields and white trash who had lost just about everything. There were plenty of good people in Brooklyn; there was joy and resurrection up there and some Negroes who, against all the odds, were climbing the pyramid of postwar success. But they tended to move over a few streets when they had the chance, somewhere quieter, where their kids could play. So Brooklyn kept its seamy side; juke joints and bootleg whiskey. Morphine and hopheads; arguments, desperation, beaten wives, and misery. Children who were forgotten and wouldn't be remembered until it was too late.

The Wilmington P.D. mostly ignored the area unless they were feeling particularly mean on a Saturday night. Then they'd go in and clean up what was left from a razor fight, beat up the niggers who dared to look back, or maybe push around some of the poor white mill workers who'd come down from the Blue Ridge and were still lost two generations later.

"They say that this Scowen spends some time on the edge, what I hear," Q.P. said.

"William's had his problems, that's for sure. But if you think he did this, I think you're goin' wrong before you start."

"Why's that?" Nokes said. He sounded angry for some reason.

"On account of it's a white man that killed her is what I think."

Chaffee was standing there with his hands clasped, looking down into Q.P.'s eyes. Waiting. Judging.

"And why do you say that, Reverend?"

"People saw a white man who'd been over at her house, and William was never the kind to do something like this."

"People change," Nokes said.

"Yes, they do."

"It still could have been Scowen. He's a high yellow, right?" Nokes said. Chaffee turned and looked over at the deputy. His eyes had narrowed. Nokes looked like he was getting ready to start throwing the old man around.

"William is very light complected, that's true enough, but people can still tell the difference, don't you think?"

"You goddamn right, they can," Nokes said and walked away before he said anything else. They watched him stalk outside.

"Can you give me the name of whoever it was that said they saw a white man over there?" Chaffee made the little movement that Q.P. decided was definitely what he used for a smile.

"No, sir, I can't, but if you do some detecting, I'm sure you'll find out who was over there." Chaffee turned and looked over at the women. It was time for him to get back to being a preacher.

Q.P. went out and found Nokes on the front steps smoking and pacing back and forth. "Goddamn nigger just *assumes* a white man did it, you know? Amazing," Nokes said, shaking his head. He flicked his cigarette into Beverly's boxwoods. He stood there for a second. Chaffee had been driven over, he saw. Another preacher, a younger man, was waiting; leaning on the fender of the church car, watching them closely to see what it was they were doing to justify their county salaries.

"Well, let's go ask around." Nokes didn't say anything, just nodded his head a few times. Q.P. turned and looked through the glass to where Chaffee stood talking to the women. They were looking up at him, the balls of tissue poised on the way to their eyes. Beverly and Giddings were nodding in agreement to whatever he was telling them.

"C'mon, let's go get this Scowen anyway," Q.P. said. He rolled his head around, loosening his neck. He realized that he was suddenly very angry, and he wasn't exactly sure why. He wasn't insulted that a white man might have killed Cora; he didn't care about any of that crap one way or another. Maybe it was the way the young preacher was eyeballing them, maybe it was the memory of the way Sykes had just walked off and left his tools in her, or maybe it had just been a tense morning and he needed to let loose a little.

It didn't matter. But he was ready to take it out on whoever had killed Cora Snow.

SEVEN

Red Scowen wasn't in, it turned out. No great surprise. But Q.P. and Nokes spent some time up on Castle Street walking around the house searching for him. Poking around and hoping that he might be hiding under the crawl space with the spiders.

The street was pretty quiet. Off in the distance a baby was crying and he could hear a woman trying to calm it down. A radio was playing in one of the houses. They walked all the way around Scowen's house. Everything was closed up. Under some dead honeysuckle there was a door down to the cellar, and they stood there for a minute looking at it.

"Let's just wait on that. It's got weeds all over it. Nobody's been using it," Q.P. said, and they kept going. An old woman came out on her porch and sat there eating a little something she unfolded from the wax paper in her lap.

They drove over two streets and found Cora Snow's sister, a much plainer-looking woman, who could not stop smiling. She was upset and didn't want to go in, so they sat right there and talked to her on the porch.

No, she didn't know anyone who might have it in for Cora in particular. When asked what she knew about Scowen, she wrinkled up her face. She wasn't smiling, she just looked that way all the time, he realized.

"Everybody tol' her to stay away from him, but she loved him."

"What was the matter with him?" Nokes said.

"He was bad and used girls to make his livin'." She looked up at him to see if he knew what she meant.

"And did he use her?"

"He had."

"But?"

"But she went back to him on account of she loved him." She smiled and shook her head at what love had cost her sister.

"Do you know where he is?"

"No, sir. He never come around here. I told him to stay away. If Cora went with him, that was her business."

"But she did get him to go to church with her?"

"He never go to that church but one time. She had to drag him into that church to hear her cousin preach one time."

"He ever hurt her?"

"No, sir, not that I know of. He might hit her some."

"Did he have other girlfriends besides Cora, you think?"

"He had all kinds of girls. Girls thought he was Mister Big Sweet Red. He used to give them presents and things. He give Cora some flowers and she went back to him 'cause of that. For some damn flowers." She had started to cry, but she still kept smiling.

"When did you see her last? Can you remember?"

"Day or two after Christmas I saw her. They had a big party, she told me."

"Her and Red?" Q.P. asked.

"Uh-huh. And some others, some fast friends they had. They had this big party and she didn't come over for Christmas, so she come by to say she was sorry and say she wasn't going to live with him no more."

"They had a fight?"

"They had a argument and she wanted to come home, but I told her it was up to Thelma and I'd have to ask her if we had room. So she went on back." She had really started to cry now and got up and went inside and washed her face and blew her nose.

"Why don't you go ask around about this white man that your preacher friend was talking about back at Beverly's, and call down to the P.D. and get them to put out a bulletin on Scowen, then come back and get me," Q.P. told Nokes.

"Take about three-quarters of an hour, I reckon," Nokes said as he went down the steps.

She came back out the screen door for a second to watch Nokes go. "Christmas. That's the last time I saw her," she said.

Cora hadn't been bad, the sister told him, not real bad. She was trying hard to shake off her wild life, and she thought that she could reform Red, too, that was why she'd got him into the church. She and Thelma had talked about Cora and decided to take her along with them when they worked as maids. The idea was that they would eventually be taking on all of Thelma's work. They'd be a kind of a team working for just a little bit more money until Cora learned the ropes. Then she would get her full third of whatever they brought in. Organized like that, they'd be able to clean faster and still get along all right. It was a good deal for Thelma and it was a way of getting Cora used to a different kind of life.

She went in and got the phone numbers of the white people who Thelma had cleaning arrangements with, and Q.P. copied them down. Recently they'd worked for three different women; all of them lived out in Forest Hills.

By the time Nokes pulled up, there didn't seem to be much more to talk about, and so he told her again that he was sorry about her sister and to telephone him if she heard anything about Scowen or if she saw him.

"I don't think he did it," she said, her eyes tearing up again. She was looking up the street, making that smile again.

"No? Why is that?" He turned around down at the bottom of the steps.

"No, Red loved her. I don't think he's the one you're after." She wiped her eyes on her sleeve and looked down at him. "I don't know of who would ever hurt her. I don't know who would ever hurt Cora."

"Well, it must have been somebody, right?"

"Must have been."

Back at the office, he made calls to all three numbers and found out right away that on the afternoon of the thirtieth Cora had gone out to clean up for Mrs. Irene Allison and that her husband had driven the girl home that night.

Q.P. drove straight out to the Allisons' place in Forest Hills, a residential area of huge houses and expansive front yards. The houses weren't quite mansions in the Southern sense of the word but substantial places to hang your hat, nevertheless. It was the neighborhood where the first families of Wilmington lived. The top crust, the "Hundred," the Cases, the Buells, and the Ballards. Mayor Wrenn had his place out here somewhere, Q.P. remembered. To get to the Allisons', he had to wind around past Sanders's place, an immaculate modern ranch-style house that draped itself across a two-acre lot. He checked. No Pontiac out front.

The Allison house was much more old-fashioned, he thought. Styled in red brick with fluted white wooden columns that were set right into the wall. There was no front porch to sit on. The people who lived here didn't relax out where everybody could see them. Hundred-year-old oaks shaded the front yard, and all he could see was one solitary lawn chair spread out under a mimosa tree. Well, it was early to start bringing out the yard furniture, he thought. No toys, no bikes. If there ever had been kids, they were gone.

Irene Allison met him in the front room, offered him coffee, which he refused. She was still a beautiful woman, Q.P. thought. At one time a natural blonde and now going to gray, which she'd camouflaged almost perfectly. She had clear blue eyes and good bones, perfect teeth. Back before the war she would have been a knockout.

She told him that on the spur of the moment they had decided to have people over on the Wednesday night and she'd called Thelma but there'd been no answer and out of desperation she'd finally got Cora at home, gone into town, and picked her up. After that she'd been busy getting ready for the evening and Cora had cleaned all the downstairs, and then at the end of the day her husband, Dr. Richard Allison, had taken her back home.

"That was on the night of the thirtieth, about what time?"

"About six," she said slowly. He heard a tentative tone in her voice. Was she wondering if six was late enough?

"Six?" He wrote slowly. "Earlier? Later? Something like that?" Irene Allison just shrugged.

"We're trying to trace her movements in the time leading up to her death," he said and looked up at her: a little noncommittal nod with nothing in her expression. Poker face, he thought.

"So you remember that he took her back into town around six, and then he came back—"

"Yes, that's right. He came back and we had guests at eight." Q.P. took his time writing it down.

"He would have been back by six-thirty, I'm sure," she said.

"Okay." He wrote that down, too. He didn't think that he'd get much from Irene Allison from pushing. She'd covered for her husband pretty well, and he had the sense she wouldn't implicate him in anything even if she did think there was a reason. He folded up his notebook.

"Did you and Cora ever talk?" he asked. She looked down at the carpet, just a little flash, and then hit him with those clear blues again.

"I'm very sorry about that girl," she said, "but no, we never talked, Sheriff. She was just a colored girl that did some cleaning for me."

She said that she had to go upstairs and get ready to meet her friends for bridge, and so Q.P. thanked her and walked down the flagstone steps and got in the Chevy and threaded his way out of Forest Hills. Past the triple lots, under the spindly oaks with their leaves mostly all gone. A few wisps of Spanish moss blowing in the gray January sky.

He parked in the back of the courthouse and walked through the breezeway and through the double doors to his office. Inside he looked up Dr. Richard Allison in the phone book.

"What's an *orthodontist?*" he called out to Mary Helen.

"I don't know. I'll ask Marly," she said. He heard her punch a button and get Marly at the Registry of Deeds.

"Hey, what's an orthodontist? Really? Uh-huh . . . Maybe I could get mine done . . ." She laughed at something Marly said. "Okay . . ." She stuck her head in the door.

"It's a dentist. Somebody who gives you braces."

"Oh yeah . . ." He knew that. Orthodontist. He tried to remember his high school Latin. More teeth? All teeth?

"We could use one of them around here, don't you think?" She put a red fingernail up to her teeth. They weren't all that bad, he thought.

There was a telephone call from Spud Reid wanting to know what was going on with the nigger girl the air force had fished out of the Cape Fear.

"Nothing's going on. We're working on it."

"You got a line on who did it?" Spud said. He sounded like he was trying to be casual.

"Look, we're working on it, Spud. Why?"

"I heard some bullshit that a white man is who did it."

"Yeah, who said?"

"That's what I heard round the hallways."

"Well, that's one of several things I've heard. We put out a bulletin for her boyfriend, and he's light skinned, so it might be the same thing."

"Oh, okay, then. I guess that makes sense." Reid sounded relieved, he thought. One less headache for him to deal with.

EIGHT

The Wilmington P.D. were the ones who finally found Red Billy and brought him up to the Fifth Floor for questioning.

Q.P. didn't find out about it until Scowen had been bashed around by Detective Tommy Wills, a big bruiser, one of Chief Carruthers's worst, a man who liked his work. Still he didn't ever smile.

Up on the Fifth Floor Q.P. made his way through the little L-shaped hallway that separated the cells from the rest of the Annex, said good morning to Mrs. Baker, and received a piece of bacon for his courtesy. Wills was taking a break from his exertions. He seemed as cheerful as he ever seemed to get.

"Thanks for your help, Tom-Boy," Q.P. said to him. There were little flecks of Scowen's blood splattered across Wills's white shirt. The huge cop raised his coffee cup in acknowledgment. It was always best to be nice to him.

"Couple of my boys routinely motor by his house there, saw the lights on, walked up to the porch, and there's the nigger fixin' himself breakfast in the middle of the night."

"No shit?"

"He walks right up to the door, we slap his ass 'gainst the wall, and bring him in." Wills looked over at Mr. Baker, who laughed.

"What did he say?"

"Not too damn much," Wills said flatly. He looked away from Q.P. and over to where Mr. Baker was cleaning out the little metal shower they had up there.

"Can he talk?" Q.P. asked. Wills waggled his head, snorted, and frowned.

"He can, but he won't. Right sassy asshole."

"That's not too good."

"Not too good for him at all, but hell, if that's the way he wants it . . ."

"Well, thanks again, Tommy, for bringing him in. You can take off if you want to. We figure it's our lookout."

"Sure, I don't give a shit. I gotta get some breakfast anyway." Wills stood up, a gigantic man. His stomach hung down over his belt, but his arms were tight inside his shirt. He might be fat, but it was fat that concealed plenty of muscle.

Scowen was handcuffed to a metal chair in the center of the tiny interrogation room, the only one up on the top floor. Q.P. left his revolver outside with Mrs. Baker and let himself in. Scowen looked up, which was a good sign. It meant that he was conscious and probably able to answer some questions.

Wills had beat him up pretty good; there was blood all down his chest, and his lower lip was split open and swollen.

"Okay, Red, I sent the other guy away. You're just going to talk to me now. Got it?"

Scowen looked up at him and tried to smile. It must have hurt.

"I'd like to call up my lawyer," he said quietly.

"How come you want to do that?" Q.P. looked at him steadily and Scowen did the same. Maybe he was still trying to smile. "Don't give me any shit, Red, okay?" he told Scowen quietly. Maybe the smile faded a little, it was hard to tell.

"You know why we brought you in?"

"He tol' me somebody killed Cora."

"That's right. Somebody did. Maybe the somebody that killed her was you?"

"No, sir. I been out fishin' for near 'bout a week. I didn't even know about her till that motherfucker told me about it." Scowen was sitting up straight now, fully awake. Angry. Q.P. could see where the shirt was torn and he was straining against the cuffs. He was a young man in his mid-twenties. Altogether he'd spent more than a year, served in stretches of a few months at a time, at the county farm for a variety of offenses. Pimping, aggravated assault.

Drunk and disorderly. Resisting arrest a few times. Once he'd got out to the farm, he settled down a little and seemed to behave himself. The rules of the game were different out there.

"You're gone fishing, that's your story?"

"I take people out fishing, that's what I do."

"Sure, sure."

"I'm a fisherman. I hire my boat out."

"You got a boat all of your own?"

"I don't owe nothin' on it."

"That's pretty good."

"I took this group of businessmen out all last week. We got up to Beaufort, you can check on it. I stopped and got gas up there and bought some bait. That's where I've been, up there with them men."

"Tell me about Cora. I don't give a shit about you and your boat. You're gonna probably go to the gas chamber, but I just want to know why you killed her."

"I want to see my lawyer. I want to call Mr. Whale—" Scowen's voice had climbed in pitch. He was scared and it was genuine fear over the fix he was in. "That man's got no right to mess me up. I didn't do nothin'!" Scowen could yell all he wanted, it wasn't going to do any good. He'd probably said more or less the same thing to policemen most of his life. Q.P. just sat there until he was finished. Scowen was panting. He gave up and stared down at the table. Q.P. waited until Scowen looked up at him.

"You're starting to mess with me now."

"No, I ain't, but I'm in trouble and I need my lawyer." Scowen's voice was starting to whine; he was pleading.

"That's right, that's for sure. Maybe if you tell me about Cora some, I'll go phone him for you."

"Shit . . ." Scowen hissed through his broken lips. "I love Cora," he said, shaking his head. "I love that girl."

Q.P. went out and got one of Giddings's photographs and slid it across the steel table so that Scowen could see it. He looked at it for a few minutes and shook his head quietly. Outside in the hall, Q.P. could hear Wills and Mrs. Baker laughing at some joke.

"I reckon we'll be charging you with murder, Red," Q.P. said quietly. He took back the picture and started to get up. Scowen looked up at him sharply.

"Nah . . . Hey, wait a second. Wait here just a second . . ." Scared.

"Sure. Tell me all about it and then I'll go call Mr. Whale, and if you don't try to bullshit me, maybe I'll get Mrs. Baker to fix you up some breakfast, too. Maybe get a doctor up here and fix your mouth up for you."

"Look . . . I'll tell you everything I know, all right?" Q.P. shrugged like it didn't matter to him and sat back down.

His story was that they'd been together off and on for nearly two years. And sure, they'd had arguments. And yeah, when she started acting up he might occasionally hit her, but not too hard and only if she needed it to quieten down.

"But I never hurt her, not really. I love her," Scowen said and looked at Q.P. to see if he bought it.

But Cora wasn't scared of him. She was different. She was a real outspoken girl and she never gave up if she got something in her mind, something that bothered her or she thought he ought to do.

A couple of times she'd decided that she was going to stay up with her sister at Thelma's. That's where she went sometimes. But otherwise she'd nag and nag, hang on like a snapping turtle once she got going.

"She work for you?" Q.P. asked him quietly. Scowen looked up at him, not knowing what to say. "You know what I mean, don't you, Red? She went out and did all the fucking and you were her manager, right? You handled all the family finances, made sure she paid her Social Security?" Scowen looked down at the floor for a second or two. A long string of red drool was hanging out of the corner of his mouth.

"Yeah . . ." was all he said.

"And so she decided that she didn't want to do that anymore and you beat her up—"

"No . . . It wasn't like that."

"Sure, sure. How was it, then?"

"Well, yeah, she didn't want to go out anymore, you know."

"Uh-huh."

"So I wanted her to keep on goin'. 'Cause we were doing good, you know? And I had all these men, these men who wanted to go out fishing."

"Did they actually catch any fish, or did they just stay down below with Cora?"

"Yeah, we catch some fish."

"Sure, I bet." Q.P. started laughing. Scowen smiled on one side of his face.

"Well, you gotta do something while you're waitin', and some of those men caught a mess of fish."

"Okay, whatever you say . . ."

"Those men like her and treated her real good. She always took good care of herself and she was clean, you know?"

"Uh-huh."

"And she was young lookin', and some of them men like that 'cause she was little. Real young lookin'. You know, they'd see her and they'd get all scared, some of them, and ask how old she was."

"She was twenty?"

"She was near 'bout *twenty-two*."

"Okay."

"Cora didn't want to go out. She had been talking to Thelma and decided that I was a bad influence, so she started doing this cleaning work. Cleaning up for white women. So I was all set up to go out with these men and bring three girls, so that put me in the hole, you see."

"I can see how something like that might mess things up."

"You know, they be arguing about the price and everything and be angry at me all the time if she don't come along."

"So?"

"So I *needed* her right then, you know? So she said she ain't goin'. Ain't no way that she is goin' out on that boat and that I'm a bad influence on her and she's movin' back in with her sister and that I can go to hell."

Q.P. started laughing.

"She lit into me good, boy . . ."

"I bet."

"And so we're yelling and fighting and I told her to go ahead and move out, that I don't give a shit what happens to her—" He fell silent for a long moment.

"And?"

"So I went out with these men and she stayed back in town and that's what I was doing for all that week, and I come back last night and she's gone, which I thought was fine; I thought she run off on me, but I figure she's comin' back because she didn't take none of her clothes and stuff."

"And—"

"And then these motherfuckers are knocking my door in and beatin' on me." Q.P. looked at him for a long stretch. Scowen looked down, shook his head in frustration. He knew he was in a bad fix.

"You go call Mr. Whale for me now?"

"So that's all you've got to tell me?"

"Yes, sir. I was out fishin' with some men from up in Raleigh. I don't know nothin' about whatever happened to Cora, that's the whole truth."

"Who the fuck are these 'men from Raleigh'? Maybe I'd like to talk to them, Red. Just to see if you're just stringing me along, you know?"

Scowen writhed in the chair, his voice started climbing up into a whine. "Those men call *me* up every time, you know? They don't want me calling them and maybe talking to their wife or like that? They're white men and they're embarrassed, you know?"

"White men? Is that who you were out on the boat with?"

"That's right, and they call *me*, I don't ever phone *them*, on account of their wives."

"Oh, yeah, I see, I catch on. You're saying that there's no way you can get in touch with them, right?"

"Please, now I got to talk to Mr. Whale."

"I told you not to mess with me, right? Isn't that what I told you? Didn't I say that right at first?" Q.P. said and got up and left.

"He's dressed pretty good for some nigger that goes fishing, ain't he?" Wills said outside. Q.P. realized that he had gotten angry in there just from talking to Scowen. He looked up at Wills for a minute trying to think of something to say that wouldn't lead to a fistfight. He turned to Mrs. Baker instead. "Just put him down there at the end and don't let anybody else talk to him, all right?"

"Sure, Kewpie," she said. He dug down and made the effort to grin at Wills.

"I just want him to cook in there for a little while, you know? So leave him alone for now, okay?"

Wills shrugged; he didn't care. "Let him stew, sure."

"I'd like him to be awake the next time I have to ask him some questions, okay?"

Wills cocked his head over and looked down at him. "What's your problem?" he said quietly.

"You hear what I said?"

"You got something bothering you, Kewpie, I'll be glad—" But Q.P. just stopped him by jabbing a finger into his chest. Wills's jaw fell open at the apparent insanity of it; he could easily kill Q.P. with one blow, and they both knew it.

"You hear what I said?" Q.P. said again, mostly because he couldn't think of a threat he could make stick.

Wills's eyebrows popped up and he started laughing. "Kewpie, your brain is on the blink. You need to take a rest, boy," he said and went out to the bathroom to wash off his knuckles.

Mary Helen had finished the paper and it was on his desk when he got downstairs. He set it aside and closed the door and just thought for a while.

He would still have to wait for anything that Sykes might include in his coroner's report. The only physical evidence were the ropes that had been used to tie the girl up. Nokes had gone over to Houldings Hardware to ask about them and found out what everybody already knew: that they were lengths of common window cords. *Sash cord,* Houldings called it because it was used to raise up your windows.

He telephoned Reid's office and got a search warrant to go through Scowen's house and boat, and then had his coffee and went through the *Morning Star.*

Up in Columbus County sheriff's deputies had raided a fish grill and found sixty bottles of bootleg whiskey hidden in a trapdoor in the ceiling; in Pender County the court term was starting and he scanned through the docket. On the next page, he noticed Sears had a sale going on rebuilt five-horsepower outboard motors, which he considered for a few minutes, since the old banger he had bolted onto his boat was just about gone and fifty bucks wasn't a bad price. It would cost that much to fix his old one.

The solicitor's office called and said that they'd put through the search warrant, so he picked it up from Marly, grabbed Glen Petty, one of his deputies, and they went for a ride over to Scowen's.

While Petty put the seals up over the front door, Q.P. searched the place. There were a fair number of empty bottles, probably garbage left over from the big party they'd had at the end of the holidays. The bedroom was unmade, Cora's clothes still lying around, draped over the chair. The place was a mess, he thought. But nothing broken. It didn't look as if there'd been a struggle or a break-in. There was a big paper bucket of fresh shrimp in the icebox.

They went down a set of narrow little stairs to the cellar. There was no light. Petty shined his flashlight around, revealing an almost completely vacant dirt hole. In one corner was a pile of crab traps in various states of repair. Other than that, all Scowen was keeping down there was his spider collection.

The house had a garage out the back and a little shed built into it. The shed was nothing but a place to store tools. He had to tug on the rickety door to get it open. Scowen had probably never even looked in there. It was full of cobwebs and rusty kerosene cans. The garage held Scowen's car, a big car, a '50 Mercury, clean as a whistle. He got Petty to break into the trunk while he looked around. Nothing in the glove compartment or inside the car, and there wasn't much else in the garage. A lawn mower that was in pieces over on a bench under a broken window. No fishing gear anywhere. No sash cord.

"Okay . . ." Petty said. There was a creaking sound, and he lifted the great curved trunk lid. Q.P. looked in and saw a couple of sheets of yellowed newspaper, a slick spare tire, an empty bottle of bourbon, and a cardboard box full of onions.

"Does it look to you like somebody got tied up and strangled and then carried around in this car for a while?" he asked Petty. Petty laughed.

"Nah . . . It looks like he was gonna make some soup or something," he said.

"Yeah, me too," Q.P. said. And so they sealed the garage and then went back to the courthouse.

"Now, if you were smart," Mary Helen said, giving him a significant look, cupping her hand over the telephone mouthpiece, "you'd put your money in real estate at Carolina Beach."

"Oh yeah? Why is that?"

"They're changing the entire town around. They're putting in a reservoir down there, Kewpie. It's going to hold a million gallons of water."

"You're kidding." He had no idea if that was a lot of water or not. It sounded like it was.

"They're building new streets, they're putting in sewers, it's going to be ready in June . . . I'm going to talk to Mr. Reeves at the savings 'n' loan. I don't know how they're goin' to pay for all these civic works, do you?" she said from around the corner.

"Nope." The last thing on his mind was putting down roots and going into hock to buy a lot down at Carolina Beach.

Nokes came in. He'd gone over the river and down to Southport and searched Scowen's boat with one of Woody Forbes's deputies.

"Didn't find a goddamn thing. Neat as a pin. He'd thrown out all the garbage. But I found some of this tied up on to some of his nets." Nokes opened up a manilla envelope and dumped a length of sash cord out on Q.P.'s blotter.

"It's not the same kind."

"Yeah. I know. He's got some more of this window cord on the boat, but it's all old and worn out, like this, and it's bigger around . . ."

"Yeah."

"And . . . I was thinking, you know, that the knots on the girl were funny. They're not very good."

"What do you mean?"

"Well, Scowen's enough of a fisherman to have a boat and he knows how to work with rope and look at this." He had gone down to the evidence room and pulled the ropes that Sykes had cut off Cora Snow.

"See here?"

"Yeah . . ." The knots were just overhand knots. Hitches and bow knots repeated on top of themselves. "These things'd come loose after a while, don't you think?"

Nokes poked gently at the knots to turn them over. They were just a mess, nothing like the large cords taken from the nets.

"Call for you, Kewpie," Mary Helen said. Nokes slid both sets of ropes off the blotter and into their respective envelopes.

"Hello, Sheriff Waldeau?" said the voice on the line.

"Speaking."

"This is Sergeant Horne, Raleigh Police Department. How y'all doin'?"

"Real good so far," he said.

"Well, that's good. We did some phonin' around for you about some men that went fishin' down that way over the holiday season?"

"Uh-huh."

"Well, I talked to all of 'em. They hired a colored man from down there in Wilmington, name of William Scowen, and went out on his fishin' boat, name of . . . the *St. Elmo*, he calls it."

"And Scowen was there the whole time? He didn't drop them off or anything?"

"Nah, didn't none of them say nothin' about that. They were out fishin' for five days. They drove down your way and got on his boat and then ended up in Beaufort. Scowen fixed them up real good . . ." Over the phone the man's tone of voice changed. "You know, I don't think them boys did too much fishin' out there."

"Scowen fixed them up?"

"Yeah, he fixed 'em up pretty good. They didn't want to talk a whole lot about it. But it's obvious, there were some poontang acquired on the voyage, you know what I mean?"

"Uh-huh."

"So I reckon that's the story there, Sheriff . . ."

"Yeah, I guess that about does it. We're trying to confirm an alibi for Scowen, so . . ."

"Well, these men were out there with him. Smokin' and jokin'."
There was a pause.

"Okay. I appreciate your work."

"Maybe I might come down there and catch a few fish myself."
The cop was laughing on the other end of the line.

"Yeah, well, just be careful or you might catch more than that," Q.P. said and hung up. "Well, that just about takes the goddamn cake," he said to Nokes.

"Let him go?"

"Yeah, go up and tell Mrs. Baker to give him something to eat and let him go. He can unseal the house and everything."

That evening just before quitting time Mary Helen leaned into the room and slipped Sykes's coroner's report across his blotter. "Unidentified Negro Female" had been scratched out and "Snow, Cora" written in above it. The report was basically a receipt. As far as Sykes was concerned, no further examination was required, and it meant that the county was releasing the body to the Beverly brothers and they could continue normally and have a service and finally lay her to rest.

So just like the Raleigh cop had said, that was the story.

But then if Red Billy Scowen didn't kill her, Q.P. thought, who did? He reached over and got his pad to make a note for the morning. On the top page were the notes he'd made earlier. He'd been on the phone and doodled all around the word:

.*Orthodontist* .

Around it he had drawn a cloud and made it so that sun rays were shooting out in all directions.

NINE

The Cape Fear Country Club was the kind of place he was supposed to be spending time, Mary Helen had said. He had been there before a couple of times with Franklin, and the deputies were invited to a Christmas party every year. You couldn't get in unless you were a guest and membership was expensive and just about impossible anyway. You had to be invited in and checked out before they voted on you.

The original house was over a hundred years old, and the big oaks out front were even older. Wings had been added on for the dining rooms and bar. There were locker rooms in the back for members on their way from the golf course and showers that flanked the pool.

He waited out under the veranda for Allison to come off the back nine. They'd sent a caddy out to warn him, and he watched Allison detach himself from two men and walk toward him, smiling.

He was a good-looking guy, and Q.P. wondered if he was younger than his wife. Playing golf didn't seem to wear him out. He was still fresh, as if he'd been for a nice walk. He had fine features and clear blue eyes, just like her. He reminded Q.P. of one of the ads for the Arrow shirts he'd seen in his childhood. He and Irene must have been a golden couple once upon a time.

"Beautiful day, isn't it?" Allison said. "Are you on duty, Sheriff, or can I interest you in a drink?"

"I'm on duty. Need to ask you a few questions if you don't mind,"

Q.P. said, standing there with his hat in his hands as the dentist brushed past him. He smelled like soap and nicotine.

"You don't mind if I . . ." Allison made a little tippling motion with his hands and kept on walking for the bar. It looked a lot cooler in there, Q.P. thought, so he nodded and they went inside.

"Thank you, Delmer," Allison said to an elderly waiter who handed him a highball that was waiting for him, and they went over to a table under the shade of the awnings.

Q.P. figured he might as well start right in. "I need to ask you some questions about a woman who used to work for you," Q.P. said. Allison took a sip and let a frown cross his tanned brow.

"You mean before Julia? That would have been . . . Caroline Pape. She was also my assistant but—"

"No, I mean a girl who worked at your house. A maid?"

"Oh . . ." Allison said. "Oh . . . a *maid?*"

"Yeah, a girl named"—he looked down at his pad—"Cora Snow. You used to drive her home after work?" Allison frowned and took another big pull on his drink.

"Mmm, let's see . . . yes, Cora . . . *Cora?*"

"That's right."

"She's the girl who was—" He couldn't say it; instead he just nodded.

"Murdered. She was murdered. Raped and murdered, we think."

"Yes . . ."

"So you used to drive her home?"

"Well, yes, I did a few times. Let's see . . ." He obviously had to think it over. "You know, I would come home from work and pick her up and give her a lift over to ah . . . over on Castle Street where she lived."

"You remember driving her home on Wednesday night, the thirtieth of December?"

Allison frowned elaborately. It was so very long ago. He gave a little hiss, not quite a chuckle, not quite a laugh.

"Christ, I'm not sure about that . . ."

"You had a party that night?" Allison looked at him. All of a sudden Q.P. realized that Irene Allison hadn't even told her husband that the sheriff had come to visit them; she hadn't prepared him at all. "You had some people come over for dinner or something . . ."

"Oh, yes. Yes, I *did*. I did take her home that night. It was a kind of a last-minute thing and I was in a hurry. I just forgot."

"Sure. Well, we're trying to trace her movements on that day up till the time she got killed, so . . . You took her home. Anything special about the trip?"

"Oh . . . I don't remember much . . ."

"Just take it easy and think about it. You might have seen something, you know?" Q.P. shrugged at the man to show that he wasn't in any trouble, that the questions weren't such a big deal. "So you gave her a lift home and . . ."

Allison grinned, made that little laugh again. "And I just . . . *dropped her off*," he said helplessly.

"Was there anybody waiting for her?"

"No. Look, I don't know. Really, I wasn't thinking about that." Allison had finished his bourbon and shook his glass at Delmer, who came right over.

"You didn't see anybody at all?"

"I really don't know. I didn't *notice* anyone."

"What about on other occasions? You'd been there before, right, to her house?" Allison looked up at him with genuine shock.

"Are you saying that I had *been to her house*?" That hadn't been what Q.P. meant, but he went along with it.

"Well, had you?"

"Christ, no. She was just a nigger maid, for chrissakes. I wouldn't have anything to do with someone like that. Jesus . . ." Allison shook his head as if he couldn't make head or tails of the whole situation. "Look, I don't know what else I can tell you, Officer."

"Here you go, Doctor . . ." Delmer slid Allison's drink onto the table.

"You sure you don't want anything? Iced tea? Lemonade?" Allison offered before Delmer got away on him.

"No, that's all right. I've got to follow this along, so . . ." He stood up, "If you remember anything that might help us out, we'd appreciate it, Doctor."

"Well . . ." Allison said. "I hope everything . . ." He'd gotten up and reached out to shake Q.P.'s hand.

"Anything at all, you know?" Q.P. started to go.

"Of course, of course . . ." Allison had his arms out as if he wanted to embrace the whole veranda. "Whatever I can do," he said. "Whatever I can do to help—" There was that smile again.

Q.P. walked out of the bar and through the carpeted front room of the clubhouse, thinking about Allison and his story of the night. There didn't seem to be much there, he thought. And if there was, he didn't think he could shake anything out of the doctor. Probably Allison was the "white man" who had been seen driving away from Cora's house. And for Allison to have been Cora's murderer he would have had to have been available for a little bit longer than an hour, he thought. The time was too short if Allison's guests had arrived on time. Why would he kill her on the night of a dinner party? Rush home, change clothes . . . It was too crazy; the orthodontist was a dead end, going nowhere, he decided.

Three women came through the lobby ahead of him. They had just come in off the course and were laughing a lot. They saw him and smiled and he nodded back at them as they came through the big doors, thrown open to catch the breeze.

"It's a beautiful day, don't y'all think?" said one of the women to him and smiled, flirting transparently. Her friends giggled and pulled her away.

"Yes, ma'am, it is. Beautiful." And he smiled and tipped his hat and watched her go, thinking that yes, maybe Mary Helen was absolutely right, this was the place he should be campaigning.

TEN

First came the food. Q.P. had got there just a little late but still in time to eat. The Wilmington Democratic Club's Campaign Kickoff was being staged in the drafty Cape Fear Hall, crammed to the rafters with the local machine. He was wearing his only dress uniform. The pants never had fit right.

He talked to Winky Peters, who was there as chairman of the school board. He was fuming over the untimely machinations on the Supreme Court and what consequences it might have for Wilmington.

"What I'm saying is that there's a right way to handle things . . ."

"Oh yeah," said Q.P. as he surveyed the long table. Democratic women were shuffling back and forth and pulling the lids off their dishes. It was noisy already and the real noise hadn't started yet.

"—and then there's the way they handle things up in Yankee land—"

"I know what you mean," he said. He began to head for the chicken.

"—you come in and just say to people that the way they've been living for a hundred years is *wrong*? And just because some assholes out in Topeka can't manage their affairs, you've got to rearrange your lives?"

"Yeah," Q.P. said. Most of the time Winky was a pretty good guy, but right now he was scared, and under his normally easygoing manner he was disturbed and angry.

"But hell, Wink, it's going to happen anyway, don't you think?" Q.P. said, trying to get the man calmed down a little. While they stood there one of the women shoved a plate in his hands.

"Yeah, sure. *Sure,* it's going to happen. It's going to happen. Yes, I know, I know that." Winky was shaking his head and staring off into the distance. "But that's what I mean, Kewpie. You don't have to destroy everything. You can do it with the *minimum*—"

Spud Reid pushed his way in between them. "I want to talk to you," he said.

"Sure."

"How come you released that nigger?"

"What nigger's that?"

"You know who I mean. Scarboro, Scarecrow . . ."

"Scowen?"

"Yeah, what's he doing out on the town?" Reid was making the nearest expression he ever made to a frown. He did it with his mouth turning down. He looked like he'd tasted something bad.

"He had an alibi."

"What kind of goddamn alibi?" Reid was getting in his way now.

"He was somewhere else at the estimated time of the murder, Spud."

Reid looked exasperated, trying to restrain himself from showing whatever emotion was threatening to bubble out of him.

"Now listen, Kewpie," Reid said quietly. "You let that boy go, you've missed your best chance right there. There's lot better ways to be spending your time than trying to solve the unsolvable, you understand me?" He had heard Reid use the phrase before. Something impressive he'd heard around City Hall probably.

"He had an *alibi* and it checked out, and whenever that happens, Spud, they get to go home or to the hospital, whichever they want." He gave Reid a hard look. "Speaking of unsolvable, what ever happened to Mrs. Talcott? Are you going to send her to the gas chamber?" Reid just shook his head and left. Q.P. took the opportunity to snag a couple of drumsticks, then squeezed along the table and loaded up a little paper bowl with Brunswick stew.

"Get some of the *ham,* Kewpie. That's Ham Heaven over there." Mary Helen called back to him as she glided past.

"All right, listen up, sailors." Hal Lutz, the assistant city manager and co-chairman of the local Democratic Party, was up on the little stage with his plate in his hand. "You can keep on eating," he said to people who would anyway. "Just keep on, just keep on feedin' from the trough there . . ." Somebody burst out laughing. Lutz let it go for a second.

"He's the craziest damn nut you ever seen." Winky had come up and stood beside Q.P. and they watched the show together. There was a group of men heckling Lutz from back by the kitchen.

"Yeah, well, none of you big boys back there are exactly going hungry right now, are you?" It got another laugh from the gang at the back of the room, a sprinkling of applause.

"Yeah, anyhow, go ahead and keep on eating, folks, but turn this way, on account of Velma Tice!"

Velma was a longtime regular. She had augmented her flame-red hair with a string mop and ran up on the stage and started singing. It was the same song she usually sang at the Democrat parties. A version of "Summertime" with the lyrics all changed around for Southern locations and political enemies. People would sing along sometimes and knew when the laughs were going to come.

While she sang Q.P. took the opportunity to get over to the barbecue, which had been made particularly hot. He was loading up as Velma ran off to laughs, and hoots, and what applause people could handle with their food in one hand.

"Did you get any of that ham?" Mary Helen said.

"Not yet, not yet."

"Oh, here he is. Jimmy!" She pulled Jim Satterwhite over to him. "You wanted to talk to him about his pictures, here he is—"

"Hey, Kewpie, you want to come in for your picture?" Jimmy said.

"Yeah, sure. I guess . . ."

"You better come in soon. Look at that." Across the room two of the wives were tacking up DEWY WRENN FOR MAYOR and ALTON LENNOX FOR SENATE posters.

"It takes a while to make those things up, you know."

"Yeah . . ." Q.P. nodded. The idea of sitting for his portrait, for some reason, made him intensely uncomfortable.

"—get a haircut, you know . . ."

"Yeah, okay."

"I'll put it in his book. It's not that much. It's only four dollars, right, Jim?" Mary Helen said as she served the three of them huge portions of potato salad.

"Yeah, it's not much. Hell, it's cheap if it gets you elected."

"You think about it like that and it makes some sense," Mary Helen said.

"Okay," Q.P. said. "Sure, I'll come on in. Sure."

Satterwhite and Mary Helen went off and he started working on the barbecue and pondered the campaign expense for the photos they'd just scheduled. Across the room he saw Mr. Pagett, the *Morning Star* editor, laughing with Mayor Wrenn. Beside them were a clutch of Atlantic Coast Line railroad men, looking stiff and uncomfortable—executive types, probably up from Jacksonville, Q.P. thought. He made up his mind he wasn't going to drink at all that night and that he would stay alert and take the first chance to make a getaway right after the speeches.

Burton Pardee came over. He was one of the New Hanover County commissioners, and as such, responsible for the budget of the sheriff's department. They hadn't had any trouble, but then again Q.P. had never had to come before the commissioners to do anything but give his monthly report. So far it had all gone along with no hitches on either side.

Pardee looked serious. "I want to know your opinion after we have all these people talk tonight. This'n comin' up might not be the smoothest election in history," he said quietly, whispering almost as if it was some kind of big secret. He put his beefy hand on Q.P.'s shoulder.

"Neck and neck with the Republicans?" Q.P. laughed. Pardee did the same and looked down and stamped his feet while he was laughing, it was so funny.

"Yeah . . . that Ikey Eisenhower is right tough to beat, you know? People like him and they think about switching over and turning themselves into Republicans. They start seriously thinkin' that maybe a little shakin' up is what we need. You know, teach-us-a-lesson kinda thing? That's what they believe, they really do."

"Well, God help us all, then. I told Jimmy I was going to get my picture done," Q.P. said.

"Goddamn, boy! You haven't done that yet?"

"Well, I've been a little busy."

"Well, hell, unless they're running off with the keys to the county, I'd go on in there and get myself together. Bein' sheriff's a hell of a lot different than just bein' a deputy, Kewpie."

"Hell, I know that already."

"Anyway, Kewpie"—he gestured to the stage—"after all this folderol is over you tell me what you think." His voice had fallen to a whisper again, then Pardee turned and waded into the crowd, stopping to grab others on the shoulders. He was a big man, very fat in the face with red cheeks. Not a drinker, just one of those shiny-faced men who carried themselves well even when forty pounds overweight.

The speeches started. He saw Ezzard Carruthers, chief of the Wilmington Police Department, standing at the edge of the stage. Like Q.P. and several other men, he was in full dress. He applauded Lutz and then took a plaque out of Bucky Nelson's custody and lightly ran up the steps to the microphone. "Folks, we wanted to take a moment this evening to pay tribute to a very special person." The crowd began to push toward the stage.

"Most of you know this person and know what she stands for, know what a *principled* person she is . . ." There was a disturbance behind him and Q.P. saw a thin little woman being wheeled through the crowd. She looked frightened. "—but not matter how tough the going gets, the example provided by Miss Minerva Goolick will—" there was a slow spreading of applause that drowned out Carruthers's voice.

Q.P. knew "Miss Minnie," as everyone called her. Her father was a veteran of Shiloh who'd scraped out a living during reconstruction as a tavern keeper. Minerva was just a little girl when the city exploded in the riots that kicked the Populists, the Fusion Democrats, and their Republican allies out of Wilmington forever. She'd stood across Seventh Street from the offices of the *Daily Record* and jumped up and down while she watched the Redshirt Democrats burn the Negro paper to the ground.

That season of rioting was the turning point in her young life. The time when she realized that the world of Wilmington city politics would be the most exciting thing she could ever hope to know. And so, full of enthusiasm, she applied herself and became a City Hall fixture long before the First World War.

"Some people impress you with how *loud* they talk," Carruthers was saying, "and some impress you with how *much* they talk, but some people impress you with what it *is* that they're saying. Miss Minnie, that's you." He paused for a second and people started clapping.

Carruthers was smooth, Q.P. thought. A real smooth Southern gentleman of the old school, who had all the tools of the professional diplomat and ruthlessly ran his domain from the basement of City Hall. He was always nice to you and then, bam, before you saw it coming, it was over. Carruthers was an old-line under-the-table type of police chief, Franklin had said. He knew everybody in the region and knew what they needed and, if he could, he made sure they got it. And he did it all quietly, neatly. Like a gentleman.

"Now, Miss Minnie, this is a little something we had made up just for you." Carruthers realized that there was no way to wheel her up on the stage to accept the plaque. "I'm going to read out what this says, all right? It simply says, 'To Miss Minnie, from Your Friends Who Love You, Wilmington City Hall, 1954.'" There was a round of sustained applause and Carruthers carefully got down on the floor and handed the old woman the plaque. He put his face down and gave her a kiss and whispered something in her ear for some several seconds. Everyone started singing "For She's a Jolly Good Fellow"; there was another wave of applause, and for a few moments various dignitaries came up to Miss Goolick and congratulated her.

Q.P. looked around the room and wondered if Dr. Richard Allison was there. He saw Winky again and asked him if he knew the man.

"Sure, yeah. He's got money and I'm sure they'd love for him to make a contribution."

"Is he here?"

"Kewpie, he never comes out." Winky shook his head at the

fund-raising tragedy. "He's been on the list for years now, but he's not a joiner. He's out there at the country club playing golf when he can, and I think he gives at the office, you know?"

"Sure," he said and let Winky circulate.

He listened to Burton Pardee introduce the guest speaker for the evening, U. S. Senator Alton Lennox, coming to the end of his term and now running hard for the Democratic nomination. Lennox was from Wilmington and Q.P. had run into him a few times, shaken his hand when he swept through the courthouse hobnobbing with his local supporters. He was a handsome man with a thick head of dark hair and bushy eyebrows beneath which he loved to glower. He tried to come off as a severe thinker, a stern and rational man who would spend the taxpayers' money frugally. He paused for a moment to let the applause die away and then addressed the crowd as he would an assembly of soldiers about to do battle.

The easy times were over, Lennox said. From now on we'd all have to be on our guard. From now on, all through North Carolina, people would have to be on their guard because now there was something here that people wanted.

"It's called *Prosperity*," he said and got his first ripple of applause. "It's everything we stand for. It's our lives and our families and our fine businesses, and our churches, and it's our way of life, and we've got to stand together. We've got to stand together and protect it!" Lennox's voice had grown, and when he shouted "protect," he raised his fist. He was illuminated by Jimmy Satterwhite's flashbulb.

The whole world was pressing in on the South, Lennox told them. And that meant that everyone would have to renew their efforts to be vigilant. At home, in the schools, and especially in the workplaces around the district.

"It's really, when you get right down to it, a simple question of what it means to be an American. It's a question of *Americanism*," he said and got his second big round of applause. Lennox was a one hundred percent red-blooded proud American. Not afraid to express his loyalty.

He was proud, he said, to stand up for the state's tobacco farmers; he was proud to oppose Eisenhower's job plan, which would prop up Northern businesses and ruin the livelihood of Southern textile workers; he was against spending money on the Saint Lawrence Seaway, against bringing in Hawaii and Alaska as states and against anyone who would tear down the reputation of the United States of America. The hall erupted into applause. Somewhere someone began to play a march on the piano, and Jimmy Satterwhite took another picture as Lennox raised his arms in triumph and made his way down off the stage to the faithful.

Q.P. had finished his food and decided that this was as good a time as any to get out. Across the room Lennox stood sipping at his beer. Wrenn was giggling and gesturing like a puppet at something Burton Pardee was telling him. Q.P. edged to the back, retrieved his hat from the girls at the coat check, and was starting to congratulate himself on his escape as he skipped down the front steps into the wet night.

He was just down to the sidewalk when he saw the man in the raincoat.

Walking along the street trying to look casual, slowing down when he got in between cars. Checking plates, it looked like. He finished a row of cars and took up a position at the mouth of an alley, where he could watch anyone entering or leaving by the front of the Cape Fear Hall.

Q.P. turned and walked the other direction, all the way to the corner and around the block. Then he went to his car for his revolver and cut up through the alley and came up behind Hong's Chinese restaurant.

He took his time. He could see the man leaning there at the end of the alley, silhouetted by the streetlight, still watching. The alley was ancient, paved with old cobbles unchanged since the Civil War. There was a nauseating smell of rotten garbage from Hong's. He took it nice and quiet until he was right behind the guy.

"Good evening. Sheriff's Department. Don't move and put your hands up where I can see them." For a second, after jumping out of his shoes, the young man put up his hands, but when Q.P. started feeling along his belt to see if he was armed, he spun and tried a stupid move, slashing at Q.P.'s gun hand.

As stupid moves went, it worked pretty good. Q.P.'s arm went numb and he dropped the revolver and the guy nailed him with a left cross. He stepped back on the cobbles and the young man came right in with a hard blow to his stomach that knocked the wind out of him and buckled his knees and sent him back across the alley into the brick wall.

Q.P. managed to block the right hand that was coming in to finish him off and brought his knee up into the guy's crotch, only just missing, and at the same time threw an uppercut that by accident landed in the guy's throat. He grunted and choked and Q.P. pushed off him and got in a good whack to the guy's jaw that straightened him up. He tried to slide along the bricks and get some fighting room, but the young guy had a longer reach and for a few seconds they both went at it toe to toe.

He was kicking himself for underestimating the young guy, who was a pretty hard boy, strong and efficient. He knew it was going to be over as soon as one of them connected, and he figured his best chance was to get it over early. He started to unload his good right but somehow he felt it blaze right over the guy's head and something happened and he felt himself sailing through the air upside down, crashing into the trash cans on the other side of the alley.

He was getting to his feet and he saw the young guy pause for a second and then start to come in for the finish, and Q.P. was on his hands and knees on the cobbles, watching the guy's feet coming at him, and just as he drew back to kick, Q.P. got up and smashed him in the face with the revolver.

It stunned him and Q.P. took the opportunity to kick him in the balls, not missing this time, and the young guy fell down and Q.P. did the same, staggering out and slipping down into the garbage that had spilled out into the street.

He got up and grabbed the young guy by the collar and slammed him into the side of a car that was parked there, cocked the revolver, and put it up against his ear.

"You about done?" he said. It came out as a sort of breathless growl. And because he wasn't sure the young guy could understand him, he said it again. "You about done now?" The young guy just moaned. Blood was running all down his face.

He pulled him up and got him walking. They went across the street, where a crowd of Democrats watched them stagger past. His dress uniform was torn and covered with garbage and blood. They were just past the front steps of the Cape Fear Hall and only a half block away from the Annex when the young guy said something and tried to turn around again and Q.P. spun him around and hit him hard in the face, which sent him sliding along the length of somebody's Cadillac and into the gutter.

"My God . . ." a woman said behind them. There was the sound of high heels fleeing along the sidewalk.

He pulled the young guy up and cuffed him, which he should have done earlier, he realized. Cars stopped for them as they staggered across Princess Street like a couple of drunks. He got him up onto the sidewalk and through the doors to the Annex.

The young guy was talking to him now . . . angry, cursing. Q.P. couldn't make out any of the words. Threats. Up on the Fifth Floor they crashed in and woke up Mr. Baker, who came out of his little night room in his robe, blinking, wondering what the hell was going on.

"You need any hep, Kewpie?" he asked.

"Wouldn't mind . . ." Mr. Baker came over and put a nightstick around the young guy's throat and Q.P. came up behind him and tossed his keys and billfold in a drawer. Then the two of them carried him down into a cell at the end of the room and shoved him inside. As soon as the heavy door slammed shut, the young guy yelled something at him. It was a threat, about making phone calls and destroying Q.P.'s life forever.

"Don't mess with me, son, if you want to get anything to eat round here," Baker said and went back to his room.

Q.P. turned on the tap and got the hose they used to wash the place out and pulled it over to the end cell. He twisted the nozzle and widened out the spray and wet the man down good.

"Fuck you!" the young guy started screaming out of his bloody mouth. "Fuck you! Fuck you! *Fuck you!*"

Q.P. held the hose on him until he was soaked through and then went over to the window and pulled it open to let the cold January air blow in.

"Sleep tight," he said as he stumbled out of the cell block.

He didn't sleep much that night. Around two in the morning, after he had finally been able to relax, things started to hurt. He finished off his bottle of aspirin by dawn. His right eye was still puffy and had gone deep purple like a blood blister. When he went to put on his shirt, he couldn't lift his arms to do up the top button they were so sore.

He eased himself into the Chevy and tried to back out. He did it by faith and looking in the rearview mirror, since he couldn't twist around to look out the back window. Downtown he stopped at Ripley's, which was just opening up, and went in and got a big bottle of aspirin. Old Man Ripley didn't say a word. Almost like a sleepwalker back behind his counter, humming to himself. Taking the money, handing out the pills.

Mary Helen met him at the back door of the Annex. She had a watering can in her hand and had been pretending to be taking care of the azaleas. As soon as he drove up, she set it down on the brick wall and ran up to him and then recoiled.

"My God, Kewpie. You oughta be in the hospital. How can you drive like that?"

"I can drive okay. I just can't put on my necktie."

"Your eye looks like an eggplant."

"Yeah, well . . ."

"I'll phone over and see if Doc Elkins can squeeze you in after lunch. Now . . . *listen*," she said, blocking his way so he'd have to pay attention to her. "Bucky Nelson came in this morning and he wasn't exactly happy—"

"Well, that make two of us," he said and tried to shuffle past her into the courthouse.

"Just hold on. What happened was that he released Mr. Saldera—"

"Mr. *who?*"

"Your prisoner?"

That stopped him. He stood there in the foyer trying to focus on Mary Helen's glasses. She was just a blur backlit by the double doors.

"Which prisoner? You mean the *guy* . . ."

"Yeah . . ." She reached up to lightly touch her own eye. "Spud phoned over and said to drop any charges and let him go because he's . . ." She looked around and grimaced. "On account of he's working for the *city*," she whispered.

"Goddamn," he muttered and staggered into his office.

He had to wait to get Bucky Nelson on the phone, fumbling with the aspirin bottle and nearly falling asleep while he tried to fish the cotton out with Franklin's letter opener.

"Deputy Mayor," Nelson said, casually, as if he didn't know who had called him.

"What the fuck is goin' on, Buck?"

"Now, Kewpie—"

"I practically had to *shoot* that guy last night—"

"We have to have a chat, Kewpie."

"We do?"

"Mr. Saldera, the man you arrested, his firm is working for us. He's working on a . . . contract for the city, Kewpie."

"In what *capacity* exactly?"

"First, I can't tell you anything about it. I'm sorry but it's off limits," Nelson said flatly as if that would put an end to it.

"Oh, I see." He was thinking about going over to City Hall and ransacking Bucky Nelson's office. Absentmindedly he pulled open the top drawer of the desk; Franklin's gun was still in there, an old army automatic somebody had given him, an original 1911 model .45, all crudded up with dirt and rust, but a *big* gun. Huge. For a second Q.P. thought about putting it up to his temple and getting rid of his headache.

"You fractured Mr. Saldera's skull. Did you know that?" Nelson's voice sounded angry and hurt. Betrayed. "Now Kewpie, what this is . . . is an *internal investigation*. We've hired some professionals to give us a little help with our subversive problem, strictly on a need-to-know basis and—"

"Some professionals?"

"Yessir, some very qualified people from up in Virginia—"

"And I didn't need to know about all this, I guess? What goddamn subversive problem anyway?" There was just silence on the other end of the line.

"I'm sorry, Kewpie . . . " Nelson began.

"Hey, Bucky, I feel just fine. You want to be sorry for somebody, be sorry for your Virginia rent-a-dick," he said and slammed down the phone.

"Oh, Lord have mercy." Mary Helen sighed. She must have come into the office. He hadn't even seen her. Maybe the fight had given him a blind spot? She had an ice pack and pushed him back in the big chair and put it over his face.

"I didn't know he was working for the city. I thought he was a safecracker . . ." he muttered up to her.

"Oh, God, Kewpie. Why don't you use some common sense and just look after yourself once in a while?" she said as his head went numb.

ELEVEN

For some hours Nina Mendelson had been cutting out decorations: cupids and Valentine's Day hearts out of red construction paper in a corner of the Wilmington Public Library. The library occupied the top floor of Thalian Hall, more often known as City Hall. But in Nina's mind it was and would always be *Thalian* Hall, and she considered the other portions, the front where the council chamber and the city offices were, and the basement, which housed the police department, unwelcome interlopers. Most of the *volume* of the building, after all, was occupied by Thalian Hall, a lovely old theater built in 1855 and in continuous operation since that time, mounting productions right through the Civil War, or as some locals liked to call it, the War of Northern Aggression.

The library had been given the top floor, and with its high windows flung open it was a pleasant, breezy place to read on a summer afternoon. Almost perfection, she thought. Children liked entering beneath the huge columns that supported the Greek facade of the building; they liked climbing the stairs to the dizzy heights of the top floor. There were more and more of them every year, and the Kids Korner was the most used portion of the library, she thought. Along with Kate Pullam, the most senior of the assistant librarians, she made a space with mattresses up there for the kids if they got tired. From the nest you could lie on your stomach and have a view out from under the huge columned porch of the hall and see right down to the river.

But on this day Nina was content to occupy a corner table and clip out her hearts. It kept her away from any conflicts with Miss Hawking, who she had come to realize was a deeply sick woman, capable of anything in her paranoia. The secret to dealing with her was to avoid her, to circumvent her at every opportunity, and to combine with Kate Pullam, a smart, lovely woman who one day would become head librarian if there was any justice. But sitting there in the sun with scissors and paste gave her something to do, it kept her out of trouble, and it gave her time to think.

She had left the South as soon as she could. She thought that maybe it had something to do with being a Jew, or maybe it had something to do with being a woman and too smart to keep her mouth shut. Being willing to speak out was a trait she admired in herself, but it seemed to win her few friends, especially in Wilmington, where girls were supposed to be pretty, virtuous, and compliant. And where, she had found, being compliant was a pretty good survival strategy, since that was all the men seemed to want in a woman.

As far back as she could remember she'd felt the same way about Wilmington: It was a place to one day leave. As a child it had begun with vague stirrings and doubts. As an adolescent the doubts had grown into quiet, only partially stifled, anger. By the time she was done carving her way through high school, she'd had enough time to arrive at the conclusion that there was no future for her in the South. At least no future that she wanted.

And one day she *had* left. Gone up north to Chicago, where they had relatives and where she went to the university and threw herself into anthropology so deeply she'd almost forgotten about her parents' broken marriage, about her meddling sister Sarah and all the expectations back "home."

And for quite some time she had been happy.

Happy was what she called it, even when she was learning what she'd always suspected; that power flowed directly from the barrels of guns, that the nail that tried to rise up would always be beaten down, that justice could be bought with money, that freedom was an illusion, and that, even considering the frequency of Stalin's betrayals, America was often the oppressor, not the victim.

Knowing all these forbidden things exacted a price; it was harder to have fun anymore, harder to be blind. Harder to look away and ignore the hypocrisy all around her. So, when Sarah phoned to beg her to come back and nurse Milton through the final stages of cancer, explaining that she simply couldn't be the one to do it because of Bob and the girls, Nina found that there was very little she could say. The vitriol of the superpatriots had shaken her and, truthfully, there really was no one else. She needed the time to finish her thesis anyway and so she budgeted a year; a year to keep her head down, a year to come home and help Pop die. Over a couple of phone calls she let herself be persuaded into coming back, and for the first time it was just the two of them in the house.

And for the first time she was the strong one.

She had quickly organized this new chapter of her life; she would work part-time in the library, filling in when anyone was sick and during lunch hours. Mornings she would nurse Milton and then she'd come back in time to get ready for their dinner. She cleaned the house and tried to arrange his estate, holding his hand, helping him make his signature. They talked, not much, but they did talk. Without expecting a reply, she sent a letter to her mother. She didn't tell Milton about it but it probably wouldn't have mattered. Milton was either brave or very detached. He seemed to accept his impending death easily, and despite all Nina's hesitations, they got along. Maybe he had forgiven his errant daughter or maybe he just didn't notice her, she thought. Maybe he, too, had a lot on his mind.

It felt good to be home without family. Finally the city was hers; no one was telling her how to dress, or how to behave, or how to be more what they had always wanted, which was more like Sarah—married and pretty, with twins and a mortgage. More happy. More in order.

Taking care of a dying father felt a little like being free, and her life, she thought, as she snipped out another perfect heart, could go on like this for some time. Sometimes you had to put yourself in a place where you had no freedom in order to understand what it really was. Strange, she thought as she made the last cuts and the heart fell away from the construction paper and left its silhouette there on the table in front of her.

She had noticed when the policeman came in. He'd picked out a table across the reading room and looked around trying to find the card catalog. What she noticed first was that he had a bandage over his eye and that to see anything he had to turn his head from side to side. Like a bird.

For a few minutes she lost herself in inventing catchy slogans for the hearts, *I Love to Read!* and *Romance Beneath the Covers!,* and lettering them neatly across the hearts.

"Excuse me . . ." Now the policeman was standing there across her table. Lost.

"Uh-huh?"

"Ah . . . Do you work here?" He gestured to the pile of hearts.

"What can I do for you?"

He was looking around. Helplessly, suspiciously? "Ah . . . I'm new here and I'm trying to get some information . . ."

Good start, she thought.

"I've got to take this test and it's all about North Carolina criminal law and so I thought I oughta brush up a little, so I came here and . . ."

"Ahh . . ." She got up and walked him over to the reference stacks.

"Law, is that right?"

"Yeah . . . I'm going to take the SBI test."

"Okay . . . this right here is the *Criminal Code of North Carolina.*" It was a series of six thick brown volumes. "And it's out of date, that's the first thing I ought to tell you—"

"Oh . . ." His face fell, at least the part she could see. She wondered what the patch covered. All around it, the skin was a blend of yellow and brown bruises. Whatever had happened to him, it must have hurt.

"I guess I could start there at least . . ." He looked at the books, doubtfully, she thought.

"You could try asking Judge Burke for help. I think they've probably got everything over in his chambers. They probably are required to have those books somewhere over in the courthouse. It's probably a law." She laughed for some reason. He did, too.

"Come on, let's get you started." Together they took the *Criminal Code* over to his table.

"Do you know anything about the test, about what kind of questions they're going to ask you?" He frowned and pulled out a sheet of paper from his breast pocket and unfolded it for her. It was an invitation to be interviewed for the position of field agent with the

North Carolina State Bureau of Investigation. It would be held in Raleigh on August 2, 1954, from 8:30 A.M. until 5:00 with an hour lunch break. There was an ambiguous statement that said that SBI "agents" were required to have an excellent knowledge of the law.

"It says here you have to know all about accounting?"

"Yeah."

"This looks pretty tough," she said.

"Yeah."

She pushed the page over to him. "Well, I know somebody who might be able to help you with the accounting part, or at least get you started. Just a sec—" She got up and went across the room and started searching for something.

Q.P. watched her as she looked around on the shelves at the end of the library. A tall girl, black hair pinned back on the sides with barrettes. She had a pair of reading glasses she kept around her neck with a little gold chain. Dressed like a bobby-soxer, long pleated dress, a sweater and blouse, saddle shoes. She took a book down, opened it up, put it back again, looked somewhere else again. Found something good, looked over his way. And smiled.

He spent most of the afternoon there, browsing through *Accounting for Beginners* and making an attempt at the N.C. *Criminal Code,* which was incomprehensible, he decided.

Nina finished her hearts and began putting them up with push-pins on the pillars between each of the windows. She worked her way along the end of the building and ultimately she got to his table.

"How's it going?" she asked. Q.P. made a face and stretched.

"You should take a break before you fall asleep," she said. He thought that was funny. His smile was all crooked, she noticed.

"I guess Valentine's Day is coming up," he said.

"Yep, every year, whether you want it to or not . . ."

He stood up and she saw that they were just about the same size.

"You want to go get a Sno-Kone?" he asked.

She laughed and for some reason looked around for Miss Hawking. "It's February, not exactly the time of year for a Sno-Kone."

"No, I guess not."

"Sure. A Sno-Kone in the middle of winter?" she said. "Sure, let's go." Wild girl. Up for anything.

She had to slow up for him on the stairs because every time he took a step down it hurt.

"What happened to you?" she whispered to him as they were going down the cool stairwell.

"Oh . . . little political meeting that turned sour," he said. She stared at him for a few stairs. Was he pretending or was this his idea of a real dry joke?

"It hurts when I stand up too fast, or if I bump into anything, or try and twist, or . . . It hurts most of the time, actually," he said with a little laugh. She thought she ought to reach out and grab his elbow and help him along. Be his nurse, too. What was she doing this for? Now she was helping this cop down the stairs, starting to worry about his health. Nina turns into Florence Nightingale, she thought, starting to feel just a little panicky there in the stairwell.

"Why don't you call in sick, or something?" she said, and without meaning to she found herself almost admonishing him.

"Well, maybe I will if it really starts to hurt," he said.

They went across the street to Runt's Pool Room, a place she had never gone into in her life.

"What can I do you for today, Kewpie?" the man behind the counter called out. He was huge with a gigantic stomach that was exploding from his shirt and hanging over his pants. Suspenders about to pop. There was hardly anybody in there. A couple of black men were strolling around the tables at the end of the room. The Pool Room must be integrated, she thought.

"We'd like a couple of Sno-Kones, I think. Yeah?" he asked her.

"Aren't you Milt's little girl?" the man asked. She found herself blushing. Q.P. looked over at her.

"Uh-huh," she said, smiling. She was acting like an idiot, she thought. She tried to calm down.

"'Fore he got sick your daddy's been doing my taxes for me, oh, Lord . . . for near 'bout ten years there."

"If you're still in business he must have done a good job," she said and everybody laughed, even the men in the back who had started looking at her.

It turned out the huge man was "Runt" himself, and in gratitude for services her father had at one time rendered, the Sno-Kones were on the house. They walked along Third Street and nibbled on the ice and talked.

She told him about her father and he told her about his eye and from little clues that they each sprinkled through their conversation they discovered their mutual distaste for Wilmington.

"I don't hate it here, exactly," she said. They were standing at the corner of Fifth and Market, watching the cars navigate around the fountain. "But . . . I guess, I loved it here when I was just a kid. I really did, and now I've learned a little too much. I've learned how much it costs if you want to be different, or feel different or think differently. All I see now is the ugly parts. It makes me nuts." She stopped, afraid of being depressing. *Now he thinks I'm a neurotic case*, she was thinking, watching Q.P. stare around the downtown with a little smile across his battered face.

"I guess I should get back," she said. "The Hawk'll be having a fit."

"Yeah. I've got some real work to do, too."

They walked down the hill heading back toward Thalian Hall. Back in the library he gathered up his notes and helped her put the law books back where they'd come from. He was starting for the steps and then turned around to her.

"Do you know anything about voodoo?" he asked. She started laughing again.

"No, but—" She gestured to the stacks. "I can probably find out."

"Well, I can't do it today . . ." he said.

"Well, come back, then," she said.

"Okay . . ." he said. It was a contract.

He started out again, a few more steps this time, and then came back closer to her this time.

"Do you want to go visit the monstrosity collection?" he said quietly. She found herself smiling. This time he was the one who started laughing.

"The monstrosity collection, sure . . ." she heard herself saying. "Sure, I love monstrosities of all kinds."

Wild girl, she thought. *Wild, wild girl.*

Q.P. went directly to a late-afternoon court appearance, which went all right for once. He managed to give some testimony that didn't crumble under cross-examination and get out of there in time to get back to his paperwork.

And then right at the end of the day Mary Helen came in his office and closed the door behind her. "I just thought you might want to know," she said quietly. "I was up talking to Marly and she said that there's, well . . ."

"What?"

"Oh, she said that somebody . . . *Somebody* . . . she really didn't know *who* . . ." Mary Helen made a face and shrugged.

"What, for chrissakes?" he said.

"Oh, Kewpie . . . I told you this was going to happen," she said sadly.

"What!" He had just about had it today, he thought.

"There's somebody else gonna be looking for your job," she said.

"*What?*"

"Marly said 'somebody else is lookin' for Kewpie's job.' That's what she said."

"Who?"

"She didn't hear. We ought to know all about it in a day or two. Deadline to file is next week, after all . . ."

He stood in the middle of the office shaking his head back and forth. If it wasn't one damn thing, it was something else. "She doesn't have any idea who's after me?" he said. His voice was high, like a kid's.

Mary Helen just shrugged.

He sighed. Politics . . . "Well, if that doesn't just take the goddamn cake," he said.

"I just thought you ought to know, Kewpie," Mary Helen said as she turned and left. A little too quickly, he thought.

Were those tears he had seen in her eyes?

TWELVE

There was a tiny clicking sound and the lock turned in its cylinder. "Okay . . ." Q.P. whispered. "We're in!"

Nina Mendelson smiled as he swung open the door to the monstrosity collection, closing it behind them before he turned on the lights. It was a musty, spooky little room down in the basement of the Community Memorial Hospital.

"You come here often?" she said, giggling. It was scary and exciting, just the breaking-in part all by itself.

"Couple of times. Doc Sykes took me down here once," he said. They were still whispering.

They walked slowly down the aisles between the shelves. Each had rows of jars, each containing a fetus or stillborn child. Each one was horrifically deformed. Is this a *date?* she thought as she looked into the little faces.

"See this one?" he said. She went over and looked at what would have been a boy with no limbs, just stubs that protruded from the body. Fins, like a fish or a seal. The eyes were open and it almost looked like the child was smiling.

"It's beautiful . . . sort of."

"Yeah, I know, that sounds crazy, but it's true. He doesn't know he's a monster," Q.P. said. He turned to her and gave a little shrug. They were standing very close to each other. Maybe this was just too strange, she was thinking. "You must work on a lot of . . . awful cases," she said to him.

"Car wrecks." They started walking along again. "They can be

pretty bad, sometimes. You know, sometimes there's children . . ."
Was he abnormally preoccupied by children and fetuses? She lifted
her hand to the jars and let her fingers move from glass to glass as
she walked down the aisles.

"I guess everybody has to die sooner or later." She was thinking
of Milton back at the house listening to the radio, sliding in and out
of his dreams. "Maybe if you've only got one life to live, it would be
okay to die right at birth." She was looking at something she
thought at first was a coconut shell, then she saw that it was an un-
born child, squeezed and twisted like a nut-brown root system.
Long hairs were matted over the skin. It was absolutely horrible.
She was glad it was cool in the little room.

"Now, this is interesting, over here," she heard him say behind
her.

It was a jar, set apart from the others, and inside was an adult
woman's hand. The nails still had polish and in the green fluid they
were a dark purple color. The hand has been severed at the wrist;
there was a long wisp of skin floating there. She could see individual hairs.

"It's an engagement ring. This was back in the twenties, sometime. She was rich. They'd followed her to this party and knocked
her fiancé on the head and then kidnapped her . . ." Q.P. was looking at her.

"Uh-huh . . ." She nodded at the hand, trying to seem detached
about it all.

"—so, after they killed her they tried to get the ring off but it was
stuck on. And so they cut off the *hand* and got rid of the body. And
the police never could find her, but the kidnappers had taken the
hand thinking they'd get the ring off later and they got caught with
that. That's how they got convicted. The hand was the evidence,
see?" He turned the jar around to show her a faded red sticker with
Coates—#4 written on it in ink.

"That's . . . that's . . ."

"Pretty awful, huh?"

"Yeah . . ." she said quietly.

"But at least they got caught," he said with a shrug.

"Is there a lot of . . . murder? Killing, or homicide, or whatever
you . . ."

"Murder. That's what it is." He laughed. She looked at him there, one arm leaning up against the shelves, the little babies floating all around him. He looked like a nice guy, she thought, strong in the chin and clear in the eyes. Ready to laugh if he got the chance. She liked the sound of his voice, she decided.

"Yeah . . . there's enough of it to go around, all right. It's pretty obvious mostly. Husbands kill their wives, wives kill their husbands. It's not like Boston Blackie." He laughed again.

She was trying to laugh along with him. Standing there next to a reassembled skeleton that hung from a coatrack, hugging herself. All of a sudden it was too cold in the little room.

"You want to go get some pie?"

"Yes, I think so. I think pie would be nice."

He drove out to Pic's, a diner out on the road to Wrightsville Beach that was open all night, and they got pie and coffee and talked.

He told her about Franklin and how much he missed the man, and she talked about Milton and about how she hoped that when she got old she could handle dying with as much grace.

A couple of Wrightsville Beach police came in and said hello. After they teased Nina about being in Q.P.'s custody, they moved down to the end of the counter with hot coffees and pie; just two cops bleary-eyed from their shift and with their own business to discuss.

She told him about anthropology at the University of Chicago and how her dream was to go to India someday. He told her about how he always thought he wanted to be a private eye in Manhattan.

"What's the strangest thing, the strangest case, you've ever had?" She pushed her plate away and leaned one elbow on the counter and watched him. The patch had been taken off and the bruise was going away. He had nice eyes, she thought.

"Well . . ." He thought about it for a minute, looked over at her, and got distracted by her face. They laughed and she poked him in the ribs.

"Okay . . . the strangest . . ." The Bladenboro Beast was just about the most bizarre thing he could think of. Then he had a picture of the Cape Fear River running high and the air force sentries pulling the tarp off of Cora Snow.

He turned and saw Nina watching him, her face gone serious because he'd drifted away for a few seconds there. So he shrugged and started telling her all he knew about Cora Snow.

About how it wasn't so *strange,* really, just that it had come out of nowhere early one morning before he was awake enough, and now it looked like the case was dead, as dead as the girl was. About how there had been a couple of suspects, but both had alibis; one was solid, the other maybe a little weaker.

"Sometimes," he said with a little grimace, "you have to wait. And then wait some more."

"You could wait forever," she said.

"Yeah." And unless something turned up the murder would never be solved. There were no leads to follow. The trail had just about gone cold.

"You know how you read about some detective who stays with a case and finally pieces it together after thirty or forty years and everybody's forgotten about it except him, and then he finally finds some little piece of evidence and goes and arrests the guy for murder and it's a big surprise?"

"Yeah."

"That just doesn't ever happen. If you don't get them right away, whatever the crime is, most times it's over. They're gone." He shrugged. "So, we'll never find out who killed her, probably."

"That's awful."

"Yeah, it is. It's an awful world."

"You can't just stop."

"Well, there's always new crimes being committed."

"But . . . I mean, you just can't give up."

"Well, we don't give up exactly, the case is still open . . ."

"But you said there's hardly any chance?"

"Yeah, there's women that are killed all the time. All of a sudden she goes missing. Nobody knows where. Maybe she doesn't want to be found, you know?"

"Yeah, sure, I can see that, but—"

"There's women that just . . . drop right off the edge of the earth. You know, most of them are poor or alone or in the middle of a bad home situation . . ." His voice trailed off. Somehow he felt guilty about what he was trying to explain to her. Like it was all his fault. "It keeps you awake at night . . ."

"A lot of them?" she asked.

"Yeah, I guess. I guess there is a lot of them; it's a universal phenomenon. Throw a rock, you hit a missing woman. Maybe somebody catches up to them before we do, then they're not missing anymore." He had a mental flash of Cora Snow down by the riverbank again, shook his head to drive the image away.

Nina had straightened up on the stool. The two Beach cops were joking with the waitress down at the end of the bar and all of a sudden she felt a little too warm. This whole thing was swerving into a big mistake, she was starting to think. ". . . and I wish we could do more and I'm sorry," he was saying, "but that's just the way it is."

He looked over and saw that she was upset. She hugged herself when she was upset. She turned to him and he realized that she wasn't just upset, she was angry.

"You can't just give up, Kewpie."

"Well . . ."

"No. Listen to me—" She reached over and grabbed his arm. She was squeezing him; he could feel her fingernails biting into his bicep.

"You can't *give up*. They could be anybody, these women. They could be *me*. You can't quit on them. That's not fair. That would be just as bad as murder. That would be letting the killers get away with it . . ."

He looked into her eyes. She meant it. She meant all of it.

"Okay," he said. "Okay . . ."

They didn't talk much on the way back into town. He drove along, chewing the inside of his mouth, kicking himself for taking her on such a stupid date. Why on earth he thought that anything good could come out of going to the monstrosity collection he'd never know. Idiot.

But when he pulled up slowly in front of her father's house she leaned over and gave him a soft little kiss.

"You're a nice sheriff," she said and then she was out of the car and through the little gate, waving good-bye to him under the porch light. And because he liked that she thought he was such a

nice sheriff, he watched her fiddle with the lock and waited until
she was safe inside before he put the Chevy in gear.

Inside she found that her father was still awake. His timing was all
off because of the painkillers. "Good time?" Milton asked. His voice
was just a whisper now.

"Mmm-hmm. Can I get you anything, Pop?"

"Tea, if you're going to stay up." She went to the kitchen and put
on the kettle and made the tea for him. Took it back on a tray.

"Papa," she asked, "do you know a man named Runt?" Milton
opened his eyes.

"Runt? Where'd you meet him?"

"He's got the Pool Room over there—"

"My God . . . You went into Runt's?" Milton was awake, looking
at her now, surprised.

"It seems like a nice place . . ."

"You didn't go in alone?" he said. She laughed. Now he starts
worrying, she thought.

"No, I had police protection."

"Runt . . . *Alexander* is his real name. I went to school with him.
Alexander Newell. He and his brother Jeff used to beat me up because I was a Jew. They used to wait for me after school, beat me up
almost every day. I started carrying a knife. I stuck him with it
once . . ."

"He said you did his taxes."

"Yes, that was after."

"After what?"

"After he was one of the infantry boys in Germany that first arrived over at the Dachau camp. We were friends after that. I don't
know what happened to his big brother." Milton had closed his eyes
now. She held the tea up for him.

"Going through all that turned him round. Changed him completely. He gave money to the synagogue after that. Go over and
look at the plaque. He's the only Presbyterian on there. Gave a
thousand dollars. In 1945 he came up to the office and I thought he
was going to beat me up again. Still had his uniform on. Sat there in
the chair and cried like a baby. We went out and got a fifth and

drank the whole thing down. People can change, you know," he said.

He reached down and held her hand. Just a light touch, no strength at all. He was smiling at her.

Her father, she thought, her strange, aloof, self-absorbed father. The man she'd hated all that time. He was smiling at her.

"People change all the time," he said.

THIRTEEN

"All right, I've got it," Mary Helen said. She came in and spread the *Morning Star* out across his blotter. "I want you to look at this, Kewpie. This, right here, is your winning ticket."

The headline said:

Beast Reappears!

"Aw, man . . ."

"That thing is still out there and those rednecks in Bladenboro can't catch it. Now, what you do is you and Donny and George Foster go out and get his coon dogs and go out there and catch it."

"Mary Helen . . ."

"Listen!" She was serious. "What you need is publicity. *Good* publicity. You need to drive over there and *kill* the Bladenboro Beast. That'd be worth five hundred votes right there."

"Suppose I don't get it?"

"Oh, come on, Kewpie . . ."

"There's all kinds of people out trying to kill that thing. What makes you think that we've got a better chance than they do?"

"George has got the best coon dogs in the county. Now look." She straightened up from the desk. "I'm not going to say any more—"

"Okay, don't."

"I'm not going to force this down your craw, but I really don't think you're going to win the primary with these." She reached over

and grabbed some ballpoint pens out of a mason jar he'd put out
on his desk.

"Hey . . . those cost fifteen cents apiece—"

"This is . . . just . . . tacky, Kewpie. This is not at all what is required."

"I thought it was kinda different. You know, every time somebody writes a check, or a note, or something, they see your name."
The pens were red with white lettering printed down the barrel:

Q.P. For Sherriff!

"Okay. You're the big-league politician," she said and went back
out to her desk. "Your face is fine now. You could go in and get
Jimmy to do your picture anytime at all," he heard her say from
outside.

He took one of the red pens and figured out how much pictures
would cost. The whole venture was going to run a hundred bucks
with printing costs. He started thinking that was why they had elections, so that all the photographers and pen manufacturers could
get rich every few years.

Mary Helen came back in. He could tell by the way she was walking that she was pissed off. She tossed one of the pens down on his
blotter.

"The paint is already coming off on these things," she said and
then left to get the telephone.

He spun the red pen around on the blotter. The white lettering
was all smeared, worn away after just a couple of days. They'd
spelled "Sheriff" wrong, too, he realized.

"It's Ezzard." She leaned in. He picked up the phone.

"How you doin', Chief?"

"It's tonight, Kewpie" was all he said.

They assembled in the City Garage, which was back behind Thalian
Hall. It had a long fence along one side and gates that had been
closed so that the Combined Team could gather without causing a
fuss.

He leaned on one of the city prowl cars and mooched an Old Gold from Donny, instantly regretted the foul taste in his mouth, but finished it anyway.

Carruthers had a couple of his cops wheel out a blackboard from the basement and they all sat there and looked at the plan that had been devised to finally catch the safecrackers. Technically the Combined Team was being led by Mookie Pritchard, chief of the Wrightsville Beach police, but in reality they didn't have the experience or the resources to pull it off, so Carruthers had taken charge.

The way Carruthers explained it, everything was going to go off without a hitch. The Wrightsville Beach police had been tipped off to where the men were holed up, had cased the place, and recognized one of the men when he drove up with four or five bags of groceries. They thought there were six men inside, but nobody knew for sure. Nobody knew how many guns they had. Nobody knew a lot of things. He and his boys were assigned to block the two bridges over the canal, and when it was all over they would be the ones who brought the safecrackers back to the Fifth Floor.

Q.P. looked over and saw Wills showing one of the highway patrolmen how he'd filed down the front sight of his revolver so he could get it out of his holster quick. Lingering by the side door was Errol Tate, the Negro rookie cop. His blue uniform shirt was devoid of insignia, probably to indicate that he was still in training, but it had been pressed so that the seams were razor sharp, and his shoes had been spit shined to where they looked like patent leather. Tate was on the tall side. Lanky, long muscled with an open face. Every now and then someone would come by and say something to him and he'd smile. Tate wasn't eating anything, or maybe he'd eaten before, or maybe they'd made him eat somewhere else.

He was glad all he had to do was wait down by the bridges, he decided. He was aware of a sudden sour feeling in his stomach, and he looked around at the men and wondered if somebody wasn't maybe going to get killed tonight.

Carruthers asked if anybody had questions and nobody did. He told everyone again to stay off the radios for the whole time until the raid was actually in progress. There was an antenna on top of the beach house and the safecrackers might have a short-wave radio and be listening in. No one was to be in position until midnight, which left them a lot of time to kill, so they went inside and ate Brunswick stew, barbecue, and hush puppies out of cardboard containers that had been sent over.

He cornered Carruthers by the Coke machine and asked him if he might borrow a couple of his men for a few days. Carruthers didn't like the idea one bit.

"Hell, I'm using everybody all the time. I don't have any men left over for you."

"I need to do a surveillance and I don't have enough resources . . ."

"A what?"

"A surveillance. A stakeout."

"Well, don't come crying to me. If you need more men or more bullets or more writin' paper or more anything, go to the goddamn county commissioners, that's who's supposed to pay your bills. What's this *surveillance* for, anyhow?"

"I want to watch Red Billy for a couple of days—"

"That ain't a goddamn case, that's bullshit. The only suspect you ever had's got five white men from Raleigh who will testify to anything you ask them except for the whores. They already said they were out fishin', so there's no case, Kewpie. So who cares?"

"I care, Chief. I got to solve this thing. It's my responsibility. It's what I'm paid to do." He was getting angry at Carruthers. "It's my case and I care. That's enough."

"Well, you can stick that up your ass. Make all this trouble over some dead nigger whore, I swear to God . . ." He turned and walked away from the machine. "Good luck, Dick Tracy," Carruthers called back over his shoulder, loud enough for the other cops' heads to turn, tipping his Coke up for a last long drink, shaking his head at the stupidity of their "Acting Sheriff."

He only woke up when Donny parked the Chevy on the bridge that crossed the canal to Wrightsville Beach, backing the car up carefully so that it was blocking the road.

"Okay . . . the radio is *on*," Nokes said. He turned the volume up on the speaker, got out, and came over to where Q.P. was leaning against the bridge rail looking down into the water.

"You can't catch a goddamn thing in there anymore," Nokes was saying, and right at that moment there was a blast of static from the radio and from down on the beach Q.P. heard a couple of popping sounds—like cherry bombs, only he knew they weren't fireworks. "Shit," he heard Nokes say behind him.

A siren had started up across the dunes; they could see headlights, and there were another couple of gunshots. The speaker inside the Chevy erupted with a sound of radio traffic. Q.P. walked out in front of the Chevy and looked across to the other bridge, where Glen Petty and a second deputy, Ellis Strickland, had parked.

"They're running for it," he said to Nokes, and even as he said it he could see the safecrackers' headlights coming at them, slewing around a corner, desperate to get out of Wrightsville. Behind him Nokes turned on their flasher and he could see the dunes in front of him flicker in the red light.

He could see the car now, a beat-up Nash, and he took out his revolver and raised it, hoping for a clear shot if the prowl cars got out of the way. The Nash came to the intersection, saw them blocking the bridge, and the driver turned, but Petty's car was sitting right there, so he jammed on the brakes and spun around backwards on the sandy asphalt.

One man jumped out of the car and started to run up the dune but only got as far as a big real-estate sign, and then he turned and started shooting. The driver was spinning his wheels in the soft sand. And that was when Q.P. heard the bullet go by—

It was like an electric bolt, or a big june bug; a low buzzing that blew right by his ear, and then there were some enormous explosions and he realized that Nokes was shooting behind him.

Now the air was alive with sirens. There was the sound of something smacking into the pilings below his feet, and he pointed his gun at the man running across the dunes and started firing, walking forward along the bridge toward the man as he pulled the trigger over and over until he ran out of bullets.

One of the P.D.'s prowl cars drove up and skidded to a stop at the intersection, and when the safecracker saw that, he threw down his gun and stood up. Q.P. saw that Petty had driven right up to the Nash. There was a cloud of smoke and it looked like the safecrackers' car had blown its engine. Petty had his M1 out and big Ellis Strickland ran around and vanished into the cloud of steam.

All of a sudden everybody was yelling all at the same time.

"Well, they don't say anything about how it got screwed up," Glen Petty was saying. "They don't say about how the P.D. drove its paddy wagon into the ditch, or how much they're going to have to pay those people for breaking down the doors of their beach house . . ."

"How did they get the address wrong? How could they do something like that?" Nokes said. He was pacing back and forth across the carpet. His pants were still stained up to the knee from wading through a ditch to apprehend the man on the sand. The entire department was reading over Nokes's shoulders the lead article in a special *Morning Star* extra edition:

Theft Ring Cracked!

Nokes stood up and made a disgusted expression. "We're not even mentioned in there. I'm going home," he said and left the room. Q.P. couldn't blame him. The night had just about worn him out.

"I mean . . . that's just not *fair*," Petty said and looked up at Q.P. "If it hadn't been for us, them boys'd be in Georgia by now."

"Here we are," Mary Helen said and started reading, "' . . . the investigations are not yet complete following arrests in which members of the highway patrol and the sheriff's department also participated.'"

"Well, from the looks of this, I think Ezzard is going to run for mayor next time, you know." Mary Helen looked up at him.

"You were shot!" He heard Nina's voice behind him. Everybody stopped and looked up. She had rushed through the wide basement doors and stood there, her mouth open staring at him.

"No, I'm okay . . . just a little—"

"Hell, they shot him right through the *collar*. Looky here." Strickland grabbed him by the shoulders, spun him around so he faced Nina, and then poked his finger through the hole.

"My God! . . . I heard . . . I mean, they were talking about the . . . and they said that you'd . . . so I thought . . ." And then all of a sudden she turned around and ran back out.

"Who's that?" Petty said.

"That is what is called an 'interested party,' I think," Mary Helen said softly, and looked back down at the paper to keep from smiling.

"I'll be right back," Q.P. said, and left, heading for the library.

They walked along talking in whispers through the stacks while she shelved returns and he tried to explain the messed-up raid and the bullet hole in his shirt.

"Look, Sheriff," she whispered. "Don't flatter yourself. I happened to hear downstairs that you'd been shot. I guess I never thought about that before. I guess that maybe I got a little scared and maybe . . . I acted a little foolishly. It won't happen again." She slammed a couple of books back into the stacks.

"Well, I'm glad you didn't want me to get killed."

"Of *course* I don't want you to get killed." Her voice had risen and she fought to get it back down to a whisper. "I don't want *anybody* to get killed! I just . . . forgot what you do for a living, that's all."

"Most of the time it's boring—"

"Ahem—" They turned and saw Miss Hawking at the end of the aisle.

"How are you this morning, ma'am?" Q.P. said, raising his hand to tip an invisible hat.

"I'm quite well. When you're done there, Miss Mendelson, I'd like to have a word with you," she said and went back to her office.

"Would you just go? I'll call you later."

"Want to go to a movie, or something?"

"No. I don't. I want to be alone. I want to think about this . . ." He thought for a second she was going to cry. "Okay?" she said. "Why don't you go arrest someone before I get fired. I'll call you."

And she did call, later, and they did go out to the movies, to catch *From Here to Eternity* at the Colony.

And the romance of the movie had the power of getting them back a little closer to the same wavelength. And after it was over

they walked all the way back up to Milton's in weather that had become unseasonably warm, a promise of spring.

"I like you, Mr. Sheriff," she said at the gate.

"I like you, too," Q.P. said. His voice was thin. Weak sounding, he
thought. Sappy. Not at all like Burt Lancaster.

"Well, that's good, I guess."

"I think it is."

She looked at him, her face gone very serious for a moment,
thinking it out. She shook her head and then kissed him softly.

"I promised myself I wasn't going to get involved with anyone,"
she said. "I promised myself I wasn't going to . . . just get carried
away, that I was going to approach things *scientifically* . . ."

He smiled a little at that, having done more or less the same thing
about a million times after Marie and all the shit they'd gone
through.

"And I was happy—" she said, reaching up to touch his cheek
and kiss him once more.

"—I was happy until I met you."

FOURTEEN

The loading door in the back of Beverly's was open, so he and Nokes walked in. There were two tables and Detective Tommy Wills was lying on one snoring. On the other was something covered by a blue sheet. The door was open for the smell, he figured. Most of it came from a pile of carpeting that had been dragged over in the corner and was pretty high.

The lights were off and the place was quiet except for Wills.

"There's Doc," Nokes said.

Sykes was over at a metal desk in the corner of Beverly's writing up his report.

"What's the scoop, Doc?"

"Well . . ." Sykes paused to stub out his cigarette and flick the ashes off the report. "Just lookin' at it, your strangler's struck again, Mr. Waldeau." Sykes waved the report around for a second to let the ink dry before he turned it over and started drawing on the diagram. "Strangulation's cause of death. Maybe up to a week ago, hard to tell exactly. Found her wrapped up in a rug."

"They know who she is already?" Q.P. asked.

"Wills says they're checking on the spelling. 'Mitchell' maybe, or 'Mee-chew'? Something like that."

"She was tied up . . ."

"In fact she *was* tied up, and then she was tied up *again* into that carpet over there," Sykes said. "Found her down by State Ports there."

They walked over to where Wills was sleeping on the table. They looked at him for a second and then went over and lifted the sheet off the woman. Nokes stepped away from the light. There was a dark mark that had blossomed around her neck or wrists. She was in her thirties, maybe middle thirties, Q.P. thought. No makeup. Her eyes were open.

"You see what I mean?" Sykes said from across the room. He hadn't even turned around.

"Is this what she was tied up with?" There was a porcelain dish with a pile of muddy baling string coiled up in it. The twine was dirty but relatively new. Still yellow inside where it was cut away.

"That's it, and"—Sykes turned around and pointed at the carpet—"there's more wrapped round the rug over there." Q.P. snapped on the lamp and moved the twine over to the dish, reached out a finger, and turned it over so they could see the knots.

"It's not the same," Nokes said.

"Not the string, but the knots are about the same . . ." He turned the cords over; they were still curved from the shape of the woman's wrists.

"Yeah, maybe," said Nokes. "I'll go get Nate." He left to look around for Giddings and his camera. Q.P. walked around Wills and over to the carpet.

"Wooff! Goddamn!" he said. For a second he thought he was going to throw up.

"Just by accident she got dumped in a place that somebody had disposed of some renderings, you know? Chickens . . . *hawgs* . . . all kinds a shit," Sykes said lazily. He fanned dry another official document.

"What about—"

"Don't get your bowels in an uproar. I took samples. For the record, I'm sayin' she was assaulted," Sykes said from his desk without turning around.

Wills was still snoring. His sleeves were rolled up and he had crossed his arms under his suspenders to keep them from dangling over the side. Giddings and Donny came back; Giddings wrinkled up his nose and made a face.

"Mmmm-*mmm*, I heard about this out in the street," said Giddings, wincing. "We'll have to burn that."

"Take a picture of this first," said Q.P. He reached out with a broom handle and pulled at the mess until the ropes came out.

"Is that what I think it looks like?" said Nokes when he saw the knots.

"Yeah, looks like it. Hey, Nate, take a picture of this right here," said Q.P., poking at the knots. "We want this part right here, picture of this knot. We want a sample of these ropes to use for evidence, Doc."

"I'll wrap it in wax paper and you can take it home," Sykes said. It was his idea of a joke. Q.P. took the broom and turned the rug over and slid it around to where he could see better.

"That's some of the window cord, right there," said Nokes beside him.

"That right there?" asked Giddings over his shoulder. "That's casement cord, pull the windows up 'n' down."

"Yeah, get me a good picture of the way it's tied up there, Nate. Same with that stuff in the dish over there."

"Nothin' is too good for our friends in law enforcement." Giddings bent over and took a photograph of the knots, then he walked away and came back with a piece of shirt cardboard that he slipped down between the cords and the dirty rug.

Nokes was standing by the side of the big door, out in the air, staring up at the clouds.

"Dr. Sykes says you got a lady-killer loose out there," Giddings said softly.

"Yeah," he said. "That's what it looks like."

Giddings took his time, using a tissue to clean the mud off the white cardboard so he could get a good picture of the knots. He finished and stepped back to look at his arrangement and then hefted his big camera and took a couple of exposures of the knots.

"That's going to come out real nice," he said.

"Okay, thanks for your work, Nate," he said. Nokes was already out in the alley where he could breathe again.

FIFTEEN

Outside the word had already got around that there was a nigger murderer stalking the north side of town, some kind of maniac who had killed once and now had killed again. First thing the next day the *Morning Star* descended on the basement offices of the department. Noppy Leigh wanted to interview Q.P. and Jimmy Satterwhite came along to take his picture.

"You could have warned me," he said to Jimmy. He was smiling but he still meant it.

"That's right, Jimmy, then he could have got himself that haircut." Mary Helen was vexed by the whole thing.

"He looks okay," said Noppy Leigh, who was generally the most awake of the *Morning Star*'s reporters.

"That's good, right there," said Jimmy. "Okay, smile . . ."

"Don't smile," said Mary Helen.

"Try to look like you know what you're doing," said Nokes, who had come up to the door and was peeking in.

"Don't smile. This is serious, this is *homicide.*" Mary Helen got in. He stopped himself from laughing and Jimmy took the picture.

"Okay, is that good?" Noppy asked.

"No, he was laughing." Mary Helen came in and straightened his collar. "Take another one, Jimmy, he was *laughing.*"

"He's not selling Wheaties," said Jimmy.

"This is an article about *murder.*" She whirled on Jimmy. "What do you want to put in the paper, his face or a bunch of weeds at the crime scene?"

"Okay, okay . . . better wipe him off, then," Jimmy said. They all waited while Mary Helen went out and got a Kleenex to keep his forehead from shining. When everybody was satisfied with his portrait, Noppy started asking questions. Q.P. could see already what kind of article it would be.

"What steps are being taken to apprehend the rapist?" Leigh said over his glasses.

"Hold on right there. We still don't know about that. We're waiting on tests."

Noppy was busily writing in his pad. " . . . Waiting on tests to confirm the rapes . . ."

"Well . . . yes, basically."

"Do you have a suspect in the rapes?"

"Noppy, what we've got is two *murders*. They might be the same person did it, but it might not. The P.D. has done all the investigating on the second one, since it happened in the city."

"Okay . . . sure." Leigh brushed the idea away. "And you say this suspect is still at large and roaming through Wilmington?"

"No . . . no, I didn't say that—"

"He didn't say that at all, Mr. Leigh." Nokes was getting angry. Noppy looked up at him just for a second.

"They're two separate crimes, Noppy. Will y'all try to get that out in the paper, please."

"Sure, sure . . ."

"There's no sense in starting some kind of panic."

Leigh looked up like he'd been slapped. "People ought to be warned about locking their doors if there's some kind of blood-thirsty nigger out killin' women, Kewpie. Don't you think?"

"Don't answer that," said Mary Helen. Nokes came into the room. Leigh was standing up already. "We've got a meeting with the P.D., so that'll have to do, Mr. Leigh." Q.P. stood up and tried to look like he was getting ready for a meeting.

"It's two different events right now, Noppy. Don't forget, okay?"

"Sure . . ." said Leigh over his shoulder. Nokes shut the door behind him. "That man is a real big argument against freedom of the press, you know?"

Noppy's big article came out in the paper the next morning.

"I hate them over there," Mary Helen said. "They used that *first* picture, you can't tell me they didn't. Just look at that—" It showed him sitting there leaning forward in Franklin's chair. The lens made it look like it had been taken from the viewpoint of an ant looking up from Q.P.'s blotter.

"It makes my nose look . . ."

"Looks like a blimp," said Nokes, "or some kind of big sausage." Q.P. thought it looked like he was trying to take a bowel movement or suffering from cramps or something.

"And then they've left out just about everything you said until the end. All he has in here is that you say there's *more than one* killer." She looked up.

"I never, ever, said that."

"He never said anything like that. He said the *opposite* of that," Nokes complained.

"I was trying to tell him as little as possible," Q.P. said.

"God . . ." Mary Helen said, softly, and went back to her desk.

And if that wasn't enough, later that night all the way across town, over on Rankin Street, not a particularly rough part of the city, a Negro woman was doing the dishes when she saw a face looking in her window. She immediately screamed at the man and, because her husband wasn't home, went out to chase him away, grabbing the first thing that came to hand, which happened to be a brand-new steam iron.

Later a neighbor threw a shoe at him as he went around the corner and started running down the middle of Rankin Street.

By then more people had heard the noise, and some saw him running by, and by that point an estimated crowd of as many as thirty or forty people were running down the street, most of them not quite knowing exactly who they were after.

The man they were chasing turned out to be a Negro, a railroad worker, Lawrence "Kaiser" Smith, forty-one years old, and he made it worse by running when he saw the mass of angry faces coming his way. He didn't get far before they caught him, threw him down on the pavement, and, as he was screaming, began to beat him senseless right in the center of Seventh Street. And it might have been fatal had not the ever-vigilant Wilmington P.D.

eventually responded to the ruckus and pulled Smith away from the mob.

Early the next morning, in the second-floor offices of Utner, Whale & Terry, Dr. Terry and his brother D.L. had their breakfast while they waited for Oscar Whale to come in.

"I went over there and talked to the woman myself," D.L. said. He was wide awake, running on coffee. "She admitted she just got a *glance,* that's all she saw, she just looked up and caught sight of someone or something, and she admitted that it could have even been her own reflection she saw on the glass. There's no light out back of there."

"Didn't that woman say the prowler was wearing a shirt, light-colored shirt?"

"Yeah . . ." D.L. said. "I saw Mr. Smith's clothes in the hospital. He had on a bloody T-shirt. That's what they took off him. I didn't see anything else."

"Well, that woman's probably not sure of anything now," Terry said. "She just saw a face, some kind of face. She'd heard about all these killings, she's scared to death, she looks up, she's already *pre-disposed . . .*"

"That's right, that's right," said D.L.

Oscar Whale came in. He was a tall man, dressed in a gray double-breasted suit. His hair was cut close against his skull and he had thick glasses that he tried to avoid wearing unless he was reading.

"Well?" said D.L. after a few seconds. He was moving at about seven times the rate of Whale.

"Well, what?"

"Are they charging him or not?" D.L. was almost frantic in his impatience.

"No . . . no, not yet," Whale said quietly. He was off in the clouds, thinking about something else.

D.L. went over to the window and stared down onto the street and chewed the insides of his cheeks for a minute. "Well, as long as he is in the hospital . . ." he said.

"That's right," said the doctor, looking up from the box scores,

"He's got guards around him. Errol Tate's over there. Safest place for him, right now." But then he looked up. "You know, however, D.L., there's one thing you haven't been thinking of."

"What's that?" his brother said.

"Well, what if he did it? What if he *is* the one that killed those women?"

D.L. just stood there for a moment. He didn't know what to say; the man was innocent. He knew people who were acquainted with Smith; he was an upright man, not much of a churchgoer, and childless, but an honest man, a hard worker.

"It wasn't him," he said.

"Fine, so let's say he's innocent, that means that somebody else is killing these women, correct?"

"Doesn't matter who it is, if it's a black man we'll have trouble," D.L. said.

"We certainly will," said Whale quietly.

Down on the street Whale could see a man standing on the sidewalk holding a bag of groceries. Talking to someone but watching something else. Whale couldn't see who he was talking to, another man hidden from view by the corner of an awning. Whatever the man was staring at, it held his attention almost completely.

"So," said the doctor, "do either of you two legal geniuses have a solution, or is it time for me to purchase my train ticket north?" and he flipped back to his baseball.

"We can leave things in the hands of the law . . ." D.L. started.

"I think not, councillor," Whale said.

"That's exactly *my* point," the doctor said from behind his paper.

"Well, *councillor,* if we don't leave it to the law, then who do we leave it to?" D.L. was twisting around in his chair like it was heating up.

The doctor slapped his paper down. "Oscar, what you have to do is call in any favors you have, talk to some of your clients you've saved from the *gas chamber,* ask them to look around and see if it *is* a black man that's doing these killings . . . You find someone to go find him *first.* That's what you do. This is too important to leave up to white people." He flipped the paper back up again. "Am I right?" he said.

Below D.L. the man on the street had turned back over his shoulder and made a joke. He was laughing but still staring at whatever it was across the street.

". . . ounce of damn prevention . . ." the doctor was muttering behind him.

It was her shadow that Whale saw first.

Moving across the pavement, a step at a time. Saw the shadow before he saw the girl. Walking along briskly. Going home probably, hugging her own groceries tight to her chest. A pretty girl, who didn't want to stop and talk and joke around. Or feel the man looking at her as she crossed the street.

Or hear him laugh.

Or be what it was the man was looking at.

Or have whatever it was the man thought he wanted.

All she wanted to do was just get across the street and get away from all of it. Just get away.

Finally she was around the corner and gone where the men on the corner couldn't see her. Whale watched the man below relax, finally released from his vision, rocking back and forth against the shady brick wall, laughing with his friend.

"I know someone," Whale said to the others.

SIXTEEN

"Now, I just don't believe that, I don't believe that at all." Ellis Strickland's finger was tapping the *Morning Star* in front of Nina.

She had gotten the name of the woman from Mary Helen, made herself a space on the bench by the double doors, and started to scan through the paper. But now Ellis had come and pulled the paper around to show her the front page.

It was dominated by the jubilant news of the killing of the Bladenboro Beast. There was a photograph of two brothers from Lumberton, holding what looked like a large bullet-riddled cat aloft between them. It had taken them almost two full nights of waiting, they said, and their secret was that they hadn't used dogs, just staked out a stunted calf to draw the Beast in their direction.

"I don't believe that, Nina. Do you?" Ellis said, genuinely perplexed.

"Well . . ." She really had no opinion.

"What did they call that damn thing?" Ellis scanned through the article with his finger and pointed out the relevant paragraph. A scientist from Raleigh had come down and pronounced the Beast to be a *catamount,* an almost extinct species of ocelot that hadn't been seen in eastern Carolina for decades.

"I've never heard of that," she said.

"Nah . . ." Ellis said sourly. "You watch, something else'll come along and kill some chickens an' them boys'll have egg all over their face," he said, and gave her back the paper.

She went back to her search and leafed through right to the back pages before she found what she was looking for, an announcement that funeral services for Ruth Jewel Micheaux would be held at Holiness Tabernacle across town high up on Red Cross Street later that afternoon.

Mrs. Micheaux had been popular and the church was surrounded by cars. From outside as Nina approached she could hear the singing. She nodded to the other mourners; all were Negroes. She was the only white face in the crowd; it wasn't the first time, she thought. There was an overwhelming atmosphere of grief; Ruth Micheaux hadn't died like Milton would die, with a long time to get prepared, a long time for his family to adjust to the idea. She had been killed after supper one night by someone who put her through hell before strangling her. If it hadn't been for the recent murder of Cora Snow, most people would have been ready to suspect her Louisiana husband, who'd never been any damn good, except that he'd been gone for more than a year and nobody knew where.

Nina hung back at the rear of the church. It was a warm morning and some of the women had brought out fans.

The church itself was not very large, a building with a balcony at the back, over the foyer and cloakrooms, large doors that were thrown open and twin rows of pews. Perhaps a dozen pews on each side. Five tall arched windows on each side. A small circle of stained glass high in the arch over the choir. In the *apse,* she recalled.

"... *no sister of God has left us, no sister of God is passed away,*" a young preacher was calling to them from the pulpit. There were answering amens from the mourners. At the head of the aisle there was the casket surrounded by wreathes of flowers.

"... *No sister is removed from the bosom of Jesus. No one can break those bonds ... No one can remove those bonds ... Those bonds are forever! No one can cast those bonds asunder ... Because those bonds have been forged. They have been forged in the furnace of God's love ...*"

The mourners answered with their amens, and the young minister went on. When the responses had grown, spiraled into a regular rhythmic chorus, the young minister stepped aside and the choir began.

With one part of her mind she watched the congregation and with the other she simply gave herself over to the music. Gathered at the front were the closest relatives, all on the mother's side of the family, dressed in their immaculate finest, free in their grief, recipients of everyone's support. The tightest circle. And outward, in concentric rings, were neighbors, more distant kin, coworkers, and their families. At the outermost ring were people who might have known Ruth Micheaux but were not particular friends, regular functionaries of the church who had to be there, and at the very back, the drivers of the hearse, the custodian of the church, and her. The stranger, the only white face.

There were prayers, led by the young angry preacher, and more singing by the remarkable choir; remarkable not only for the music but also because it had a strong bass section, something she remembered as being unusual in the matriarchal black South.

Why was she here? The thought continued to shiver through her just as it had the time she had begun going on her first anthropological field trips. She knew it was a kind of heightened shyness, a natural fear of the unknown, of going where you weren't wanted or even expected. Like entering a room full of strangers. Confronting it produced a jazzy kind of adrenaline charge that made her feel like she'd been drinking coffee all night long. The challenge of breaking through that fear was partly what she had come to love about anthropology. She knew from experience that trying to suppress her nervousness would only create more anxiety. Anxiety that would cause her to compensate in her own behavior, anxiety that would cause her to lose her objectivity and inevitably lead to bias. You always had to remember that your subjects were probably as nervous as you were; you had to remember to stay calm and use your posture, your tone of voice, your entire *being,* to lessen the intrusion. She took a deep breath and tried to let her shoulders relax and let all the fear and stage fright just slough away so she could get on with the job, which was *to observe.*

There was a prayer and the young preacher assisted Ruth's mother to the casket and oversaw her sobbing embrace of her daughter. Along with her were the two children, who held each other's hand and stood numbly before the casket. There were sobs from the congregation and from somewhere an organist began playing her dirge. In ones and twos and then in a long queue the community filed past the casket.

As the choir began to sing a processional, the young preacher and the innermost family members began to file down the center aisle. Nina quickly slipped away from the doors as the invisible outer ring altered its shape to allow the most important people present to, in effect, penetrate it; to enter and perform a kind of blessing and transformation. Now men from the choir and a boy, a teenage relative of Ruth Micheaux, mounted the casket on their shoulders. She watched them walk down the aisle, absorbing the protocol, now able to identify the rank of nearly each individual in the building.

As the assembled mourners began to file out of the church, she pushed her way to the very back of the narthex, near the stairs to the balcony, and watched the pallbearers in their black suits carry Ruth Micheaux's casket down the stairs.

The processional came to its stirring conclusion. A song of affirmation, she thought, an expression of optimism in the face of implacable reality. In some societies the bereaved would be expected to make physical contact with each mourner, but here Ruth Micheaux's closest relatives were actually *parading*, displaying themselves by walking through the center of the community group.

Now the formality phase was over and she watched as the lean young preacher escorted Ruth Micheaux's mother outside, where the community was clustering, unconsciously reestablishing its pattern under the trees.

From her corner of the narthex she watched the young preacher as he stood beneath the trees, his dignity as severe as a lightning rod. His function, she realized, was somewhat different than she had anticipated. He gave no embraces, she noticed. Any comfort he gave certainly wasn't physical. At an event notable for the presence of physical consolation—hugs, embraces, kissing, and the exchange of intimate expressions of grief—he maintained a special proximity, a measurable social distance that rarely varied. Occasionally she would see a foray, to her eyes an obvious mating attempt of one of the younger single women seeking his attention and approval, a kind of display behavior. He was polite and, from all appearances, kind to the supplicants, but his guard would never relax. Each attempt at intimacy met with a rejection so subtle that it might even go unrecognized by the girls. Fascinating, she thought.

She was witnessing two different behaviors clashing, the signals by one party being misread, or perhaps invisible to the other part of the transaction. What an interesting young man. *Who is he?* she wondered.

"Oh . . . excuse me," came a low voice behind her. She turned to see a tall man, from his collar another preacher but much older and with a face that seemed scarred by time or events. She extended her hand and he took it. "Were you a friend of Sister Ruth?" he asked. Here it was, she thought, the question of her credentials.

"No, I just heard about her death. I wanted to come and pay my respects." It was true enough, she thought.

"It's very sad," the old preacher said, looking out onto the lawn. "It's all very sad indeed." His voice was smoky, she thought; a quiet man, not an orator like the sleek young man out front.

"No one deserves to die like that," Nina said, moving so she could see through the little facets of clear glass and watch as the young preacher detached himself and helped Ruth Micheaux's family into the limousines for the drive to the cemetery.

"Devil is all around us," the old preacher said. He sounded weary, she thought. She wondered if he had retired, passed on the preaching duties to the other, younger pastor. "Sometimes you can see him before he gets in, and sometime you don't see him and he gets in and has his way," he said.

"Could I come and speak to you sometime about your choir?" she said to the preacher. He turned and raised an eyebrow.

"Yes, ma'am, anytime at all."

"They sing so well, and I think that someone should record them." It was a kind of bribe, she knew, and it didn't come out well. The preacher almost seemed to stiffen. Idiot white woman, he was probably thinking.

"We're not in the record music business . . ."

"Oh, I don't mean like that, it's just that . . . You see, I'm a librarian and an archivist. Cultural anthropology, actually. Part of my

work is to collect oral histories, to trace influences from one mar-
ginal group to another while they're still viable." She smiled and
shrugged, not wanting to overwhelm the man with details he
wouldn't be able to understand.

"Is that right?"

"And, well, it's just that I've never heard any of those hymns."

The old man looked around for a moment. "Everything in this
church is old. Older than me even." She thought she saw him smile
for a moment. "I don't even know if those hymns are in the book.
We did put some of those songs on the mimeograph machine a
while back . . ."

"That would be a good start." She smiled up at him and thought
for a second that he nodded his assent. "Perhaps I could phone you
sometime during the week, or you could always get me at the library," she told him before she remembered that he wouldn't be allowed up to the white-only third floor.

"That would be fine. Just come on by. There's always someone
here," he said. The eyes were incredibly deep. "I'm Reverend Chaffee," he said, taking her hand again in his warm, leathery grasp.

"Nina Mendelson." She smiled. "I'm so sorry to have to make
your acquaintance on such a sad occasion," she said. He nodded
and let go of her hand and together they moved to the entrance and
stood looking down on the lawn. Several people looked up at them
standing there. She knew that it was a gesture of acceptance, them
appearing together. He was vouching for her.

"I s'pose I'd better be going now. Do you have transportation?"
he asked.

"No, I thought . . ." At graveside she would be too obvious. No
place to hide.

"God bless you, then, sister," said Reverend Chaffee, and he left
her there and went down to the cars while she moved outside,
through the rings of black faces. Now she saw that they were nodding at her when she looked their way. She had been accepted; she'd
moved inward at least by one level. And now she moved through
Ruth Micheaux's community, returning their glances with nods of
condolences, her progress reverential, every movement of her tall
body in a posture of gratitude for being let in to share their grief.

A little round woman came up to her and took both of her hands in her own. "I just want to thank you," she said. "I just want to thank you for comin' here today." The little woman was crying.

"Thank *you*," Nina said, whispering to her. The woman hugged her, a surprisingly strong embrace; Nina felt her smooth cheek, could smell the gardenia in her hair, the scratch of her veil. The grief was contagious. All of a sudden something cracked inside. She felt tears welling up in her eyes.

"God bless you," she said to the woman and moved past and started walking again toward her car. Now she could feel them watching her go. Now she was aware that she was blushing, that there were tears running down her cheeks, and she was trying to walk faster, trying to get away.

Running. Running away.

Why had she come? She was acutely embarrassed, brought down to the ignominy of a child caught in a lie. Why? She could no longer control the tears as she pressed her lips together and almost managed to hold back a sob.

Why? Was it to observe them? Who did she think she was fooling? What arrogance, she thought. What damn idiotic patronizing arrogance. To *study* them, was that why she'd come? Like lab rats? Like some kind of curiosities, some relics of the past?

What did she think she was looking for? Fool, she thought. *Fool, fool, fool.*

She finally got down to the sidewalk. Milton's Buick was just a blur ahead of her. She told herself to do everything slowly, to keep in control. Not make it worse. She stood there and fished around until she felt the keys in the bottom of her purse, then got in the car and made an effort to drive away as discreetly as she could.

SEVENTEEN

The capture of Lawrence "Kaiser" Smith, but not the beating, was revealed in the weekend edition of the *Morning Star* together with an editorial calling for more efficient policing of the city's streets at night. It was clear that living standards in the city were on the wane and things had come to a pretty mess when a responsible woman in one of the better colored neighborhoods couldn't even do her dishes, the paper said.

"There is nothing *silly* about this, Kewpie," Mary Helen said. "All of a sudden people are worried. All the niggers especially. They're lockin' their doors at night and they're ready to jump at anything. I mean, this telephone—" She put both hands on the receiver as if to hold it down on the cradle.

"—I've been in here *all* morning and this phone has been *ringin' off the hook.* It's a panic, Kewpie, a real panic. It's like the scales have fallen from their eyes, and now they're all scared."

"Well, maybe they have reason to be," he said. He decided to hide out in the office and maybe get some work done on his campaign.

"Oh, and this just came in." Now all of a sudden she was smiling. "You certainly have arrived, I'd say." She looked like she was going to break out laughing.

"What?"

"The local chapter of the N double-A C P has invited you for lunch." She slid a small envelope across his blotter.

"*What?*"

"That's what it says. Dinner on Wednesday. Reverend Fontaine and his pals want to break a little bread with you and probably listen to whatever it is you want to say. After all, you are a candidate for high political office." She actually did start laughing at him then, sitting there with his mouth hanging open.

"That oughta be some speech," she said. "I'd really like to come along, Kewpie, and listen to you explain the poll tax, but . . ."

About the same time the phone rang and he learned that he would miss lunch because Spud Reid was going to go over for an interview with Kaiser Smith, who was suddenly healed enough to where he could speak, according to the doctors.

When they all met at the hospital Smith looked lumpy, sore, and middle-aged. He didn't look like he was the kind of man who'd peeked in anybody's window in about twenty years.

"Look, Mr. Smith. I know D.L. has told you that you might be in a lot of trouble, but I think I can get this figured out real quick." He had brought a yard-long piece of parachute cord over with him. It was nice rope, some kind of silky fiber that could make tight knots that would hold.

"What are you talking about here?" said D.L. He was thrown by the whole thing. He hadn't paid much attention to the details of the murders of the women and nothing had been written down about the knots. He'd have to have seen the photographs to know anything about them, and that wouldn't happen unless and until Reid charged his client with murder.

"Can you just tie my hands up, Mr. Smith? Can you do that for me?" Smith looked back and forth between them for a second and then took the rope. Smith made a quick little loop around Q.P.'s wrist and then a square knot, then cinched the other wrist up to it with a half hitch. He'd left enough room to coil the end of the rope around the junction, hiding the first knots, and to finish it tightly so that Q.P. would have to bend around and inside to pull it apart with his teeth. All the knots were good. He turned to Spud and held out his wrists.

"There you go. You see how he did that?"

"Yeah," Reid said. Terry and Smith just stared at him. They had passed some kind of test but they didn't know what.

"What do you do down there at the rail yards, Mr. Smith?" Q.P. asked him.

"I do a little bit of everything they got down there."

"You got a boat? Ever been a fisherman?"

"Well, I've been fishin' but I ain't never caught too much," Smith said. They all laughed at that.

"Good afternoon, Mr. Terry," said Reid, a little too briskly. He had got to his feet and was closing his briefcase. "Good after*noon,*" said Terry as they walked out.

"Well, Kewpie," Reid said as soon as they were in the elevator. "I guess you killed that case pretty good." Reid just looked straight ahead, like he was trying to stare a hole in the elevator door.

"Do you really think he did it?" Q.P. said without trying to hide his irritation. Reid shrugged and looked up to the wand that measured their descent.

"Nah," he said quietly, "wasn't him. He's just some nigger got in the way." Reid fell silent all the rest of the way down the elevator and out into the parking lot. "Good luck, Kewpie," he said on the way to his car, but he didn't look back.

Campaign-wise, besides the NAACP lunch there was a speech that he was expected to give to the Lions Club. He pulled out a piece of stationery and started trying to write down what he thought the Lions might be interested in hearing. He had nearly joined the Lions a year ago; it was the expected thing for the sheriff to do. If he had ever thought he'd be running for office, he would have done it a long time ago. But now it was uncomfortably late; if he tried to join now, the Lions would think he was joining just to get their votes. And they'd be *right.* It was a lousy situation. Even though they'd accept him right away, he just felt that he couldn't rush out and try to join. If he *won,* he'd join.

He looked down at the paper and realized he hadn't written anything at all. There was a little Kilroy face he'd drawn and a row of his houses; simple cartoon houses with a door, two windows, and a chimney. Little houses overlapping like a chorus line, getting smaller and smaller into infinity.

He balled the paper up and pulled out another and started all over again. He thought about Alton Lennox and how effortlessly he had talked about Prosperity! And Americanism! How he managed to be happy and angry all at the same time. He tried to imagine that he could hear Lennox speaking for him. What came out were a series of slogans. They all looked good with exclamation marks beside them.

Freedom!
No Taxes!
Fun!

Well, that was great, but what was he going to do, just stand up there and shout at them like a cheerleader? He started writing out phrases that sounded catchy. They all circled around and came back to zero, like: "It doesn't matter how hard you work as long as you work hard!" or "What you get out of life depends on what you put into it!" He wrote down five or six of them. If he could string a few together, it might work.

He stood up and walked around his desk practicing them a few times. He wondered if there'd be a microphone.

"Never go looking for a break if you're not willing to work hard for the breaks you get!" he said. He tried it again louder. The trouble was that when he shouted his voice got higher. Shrill almost. It would all sound better over a microphone or on the radio.

"We've got a whole new world of prosperity and freedom just around the corner!" he said with a big smile, throwing his arms wide and waiting for the applause. The door opened and Mary Helen looked in.

"Are you okay?"

"Yeah, sure. I was just practicing."

"Oh, yeah. Okay. Sure, good. That's good," she said.

"Did you hear it?"

"Yeah, it sounded good," she said. She was lying, he could tell. "You just keep working on it. That's good. Really. It's coming along."

"Okay," he said. She closed the door, but it was too much knowing she would be listening as soon as he said something.

He went back to the desk and worked on more complicated phrases about law and order, but all of it sounded stupid. He sat there for a while trying to think of some good things to add. The piece of stationery was a mess, filled with his little lists and places where he'd scratched out his mistakes.

As he was looking at it, he had a vision of Sykes's diagram of the Micheaux woman's wounds, the line inked across her neck, and Nina's voice echoing in his head telling him that, yes, he *could* save the world if only he'd try.

Milton was already installed on the sofa when Q.P. got there. Nina came out and gave him a peck and didn't seem nervous at all, and he shook Milton's hand and sat down in the middle of *Topper*.

"That's a real nice set you've got there," he said to Milton. It was a brand-new Philco with a cabinet of blond oak and golden knobs on the front to change the channels and adjust the reception. Milton turned to him. "I'm dying of cancer and I thought I'd get one of these before I pop off, to see what all the fuss is about."

"They're ghosts, right?"

"The young folks're the ghosts. Yeah, I'm gonna be like them soon."

"I asked Kewpie to come over to have fun, Pop." Nina looked in, trying to be stern.

"I'm havin' fun. Are you havin' fun?" Milton turned to him, grinning.

"Sure," he said.

"Do you like garlic?" Nina smiled.

"Sure. Great."

During the ads Milton asked him all the requisite questions and took advantage of his situation, not only as father but as father-near-death, to probe for all sorts of intimate details about his aunt Yvonne's marital status.

"She got a job testing adding machines," Q.P. said, thinking that might make sense to an accountant.

"All day long?" Milton asked.

"Yep. You can't even see her fingers move, she goes so fast."

"Awful," Milton said. Douglas Edwards came on and Milton watched the news while Q.P. escaped to the kitchen to help get out the plates and take an opportunity to kiss the cook. They talked and he stirred things to help out.

"So you think this guy in the hospital is the maniac that did it?" she asked.

"Nope. What happened was they chased this guy down who was maybe, nobody knows for sure, looking in some woman's window."

"But probably he's the killer, right?" She had stopped cooking for a second and was looking at him with a worried expression.

"No . . . it's somebody else," he said quietly.

"The same one that killed the other girl? *Cora?*" She remembered the name.

He took a deep breath before he answered. She had gone back to cooking. "Yeah," he said finally; he shook his head to keep it away. Sometimes it was like being out in a marsh with flies biting at you all the time.

But he had to go through it all again for Milton while he set out the trays. People had started to telephone the department, they were seeing the killer everywhere.

"Hysteria, mob behavior," Nina said.

"Well, ever since they shot that poor animal over there in Bladen County," Milton said, "people have been hankering for something new to be afraid of when the lights go down. They'll take anything they can get."

"I guess," he said.

Nina had made Italian dishes she'd learned in Chicago, rolling out the dough herself and putting together everything she needed from the Piggly Wiggly. She was a good cook, but they ate fast so they could pay all of their attention to the new television.

All along they talked; about the mills in Lowell, Massachusetts, and Nina's time up North and how the Yankees had infected her with northern ideas. They talked about the H-bomb, which had been set off in the Pacific and mistakenly showered fallout over a couple of hundred sailors and a Japanese fishing boat.

"That's what they wanted to do with me, you know?" Milton said, pointing to his chest. "Bombard me with atomic rays? Forget it."

They watched *Our Miss Brooks* and after that Milton said he was tired and they helped him back to his room. The two of them did the dishes and went back out to the living room and spun around the channels and watched *The Life of Riley* and started to watch the news, but he said he should probably be going, and she put her arms around him and they kissed.

A few minutes later they pulled themselves apart and Q.P. said that he probably thought he really should go.

"Pop sleeps through the night now, so I'll walk you home, how's that?" she said. Wild girl returns, she thought.

They walked to his place, not that many blocks, under the trees, looking in the windows to see all the other televisions flickering, people huddled around. He opened the screen door and kneed the front door open and then thought it best to leave the lights off, mostly so she wouldn't see the mess.

In the back he showed her the view of the river and stood behind her and put his arms around her and breathed in the smell of her hair and she turned her head and they kissed again. His hands had begun to move around her sweater and she let him, and when it got to be too much she turned in his arms and kissed him hard on the mouth.

"I guess we're starting something," she said. She was breathless. They both were.

"Yes, I think we are. We're definitely starting something."

"I knew we were." She pulled back and gave him a long look. He was smiling. It was contagious. "I don't want to get pregnant, okay?" she said.

"I don't either," he said, and she laughed and kissed him again and bit his lip, and twined herself around him as tightly as a boa constrictor. Held him to herself as if she'd never let go.

"I think . . . we can probably work something out," he said.

"I'm sure we can," she said a minute or two after that.

And so they went back to his bedroom, arm in arm, one step at a time.

EIGHTEEN

By the time of the NAACP lunch on Wednesday, Smith had been officially cleared. He was hobbling around and neighbors were bringing him covered dishes to help out. With the pressure lowered a few notches, Q.P. was free to actually enjoy lunch with the NAACP, which turned out to be cordial in the extreme, he thought. A real high point.

The famous lunch was held in the large back room at Castle's Fine Restaurant, the city's best colored dining establishment, and Q.P. regretted that he was the guest of honor, mostly because he couldn't ever finish his seconds or thirds when they were pressed on him.

It was a large gathering around the dinner table. Something around twenty, and a couple of chairs pulled up later as various members arrived late but sat in on the action. Reverend Fontaine was presiding, and he was all smiles, sitting at the head of the table and lashing them into talkativeness whenever the conversation started to flag. The story had gotten around, via some of the black nurses or maybe D. L. Terry himself, about Sheriff Waldeau's rope trick. It was the kind of act that Smith could easily repeat in a courtroom, and thus was generally credited with getting him off the hook.

It was after the main course and many of the men had lit up and were waiting for the dessert when Oscar Whale straightened up from where he had been dozing at the corner of the table.

"What I want to know is why everyone thinks the killer is a *black* man?" The question stilled the table, the kind of thing everybody had been waiting for all afternoon. It had caught Q.P. as he mopped up the last of his okra with a hush puppy, so he had a long time to chew it over.

"Well, there's nothing to prove he's black *or* white." He said it as matter-of-factly as he could. "I've been trying to let people know about that from the beginning. I told Noppy Leigh that, and as soon as I did, he put in the paper that there might be *two* killers running around, so . . ."

"Well, then what efforts have you made to find a *white* suspect?" Whale said. He was leaning back in his chair with his eyes half closed. Like he was in some kind of trance or had been playing piano in a club all night.

"Can't tell you. There's some tests we're waiting on," he said, wondering how much longer he would have to wait for the SBI lab in Raleigh to get around to analyzing the swipes taken from Ruth Micheaux's vagina.

"But, Sheriff, aren't there eyewitnesses who *saw* a white man?" said Dr. Terry, sitting all the way down at the end, as far away from Fontaine as he could get.

"Yes, Doctor, it's true that there was one person who saw a white man, but at the moment we've accounted for that suspect and he has an alibi. Right now his alibi is reasonably solid, and so there's no more evidence to suspect him than there was Mr. Smith"—he looked around at the men—"or anybody else for that matter. We're still investigating both of the homicides. Wilmington P.D. is on it, too. We're going to get some scientific help from the SBI—"

"All the normal things," Reverend Fontaine said to help it along.

"That's right. All the normal things and then some. But right now it could be anybody. Anybody at all. Black, white, no evidence either way. I'm sorry. I'd love to catch the guy this afternoon, but that's as far as I can go right now," he said and went back to his hush puppy.

"Hmmph." Whale raised his eyebrows with the attitude that he was satisfied for now, and the table returned to general discussion.

When he got back to the courthouse, everybody wanted to know how it had gone and he just shrugged it all off. It was obvious he had gotten through the dinner with minimum damage and Mary Helen started calling him "Honest Abe" and making jokes about how he was going to take the Negro vote for sheriff.

"And, you know," she said pensively, "that could backfire on you. It could," and she went away thinking.

Nina came in and he heard her and Mary Helen talking about the lunch. He came to the door and courteously shook her hand. Nina leaned against the desk and gave him the once-over. "Well, I understand you were out politicking today," she said softly.

There was a pile of paperwork on the desk that had ended up there while he was out eating. He moved one pile and put another pile on top of it.

"Oh, that's good. That's real efficient," Nina said, rolling her eyes. He looked around and saw the office through her eyes for a split second. The whole place was a mess, he thought.

"I was *working*. That was a working dinner. I figured I'd check in and then go home and clean up." He looked at her and tried hard not to raise an eyebrow.

"Hmmmm," she said and kind of smiled. "You know, I was looking some stuff up the other day at City Records," she said. "I just happened to glance through some of your recent missing persons stats and they're *way* off, you know?" She had been trying to dig out missing persons statistics and country-wide death certificates.

"Still pokin' around?"

"*Research* is what it's called, pardner. I found more than a few anomalies."

"Anomalies?" His eyebrows shot up.

"Oh yeah. I found the files easily enough, but brother . . ." She wasn't really supposed to have access to the files. But everyone had seen her around Thalian Hall, and more recently in Q.P.'s company, and without actually saying it, she had implied that she was working for the sheriff's department. Nepotism. Everybody does it probably, most of the staff thought; sheriff has a new girlfriend, sheriff puts her on the payroll.

". . . after you sift through the maze of different statistical methods, you discover that a *lot* of women have gone missing over the last ten years," she said. He was frowning at her.

"Well, yeah," he said. "People go missing all the time—"

She made a face. "I know, I know. But when that first girl got killed—"

"Cora?"

"When she got killed you said you had done a search for missing women and she wasn't even in the files. So, statistically, this sample"—she waved a thick folder at him; he hadn't even noticed it before—"this sample is underreported by your own admission."

He was starting to feel like he was on the witness stand. "Yes . . . yes . . . So?" He tried to look smart and not squirm around in the chair.

"So . . . I started digging around and I think you should ask a few more questions about who knew and who didn't know Cora Snow. These people—" She waved the folder at him again as if it were magic and would transform him into a frog. "These people are all part of a *community*, Kewpie. They are all intertwined. If you pull on the loose ends of the string, it'll unravel."

"The guy we thought killed her has an alibi . . ."

"It's a lot bigger than that. You've got to realize that this girl, Cora Snow, she had just as sophisticated a life as yours. How many people do you know?"

"Oh, hell, Nina . . ." He was tired. He wanted to go home and have a drink and sleep off the meal.

"How many?"

"I don't know, a couple hundred."

"Most North Americans, unless they live in extremely remote locations, have between five hundred to a thousand acquaintances. People they recognize and can name. Well, Cora was the same way. You said she had employers, she worked as a domestic?"

"She cleaned for some white women, yes."

"Okay, that right there is a link to a whole other community. That's a different circle, you see?" She was enthusiastic, smiling at him. On fire with her ideas. He loved her when she got like this. "See, she was *involved*. We usually think of people like her, prostitutes and addicts, we think of them as being out on the periphery. They are supposed to live and be somewhere that we don't ever go; they don't have friends like us, they don't feel like we do, they're not as smart, they don't have *lives*, they're invisible. But that's never the case. That's just our academic prejudice."

"Right, okay . . ."

"So . . ."

She wanted him to do something, but he didn't know what yet. "So," he said, "I guess you want me to dig a little deeper into her life, right?"

"Absolutely."

"Okay, okay." He thought back, trying to remember if they'd left anything out.

"What about the dentist who drove her home?"

"He's got an alibi from his wife."

She smiled at him, leaned over the desk, and put one finger under his stubbly chin. "Darling," she said, "don't you think that a man's wife would tell a little lie if she thought it would help him?" she said, tweaking him with her fingernail. "Why don't you go have that shower," she said and left the office.

"Did you straighten him out yet?" Mary Helen said to her out in the front.

"Did my best, Queen Bee."

"Well, would you tell him it's too late to get his pictures now?" She shook her head.

"He's real shy about that, I think," Nina said.

"He looks *good*, Nina. He's a handsome man." Mary Helen was talking loudly so that he could hear them. They looked in at him to see if he got the message. He was shaking his head. "And his eye's all healed up . . ."

"He's going to have to give that speech sooner or later . . ." she said. Q.P. made a big sigh and got up from the chair. "Do you think he looks French?" she said to Mary Helen.

"Come on, let's do some work around here, okay?" he said.

"Yes, sir," Nina said and gave him a kiss and left.

"You, too," he said to Mary Helen.

"You'd better have that shower," she said. "And a shave, too, I'd say . . ."

Afterward she teased him by rolling grapes from the V down between his buttocks up his spine and then eating them when they got to the nape of his neck.

"Donny and Kay invited us to go on a coon hunt," he said sleepily.

"You're kidding."

"No . . . Her father's got coon dogs and Glen's probably going."

"I don't know anything about hunting raccoons. I always thought it was a disgusting idea."

"Well, they invited us."

"She's going out there, too? Don't you run around all night or something?"

"I don't know. We didn't go hunting much in Baltimore. You're the one who grew up down here in the swamps."

"You wait in the rain until the dogs smell something and then you run around in the dark trying not to kill each other with shotguns. Can't I just stay in the kitchen with the other girls?"

"Not from the way he was talking."

"I think I'm getting a cold . . ."

"We don't have to go, but Glen loves that stuff."

"I'd rather stay inside." Another grape made the journey to its ultimate destination. He rolled over and nearly fell asleep while she twirled her fingers around in the dark hair that covered his chest. "Maybe I can find some obscure Jewish holiday to use as an excuse, but you . . ."

"I'll just tell 'em we're having dinner with your dad," he said sleepily.

"Good! We can watch TV and stay warm, that's a much better idea. You're smart, Sheriff."

"Mmmm." He was starting to drop off. She propped herself up on one elbow and watched him. His mouth opened a little.

"I think I love you, Quentin," she said.

"Mmmm . . ."

"Horizontally speaking, at least." She gave him a little pinch, got up, and walked over to the window and started getting her things.

"You oughta pull the blinds on that window," he said. "People'll look up here and see you . . ." His voice was soft, like it was coming from a long way away.

"I don't care. I'm not ashamed of my body. They can look all they want to." She looked down onto Orange Street. There were a couple of kids coming home from school, carrying old army book bags, little Lone Ranger and Superman lunch boxes dangling from their hands.

". . . 'gainst the law . . ." His voice had fallen to a mumble.

"You can sell tickets," she said. "You could live off the proceeds of my exotic dancing." She started getting dressed.

"I'm gonna do what you said," he murmured.

"What's that?" She turned to look at him. He had pulled the pillow over his eyes to keep out the light.

"I think . . . what you said's a good idea," he said quietly and sighed for a moment. There was a pause and she thought he might start snoring. She tried to remember what it was she had told him to do.

"Yeah . . ." he said and then fell asleep.

Out where they'd built the State Ports there was a yard, a junkyard that had grown up. It was on land owned by the State of North Carolina and one day intended for expansion of the Ports, but it had rapidly become an informal landfill and all-purpose garbage dump. There was a dilapidated chain-link fence and a plywood sign that said NO GARBAGE but people went in there anyway. If you wanted to dump a load of fill there, you were supposed to phone State Ports and ask permission. In practice most of the local construction firms had a blanket permission to use the place.

No one had ever made any kind of plan or layout of the yard. The road in had been "paved" with occasional loads of gravel and shell and went straight toward the river, looped around, and came right back out again. There was an informal area for the fill dirt, broken concrete, and old bricks over near the swampy lowland. Everything else was on the high ground. Most of it was salvage, great cylinders of smokestacks, ruined valves, and rusty pipe destined to be carted to a steelyard if the price for scrap metal ever got out of the cellar again, piles of shingles, old oil drums, a lattice of salvaged creosoted beams that would never rot.

At the corner of the yard was a row of olive-colored army buses, discarded now for more than a decade. They were old vehicles, from the late thirties and early years of the war. With high radiators and wing hoods. The wheels and tires had been taken off all of them and the glass broken out by accident or by wandering boys bored with plinking rats with their .22s. The buses had oblong windows over the cabs that said NO SERVICE or CHARLOTTE or else were permanently stuck between destinations. Without their wheels the buses sat on their axles, low to the ground. Their great broken headlights peeked out of the thorns like animals, like the eyes of lions waiting in the grass, Q.P. thought as he pulled up.

There were the various police cars parked down there, a gray State Ports GMC panel truck, and driving in right behind him came the ambulance.

Two truck drivers had found the woman. They had stopped to unload some old wringer washers and had caught the smell. They looked over and saw that the brush had been pushed down between the buses, and then they saw something else under there.

Neither one of them had walked any closer, the drivers said. They'd gone out right away, told the man running the gate at State Ports, and he had made the call. It was only about a mile, maybe a mile and a half away from the little bog where they'd pulled Ruth Micheaux and her carpet out of the muck, Q.P. thought.

The path to where she had been stuffed under the side of the bus had been used, he could tell, but the grass had started to spring back from where it had been trampled down. He tried to walk slowly, keeping to the side in case there were any footprints. It was wet and grassy there and there was nothing he could find that could be lifted by a plaster cast. The road circling in front of the buses had been chewed up with each passing dump truck. The smell was familiar and unbelievable, a sweet smell that went right to his soul. He had to force himself to walk back down between the buses to get to the body.

He could see her now, swollen and turned a waxy yellow color. There were bugs crawling all over her and he straightened up to turn around and get out of there before he threw up all over the crime scene.

But he had seen enough. He had seen the ropes. Trailing out onto the muddy grass. Common window sash cords, tied round the woman's ankles and wrists. It had been done awkwardly, like a bad Christmas package, in looping half hitches, over and over again.

And he had seen more.

He'd seen that it was a white woman.

NINETEEN

Waddell Memorial was the white funeral parlor that the city used for their morgue. Jimmy Satterwhite had got there ahead of everybody except Sykes and hung around the back door hoping that the coroner would let him inside to take a picture. It meant that Sykes was angry, since he'd have to keep the doors closed. People had started to gather in the alley. One of Mr. Waddell's sons came over with a little can of camphor in his hand, like a shoe polish tin. He held it out to the cops.

"You just put this right up at the edge of your nose, gentlemen, make it a little better in here."

They all daubed their nostrils and stood around while Sykes did the autopsy. Under the lights it looked like he was cutting open a huge yellow larva, Q.P. thought. Except for the limbs, the woman was almost unrecognizable as a human. Her features were both swollen and compressed where she had been pushed facedown onto the hard dirt under the side of the bus. There were bugs still crawling out of her.

"Goddamn . . . goddamn . . . Shit . . ."

The whole time people kept coming in and out. Wills arrived looking like a mammoth in one of his cheap suits. He didn't even take off his hat and went straight to the table. Reluctantly Q.P. moved over beside them so he could hear what Sykes was telling him.

"All right . . . She was killed by strangulation." He looked up as Q.P. moved to the other side of the table. "All tied up just like you like 'em, Sheriff."

Wills looked up at him. "I know her," he said; he was breathing hard. Astounded. Amazed. Angry.

"You *knew* her," Sykes said.

"That's what I mean," Wills said.

"There's a big difference, Tom-Boy," Sykes said. "Can I cut these, Kewpie?" he asked, pointing at the ropes.

Wills looked around. "What the fuck is all this shit?" He sounded confused and lost.

"You knew her?" Q.P. asked.

"Yeah . . ." Wills was standing there shaking his head. "That's Millie. She lives over there . . ."

"We had *two* nigger gals tied up before this, just the way Kewpie likes 'em, and this here is number *three*, looks like," said Sykes around his cigarette. "Yeah, I'd say it looks like the same. Don't you think, Kewpie?" Sykes stood back for a second. The camphor wasn't working too well, Q.P. thought. He could almost *see* the vapors coming out of the woman.

"Can I cut these now?" Sykes said.

"Did you get pictures?" Q.P. asked Wills, who came out of it and turned around.

"Hey, meathead! Get your butt over here." A thin young man, almost a teenager, came over with his camera. "Right there, yeah?" Wills asked Q.P., pointing at the knots for the teenager.

"Yeah," he said and stepped back so the kid could get into the table to take his pictures.

"Millie lives over there . . . around Grace Street," said Wills, shaking his head sadly.

Sykes looked doubtfully at the woman. Now that her legs were freed, they had begun to spread slowly of their own accord. Sykes sighed and shook his head. "Look, Kewpie . . . you want me to look inside?"

"Evidence of rape would be nice," he said.

"Ain't gonna be able to find anything, I'm tellin' y'all," Sykes muttered and went over to the sink to get his tools.

"I think I'll step out for this," Q.P. said to Wills.

Out in the alley more and more civilians were finding excuses to walk along back of Waddell's. Wills came out a minute or so later.

"Doc says as far as he's concerned she was raped."

"God*damn!*" a man said who was walking down the alley with a box of cabbages on his shoulder. "Did I hear y'all right?" He stood there, spun around. "Raped a goddamn *white* woman?" the man said, his voice shrill with indignation. Wills just looked at him until the man turned away and started back down the alley.

"You got some information on this?" Wills asked Q.P.

"Not anything that you haven't already heard."

"This goddamn town is gonna pop wide open," Wills said. The muscles in his cheeks were flinching with anger. "Goddamn niggers," he said tiredly. "It's about goddamn time somebody up and did something 'bout this shit," he said quietly. It came out almost like a whisper and then Wills said it again: "About goddamn time . . ."

Q.P. didn't see any reason to help Wills out; he should have known all about the murders. But he looked so sad over the woman's death that Kewpie waited a few minutes before he filled Wills in on Snow/Micheaux and the knots. Now it looked like they had somebody who was killing just for the fun of it.

"You said you knew her?" Q.P. asked the huge detective. Wills looked over at him, almost wincing.

"Yeah," he said, "I knew her. I knew who she was, I mean. I didn't *know* her."

Wills said she was named Millie, for Mildred, Garnet, and she was officially identified that same day via a missing persons report filed at the police department ten days earlier by the woman who shared a duplex with her. A search of her side of the house turned up nothing unusual.

She was a widow; her husband had been a mill worker who'd righteously signed up right after Pearl Harbor and who ended up getting erased on some beach in Normandy. Mildred had been killed just a few months shy of turning forty, the possessor of a criminal record amounting to two convictions, one for running a common bawdy house, served back in '47, and the second, a year later, for possessing lewd pictures.

Because the remains had been found on land that belonged to State Ports, Q.P. informed the SBI in Raleigh of the homicide. Sykes got to his paperwork right away and Mildred was sealed into a vault at Waddell's awaiting a ruling on her estate and to see if anyone would claim her remains.

And so, barely twenty-four hours after the truck drivers had discovered her, Q.P. and the Wilmington Police knew all about the woman who had been found in the yard down by State Ports. But just as in the Snow case, there were no clues beyond the knots. Nothing solid, nothing to back up Wills's assertion that a crazy nigger had been responsible.

But Wills was right about the town popping wide open. The headline in the *Morning Star* read:

White Woman New Victim!

He read the newspaper over and over again, but it never got any better. He and Mary Helen spent most of the day on the telephone with the SBI, Carruthers, and various interested city officials. She went out to lunch, came back with a chili dog for him, and reported that according to the gossip the local VFW legion was planning a series of self-defense classes in pistol shooting to help people if they should encounter the psycho-killer who the New Hanover Sheriff's Department had been pursuing since Christmas.

"Oh, shit . . ." he said.

"And they says it's a crazy nigger that done it, and that we already know who he is, but we can't find him," she said.

"We don't have the slightest idea who did it. I told you that! They could be chartreuse for all I know."

"You don't have to get touchy."

"God*damn*, Mary Helen—"

"Well, anyway, Kewpie, I'm just telling you what people think," she said.

That night Glen Petty arrested a carload of white men who were driving down the highway. All of the men in the car were drunk and he was forced to call in for assistance. When George Foster got there in a second car, they ended up arresting all the men and confiscating three shotguns, two pistols, a sock filled with gravel, a mattock handle, and a butcher knife. They were out trying to find the killer, they said.

The next morning he went over to Milton's and had breakfast with Nina and she showed him the editorial that Mr. Pagett at the *Morning Star* had written. With mysterious logic Pagett somehow managed to lump in the Communist menace in Indochina with "several" unexplained local stranglings, and then leapt ahead to complain that the only local crime-fighting had come from neighboring police forces doing work that was the responsibility of the New Hanover County Sheriff's Department all along. Such a situation was embarrassing and should not be allowed to continue and Wilmingtonians should thank their lucky stars that an election was coming up soon.

"Now, that right there is pretty low, I say." Nina looked up at him.

There wasn't much he could say. He went into work feeling like everyone he saw was avoiding him. The atmosphere in the basement of the courthouse was leaden. The white men who Petty had brought in got off after the driver paid his fine for driving under the influence, and then pranced around griping while they signed for their guns at the Evidence Room counter.

A little after three in the afternoon, he got a call from an SBI agent in Charlotte who had been assigned to the junkyard case. He'd be driving down that night and asked if they could meet at the Carolina Inn the next morning.

The SBI guy's name was Keating and Q.P. didn't think he was very much. Brand-new to the job and almost the same age as Q.P. Being unmarried was an advantage, Keating said. It made being on the road a lot easier. They went over to Binky's and Keating ordered grits, which he said he didn't get much up in Charlotte.

They talked about the SBI and how Keating had nearly not got in. "There's an incredible amount of paperwork. It's—" Keating shook his head; he looked like he'd had trouble sleeping. "It's *ungodly* the amount of reports we have to do. When we're not doing that, we're collecting data. Everything is about 'collecting data'; graphs and charts all over the place. Everything is *scientific*." Binky came over and topped up their coffees.

Then Q.P. filled him in about Snow/Micheaux/Garnet and the ropes. The young agent frowned and nodded as if he were digesting the information. So much data, all at once. "And you have no suspects at all?"

"Well . . ." Q.P. took the opportunity to talk about the background of Scowen and the Smith fiasco, and then in a quieter voice he told him about Allison.

"According to his secretary, who for right now we'll assume is telling the truth, Allison was visiting with his relatives in Charlotte at the probable time of Mrs. Garnet's death. We took this—" He pulled a photograph of Allison that had been clipped from the society page of the *Morning Star*. "We took it and showed it around over in the neighborhood around Grace Street. Mildred Garnet's duplex neighbor had never seen him before. So far we can't place him with her."

"A white man?"

"Yeah."

"Hmmm," the agent said, frowning and nodding. "Maybe it's good that he's off the hook. Y'all might have a real mess on your hands down here." Binky came over with the bill and Keating picked it up.

"Well, I tell you what, Sheriff," he said. "Just for starters, suppose we take a couple of clippings from all your different sets of rope and window cords and send 'em up to the lab in Raleigh. What about that?"

"Might help," Q.P. admitted.

"Well, it's *data*, right?"

"Yeah, it's data at least."

They went outside. It was raining but the sun was out. It made a fine mist and little wispy rainbows. People were walking along Front Street with their faces turned to the sky, pausing to wipe their glasses off and laughing for no reason. The agent shook his hand and thanked him and promised to stay in touch about the ropes. He was being driven down to State Ports by Errol Tate, the Negro patrolman.

By now Tate had become a fixture in the city, a quiet man who managed his duties (giving parking tickets, directing traffic in the late hours after baseball games, et cetera) with a kind of stolid grace, his uniform as perfectly pressed as ever. Q.P. watched Tate open and close the door for Keating and drive away from the curb. An older man was standing there on the sidewalk looking at them go.

"That's what you get," the old man said. And then he spat on the sidewalk.

TWENTY

Two mornings later he wasn't even in the double doors before he heard the man's voice behind him.

"What are you doing to find the nigger 'at killed my Millie?" Q.P. turned to see a little man who was standing there holding a straw hat in his hands. He was sunburned and wore overalls under his jacket. There was an old woman—she looked almost ninety—sitting behind him, struggling to get to her feet. Helping her get up was the little man's wife, and from the color of her face, she was the one who was truly angry.

"Excuse me?"

"Comin' in pretty damn late, aren't ya?" the wife said, pointing at him.

"Kewpie, I'd like you to meet Mr. and Mrs. Vaughan, and Mrs. Mangum, Mildred Garnet's grandmother," Mary Helen said in her sweetest tones. She had come around and was helping the old woman to stand up.

"I'm not that old," the old woman said, shaking her away.

"You either get off your ass and go git these goddamn nigger killers or I know some boys who'll go get 'em for you," Vaughan said.

"Why should we be always waitin' on you people up here?" the wife asked the whole room. Mary Helen had continued to help Mrs. Mangum in her slow shuffle up to Q.P.

"I loved that girl no matter what," the old woman said. She

tapped Q.P. on the chest with her little bird finger. "I loved her day an' night."

"We *all* loved her," the wife said, but it didn't sound like she meant it that much.

Mr. Vaughan had gone completely red in the face. He looked around the office and squeezed the brim of his hat. "*Damn* it!" he said through gritted teeth. "Damn it *all!*"

"You people ought to really have to work for a livin'. Work for a livin' just *once* in a while," said his wife. She had begun to cry.

"You know what this is? This is a goddamn waste of time," Vaughan blurted out. Q.P. could see little flecks of tobacco spit flying out into the office. Vaughan gave him a last dirty look and spun away with his family. Q.P. stood there watching as they all headed for the double doors.

"You'll have this on your head, glory-boy. You have this on your head unto *eternity*," Vaughan shouted back to him as he followed the women outside. Q.P. turned around with his mouth open. It had only taken a few seconds. Everything in the office had come to a dead stop.

"The Vaughans drove up from New Zion, South Carolina, early this morning just to see *you*," said Mary Helen. "Wasn't that nice?"

"Yeah, that was swell," he said and went into the office, leaving Mary Helen and Ellis to compare redneck stories.

Paper-clipped to the top of his mail was a leaflet that looked like it had been passed around a few times and then stepped on. It was printed with a picture of a Negro with his jeans undone and a shotgun in his hand. In his other arm was a blond white woman. Her blouse was torn open and one breast was exposed. The only other clothing she was wearing was her apron, which was just a little too small to keep any spills away.

"Where'd this come from?" he called out to Mary Helen.

"Ellis brought that in. They were puttin' them out down at the railroad. I thought you might like to add that to your collection of campaign fan mail . . ."

Below the picture was a banner that read:

Klarion Kall to Arms!

The phone rang. It was a call from Keating from the SBI. He was cheerful. He was back home, it was a nice day in Charlotte. He was going golfing later in the day if he could clear up a few more of his cases.

"That's nice," said Q.P. He ran his tongue around the inside of his mouth. It tasted like rotten mushrooms. Compost. He closed his eyes and listened to Keating and the sounds of the busy SBI office.

"—anyway, as regards the report on those ropes, you ought to be getting a photostat of it real soon."

"They're the same?"

"Yep, so far they say they're the same. Same *piece* of rope."

"Altogether he's used about twenty-five feet of rope."

"Well, they make the stuff in *lots*. I guess it can be thousands of yards they make at the time. But it's all made out of cotton and they can see the fibers under the microscope, so that's how they know."

"That's amazing," he said to Keating, who started rhapsodizing about scientific things.

"—they coat the stuff when it's new with paste; *sizing* is what it is. And they can scrape that off and tell if it's the same chemical composition, and they're working on that over this next week, so . . ."

"So he bought a whole bunch of rope, then."

"And the other thing that's come up is that the carpet that he used to dispose of the Micheaux woman was new."

"New?"

"Brand-new piece of carpet, seven by ten. Brand-new, never been laid," Keating said.

"That's something."

"Yeah, that sticks out to me. Didn't have any particular pattern to it and we're trying to find the brand name and all that right now. Might have to go to Washington for that. Takes a while. So I'm sending you a piece down so you can have it as a sample."

"I hope you cleaned it first."

"Oh, hell yeah, that carpet is legendary in Charlotte already." They both laughed about that for a minute. "Anyway, Kewpie, I just wanted to let you know that we're on the job up here in the big city."

"Oh yeah?" He found that he was starting to like Keating for his honest embrace of the good life. "Well, I like the pace of your work-day so much I'm definitely coming up to take the test, first chance I get."

"Well, bring your clubs and practice up on your spelling, then," said Keating and hung up.

The next day the Wilmington *Morning Star* ran a profile of Mildred Garnet and the Vaughan family. There was a photograph of Mildred when she was young and attractive back in the thirties. In the picture she smiled shyly and looked away from the photographer, up toward heaven beyond the corner of the page. She looked like she was just going off somewhere to have fun. Beside her was a badly lit photograph of Mr. Asa Vaughan, a farmer from South Carolina who had come all the way up to Wilmington to claim his baby cousin's mortal remains. It looked like it had been taken at night with Vaughan posed sitting on the tailgate of his truck.

According to the paper, Mildred Garnet was a long-suffering war widow cut down in the prime of her life by the same killer who had been stalking the north side of Wilmington for months. At press time the New Hanover County Sheriff's Department, which had originated the investigation, had *no* suspects. Noppy Leigh had portrayed Millie Garnet as a well-liked and accomplished piano instructor. Leigh had discovered she had worked as a dancer in Miami before the war, and after her husband's heroic death in the D-Day invasion, she had dedicated herself to church affairs. The Vaughans were described as "devastated" and "inconsolable" over the loss.

A coalition of various groups including the Lions Club and the local VFW held a memorial march down Front Street to mourn Millie Garnet. A large blowup of her old portrait was carried in the backseat of a shiny black Cadillac convertible, held by two little girls. The Vaughans had been persuaded to stay in town for the parade and they rode in the next car back, another Cadillac convertible. All the freshly waxed cars had been donated by Oleander Motors, the local Oldsmobile, Buick, Cadillac dealer.

It didn't seem to him that the city was grieving exactly. Most of

Wilmington's white citizens seemed tight-mouthed and angry. Most of the Negroes had stayed indoors, but those who'd been caught out on the sidewalk stood there looking properly mournful, holding their hats in their hands while the cars went slowly by.

Later the same afternoon Burton Pardee threw a little party out at the golf club and announced that after a long period of soul-searching he was giving up his post as county commissioner and entering the arena to run for election as the next sheriff of New Hanover County.

Mary Helen knew all about it within half an hour after the party ended. "Well . . . *allegedly*," Mary Helen said, "he didn't say anything bad about you, exactly."

"What do you mean, *exactly?*"

"He didn't mention your name. He never came right out and said, you know, 'Kewpie Waldeau is a terrible sheriff,' or anything explicit like that."

"I guess that's good," he said.

"There were about twenty or thirty people there—Cammie's friends, I guess mostly." Cammie Pardee was a big mover out in Forest Hills and the beach-house set, a society woman with energy to spare. She liked getting out and boosting her husband. Burton held up his side of the bargain. He knew what he was supposed to do and glided like a tamed whale through the parties and promotions she organized on his behalf.

"Burton . . ." Q.P. muttered; the man who'd wanted his opinion. The man with the smile and the happy handshake. Q.P. stood there. Stunned, looking round at Franklin's office, the mountains of unfinished police business. There was nothing of him in the room, except his raincoat up on the hat rack. "Damn . . ." he said.

"It's not too late . . ."

He was going to lose his job.

"Damn . . ."

"It's not too late . . . you can get out there and *fight*. You can fight hard, and, you know . . ." Mary Helen was babbling, staring around the room like a chicken looking for a target.

"Is it too late to call Jimmy Satterwhite?" he asked.

"Just a little," Mary Helen said, rolling her eyes.

"Okay . . ." He got up and grabbed the red pens out of the mason jar and walked down the street to A-1 Printers.

"You see these." He put one of the pens on the counter in front of the man who ran the place.

"This is what I want, some cards printed up like this, except spelled right."

"Okay, just slow down . . ." The man got an invoice from under the counter. Back along the wall there were huge posters leaning against the cheap paneling. They were turned on their sides. He saw Pardee's chin sticking out and a curvy slogan:

Time for a Change!

"Okay . . . just like *this*"—the man dangled the pen—"but spelled right. What part of it do you want spelled right?"

"All of it."

"I mean—" The man turned the pen around so Q.P. could see it. The paint had gotten smudged.

"I'll write it out," Q.P. said. He grabbed a piece of pink scrap paper and drew a rectangle on it and then wrote in block letters across the top:

Vote for Q.P.

"That's good," the man said.

"Yeah . . . I want to add a . . ."

"Slogan?"

"Yeah, a slogan. A *phrase*, you know? Something that people'll remember, you know?

"Sure . . ."

"Something catchy . . ."

"Sure."

"Something that'll sort of sum up my whole . . . approach to law enforcement, you know?"

"Right," said the man.

He thought about it for a while but nothing sprang to mind.

"How 'bout 'A Candidate with a Future'?" the man said.

"That's pretty good," he said.

"Or . . . 'Keep Up the Good Work.'" The man turned the card around, lettered it in, and then showed it to him:

Vote for Q.P.
Keep Up the Good Work

"Mmmnn . . ."

"You want to think about it for a while? I've got some stuff that's just coming off the press, so . . ."

"Sure, sure. I'll just take a second here and try to figure it out." He sat down at a coffee table with magazines spread out across it. He opened up an issue of *Holiday* and thumbed through it looking for inspiration. He tried placing his name over every ad in the magazine.

Vote for Q.P.
Add Glamour to Better Coffee

Obviously some of the choices were no good, but he did find an ad for Evinrude motors and inserted himself:

Vote for Q.P.
All's Quiet on the Waterfront

But after a few more pages he found something that seemed to leap out at him and make sense right off. It was an advertisement for the new '54 Chrysler. A man in a tuxedo was exiting the bright red car and chatting with a woman who looked amazingly like Nina, only with red hair. He went up to the counter.

"Okay, I got it," he said to the printer, who was boxing up another job. "What do you think about that?" he said, turning his mock-up of the card around on the counter.

"Now, I *like* that. That's classy," the man said. "How many?"

"Five hundred?"

"Fifteen dollars plus tax, okay?"

"No way out of it," Q.P. said.

"That's democracy for you," the man said.

"I guess it's cheap if it helps me get elected."

"Sure . . ." the printer said and wrote up the order, promising the cards for the next afternoon. Q.P. went back up Princess Street to the courthouse, thinking that maybe his campaign might just have a spark of life left. He could see the card floating in front of him. Maybe he'd splurge and get a few posters printed, too:

Vote for Q.P.
The Look of Leadership!

TWENTY-ONE

Mary Helen was just finishing her sandwich when she heard something in the voice of the announcer.

Everything stopped and people were staring at the television Binky had hung up in there near the ceiling. It was like when they announced FDR was dead, she thought. That sudden chill and that spontaneous silence; that shock. So she looked up, too.

It was Douglas Edwards reporting the news. He looked down at his papers and announced that the United States Supreme Court had finally handed down a decision in the case about integrating the public schools. It was the end of an era, he explained. The court had held that racial segregation of public schools was a violation of the Fourteenth Amendment.

All of a sudden she became aware of the silence and she looked around. Binky was standing there with his towel tucked in his belt, dirty dishes in each hand.

A state could no longer justify segregation simply by providing separate but equal facilities for Negro children, Edwards told them. The court had made it clear, he said, that segregation of children on the basis of race was a denial of equal educational opportunities.

Through the window to the kitchen she could see the backs of Binky's kitchen help. One man was briskly cleaning up the first wave of lunch dishes. He and the cook were the only people in the place who couldn't hear the television.

The verdict was unanimous, Edwards said. He finished the report and without commenting put one page aside and continued on with other news. Binky's restaurant started buzzing right away; there was a burst of loud laughter and she turned around to look at a table of red-faced men in business suits. Binky continued on his way. "Holy taloodle," he said as he passed her table.

Why was everybody laughing? she wondered. Did they think this was just a joke, something that would blow over like yesterday's news? Did they think that this was a fad? She didn't even have children and she was concerned. She did what she could. She worked, she volunteered. Didn't all of the rest of them see the seriousness of what was happening? She couldn't eat anymore. It was like she was suddenly on the ceiling. The table looked like it was an impossible distance below her.

"Holy taloodle is right," she said to herself, and just before she got up to pay, she saw Mrs. Gates, a widow who worked at Pickard's and came in every day and ate alone, sitting at her booth all alone, tears streaming down her face.

And now she was walking.

Walking back as fast as she could, trying not to run because she couldn't run in those damn shoes, but still—walking as hard and as fast as she could down the corner at Front Street. On the surface life looked the same. Cars put on their brakes for the red light, people went about their shopping, unaware of the changing of the tide.

Maybe no one knew yet? Waiting at the corner, she looked around at the city of Wilmington. Everything would change soon, she thought, everything. The street itself would look different; all the people would change. The city wouldn't be like the city anymore.

She had realized the importance of the case the very first time she'd heard anything about it. She asked everyone about it, asked what they thought would happen, what they'd *do*. As the case made its way through the courts, more and more people around the courthouse and over at City Hall were aware of it. Watching, waiting.

It was as if they were looking up to see the signs of an approaching storm. The case had gone to the high court incredibly quickly. It was like the decision had already been made somewhere in Washington. How could you help but not think that? Vinson dies, Earl Warren takes over, and quicker than you can say N double-A CP, the case is being tried by the Supreme Court. How did that look?

How had things come to such a point? She and Marly had been talking about it upstairs just yesterday with Hal Lutz.

"I'm not worried about it all that much," Lutz said, but he always tried to laugh his problems away, she thought. "After all, it's impossible," he said. "It's impossible to implement. They don't have a plan, nobody's every done it. It'll take years, Mary Helen. Years."

Winky Peters, who was a member of the school board, hadn't agreed. It was going to be the end of everything, he said. "We don't have any power. We can't secede from the union a second time, so you've got this much of a choice," Winky said, obviously frustrated. "You can burn the whole buildin' down or you can stand off and watch it die from deterioration, because that's what's goin' to happen now that they've won."

"Well, however you cut it, there really isn't enough money for the county or Wilmington to fight it in the courts," Hal said.

"I know, I know," Winky said sadly, remembering the good old days in the war when the Wilmington city coffers were overflowing with tax revenues.

"But look, y'all, there isn't any point worrying about any of this." That was vintage Hal, smiling at the face of doom.

"Yeah, the state might have a little something to say about it," Winky said.

"That's right . . ."

"Maybe a *couple* of states. Georgia'll fight it. They got enough money and a governor that gives a damn down there," Winky said. He had no idea what the teachers would decide to do. He knew what he thought they'd do, and he figured he had a good idea what the *Board* would do, but everything was up for grabs now. Unpredictable, he said. At the end of the conversation they had laughed, she remembered. Laughed at the unreality of it all, at how absurd and chaotic life might suddenly turn out to be.

And then they had all gone back to work.

Brown, she remembered. That was it; somebody named Brown vs. the Board of Education in Topeka, Kansas. That was the name of the case.

Topeka, she thought. What a crazy place to be deciding the fate of the whole South.

And she remembered another thing. It was the particular phrase and the wording; the essence of the verdict, and why Winky and Hal and any thinking person who knew anything about government would be so distraught. She remembered Douglas Edwards as he announced in his grim voice: The Court had decided, for once and for all, that there could be no such thing as separate *and* equal.

Black Monday, she was thinking. Black, black Monday. She stepped off the curb the moment the light changed and got across Princess Street handily and went in the front entrance. It would be crowded right after lunch and she'd be able to tell more people that way.

TWENTY-TWO

The boy had been beaten. It was obvious from his lip that had been stitched up. It had happened quickly, on impulse. He was with his friend, he said, walking down Shipyard Road on his way to his mother's house. He was a big boy, with strong broad shoulders and a thick neck.

"He fought 'em off and ran. Three white men in a black car," Chaffee said, as solemn as ever. Looking at the boy's big arms, Q.P. could believe it.

"What happened to your friend?" Q.P. asked.

"He run off while they were getting out of the car. I just heard him go by me running and didn't see him after that."

"He's probably at home," Chaffee said.

"Anything you can tell me about these men? Can you describe them?" The boy looked up at him with his wide young eyes. He was thinking about it.

"I didn't see the man who was drivin' but I sure saw the other two." The boy gave a little gasp; it was almost a laugh of amazement at how close he'd come.

Q.P. wrote out the description the boy gave him, but already he could tell there was nothing much to go on. Two adult white men and a third driving. One man had on a hat. The boy said he could smell that they'd been drinking. They had run him off through the swamp and they didn't want to get their pants and shoes all messed up, so they didn't follow him.

"Did they have any guns?"

"One man, the man who was drivin', he had a stick, like one of these sticks out here."

"A nightstick like?"

"A billy club, yes, sir. Like what a policeman uses."

Q.P. looked up to meet Chaffee's eyes, trying to see if the whole thing was some kind of setup. "You think maybe this person was a policeman of some kind?" Q.P. asked quietly.

The boy sighed and looked down at his feet. "None of them was wearing a uniform," he said finally.

"All right," he sighed. "I guess if you *see* these men again, or if you see the car and can be sure you recognize it, or if you can get the license number off it, then we could go out and get 'em, but right now, all I can say is if we find people who match, we'll ask you to come in and identify them. Would you be willing to come down here and do that?"

The boy looked at him for a long moment and then over at Chaffee. They all knew what was being asked. He'd be foolhardy to come in and try to identify three white men he'd only seen out on some dark road. If one of them did turn out to be some kind of policeman, from Wilmington or from a neighboring town, Q.P. and Chaffee would be asking the boy to trade his life in an attempt to see some justice done. He wasn't sure he'd let the kid do it even if he was willing; if they couldn't make a case stick, it would be the same as suicide for the boy.

"I'll try to do whatever I can, sir," the boy said quietly; his voice was low. Purring almost like a cat, he said it so softly, looking down at the linoleum.

"You can go wait outside, Luther," Chaffee said to the boy, who stood up, all legs and elbows, and slipped out the door.

"I want to emphasize that black people are scared right now," Chaffee said. "It's all because of these murders, you understand?"

"Yes . . ."

"All of us, we're scared of being the target of white folks' revenge." Q.P. smiled at the older man. Most county sheriffs would have thrown Chaffee out by now. They both knew it.

"These newspapers have been sayin' that it's a black man who is doing this. But there's no proof of that," Chaffee said. His voice was strong and level.

"We don't have any idea who it is. I've been telling people that all along. I told the newspaper all that." He was getting frustrated. Caught in between. Now he was supposed to defend Noppy Leigh?

"We expect protection, Sheriff, just like everybody else. We expect you to do what's right and we're willing to help you any way we can."

"Okay . . . Well, I'll try to provide it."

"We know what a difficult situation you are in. You know the girl who works for you?"

"Mary Helen, the secretary?"

"No, sir. The other girl from the library who does the research for you and the police department?"

"Yes . . ."

"Miss Nina, she came out to put our choir's songs on her tape recorder."

"She did?"

"Yes, sir. She's encouraged us to do whatever we can to augment your efforts."

"She *has?*"

"Yes, sir. We had a meetin' the other night and decided for our own protection to start a system of neighborhood patrols."

"Now, hold on. Just wait a minute, Reverend—"

"Not only to help the sheriff's department, but also to protect ourselves—"

"—this is getting way out of hand. This is crazy. You say you're afraid of these rednecks comin' after your people, but when they find out you folks are out there *patrolling,* they're just going to come into town looking for a fight."

"Well, what are we supposed to do while you try to catch the man who's been killing these women?"

"I don't know, but that's not the answer."

"Just wait around like good little niggers?"

"I don't know. I don't—"

"We've got the right to protect ourselves the same as white people, we've got the right to bear arms and defend our homes. How else we're supposed to get justice? We're not going to let these people beat us down, Sheriff. Those days are gone now, I guarantee *you.*"

"Look, Reverend, patrolling the streets is a *police* function. In the city, that's up to the Wilmington P.D.; in the county, it's up to me. Now, I appreciate what you're trying to do, and I have told you how nuts I think it is. For my part I'll do what's right, but I can assure you that the P.D. doesn't especially like any competition."

Chaffee looked at him for a long moment. His face was stony still, like he was waiting for something else, or making up his mind. He took a breath and stood up.

"Blessed is he who considers the poor and the needy," Chaffee said, "for the Lord shall deliver him in the time of trouble." He was standing in the office doorway now, almost filling it. From her desk Mary Helen was looking up at him, her mouth was open a little, like she was startled to see the preacher standing there.

"But there *will* be trouble, and when trouble comes, we're all going to need some help, aren't we?" Chaffee said to her.

"Yes . . . I guess we will," Mary Helen said weakly.

"God bless you, then, sister," Chaffee said and turned away, heading for the parking lot to take the boy safely back home.

He found her walking along in a clutch of influential people who had been assembled by the chamber of commerce for a tour of the dilapidated Wilmington Light Infantry Building. The room was open and high with large windows that surrounded it. Most of the library committee was there, and he nodded politely at the Hawk, who simply ignored him. Obviously the idea was to get all the city leaders to agree to sponsor a bond issue for a new library. They were being led around the treacherous floors by Mr. Hopkins, the caretaker, who walked ahead of them with a large flashlight, helping them avoid the nails and little landslides of plaster and lath.

Lamont Sanders had come to the tour straight from the golf course, and Ralph Pagett was there for publicity purposes, to get the *Morning Star* behind the whole idea. As he found his way inside, they were discussing an estimate for the costs of renovating the building. Sanders was standing there rubbing his chin, making up his mind whether it was to his advantage to bleed all he could out of the library contract or donate some of his services and take the tax breaks and the prestige. You could hear the adding machine in his brain all the way across the room, Q.P. thought.

Nina saw him, smiled, and then frowned a little when she saw his expression. She disentangled herself from Pagett, who was almost drooling over her, and worked her way around the group.

"What are you doing here?" she whispered to him.

"I was just having a little meeting with your *friend* Reverend Chaffee."

"Oh?"

"He says you told him to start patrolling their neighborhood." He was looking daggers right through her. He was so tense he was humming.

"Well, that's not *quite* what I said . . ." She rolled her eyes. She tried to remember the text of her conversations with Chaffee. She had implied as much, she realized.

"That wasn't such a hot idea, Nina."

"What am I supposed to say to the man, Kewpie?"

"There's enough trouble starting up now without word getting around that there's posses of angry niggers running around—"

She stepped back and eyed him as coolly as she could imagine. "Well, aren't all posses created equal—"

"Goddamn, Nina . . ." Q.P. whispered. He looked down at the floor and walked behind her and quietly kicked a pile of broken window frames. She saw Pagett look over their way. She tried to smile back.

"I told him that they should *stick up for themselves.* I think they should, Kewpie. I didn't tell them to start shooting people—"

"Yeah, yeah . . . You told them you were working for the department?" She turned and looked at him.

"No . . ." she lied. In fact she had taken advantage of everyone's misconceptions as soon as she could.

"I got my friend Conrad to come down. We've been tape-recording their choir for UNC's culture program . . ."

"Conrad?"

"Conrad Ashbaugh, he's getting his fudd at Carolina. I told you about him."

"His what?"

"His fudd, his *Ph.D.*—"

"You never told me about him," Q.P. said. He looked shocked, she thought. Bewildered. Like a cow somebody had hit on the head.

"I did, too. I knew him in Chicago," she protested. It didn't come out as innocent as she'd hoped.

"Right, right . . . *Conrad.*"

"Kewpie, for God's sakes—"

"Okay, look. I am still the sheriff of this county, okay?" he said. He was pointing his finger at her. She saw Kate Pullam smile at Champ Evans and look over their way.

"All we are doing is collecting indigenous Southern hymns for this tape collection," she said. They were facing each other directly now; she was starting to lose control. She could feel it. Q.P. had put on his scowl-face. "They are singing things that have never been written down. Conrad is an old *friend*—"

"And keeping the streets more or less safe is still my responsibility until election day." He was hissing his words at her.

"You certainly have been a lot of fun lately," she said, starting to cry in spite of everything. Starting to cry because she had been angry when she had heard about the beatings and harassment that was starting to happen around town, starting to cry because— Because she *had* been happy to see Conrad again. Happy because he was the good Conrad again and totally immersed in his work and she liked to see him like that. Starting to cry because—

"Why don't we all go around to the basement entrance. That's where we were talking about putting the children's room," the Hawk was saying in a loud voice and gesturing to the doors. The group all began to herd toward the front of the building. Nina turned from Q.P. and started walking toward the group.

"Shit," Q.P. said, following along behind her. "Shit, *shit!*" And he brushed past her out the door.

Conrad had been so happy when she called. It wasn't that he was friendless at Chapel Hill; it was just that the program was all stretched out ahead of him and he was bored silly with two years to go. The chance to gather the hymns came out of the blue, and he grabbed it.

And yes, it was good to see him step off the train, and it was good to have him hug her, and to smell his funny smell, something in his hair tonic, maybe. Hear his funny accent; somewhere between Maine and Minsk. Watch him laugh.

They had gone right from the station out to the church and poked around. They waited in the front yard until Miss Selma Bird came down the block and showed them around the building. She was the woman who'd hugged her and turned her inside out at the service for Ruth Micheaux. It turned out she ran the church, and everybody knew it, but she did things with such subtle force that Nina had missed it completely. Miss Selma spotted Conrad out for the imp he was in about three seconds and shamelessly flirted with him as they looked for good places for the microphones. They made their first tapes that same night.

The choir was careful, nervous, and a little overly precise. They got a good recording of the hymns, but not very much emotion. Maybe they'd get a freer performance when the choir loosened up, probably right at the end of the sessions, she thought.

She watched Conrad as he inserted himself into the congregation. Seamlessly. He was an innocent, or at least *seemed* innocent. He had no guile at all and that radiated around him, she saw. People sized him up instantly, accepting him. He could get in anywhere because nobody was afraid of him.

They made a little station at a folding table and took down names and addresses of the choir, since a large part of Conrad's project was tracing the kinship groups that made up the congregation. The singers sat around waiting for their turn to come up to the table and give thumbnail sketches of their lives. Little vest pocket oral histories that he'd use later to flesh out his thesis. First they worked their way through the men, a collection of proud, dignified basses, a few smooth-voiced baritones and tenors, and then they moved on to the altos and sopranos.

A young girl came up. She had great wide eyes and was smiling.

"Okay," Conrad said as he pointed the microphone her way. "What's your name?"

"Elaine," she said.

"Okay . . ." Conrad spelled it back to her. "Last name?"

"Snow," the girl said. Nina looked up at her.

"Okay . . . Snow, like on the Christmas tree?" Conrad asked her.

"Mmm-hmm." The girl smiled.

"You have a middle name?"

"Littelle." She spelled it, and Nina wrote it out. Conrad got her age and place of birth and then started asking questions about her extended family.

"Are you kin to Cora?" she asked the girl softly.

"Yes'm. I'm her sister."

"I—I'm very sorry about your sister," she said. Conrad looked up.

"Thank you."

"What's the matter with your sister?" he asked the girl.

"She's killed by somebody. They don't know who."

"That's *awful* . . ." he said.

"I'm sorry," Nina said again.

"Yeah, oh . . . God, that's *awful*. That's really *terrible*," Conrad said. They began to record her family. Mother deceased, father gone. A lot of uncles and aunts on her mother's side.

"That's my cousin, right over there." The girl had started laughing at Conrad, who was trying to cheer her up by spelling everything wrong on purpose. Nina followed to where she was pointing. Across the church she recognized the lean young preacher who had angrily presided over Ruth Micheaux's funeral.

"Him?" Nina asked.

"Yes'm, that's him." The girl standing behind her giggled and Elaine broke up, too, as they both turned to stare at the sleek young man. "He's the preachinest preacher round here."

"Okay," said Conrad, looking at the line of singers waiting for their interviews. "Your cousin over there, what's his name?"

"Otha," she said. "Otha Snow."

Nina wrote it down in the little box.

"S-N-O-W," Conrad was repeating. "Is that French?" he asked the girl. She started laughing now and poked him in the shoulder.

"No, that ain't French, that's *American!*" And she left their table laughing and shaking her head at the crazy white folks.

"Okay," Conrad said, looking around at the rest of the women who were waiting there. "Okay, girls. Who's next?"

TWENTY-THREE

The crows were setting up a racket down below them where the road came out through the woods and opened out on a cornfield.

"You know what he was? He was just the first installment on the price that the niggers'll have to pay," Braidwood said. He was with Donny Nokes standing in the wet pine woods just over the line in Pender County. They were looking at the naked body of William "Red Billy" Scowen hanging there in the shade. Absolutely still.

Scowen had been stripped, flogged until he bled, and his penis had been severed. Where it had been looked like a black two-bit piece there in his pubic hair.

"Hell of a price," Nokes said.

Sheriff F. Tilton Braidwood was an amazingly little man to have made a career in law enforcement. Not only was he little, but he was angry all the time. Ugly with bad teeth. He must have got beat up a lot as a kid to be so mean, Nokes thought. Some of Braidwood's deputies had come up behind him. "I don't want to wait out here all day for goddamn Kewpie," said Braidwood. He spat some tobacco toward Scowen.

"I'd like to preserve the crime scene, if you don't mind, Sheriff." Nokes turned to him angrily.

"I'll preserve your goddamn crime scene, you fucking little piece of shit." Braidwood had actually taken a step toward Nokes, who, in turn, was forced to step back to where Scowen's feet were hanging down in the middle of the road. He'd thought that handling Braidwood would be easy, but now he felt himself bending over and walking backwards. It felt like he was trying to fight some kind of crazy little dog. Fortunately the deputies held Braidwood back just in time.

"Why don't you go home to bed, Sheriff," Nokes said. "We have reason to believe he was killed in New Hanover, so we'll take it. Go on home and, if you can, try not to walk on the evidence."

"Y'all tell Kewpie to keep his shit in his own bucket."

"Yes, sir. You can tell him yourself, you're such a big shot," said Nokes because he saw Q.P.'s Chevy pulling in up at the head of the road.

"It's all you goddamn people's fault anyway. You'd been doin' your goddamn job, that woman wouldn't been killed in the first place and force somebody to clean your mess up for you."

"You got a complaint about my work, you can always take it up with my boss," Nokes said. Q.P. wasn't scared of Braidwood, and Nokes couldn't think of anything else to tell the man, he was such a moron.

"You goddamn people are lucky to even have a goddamn job!" he yelled back to Nokes and walked up toward the highway to throw his weight around some more. Nokes stood in the clearing and shook his head and tried to imagine how nice it must feel to be Braidwood's wife.

There wasn't much he could do about the top of the road and the area right where he was standing, but he could stop people from going down to the cornfield, traipsing through the scene, at least until Q.P. got down there.

"Boy, has he got a hard-on this morning, huh?" Q.P. said when he got down the road.

"Oh, God . . ."

"He said you took it."

"Yeah, I figured Red Bill was all ours."

"Yeah." Q.P. squatted down and looked at the ground all around Scowen. At least there wasn't any smell. They'd gotten there maybe within a calendar day, he thought.

"Man, this is the goddamndest thing . . ." Q.P. said but Nokes didn't answer him. He had gotten very quiet. "Braidwood says the Klan did it," Q.P. tried again.

"Maybe . . ." Nokes shrugged. "I guess he'd probably be the first to know." Braidwood had told him his theory about the Klan in detail, saying how he knew way back when he first heard about the Garnet woman, and then right after that, when he heard the outrageous news about the Supreme Court decision, how he *knew* there was going to have to be some blood. It was just natural and he wasn't surprised at all, he'd said. "They forced our hand" was the way he'd put it to Nokes.

Q.P. saw that it was getting lighter. He could see down the road. It petered out in a growth of little pine trees and blackberry bushes at the edge of the cornfield. Just a few yards down past where Scowen was hanging.

"Well, you know, Donny, if nobody drove down here, I think we might be able to lift a tire print over there." Q.P. pointed to a line of tracks that ran along under Scowen.

"You know," Nokes said quietly, "I don't think this was a lynching, Kewpie. I've been to a lynching and it wasn't nothing like this."

Q.P. looked up at that. After about ten seconds Nokes looked back over at him. "Yeah," he said, remembering back. "It wasn't nothing like this at all."

"Really?"

"It was more like a party," Nokes said. He was still looking up at Scowen, whose neck had been bent over by the knots so that it looked like he was trying to see something way up in the branches.

"A *party?*"

"Ah, hell, Kewpie," Nokes said. He'd finally pulled his eyes away from the dead man and he was looking down at his feet and shaking his head. "It was way back. Way back when I was in high school, and we heard there was going to be this lynching and, you know, a bunch of us went up there." Nokes took a deep breath and looked up at Scowen again.

"I just got swept up in the whole thing," he said softly.

It had happened down a road much like this one. Just after sunset, in a grove off the blacktop road where he biked to school. He'd run up there, breathless because they all wanted to get there in time, run up there with his buddies, Al and Joe Norment. There were cars and pickup trucks parked all along the shoulder, and when they got up to the road, they saw some girls squealing and running away in horror out from the woods. Then the girls edged back, too fascinated to leave.

There had been four of them. Negroes. They could barely see them from their place on the edge of the circle, standing up on their toes to get a good look. He had time to see the ring of trampled grass, the men dangling from branches, their toes almost touching the dirt. There was a great cheer when each man got pulled up off the ground. Someone had a bugle and he kept blowing it over and over; not a song or a melody, just single blaring notes, like some animal calling. The girls were crying. "What did they do?" Al kept asking him, and when he hollered back that he didn't know, Al started asking all the people in the crowd. "What did they do?" he kept saying over and over but nobody was paying any attention to him. When a man saw them hanging around, he detached himself from the back of the crowd and angrily ran them off. "Kids shouldn't see such things," Nokes remembered him screaming at them.

". . . I guess there was near 'bout two hundred people out there. There was bottles, and cigarette butts, and, you know . . . a fire. They'd basically . . . *had a party* while they were hanging them."

Later that night the police came around and so the next day, by the time they could sneak back on their way to school, the dead men had been taken away and there was just the garbage left. He'd spent the afternoon down there with the other kids, walked all over the scene.

". . . and, you know, there's nothing like that here. Nobody had a party down here at all," Nokes said.

"No." Q.P. got up and walked around in a wide arc, thinking about Nokes and his story. Now Nokes kept on talking, like he'd decided to solve the murder and that way he wouldn't have to think about it or remember what he'd seen.

". . . and so, the thing that bothers me about the Klan idea is that it's just not messy enough, down here."

Q.P. looked around. The little road wasn't that easy to find. There was some old garbage dumped up near the entrance, but hardly anybody had ever driven back down where they were standing, where the ground was lower. The road wasn't very good down there, muddier under the big tree and there was no place to turn around.

The entrance was hidden, too. There were bushes and honeysuckle all around up there by the blacktop. He wouldn't have been able to find the entrance at all if it hadn't been for Braidwood's boys lounging around by the side of the highway on the hoods of their cars.

"You'd think there'd be some more blood," Q.P. said.

"Yeah, there's no blood at all. That's something else that's wrong, too," Nokes said and gave him just a little look.

"But this is our same guy, it looks like to me," Donny said. "Check the knots." It wasn't a noose that held Scowen up to the tree limb but a simple loop with a series of loops repeated over and over to give strength to the knot. The other end was tied around the trunk of the tree in the same way. Sash cord. Q.P. walked around so he could get a good look at the pathway to the tree. There were some footprints over there maybe.

"You better go get that kit out of the car."

"I don't feel like talkin' to that asshole," Nokes said quietly.

"It's all right, then. I'll do it," Q.P. said.

Donny didn't even notice him as he left. He was just standing there in the center of the road; standing there with the sound of the crows still fighting down in the field, looking up into the face of the dead man.

TWENTY-FOUR

He knocked off at lunch and walked back up to his place on Orange Street and climbed into his old truck. It was a Dodge that he'd bought off a friend of Glen Petty's; the tailgate was long gone, but he'd put some chain across the back and it was strong enough to hold the aluminum motorboat. He held his breath, pulled out the choke, and after a few coughs it started.

Then he drove out along River Road, trying to imagine that he'd just killed Cora Snow.

He went right past the junkyard near State Ports where Mildred Garnet had been dumped, along past the old abandoned warehouses that were fenced off from the road, until the pavement curved and he could drive right beside the river. Every so often there were little roads that ran down toward the banks that only fishermen or lovers ever used. He slowed right down to a crawl, waving past anyone who came up behind him, and watched the side of the road until he found a place that fit the requirements he had begun to imagine in his murderer's mind. It had to be a road that wasn't so sandy that he'd get stuck. And it had to have enough trees and brush around it so that nobody who happened to drive by would be able to see while he dumped the body.

He stopped at the first good place he found. After all, he had just killed someone. He was scared. He wanted to get rid of the evidence. He parked the truck with its back to the river and sat there for a second. No traffic. If it was night he'd be invisible back in the tangle of scrub. He went to the edge of the bank and tried to imagine throwing Cora Snow into the high water of the Cape Fear.

He had an inner tube in the back and he had stretched an old piece of nylon aircraft netting around it and he put in about as much as he figured Cora would weigh, a couple of concrete blocks and an old electric motor. He tied it all down inside the netting in the center of the inner tube, tied the neck together, and then lashed the whole thing around the tube with his parachute cord. Then he lugged it down the slippery bank and lay it on the sand while he manhandled the boat into the water without banging up the propeller.

He pushed the weighted inner tube as far out as he could. It got hung up on a low sandbar right away and he searched around until he found a stick to unhook it. Then he climbed in and fired up the motor and pulled out into the river and followed it as it floated down to the Atlantic. The river wasn't as swollen as it had been on the night they had found Cora. The current caused the tube to spiral around, and after a few minutes he saw that the net was dragging on all the sandbars, so he motored over and wrapped the weights together in a tighter package so that the draft of the float wasn't so great. Then he let it go into the current again.

It floated free then and he followed along, inevitably moving faster than the float. Every so often he'd cut back upriver and then just drift down again. The draft had been reduced, but still every now and then it would catch, spin around on the peak of one of the little bars for a moment—then break free.

He thought about Nina and what had gone wrong there. He wondered if there was any way he could fix it. He thought that maybe it was all for the best and that probably the two of them weren't made for each other like he had been hoping.

He hadn't thought it was too much to ask her to keep her nose out of department business. He wouldn't have let anybody else do the kinds of things he'd let her get away with. Anybody else who had represented themselves as being in the department when they weren't, he would have had Spud Reid charge them with impersonation. She wasn't even aware of how close she'd come.

She just went ahead, he thought. Just went ahead and did whatever she wanted. Went ahead and thought whatever she wanted to think. She wasn't afraid. Not afraid of nothing.

He figured it came from being privileged. With a daddy who loved her and sent her off to a college so she could study the mating habits of the Samoans. It came from never having to wade through the kind of shit he'd grown up with in Baltimore, the kind of shit he'd seen every day in Korea.

He watched the inner tube free itself from a bar and twirl its way downstream. It came from being blind, he thought. She was just blind to all the danger out there. Innocent. Like some kind of a lamb. One day she was going to get burned. She was going to stick her chin out and lay into the wrong guy, somebody who didn't care so much about seeing her cry.

The sky clouded over and the wind began to rise, and a little squall came blowing up and soaked him through. And then it was gone almost as soon as it had arrived. He shivered for a while and got down low in the boat to avoid the worst of the wind. He saw three freighters coming up the channel hurrying to get into port before nightfall. It was getting darker, but he could still see the float bobbing along ahead of him in the waves. He reached behind him and twisted the throttle and ran out into the river a few yards and was glad when he saw the huge dishes of the radar station down by Fort Fisher, perhaps a mile away. The river was wider here, the current faster. He could see the lights of Southport winking on down at the mouth of the river.

He swooped back in and idled along until he found the float again and followed it along.

He kept trying to fit all the victims in. He had started out thinking that whoever had done it was a sex fiend. Rape and kill randomly and then hide the evidence. Because of Cora Snow and Ruth Micheaux he had figured the killer probably was a Negro. Then Millie Garnet threw it all off. Then along came Scowen.

Why had Scowen been killed? he wondered. Mutilated and killed. It was too much of a coincidence that Cora and Red Bill had been targeted by accident. They must have known the killer, been into something together. Maybe they'd been witnesses; maybe they were just in the way. If so, then how did Mildred Garnet, the white prostitute, fit in? Or Ruth Micheaux? Maybe he'd have to go back to square one.

He saw the wide bank at the foot of Davis Beach Road on his left. And he turned back and circled as the float caught; once, twice, and then a final time there at the bank where the long gray snag had fallen out of the forest. The inner tube struck the snag and stopped, turned slowly, and stopped once more. He made a note of the time. The whole voyage down the river had taken nearly six hours. If he let it keep going, in about another hour it would be out by Frying Pan shoals at the mouth of the Cape Fear, and after that the Atlantic Ocean. He throttled over to the float, hauled it in, and motored over to the dock at the air force base.

As he pulled up, a couple of sentries advanced down the pier. They had their holsters unbuttoned and were waving at him, calling for him to halt right now or they'd shoot. Their faces were young and they looked scared, just the kind of people who were really dangerous, he thought.

She had made up her mind to go over there and see what he was up to. And so, after she finished up at the library, she went to the washroom and checked herself out in the mirror and then walked over to the courthouse.

And, of course, he wasn't in.

She talked to Mary Helen, who was just finishing up her morning, and asked her to cover while she ran out for lunch. Q.P. was somewhere talking to people at the hardware store, probably about his boat, she said as she grabbed her purse and headed for the doors.

Nina followed her to the steps and watched her pull out in the Studebaker. She wedged open the door and sat outside on the concrete banister and waited. Q.P. had probably been up all night on some cop adventure, she thought. What was she doing here? Trying to help? Trying to see him again? Trying to prove that she mattered? That what she thought, her suspicions and ideas, that all that ought to matter and mean something to him?

Getting a little stupid, she thought. Getting a little softheaded over this guy, she thought. *Sucker.*

She shifted the file folder and tucked it under her thigh, where it wouldn't blow away. In the file were some of Conrad's grids. They were something like family trees and then they had spaces for other details as well. He had designed an entire system where he could enter each person's vital statistics on a card and then, by punching little notches in the rim of the card, cull for any specific coded characteristic. Brown eyes, blue eyes, age, gender, birthplace. Whatever. At UNC he had a machine, a kind of typewriter with long needles, that speared a stack of the punched cards and then shook whatever had been selected free. It was amazingly effective, Conrad said, the uses of the device were limited only by the imagination of the person who was designing the punch codes for each file card.

Before Conrad had left they had discussed doing a paper together on Southern Negro church-based kinship, so she'd mimeographed copies of the grids to keep in Wilmington. The one she had brought in the folder for Q.P. to see was for the Snow family.

He came walking around the corner, surprising her even though she'd been looking for him. He opened his mouth when he saw her there, and then closed it again.

"I brought something for you," she said, holding out the folder.

"Oh yeah?" He stopped there and looked at her. He looked terrible. He hadn't shaved. He probably hadn't slept. She chewed her lip.

"What is it?"

"Some stuff that Conrad and I put together about Cora Snow's extended family group."

"Ahh . . ." He sighed and nodded. That again.

"I was going through it and thought you might be interested."

"Great."

She opened the folder and showed him the grids. "It's the Snow family with all its kinship groupings related to people here in the county. It's basically a matrix of all the people who knew the Snow girl. Kinship doesn't have to mean that they are blood related."

"Okay . . ."

"So . . ."

"Okay. Thanks," he said.

"It's just another way of looking at her world."

"Yeah, okay. This is all your friend's stuff, then? Conrad?"

"Yeah, except for what's mine," she said. She'd been there work-ing on it, too. He never seemed to pick up on that.

"Okay."

"See you, then," she said and started walking up the steps.

"Nina—" he said as she left. She stopped there at the edge of the sidewalk. A car full of shrieking children waving their beach toys out the windows drove slowly up Princess Street.

He had come up the stairs.

"Look, thanks for all you've done on this, but you're not a *cop*, you're a *librarian*."

"Right," she said. He was just standing there looking at her, dead serious. She tried to smile at him. It probably didn't turn out that way. She turned away and walked to the edge of the street and jay-walked across ahead of the traffic.

Well, at least I'm a *good* librarian, she thought.

That night he took a glass of bourbon to bed and a hot water bottle to ward off what he figured was a bad cold coming on and read himself to sleep with Nina's history of the Snow family.

At first he couldn't make anything out of it. He had to lay the pages out across his bedspread. The first and central page was headed *Cora Elizabeth Snow*. The name was lettered in handwriting that wasn't Nina's and surrounded by a box that dominated the page. Inside the box was information, some of it in abbreviations that he didn't understand. The date of her birth and approximate date of her death were there and then other notations that seemed mostly to do with religious affiliation.

Connected to Cora's box and spreading out onto the other pages were other boxes. There was an empty box for her father and an only slightly more complete one for her mother, whose family name was Rowell. There was a box for her sister and then another box made of dotted lines right beside it.

There wasn't really very much information on the Snow side of Cora's family. There was a box for Thelma Snow, Cora's aunt, who had taken her on and tried to make a maid out of her, and below it a box for Thelma's nephew, Otha. Beside that box there was another curious box made up of dotted lines and from it other dotted lines that ran off the page. On another page was a longer list of Rowell relatives connected to smaller boxes with their children. He tried rearranging the papers so that they made some kind of design, but there were dozens of them. From the looks of it, Cora was connected to a lot of people. He could ask Nina about it, he thought. It would be a good excuse to phone up and talk. At least that way he could show her he had looked at the information like he'd promised.

He turned out the light and tucked his head under the pillows and inhaled her faint smell from the pillow. It was almost gone, he thought.

How could he have been so stupid to lose a woman like that? He made up his mind to call her the next day, to thank her and rave on about how much the family tree had helped him, and to make a date for dinner. Maybe at Hong's, where the lights were low and there were candles and little booths where they could be alone without all kinds of civilians wanting to come by and slap him on the back and talk about the election.

But the next morning he got away late. His head was all stuffed up and he took seven aspirin and rushed in and pulled Nokes off of court duty and they took the Chevy and headed down to Front Street.

Because in the night he had a dream.

The Cape Fear River was in the dream, and Nina's diagrams, and he floated along all twisted up with boxes and grids, and on the banks there was a man with tire tracks where his mouth should be.

The tire tracks were like mirrors; they gleamed and reflected the sunset back at him, and he tried to turn his old boat around before it drifted away and get back to the man who was standing on the shore with his blood-red teeth.

Laughing.

TWENTY-FIVE

Allison was out when he and Nokes arrived at the office on the sixth floor of the Trust Building, on the corner of Front and Market Streets, the closest thing you could get to a skyscraper in Wilmington.

"He's canceled all his appointments for this morning, but he's got a two o'clock," the receptionist told them. He and Nokes went out into the hall.

"Hell, it doesn't matter, we can always pick him up at home."

"Yeah, I guess."

"Let's just come back at two and pick him up then."

"You stay here. If he phones in, I don't want her telling him we're here. I want him to just come on in like normal."

They went back in and told the receptionist to cancel all his afternoon appointments. She stiffened at that. "He'll be coming down to the courthouse all that time," Q.P. said.

"I don't know whether I can do that . . ." She looked at the ledger in front of her.

"Well, unless you want all these patients showing up and he's not here . . ." He smiled at her.

"Isn't there another time you could book an appointment?"

"This isn't an appointment," said Nokes.

"He's going to be coming with us. We've got a few questions that we need to ask him. It's an interview."

"Oh . . . Okay . . . Well, thank you, then." She started dialing. Q.P. stole a look at the ledger. Allison seemed to work mornings and then afternoons, off and on. Maybe braces weren't such a hot item in Wilmington, he thought. Either that or he had enough money and could play golf whenever he wanted. Pretty good life, he thought. He was starting to dislike the guy already.

He went down to Binky's Parlor and got a chili dog and a Nehi and sat down to leaf through the magazines. He read an article all about how the navy had developed a system designed to wash nuclear fallout off the flight decks of aircraft carriers before it could contaminate either steel or men. There was a photo of the *Shangri La* with gigantic sprinklers spraying the whole ship. He read for a little longer and the place started to fill up, so he went up and relieved Nokes so that he could get something to eat and be back by a quarter to.

Allison came in a little late. Made it halfway to his door before he caught sight of Q.P. and Nokes just getting to their feet.

"Ah . . . Dr. Allison, these men—" the receptionist started.

"Yes?" Allison said when he saw them. He was scared already, Q.P. thought. Push on it, he could hear Nina saying in his thoughts.

"What's this all about?" Allison asked, right on cue.

"We'd rather not discuss it here, Doc," Q.P. said easily.

"I'll drive," said Nokes, and they steered Allison to the door.

They put him in the car and didn't strike up any conversations or chat or try to put him at ease. Q.P. wanted him to be as uncomfortable as possible, but just on this side of asking for his lawyer because they had no reason to haul him in, not really.

They went into the offices and Allison, who'd probably never been there before, got a good look at the teletype machine and the dispatcher's room and the racks of shotguns and Ellis Strickland leaning on the counter of the door to the evidence room.

The interrogation room had a wooden table and three chairs and an ashtray and a two-way glass window that was set so that it faced the suspect. Nokes let him wait in there for a few minutes. Q.P. came in by himself. He had a pad and a pencil and a manila folder with him.

"Sorry about this, Doc," he said while he arranged his papers.

"Oh, that's all right." Allison smiled. Trying to be casual. He was already smoking. Q.P. eyed the cigarettes.

"Can I bum one of those?" He pointed to Allison's Tareytons. He had just unwrapped the pack; the cellophane with its little red ribbon was crumpled there in the ashtray.

"No, sure . . . . *Sure.*" He flicked the cigarettes over to Q.P., who lit one up.

"This is about Cora Snow, again," Q.P. said and spat out a stream of smoke across the table. The Tareytons were filtered and tasted like a whole lot of nothing, he thought.

"Sure . . ." said Allison.

"Okay, then . . . let's just go through it once more. Just think back. You dropped her off and you didn't see anything. Nothing?"

"I told you that already. I told you everything."

"Okay," said Q.P. and reached into his folder and slid a photograph of Millie Garnet across the table. "What about her?" Allison's eyes went wide; he'd seen the photograph in the paper.

"Ever work on her teeth, or . . ." said Q.P., trying to keep his tone helpful.

"*No* . . ." said Allison, wincing.

"What about this?" The next photograph had been recently taken by Nate Giddings after they'd cut down Red Bill Scowen.

"Jesus Christ . . ." said Allison, and then he said it again.

"You know him? Ever see him at Cora's place?"

Allison's eyes flashed up from the photograph. His face was red and his voice had risen to a shriek. "I told you! I don't even remember any of this. I don't know anything about this, or her, or . . . *any* of this!" He was holding a photograph of Ruth Micheaux when he said it.

There was a knock at the door and Nokes let in a man in a dark suit whom Q.P. recognized from court. Ed Nicholson was a trial lawyer to the Forest Hill set. Q.P. didn't get up and Nicholson didn't sit down. Nokes stood in the door and shrugged.

"Afternoon, Kewpie. Is my client under arrest?"

"No."

"Has he been charged with anything?"

"No."

"Well, then, what the fuck is this all about? You come in, cancel his customers out from under him—"

"I'm questioning him about some murders, Ed." It didn't stop Nicholson for a moment.

"What fuckin' murders, Kewpie, are you talkin' about?"

"These right here." He splayed Giddings's photos across the table. "This is your client's maid. This one is her boyfriend." Nicholson frowned at Cora's death mask; he normally dealt in cleaner territory.

"And there's these two. We're just trying to find out what happened. The Doc here says he dropped her off and didn't see anything out of the ordinary, so . . ." He stood up. "That's all, I guess, Doc." Nicholson was still looking at the pictures.

"You brought me all the way down here for *this?*" Allison said. Getting bold now that he had Nicholson in the room with him.

"Look, I'm sorry, Doc. We're just trying to establish the extent of your relationship with the dead girl—"

"*I told you!*" Allison suddenly shouted. Nicholson put out a hand to restrain him. "I didn't have a *relationship* with her! I didn't have a goddamn thing to do with her! *I told you!*"

"Come on, Rick." Nicholson helped Allison out of the room. "You're not goin' fishin' with my client, Kewpie, you understand?" Nicholson said as they left, grandstanding. Q.P. wondered how much he'd charge Allison for coming to the rescue.

"Sorry, Ed. Next time it'll be nice and official." He watched them walk down the hallway.

He was out on the porch, working his way through his third bourbon and just about to fall asleep, when the phone rang. He shakily got to his feet and went inside, handhold by handhold so he wouldn't knock anything over in the dark.

The voice was low and husky, and at first he thought it was Reverend Chaffee and that he, too, was drunk, but that idea went away fast.

"*You goddamn nigger-lovin' Commie. We're going to kill your ass . . .*"

"Yeah?" he said, waking up a little at the insults. Maybe the guy would talk long enough to give himself away.

"*Everywhere you go, everything you do, we're watchin' your ass . . .*"

"I hope you're having fun."

"We're gonna cut your nuts off, funny boy. We're gonna cut your dick off an' make your Jew Commie girlfriend eat it . . ."

And then he slammed down the phone before the man could start laughing.

TWENTY-SIX

Maybe it was the fact that he'd had to pull his phone out of the wall, maybe it was the influence of Nina's boxes and grids, or maybe it was his contempt for Braidwood and his happiness over what he thought was a Klan triumph, but Q.P. didn't have much trouble making up his mind to attend the service for Scowen. He decided to show up if for no other reason, he told himself, than his new job of putting down rumors.

It was an open-casket funeral and it was crowded with men from Red Bill's world. They all knew how to behave at church. A lot of them had heard the Klan story and their faces turned hard the moment they recognized him. Some of them were familiar to him from arrests, interrogations, and various other moments in law enforcement.

He saw "Stick" Niles, a gambler and fence for bigger Negro criminals in Raleigh and Charleston. He was lean as a post with high cheekbones and legs that were long in the thigh. He was dressed in powder blue and sitting in front of the church. Stick looked over his way and gave a barely perceptible nod, just a hint of a smile. He nodded back at Niles and walked with the others in a slow line down the aisle and waited his turn to pass the casket.

Red Bill looked peaceful, Q.P. thought. Courtesy of Mr. Beverly and Nate Giddings, he looked like he was asleep. He even looked *proud* to be asleep. His white collar covered the marks around his neck. There was no bruise because he was dead before he was hanged, Q.P. thought. The bottom half of the casket was closed over

Scowen's stomach. Q.P. put a hand on the edge of the casket, just a little pat to say good-bye to the last man to love Cora Snow.

"They really cut off his dick?" Stick whispered when Q.P. got over to him.

"They really did."

"Damn . . ."

"How did you know him?"

"I known him since I was a kid. We sold things to him, bought things from him, you know. He's okay."

"Yeah, I thought he was okay."

"Musta pissed somebody off."

While he was standing there with Niles, something caught his eye and he looked up at the back of the church and recognized Nina. She was perched on a stool under the balcony. She was concentrating on a tape recorder set up on a folding table back there. She put one hand up to her earphones and looked off into the distance and saw him, too. He nodded and after a moment of concentration she did, too, and smiled a little.

Then there were the opening chords from the organ and the choir began to sing "Satan, Your Kingdom Must Come Down." He looked around in the flowers and saw a couple of microphones and another, painted black, hanging down from the center of the arch.

He watched as Nina rocked gently to the rhythm of the hymn and resisted the urge to adjust her controls. There was a little round woman there beside her fanning herself to the pulse of the music. Nina handed her the headphones and let her listen for a moment.

Most of the mourners didn't seem to be sad at the passing of Red Bill Scowen. Probably everybody at one time or another had figured that he would wind up dead at an earlyish age anyway. Some might have bet that the Klan would get him because Red Bill had been known as a race man. Not a suit-and-tie organizer like Dr. Terry or a politico like Fontaine but the kind of man who wouldn't hesitate to put himself in the way of trouble. As a result he had a spotty employment history, and because he'd never given in much on his rights, he had taken a few beatings. He was light skinned, and that pissed a lot of people off, black and white. Altogether it was a risky way to go through life.

But it was obvious that most people had *liked* Scowen. He hadn't

162 S T E P H E N E. M I L L E R

been a bully or a mean man. He'd supplied some of their needs, stuck up for himself, been generous when he could afford to be, and had tried to have fun while he was around.

The choir fell silent and he saw that old Reverend Chaffee had come up to the pulpit and was asking them all to bow their heads and pray with him. The church went silent for a long moment and Chaffee began to speak, his soft voice carrying to every corner of the room. He thanked God for bringing everyone here today to pay tribute to their fallen brother William.

He asked God to help them all remember the lessons of Brother William's short and tragic life, condemned those at whose hands Brother William was brought down so cruelly, and proclaimed his faith that God would continue to comfort them in their grief.

A second preacher came up and spoke, a young man, perhaps as young as Q.P. His attitude was in complete contrast to Chaffee; where Chaffee was rumpled, the young preacher was smooth; where Chaffee was quiet, the young preacher was loud. Chaffee might still be a strong man, but it was old strength, strength carried inside. This young preacher was gifted with an amazing power that was obvious the first time you laid eyes on him. He had that thin whippy strength that some lightweights have. The preacher would work quick, Q.P. thought, he'd come right to the point.

Now his words had worked the congregation up into a chorus of amens—". . . and I looked unto you, and I searched your faces, and I asked, 'Who would deny me?' . . ."

There was no answer, and the young preacher went on to describe how Brother William had been killed by brutal agents of Satan. Brother William had been killed by those who would beat down all of God's brown children, and God Himself was angry about it. He was furious about it, the young preacher said, and he was looking to find the culprit—". . . who would seek to part the lamb from the shepherd, who would seek to part me from my master . . ."

Q.P. looked over to where Nina was getting it all on tape.

". . . my sight will uncover you, my ears will not listen to your apologies, my vengeance will be swift and my scourge will be pure . . ."

The time was coming, the preacher said, when all those who made their combination against the workings of God were going to be hurled into the fire—"*. . . and I will find you. I will discover you. Wherever you run, wherever you hide . . . you will quake with fear in the blinding light of the eye of God . . .*"

The young preacher looked around at all of them and, just for a moment, his eyes picked out Q.P.'s white face.

"*. . . and I will be the right hand of the Lord God Almighty, I will be a vessel for his will, for his righteousness . . . I will walk the earth and I will do his bidding . . .*"

Maybe the preacher was one of the ones who thought the Klan had done it and that Q.P. and the handful of white faces had come to the service to gloat.

"*I am the Alpha and the Omega and it is* my *word . . . it is* my *word to say or not to say . . . and if he should come and stop* my *mouth . . . if he should make me fall silent . . . And I could not cry out, my word could* not *be heard, then* you *must be my word—*" There was a great rush of response from the congregation that must have sent Nina's machine right off the dials.

"*And for you—a thousand years shall be as one hour!*"

Outside he went over to her as she packed her machine into the trunk of Milton's big car.

"That was something, huh?" he said to her.

"Oh yeah. That last preacher's the guy who is Cora's cousin," she said as she stowed the tape recorder in with some old pillows to protect it from sliding around. A series of her diagrams went through his mind and he saw the boxes with their confusing lines.

"Oscar?"

"Otha," she said. "He's been preaching since he was twelve. He's what they call a 'natural' preacher."

"And he was her cousin?"

"Those charts I brought over for you, did you ever look at them?" She sounded irritated.

"Yes, I looked at them. I couldn't figure them out but I looked at them."

"It's not that hard. Everybody is a box, they're connected some-how to everybody else, and if there's enough information that it runs out of the box, you make a supplementary sheet—"

"What does it mean if there's a dotted line?"

"Lot of those in this community," she said. "It means that there's some question about the paternity or the maternity. Orphans, bastards, stepchildren, et cetera. You were probably trying to find out about Cora's father?"

"Yeah, probably . . ."

"Well, there's not too much on him. He abandoned the family a long time ago; it's mostly Rowells on the chart; that's the stable side of the family. Thelma is about it for that generation of the Snows." They fell silent as they drew toward Chaffee. Nina moved ahead to meet him. She put the microphone stands down and took his hand.

"Thank you so much, Reverend. I think we're done."

"Well, I hope we have been of some help, Miss Nina. Did you get everything you wanted?"

"It's a wonderful collection of music, and when it's edited I'll bring you a copy and we'll play it for everybody." She smiled brightly.

"That'll be just fine," Chaffee said. As Nina packed her cables in the trunk, Chaffee turned to him. "I understand that you are investigating the lynching of Brother William?"

"That's right," he said. Chaffee was looking at him with a hard glare.

"And have you made any progress, Sheriff?"

"Well, the Klan didn't kill him, that's for starters." Chaffee hadn't wanted to hear that; his face changed and he pulled away from Q.P. and looked around in frustration.

"The man was *lynched*, Sheriff. He didn't go out there and hang himself . . ."

Q.P. stood there and waited for the reverend to simmer down. He didn't have to tell him a damn thing and they both knew it.

"In fact he was killed by just one person, Reverend. He was murdered and then he was hung up out there, probably to make it *look* like a lynching. It wasn't a bunch of guys in white robes. So you can tell everybody that and maybe help cool things off around here, okay? That would be a good way to help." He moved past Chaffee with the intention to help Nina with the last of her packing, but she was in conversation with the little round woman who had been listening to the recording.

"Listen to me, Sheriff," Chaffee said behind his back. He said it quietly but firmly, like a man about to pull out a gun or a knife, like it was a last warning. "Crosses have been burned . . ."

"Yeah, I heard about that—" he started. There had been a cross burning across the river up in Brunswick County. The Klan had got a lot of new members out that night by holding a memorial burning to show their outrage over the murder of Mildred Garnet, and they weren't exactly happy about integrating their schools, either.

"Because we have now finally won the right to have an equal education, every white cracker Klan member is using this as an excuse to beat up black men, to rape black women, to abuse black children . . ." Nina and the little round woman looked up at Chaffee. He was talking with anger but quietly, utterly controlled. Q.P. put his hands in his pockets. There wasn't anything he could do to stop the old man from talking his piece.

"Now another black man has been *lynched*. Hung up to die in misery. All because you people think it's all right to let some of your boys blow off steam," Chaffee said. His face was glaring now, his eyes almost glowing, Q.P. thought. "Well, a man's life is not steam. A woman's dignity is not steam. We're not going to be your safety valve. You hear me, Sheriff?"

He didn't say anything. Chaffee's voice could be heard across the lawn and people were watching them now. "We'll protect ourselves if the sheriff's department and the police won't do it."

"I already told you what I think about that, Reverend. The Constitution gives you the right to bear arms, and freedom of speech, and the freedom to make real big mistakes, too. I can't do anything about that, either."

"Even if it was just one killer, it was still revenge. It was revenge on a black man who got in somebody's path. Everybody knows *why* it got done." Chaffee had come right up to him; he was pointing with his finger to emphasize his words. Q.P. made up his mind not to get into a fistfight with a sixty-year-old preacher at a funeral.

"Why should we keep on helping you people?" Chaffee said, almost spitting the words he was so bitter, and then he walked away. The congregation depleted, most of the solemn faces moving away from where Q.P. was standing there alone in the yard, getting into their cars for the long train out to the cemetery.

He went over and found Nina still in conversation with the little round woman. Nina introduced her as Miss Bird and she beamed up at him and took both of his hands in hers. "Thank you for coming here today. It would have meant so much to William," she said, giving his hands a little squeeze.

"Well, I'm very sorry for what happened to him," he said to her. She looked up into his eyes for a second, and then said good-bye and went away to close up the church.

"How're you doing?" Nina said. She was looking closely at him and he thought that she was all of a sudden stunningly beautiful. She was wearing her black sweater, a little ring of pearls. A little purse to hold on to, her big skirt flaring. Black shoes this time.

"I'm okay, I guess. I wanted to talk to you," he said. She smiled and looked around the yard.

"Sure, start talking, Sheriff. This is nice." She reached up and pinched the lapels of his suit jacket.

"Look, would you show me more how to read all those charts that you and what's-his-name made up?"

"Conrad?" She smiled.

"Yeah," he said.

"Sure, if you think they'll do you any good." She was still smiling at him. He realized that if they got back together he'd never get off the hook.

"It's all data," he said casually, like Keating, the SBI kid.

"Hey, from what I heard you're in a kind of tight race in the primary," she said and made a little face. It was the kind of expression you use to comfort a boy who's just skinned his knee. He couldn't think of anything to say, so he just shrugged.

"People are scared, Kewpie, and people don't think logically when they're scared."

"No, I guess not."

"You know what you're going to do . . . if in the event . . . you should lose, that is?" She was trying to be diplomatic about it all.

"Franklin's term goes up to January, then Pardee would officially come in."

"'Ex–Acting Sheriff Waldeau,'" she said. "That doesn't sound so hot."

"I was thinking that maybe I'll go up to Raleigh, try for that job with the SBI."

"Study up on your accounting?"

"Yeah. Your father said he'd help, so . . ."

She made a face and twisted the toe of her black shoe into the lawn. "Well . . ." was all she said.

"Maybe . . . how 'bout tomorrow night you and I go for dinner at Hong's?" he said. A breeze came up and riffled through the oak tree above them and the light dappled across her face.

"And you can have whatever you want," he said to her. And she looked up at him, and for a while they just stood out in front of the church like that, peering into each other's eyes.

TWENTY-SEVEN

The Klan had a meeting the very same night the news came out about the killing of Millie Garnet.

And in the weeks since the killing they had been planning their action, waiting for a chance to punish the niggers again. It was clear that the niggers and their leaders wanted to play rough. That had been clear down at the yards and you would have thought they had got the message, but it behooved the Klavern to take some serious action. There was certainly a case for it; there was certainly plenty of justification. There was an obligation to do something in Millie Garnet's name; it was just a question of where and when.

The prevailing sentiment was that it was impossible to punish all the niggers; there were far too many of them, and besides, almost everybody had some nigger that they wanted to make an exception. A maid, or somebody who worked on their car. Somebody they did business with or needed or even *liked* who just happened to be a nigger.

So if the Klavern couldn't punish all the niggers, it would settle on the nigger leaders. Run them back up to New York City to live with the Jews. There was an election coming up and whatever they did now would have the added benefit of keeping the niggers away from the polls.

So the Klavern met deep into the night and decided on a bold strategy. They'd make their first target the nigger abortionist, Dr. Terry. He was one coon who for a long time had been operating under the illusion that he could fight back and get away with it.

They had the girl all picked out. Some girl from up around San-
ford whom they'd had a serious talk with. They'd even sweetened
it up with a little cash incentive for her to confirm that Dr. Terry
had given her the abortion. Three hundred dollars he'd made
her pay; she said she'd testify to that. This was all agreed to in advance. Terry would, at the very least, have his license to practice
medicine taken away. So they voted to go ahead with that scheme,
and while their lawyers pushed their complaints through the court
system, the instrument of Terry's punishment was to be a Klan
motorcade.

Now the line of vehicles was slowly idling its way through the
black sections of town. Inside the cars and back in the beds of the
pickups were robed and armed Klansmen and friends. They had
baseball bats and ax handles and a lot of the boys had brought pistols with them just in case. Mostly it was good clean fun. They'd
wave the battle flag and share a bottle around, and then see if they
could throw it far enough to break a window in one of the rickety
nigger houses. They started way up in the north end of town and
drove through the old "Brooklyn" neighborhood. Ahead of them
the streets immediately cleared. It was comical, like a big vacuum
cleaner had suddenly hit that part of town. Any niggers who were
driving in their direction suddenly backed up and squealed their
tires as they tried to escape onto a side street.

There was an edge to all the festivities because everyone was an-
ticipating the burning of the cross, which was supposed to happen
right in front of Terry's house. All the men were thinking that there
would be a few minutes there where they'd have to get out, put the
cross up, get it lit . . .

Now as they rumbled through the dusty streets shades were
pulled, doors were locked, children were hidden in the back bed-
rooms until the cars drove past. A steady litany of honking horns,
rebel yells, and insults filled the neighborhood.

And then just as soon as they'd driven past, the neighborhood
would fill back up again, the angry niggers explaining to their kids
what had just happened, the men with their jaws clenched in im-
potent fury, standing in groups in the center of the street watching
the line of cars slowly vanishing down the hill toward the river. The
women, holding the children against their legs, shaking their heads,

once again thinking about getting out of North Carolina, going up north or out to California, where things were safer.

Everything was going according to plan until the motorcade hit the corner of Eleventh and Rankin, only about a block from Terry's house; they rolled around the corner and suddenly found an old junk wagon across their path. The drivers in the cars coming up from behind couldn't see and there was a squealing of brakes. The driver in the lead car leaned out of his window and started shouting for the stupid coons to get their wagon (a wagon, imagine!) out of the street. Right in front of him a nigger man came out of a house there, on the driver's side. He was scared and had his arms held out wide as if he was going to explain. The driver had time to see that his face was black as coal, darkened by outside work, and he wore a white shirt that gleamed dazzlingly in the bright sunlight. The driver reached out and jiggled the noose he had tied on to the side mirror to frighten niggers and started to yell something. In the reflection he saw that some of the Klansmen had gotten out of their cars and were walking forward to move the wagon out of the way so their motorcade could get moving again. And that's when he heard the first shots.

At first he didn't know what it was, but all of a sudden there was shooting all around him. It felt like gravel being thrown hard up against the side of his car, he thought.

"*Goddamn! Goddamn! Goddamn!*" the man beside him was shouting, and he ground the gears trying to back up.

And now there were niggers everywhere, standing on their porches and shooting all kinds of guns, little .22 rifles that could still kill you if they hit you in the right place, shotguns, whatever they'd managed to scrounge up. A chill welled up through the driver's body as he realized that the niggers had been waiting; they were all prepared. Perhaps tipped off in advance by some spy, or a fool who'd let word of their plans slip and be overheard by a maid. Even as he shifted into reverse, he realized that it was all over, the niggers had tricked them into an ambush.

"*—the hell outta here!*" the man beside him was screaming, his voice high and scared. The windshield disintegrated right in front of him. Some of the men were firing back at the shacks along the street, but they were in an exposed position, right out in the center of the street blocked by the goddamn wagon. He could see that the niggers were jumping out of their houses to take little potshots and then running back and hiding. And now something had gone wrong with his car because all of a sudden it wouldn't steer so good.

Everything was disintegrating into an outright panic. The boys were having to back up into the nigger yards and over the curbs. They just had to sit there waiting to back up as soon as they had a chance. He could hear the combined horns of the motorcade sending up a long howl. The man beside him was halfway out the window with a pistol in his hand. They backed up so fast he was nearly flung out of the window.

Now there was the sound of sirens and he saw two sheriff's department cars swerve around the corner and speed up the street past the Terry place. You can't even count on your own people to help you out, the driver thought as he watched that. Tears spurted in his eyes for a moment and he tried to stop himself from crying, from simple fear and frustration. Right in front of him his taxes were paying for his own people to race to the protection of the nigger doctor.

And there on the porch was the target himself, the driver realized. Terry, stepping out casually, a half-read newspaper in his hand. Smoking his pipe. As if he had no idea there was a gunfight going on at the end of the block. It was a big house, the driver saw. A big brick house with a wide porch and green-and-white striped awnings to shade it in the hot weather.

His car ran over something, making a tremendous crash as it bounced over the curb and then a hideous scraping sound as it dragged its tailpipe along for a few yards. He ducked down low behind the wheel and drove as fast as he could back up Rankin Street, trying to keep from running up the back of the man in front of him.

And it wasn't until he was hitting sixty up Chestnut Street, with the car pulling to the left the whole way and him holding on, holding on so that it wouldn't crash into the curb or the parked cars, that he realized the tire had been shot out, and that there was a hole in his radiator, and that he'd just been run out of town.

They got there and were stopped by the same wagon that had been placed across the road to block the Klan. Glen got his car up over the curb and went tearing past the driveway where Q.P. was trying to ease the Chevy around a huge Negro man who had suddenly collapsed out in front of a house on the corner. He was holding his arm and crying. People were swarming all over the street, a lot of them were laughing. Dr. Terry had come out onto the sidewalk and was looking up to where his attic window had been shot out.

D.L. Terry came running up the street, breathless and outraged. He gave Q.P. a glare as he ran up to his brother there on the sidewalk.

"You should be back inside!" he said to his brother. "These crackers are trying to kill you." He looked over suspiciously at Q.P., who was halfway up on the sidewalk in front of them.

Q.P. rocked up over the curb, forcing the men to jump out of the way. Then he was skidding around the wagon and bumping back out onto Rankin Street with the accelerator to the floor. He caught up to the last of the Klan cars and then suddenly he blew right by an accident. A pickup truck had run off the road and smashed into a telephone pole and he saw a couple of Klansmen running through the yards. Glen Petty was out of his car with his revolver in his hand, trying not to step on any live wires and waiting for the ambulance to come and pull the other Klansmen out of the wreckage.

Right up ahead of him was a big black Chevrolet. Not a new car, something from maybe '40, with a fat rear end and a trunk lid the owner had tied shut. The driver knew that the police were on his tail and he was in a panic. It looked like a cloud of steam was coming out of the radiator and Q.P. was right up on the Chevrolet's tail when suddenly for no reason the driver jammed on the brakes, and before he could react, he rear-ended the old car and smashed his forehead hard against the top arc of the steering wheel.

Next thing he knew he was out in someone's front yard and all up and down the street people had come out onto their porches to watch. He had his gun in his hand but he didn't quite know where he was. He saw a man running across the grass. The man looked like he was tangled in a clothesline and then Q.P. realized that it was one of the Klan trying to get away. He yelled something at him but the man kept on going.

He staggered up to the door of the wrecked car and pointed his gun at the driver. There was a sweet smell of steam pouring over both of them from the broken radiator. The whole front of his prowl car was caved in.

"You goddamn nigger-lovin' son of a bitch!" the man was saying to him. He stopped when Q.P. put his gun up against the man's forehead.

"This is . . . the Sheriff's Department," he managed to mumble. He realized he was shaken up from the accident. He couldn't hardly see the man sitting right there in front of him.

"A *war* is comin'," the driver said to him. He was wearing a red satin robe and his hood had been pushed back, revealing his hair, long hairs draped over his pink bald head. It was all plastered down from sweating. The man beside him was slumped back in the seat as if he were sleeping. He might have been hit by a bullet, Q.P. thought.

"And when the war comes we're gon' get *you* first. We're gon' get all the *traitors to their own race.*" The man's voice was calm. Like he was telling somebody a bedtime story.

"Get out . . ." Q.P. managed to say and pulled the door open. The man just sat there.

"We're watchin' *you,*" the man said. "We're watchin' you and all your nigger-lovin Jew friends. Y'all gon' die . . ."

"Get out!" he shouted now, but the man just sat there watching him. The car seemed to tilt on its side and Q.P. realized he'd slipped and fallen down there on the grass. He was going to pass out, he thought. Then they'd take his gun away and kill him. He cocked the hammer back and tried to threaten the Klansman one more time.

"—gon' die . . ." the driver was saying, then his eyes rolled up and he gasped suddenly like he himself was dying.

"Put your hands *up!*" screamed a voice overhead. "Right *now!*" And Q.P.'s head rolled back onto the grass and he saw Errol Tate standing over him with a pistol in his hand.

"I *said,* put your hands *up!*" Tate was screaming again at the Klansman.

And then Q.P. just closed his eyes and fell asleep until the ambulance came.

TWENTY-EIGHT

Mary Helen was looking at his forehead, her mouth in a tight smile of distaste. She looked like she was about ready to mash something to death in her garden. "How many stitches?" she asked again. The whole thing pissed her off and horrified her at the same time.

"*Eleven,*" Nina said. "Let's sit him down." Everybody crowded together and he obediently sank into Franklin's chair.

"Well, it's going to leave a scar then. Every time people look at you, they're going to think about chaos and gunplay."

"You've probably got a concussion," Nina said. She was standing back from Franklin's desk, her arms folded across her chest. She was looking at him the same way as Mary Helen, he thought.

"I'm okay, really." He put his fingers up to his forehead, where Doc Elkins had sewn him up. It didn't hurt, but it had gone puffy and leaked a little. Nina just looked at him and sighed.

"Remember, you're not supposed to go to sleep," she said, then turned to Mary Helen. "That's what they told him at the hospital."

"I already fell asleep last night," he said, getting irritated. He'd slept like a baby. Woke up and felt refreshed by the whole thing. He was on the move, he figured.

"People with concussions aren't supposed to fall asleep for twenty-four hours," she said like it was some kind of engraved commandment.

"Okay, I promise. I'm not tired, really. I'm fine, really," he said and gave them a deliberate big campaign smile. It made the stitches hurt.

"No more photographs for *you*," Mary Helen said and they left him alone.

He spent the morning until lunch fixing up what he called a "Case Room." It was an idea he'd got from the movies, and it made so much sense that he figured it must be derived from some real police technique. He thought he'd have it all ready by the next time Keating came to town, and if Noppy Leigh ever dropped by he could pose for a picture in there and it would look better.

The Case Room was just a little square room deep under the courthouse where they kept boxes of old files. There was a table in there and he cleaned it off and stacked the ledgers along one wall and made the attempt to dust the top with a paper bag.

He did the same thing with the wall, and then had to go out and get a washcloth and actually *wash* the wall before he could tape up photographs of the Sash Cord Victims. It was so dusty in the little room that he tried to open the transom window but it had been painted shut, and so he wedged the door open with a number ten can full of bottle caps that had been in there for some reason.

All morning department personnel came cruising by to give the Case Room a glance. Whoever came by would always have some justification for whatever it was they were pretending to be doing. Mary Helen poked her head in and gave it the once-over. "You can always get custodial work after the election. That's a plus right there."

"I know."

"Do you need anything?" She was looking at his forehead again.

"Could go for a coffee, maybe."

She nodded and looked around for a minute. "This looks very efficient," she said, considering it all. "It looks like you know what you're doing."

"Well, you know . . . I was hoping . . ."

Her eyes traveled up to the wall and the pictures of the dead women. Off to one side he pinned up a mug shot of William Scowen.

"Now I get it," she said, looking at the little room. "You know,

Kewpie," she said quietly, and the real sadness in her voice stopped him and he turned to look at her in the doorway. "I think that over-all you've made yourself into a fine public servant. I really do," she said and then went back outside before he saw her start to cry.

Nina came by and they had lunch out on the steps and made jokes about how he looked like some kind of Martian Frankenstein with the white rectangle of adhesive tape across his forehead. He had put the Case Room in as much order as possible and they kissed briefly there on the steps in the sunlight.

And the day would have gone on like that with nothing much happening except him sitting down in his hidey-hole staring at dead people's pictures, except that later that afternoon, just as he was about ready to pack it up, Ed Nicholson phoned.

Nicholson's voice was subdued, a lot quieter than he had been in the corridor. Casual, like he was discussing something on a menu.

"Listen, Kewpie, I was wondering if we could . . . have a little talk."

"Sure, Ed. What's up?"

"Well, I was thinking that you and I might come to an under-standing regardin' my client."

"Allison?"

"Ah . . . shit. Look. Could we just talk somewhere . . ."

"Meet you in the parking lot. I'm just on my way outta here."

"Okay." Nicholson hung up.

Nicholson had never done what he was about to do before, Q.P. thought. Never really attempted to bribe a policeman. He was ner-vous and looked around checking to see if anyone was looking at them from the windows of the Annex.

They had the conversation in the front seat of his brand-new Cadillac. It smelled of plastic that had been sitting in the sun and of new carpeting. It was hot outside. Nicholson had the windows rolled up.

". . . my client is understandably disturbed by the regrettable murder of the Snow girl, who after all was an employee in his household, and he wants to make sure"—Nicholson looked over at him to make sure he was getting it—"he wants to make sure there's no casual association between him and this girl."

"I'm sorry, Ed. I got no idea what y'all are talking about."

"Goddamn it, Kewpie." Nicholson took out a sealed envelope, pulled down a thick armrest that divided the seat in half, and put the envelope on top of it.

"He wants you to drop him outta this shit with the nigger whore."

"Why?"

"Goddamn. Look, he doesn't want people thinkin' he was fuckin' her, Kewpie. It's obvious, isn't it?"

"Was he?"

"Look . . ." Nicholson patted the envelope. "He wants some *insurance* about it. He wants to be able to sleep at night."

"I don't care whether he sleeps or not, Ed." Outside Mary Helen walked by and tapped on the glass waving good-bye to him. She turned sideways and opened the door of her little Studebaker and was careful not to scratch Nicholson's paint job.

Nicholson waited until she was inside her car and then he heaved a big sigh and swiveled around in the seat to face him.

"Now, you listen to me, Kewpie," he said. "You haven't been down here that long, but I'm tellin' you, a man in Dr. Richard Allison's position, he has a *lot* to lose. He moves in a completely different world and has completely different problems than you do. He doesn't want his reputation tarnished by the caprice of the sheriff's department. Now, I'm gonna tell you—" Nicholson was down to his last card, leveling with him now, Q.P. thought.

"You call him in, in the middle of the day, you cost him money by runnin' off his patients, you bring him down into the street where everybody can see you loadin' him into your paddy wagon, and then you grill him like a goddamn common *thief;* just right there you're in a lot of trouble. You do something like that again and all kinds of shit is going to come your way, I *promise.* Now, we can do this the easy way"—he patted the envelope—"or we can do it the hard way. It's up to you."

Q.P. looked at the man. A film of sweat had formed across his top lip. He could smell Nicholson across from him, smell his sweat and his fear seeping through his cologne. Smell the nicotine on his breath and the sweet dry-cleaning smell of his car.

"Well, hell, let's do it the hard way then, Ed. That doesn't bother me at all."

"Shit . . ." Nicholson hissed as he pocketed the envelope. He started fishing for his keys. "You don't even know what your goddamn job is, Kewpie."

"Is that right?"

"You're not supposed to be harassing the most upstanding citizens of the goddamn city. What you're supposed to be doing is looking for the depraved black nigger piece a shit that killed those women. *That's* your job, understand?"

"I understand real well, Ed. And let me tell you something. You come to me with an envelope again, I'm not going to worry about trying to get your ass disbarred, you understand?" Nicholson's face had gone white. He was just as afraid of scandal as Allison, Q.P. figured. "I'm just going to get a couple of my boys and take you on a little ride up to the bend and mess you up *real* good."

"You're in a lot of trouble, Waldeau, fuckin' threaten me!" Nicholson exploded. "You've been warned, goddamn it," he spluttered as he started up the car's big engine. "*Warned*, Kewpie, goddamn it! I mean it."

"I'm scared, Ed. I'm *terrified* . . ." Q.P. got out as Nicholson levered his car into reverse; watched him back out of the awkward little parking lot and peel out as soon as he hit the street. He stood there for a second after the Cadillac was gone and wondered how much they'd decided his price would be.

Why would Allison be so jumpy about a dead maid he used to give rides to? Why would he take the chance with the bribe if there wasn't something there somewhere?

He *was* fucking her, Q.P. thought.

He walked back into the basement wondering if there was any sash cord in Allison's garage and if he had enough cause to get a search warrant to hunt around for it. He sat in Franklin's chair and tried putting himself in the shoes of Dr. Richard Allison, a guy who had it all. A guy who was good-looking, smart. A big shot with a sharp wife and a lot of money.

He sat there trying to imagine all the different things that could come up out of nowhere and combine to make a big man like that get so afraid.

TWENTY-NINE

He and Nokes spent the next morning writing out the search warrant for Allison. Once they had it all figured out, he got Nokes to type it up and he went across the street.

Nina was standing at center stage in Thalian Hall, dwarfed by a mountain of old theater seating piled up on the floor. A crew of workmen went about their tasks, slowly removing the old seats and fitting the newer ones from New York into rows across the sloping floor of the theater. She was looking at a blueprint of the floor of the theater that was spread out on a large table. When she did finally look up and see him, she stopped for a second, moved a stray curl away from her forehead, and met him with a tight little smile as he walked up to her.

"Hi," she said. She held up one finger to get him to wait a minute while she went on with her business. Apparently the seats were not fitting into the floor of the theater as efficiently as had been hoped. They screwed together in bizarre ways; some had arms on the left, some on the right, and some had no arms at all. Some of the upholstery was punctured and frayed, although the theater in New York had vouched for their condition. The seat backs leaned back at two different angles. Nothing matched.

While she finished talking to the workmen Q.P. walked aimlessly around the stage, peered up into the heights of the fly gallery, walked out and stood at the edge of the stage, carefully avoided falling into the orchestra pit, and tried to imagine acting there with all those people looking at him.

"Well, what can I do for you, Sheriff?" she said from behind him. He turned at the sound of her voice. She was standing there waiting for him to come up with something good.

"I thought I'd come by, say hello."

"Really?"

"Yeah. And if you're willing, I've got this speech that I could use some help with. It's a political speech, so I thought you might be able to give me some advice." She laughed a little at that.

"I don't know if you'd get many votes around here with me as your speechwriter. Long time since I've seen you round these parts. Been busy roundin' up rustlers, I reckon?"

"Yep . . ." he said, trying to sound like Gary Cooper. He went over to the table and she showed him the plans and explained how the seats were all confused. They fell silent and she looked over at him.

"Strong silent type, huh?"

"Yep . . ."

"Come on," she said, feeling a little uncomfortable with all the carpenters working around them. "I bet you've never taken a tour of this place, right?"

"Nope . . ." Gary Cooper again.

She took him off the stage and up the aisle to the lobby and then upstairs to the balcony and on the way he told her about the Lions club speech and how he really didn't know what he was going to say.

"Maybe it's because you don't really know what you believe in," she said, trying to make her voice sound reasonable. "I don't know that I can help you much with that, Kewpie."

"I know what I believe in," he said. "I know exactly what I believe in," he said, and then they did finally kiss, and kissed again.

They couldn't stay there necking, so she took him out to the end of the narrow corridor and he found himself out on the highest of the balconies, looking way down onto the stage, almost at eye-level with the angels painted above the proscenium.

"These are called the 'vomitoria,'" she said, and they both laughed. She pivoted, assuming the posture of a television saleswoman, "because they *vomit* the audience into the arena—"

"Great . . ."

"All of the famous actors of the day played Thalian Hall. John Philip Sousa, Tom Thumb, Oscar Wilde, and Maud Adams, the greatest actress of her day. Frederick Douglass spoke here in 1872 and so did Booker T. Washington. Buffalo Bill Cody performed here, pardner."

"No kiddin'?"

"Do you know who Frederick Douglass was?" She pointed one finger at him and made a screwing motion.

"Uh . . ."

"We'll see if we can't work it into your speech somehow . . ." She dropped the pose and took his arm and they went down to the railing and looked over the balcony into the abyss, where the workers were crawling through the chaos on their knees.

She explained the evolution of the great chandelier, from candles to gas to electricity. Beneath the balcony was a gallery with dozens of old playbills hanging from the walls, portraits of great theatrical personalities he'd never heard of. Backstage were strange machines—a revolving drum that could be filled with dry peas to make the sound of rain, a trough above the great arch that the stage crew could roll cannon balls along to simulate thunder.

And before they parted she agreed to help with his speech, warning him that he'd almost certainly want to edit it, warning him that there were certain things she simply wouldn't say, warning him that it might end up being political suicide.

"Sure," he said. "I wouldn't want it any other way, pardner."

"Deal," she said. Another shaking of hands. She had to get back down and finish with the seats, and—too quickly—they kissed once more and he went back to the courthouse.

He stood waiting in Judge Burke's chambers while Burke read through the search warrant that Donny Nokes had typed up. Beside him stood Spud Reid, his hands clasped behind his back. Rocking gently back and forth and humming under his breath.

Sprawled behind his desk Burke didn't look happy. "Now, now, now . . ." he muttered and then read on some more. After a second or two he frowned and shuffled the papers together. "Do I understand this correctly, Kewpie? You wanna search the house, the garage, and any outbuildin's, any vehicles . . . *and* the office of Dr. Richard Allison just so you can find some *window cord?*"

Reid sighed.

"That's correct, Your Honor."

"What the hell for?" Burke sat up. He had one hand splayed out across the search warrant as if to hold it down on his blotter.

"Allison had a connection to the Snow girl. She was an occasional prostitute who lived and worked in the same neighborhood—"

"I'm sorry, I'm gonna stop you right there—"

"I told you," Reid said, turning and heading for the door.

"This here is denied," Burke said. "That's just not quite enough cause, Sheriff, and what pisses me off is *you know it.*"

"Your Honor—" Q.P. started.

"You *know* it! You *know* I can't sign something like this and drag Ricky Allison through the goddamn rumor mill for no cause. It's as obvious as the goddamn face on my wristwatch that the man who killed these women is some nigger from over in Brooklyn! Hell, everybody already *knows* that! What are you tryin' to stir up here, Kewpie?"

"With all due respect, Your Honor, it's not quite that obvious—"

"This is goddamn denied. Don't waste my time anymore, gentlemen," said Burke as he got up from his desk.

"I told him, Len," Reid said and left the room. Q.P. was right behind him. "Don't come back!" Burke yelled out as Q.P. shut the door.

Reid stopped in the middle of the corridor and turned on him. "You know." Reid dropped his voice to a near whisper. "Sometimes I think you've gone completely crazy, Kewpie."

The fire came out of nowhere.

Starting with a crude cross that was hastily planted in the sod and then burned unevenly, falling into the boxwoods, where the pine needles had piled up. It was the screaming of tires that woke her up.

The old paint went up fast and when she came to the door the little portico was in flames.

Terrified, thinking her heart was going to burst, she still did the right things: closed the door and went inside and phoned the fire department, controlling her voice, stopping her hands from shaking. Then she did the wrong thing; instead of getting Milton out first, she moved grimly through the darkened house, out the back door and along the side, screwed the garden hose on the spigot and opened it up all the way, tugged it free of the shrubbery, and went around to the front of the house. Held her finger across the hose to get a fine spray and started to put the fire out all by herself.

The street was dark and the whole time she was standing there she knew she was a target, feeling the crosshairs settling on her back. The spray blew off the front of the house back at her, and her pajamas were soaked and she didn't dare turn around. Let them go ahead and kill her, but she wasn't going to just let them burn down the house. She wasn't going to let them kill her father.

She jumped when there was a voice behind her; a man she didn't know, a new neighbor, she supposed, had routed *his* garden hose over the fence and together they stood there spraying down the front of Milton's house.

Then she ran in to get Milton ready in case he should have to get out, and telephoned Q.P. and he said he was on the way. Outside from her old bedroom she could see the fire, burning the columns on the entryway and catching under the little gable roof. Still the wind was blowing the other way. The neighbor man was walking back and forth, covering the front of their house. Then there came a great wailing and the pump truck from the Wilmington city fire department rolled up and a few minutes later a second truck arrived, the big men jumping off the trucks and casually going about their business. By then Nina and her neighbor had done most of the work.

From his bed Milton watched the firemen climbing about on the roof with mild amusement.

"Now, that would have made a nice twist in my biography, don't you think?" He was actually smiling at her. She just left him she was so angry. Q.P. squealed up just in time to watch the firemen break up the embers piled up at her front door, and that was when she fell apart, and he took her inside and held her and waited until she stopped sobbing.

The firemen coiled up their hoses, the neighbor went home. Q.P.

took her up and put her to bed and then spent the rest of the night downstairs sitting on the sofa with his revolver in his lap. The wind came up and cleaned the burned smell away for a few hours. When the adrenaline was gone she slept so soundly, so dreamlessly, that she forgot all about the fire and then woke up with a snap when it all came back to her.

She went downstairs and looked out the crudded-up windows and saw Q.P. and Keating duckwalking around the yard looking for evidence. The half-burned cross was already moved over onto a piece of plywood. He looked up and saw her standing there.

"Better not try and come out here. All that's going to come down," he said, sounding official, pointing up at the remains of the entryway.

"Well, there's no footprints. *Lots* of tire prints, but nothing . . ." Keating muttered, trailing off as he methodically looked around the trampled flowers, the muddy yard.

"I guess somebody thinks we're running down the neighborhood," she said quietly, looking down at the muddy embers of their front entrance. The ashes of the mezuzah were somewhere down there, she thought distractedly. Q.P. was looking at her strangely for some reason.

"It seems that way, I guess," Q.P. said. He walked over to the front steps; the debris of the entryway separated him from her. Climb over, she was thinking. Climb over and hold me in your arms.

"I don't think it had anything to do with you, not really. This was sent to me at the department this morning. He pulled out two photostatted pages from his jacket pocket and held them up.

The first was a title page from a book:

Red Channels
The Report of Communist Influence in Radio and Television

Paperclipped to that was another sheet, two columns of names closely printed. A lot nobody had ever heard of, but some were famous: Edward G. Robinson, Burgess Meredith, Gypsy Rose Lee.

And sandwiched in between them someone had drawn a circle around "Nina A. Mendelson."

"Yeah . . . that," she said quietly.

The bells of the Presbyterian church a few blocks away started up. Somebody was getting married, she thought. Her chin quivered and she stared at the pages until she couldn't see the type.

"Are you a . . . Communist?"

"What?" She came to life and gave him back the pages.

"Nina, somebody is using this stuff . . . I don't know. You never said anything . . ." He was looking down at the burned doorway, too. "Just tell me, that's all, Nina. That's all." She looked at him for a second, and it was like all the blood was starting to drain out of her, like just for a second she'd aged about sixty years.

"No, Your Honor, I am not, nor have I ever been—"

"Good, okay. Good . . ."

"What is wrong with you? Have you gone off your rocker?"

"Did you work for any television stations or get in with any organizations, or any . . . committees? Did you sign anything in Chicago?"

"What I'm a member of is my own business. I thought the Inquisition went out of style a few centuries ago, Sheriff."

"Nina, it might help if I knew everything."

She was standing there, awake now. And angry. Defiant. He took the pages and looked down at her name. The circle of ink around her name had begun to change to green, to blue, to brown . . .

"What happened was . . . the university had a radio station and I was the theology commentator. When he got fired from *The Goldbergs* TV show, Philip Loeb gave us a long telephone interview, and then, when we wouldn't sign their loyalty oaths, the regents shut down the station. We're all in there."

He stared down at the list of names as if some truth would emerge from the splotches. "That's it?"

"Doesn't take very much, Sheriff. My other crimes were that I joined the Americans for Democratic Action because I was sick of watching crooks run the Congress and nobody saying anything about it. When they lynched a Jew down in Georgia, I signed a petition. I think that the atomic bomb is a bad idea, and I think the Scottsboro Boys were innocent. And I'm not too crazy about people burning my house down."

"It's not you," he said, looking around the yard. "At least I don't think it's you . . . it's me. I thought it was because of the Klan all last night and then they sent this to me, see?"

The call had come right after he had stepped into the office. He had just opened the envelope and was reading the pages for the first time, trying to make sense of it.

". . . *we can get you, can get your ass anytime we want . . . mixing white men's business up with niggers . . .*" the voice had said in the second call. He had stood there in his office, listening for the rhythm of what he remembered of Allison's voice. "*. . . you get some sense, you get some goddamn sense . . . or you get a goddamn bullet in your goddamn back . . .*" The voice was purring behind three or four dishcloths.

"*. . . we're watching you . . . we're watching your ass . . .*"

Maybe it was because she was finally able to see his face, or maybe it was something in the tone of his voice, or the way he was standing there glaring across the destroyed yard.

"I'm not afraid, Kewpie," she said. "I'm not afraid of these jerks. I'm not going to change my opinions or forget what I know, or pretend that I don't *see* things or learn things. I'm not an idiot. I'm just a Jew with a brain. I just want a better life. I want a better life for everybody. Is that a crime? Maybe in some people's eyes it is, I guess."

He didn't know how to answer. "No," he finally said.

"This is America, right?" She'd finally lost control and was angrily throwing her words at him. "Here it is. This is what you get. This is the country where you're supposed to be free, right?" Keating was looking up at her, holding a long piece of rag dangling from tweezers in his hand.

"Yeah, right . . ."

"Free to *think* or *read* whatever you want, and we have a secret ballot too, right? So, okay, apparently"—she looked around at the cinders—"some people have decided that *thinking* is suddenly un-American. I'm starting to think that we're living in the land of the not-so-free, or the land of free-as-long-as-you-don't-rock-the-boat."

"No, no, Nina. It's not like that. It's not really you. They're just *using* you, he said again firmly. "This isn't from the Klan, either."

"He's right," Keating called over to her, "and I don't think so either."

She stood there, paralyzed in the doorway. Q.P. was looking up and down the row of scorched boxwoods along the facade of the house.

Then he turned and looked up at her. His face was set, he was angry, and his eyes were dark, boring into her. She almost shivered. "I'm going to get them, Nina," he said, holding up the pages at her.

"I'll get them . . ."

THIRTY

He helped Keating wrap up the fragments they had collected in the yard of the Mendelson house and paced around the Case Room while he tried to work out a strategy to build a case against Allison.

Allison was still his number-one suspect, he thought. He had friends, he'd probably heard about the failed warrant from Judge Burke or Spud Reid and when Ed Nicholson's bribery didn't work he'd decided to scare Q.P. off by striking at Nina.

"I guess that's one way to look at it." Nokes frowned. He hadn't had nearly as hard a time the last couple of days, and he was brushed up and shined. "Don't forget that there's lots of people that hate your guts, Kewpie . . ."

"Yeah . . . okay . . ." Q.P.'s election chances were a subject of open discussion around the department offices now.

"Sure, there's all the relatives of the Klan who were arrested—"

"It only took 'em about two hours to get out on bail . . ."

"There's a *burned cross* . . . that sounds like Klan to me, and you're not getting any votes from those guys . . ."

But Q.P. didn't think so and he began collecting all the information he could on the orthodontist.

At the same time he went back and did all the routine things, along with trying to keep up with the normal rate of crime in New Hanover County. When he could delegate any of his work, he did. But instead of campaigning, which Mary Helen refused to acknowledge as fruitless, he drove around, sifting over the background of the case.

He could place Cora Snow with Red Bill Scowen, and he could place Allison with Cora. Maybe they were all in some shit together that would scare Allison enough to want to keep it quiet. But then, why Ruth Micheaux?

He spent a lot of time walking around and talking to the friends and neighbors of Ruth Micheaux. It amounted to a lot of atmosphere, he thought. Various neighbors said she was not a "social butterfly" although she occasionally went out dancing. She liked to laugh and seemed to be a good mother. She was not particularly religious but attended church from time to time, mostly with her family.

The children missed her completely, and it showed mostly on the boy, who had grown very quiet. When Q.P. talked to him he only shrugged and answered yes or no. He had gone to school one day, and when he came back, his mother was gone forever. Now he was thinking about it all through the long summer.

So why did Allison kill her? There was no apparent link.

Keating looked at the autopsy information carefully, went away, and came back on his travels up and down the coast.

Q.P. went back to digging into Cora Snow's past again, and one afternoon he and Glen Petty ended up over at Cora's aunt Thelma's house on Walnut Street.

They talked while Thelma sat on the cool porch with one foot in a bath of Epsom salts. She fanned herself as she talked and she seemed short of breath. She looked so uncomfortable that Q.P. asked if she wanted him to call a doctor.

He sat there on her porch rail, and she invited Petty to take the chair beside her and said that if they wanted, they could get some tea out of her brand-new Frigidaire, "the only thing I got's that's any good at all."

They listened to her complain about the weather that had caused her foot to swell up, and how working on days like this was almost impossible but that Elaine was gone out doing it anyway. Every day Elaine had been doing all the cleaning since Thelma had been sick like she was.

They talked to her about the Snows and the Rowells and Q.P. tried to fit what she said to Nina's diagrams that he only half remembered.

Yes, Thelma had got them jobs cleaning for several different white women over the last two years. The dentist's wife, Mrs. Allison, was one, but for a long time they also cleaned the offices and the furniture showroom for businesses. And of the names she gave them, she mentioned that they had worked for Mr. Henry Houldings.

"Over at the hardware store?" Q.P. asked.

"Well, Mr. Houldings, see, he's got his fingers in a *lotta* pie," said Thelma with emphasis.

"Yeah?"

"The Houldings they got themselves the furniture business. And they sell the pipe and all that."

"And they sell steel out of there, too," Q.P. said.

"That's right, they *do*," she said. "They sell wirin' for your house. Sell you the plumbin' for your *out*house." She laughed and poked Glen Petty with her good foot and he laughed too.

"And they got that showroom over there on Oleander Drive."

"You know, her side of that family was a big family here in Wilmington," Glen said.

"It *was*," she agreed.

He made a note to get Nina to check out the Houldings family. He only knew the name from the hardware store.

"And he sold all that insurance. That was *his* business."

"Yeah," said Petty, "he had an office up there where they insure your furniture and household possessions if you're moving somewhere."

"Uh-huh, and they come and deliver your things right to you. Lord have mercy, I know them folks one way another all my life. Cora worked for them and Otha still works for him every now and then."

"Otha?" Q.P. said. "I thought he was a preacher."

"He's a *deacon*."

"Okay."

"What that is is like a preacher but he don't get no *money* off it."

"I didn't know that."

"Reverend Chaffee, he's the elder over there, and he's lettin' Otha do some of the preachin' so he can *learn*."

"But he works for Houldings at the hardware store?"

"I think he still does do some work for him."

"He drives a truck for him," said Glen.

"Whole damn Snow family work for Houldings probably one time or another."

"Okay, okay," Q.P. said, trying to remember all this so he could help Nina fill in her charts.

"I worked for his wife's mother, Old Miz Buell."

"Oh, I remember *her*," said Petty, nodding.

"I worked for Miz Buell when I was just a girl out there at the ol' house. That was an ol' cotton family, them Buells."

"They built the mill," Petty said to him.

"That's right. That's a real ol' family. They had money, they had *slaves*, they did real good all along. They'd didn't never not have no money. They built that mill and they built another mill out there, too."

"Textile industry," said Petty.

"That's right. That's what they did, sell that cotton. So Mr. Houldings, you know, it all come down to just him." She nodded sagely and fanned herself. "You don't want some ice tea?" she said to Glen.

"No, but I'll get you some, if you want."

"God bless you, you good young man," she said. Glen went inside to look for her new Frigidaire. Thelma shifted around in her chair so she could get a good look at Q.P.

"You know after that funeral the other day?"

"Uh-huh."

"I saw you talkin' to a right pretty girl. Didn't I see you two talkin' on each other, Sheriff?" Thelma laughed at him.

"Yeah, I think so. She *is* right pretty."

"Is she smart?"

"Oh, yeah. She's real smart."

"Well, what the hell does she see in you, then?" Thelma said and laughed so deeply that her foot splashed water out onto the porch.

"I don't know," said Q.P., and he was laughing, too. A couple of little Negro kids were learning to ride a bike out on the dusty lawn. It wasn't a lawn really, just a collection of bare patches with little hummocks of grass in the places where the children didn't play, some bushes that weren't quite a hedge between the houses. A garden in the back that she and the girls had tended. When they broke out laughing, the children looked over and saw them and grew quiet, and then all of a sudden ran off like a covey of doves.

"Them kids think you're gonna come lock 'em up down on the Fifth Floor," Thelma said.

"Well, maybe if they see us fooling around out here, they won't be too scared."

Thelma leaned forward in her chair. "Hey, you!" she called out. The kids returned at the sound of her voice, in ones and twos. Just poking their heads out from the bushes.

"If you children don't do what your momma says, this man here is gon' come take you *downtown!*" she yelled, and the children ran away for good this time.

"Great," he said. "That's really . . . great public relations. Thank you, Mrs. Snow."

"I know it don't help you very much, Sheriff, but maybe it'll help them kids to be scared of goin' off to jail," she said, but she didn't seem to really believe it. Glen came out with the pitcher of iced tea he'd made.

"You sit here and have tea with me, then them kids won't be afraid of you no more." Thelma smiled up at him. And so they sat there while the night went from sunset to green to the long blue and the fireflies came out under the trees.

Keating looked at the pathetic display on the Case Room wall and admitted that Houldings as a wild card suspect was possible.

"So, okay, you go and look at where things originated. There's a good chance the sash cord came from his store."

"I went over there and talked to him, showed it to him," said Donny.

"How did he act?"

"He seemed fine. He just told me what it was. He was just walking through the floor, stopped when he saw me, helped me out . . ." Nokes looked up, shrugged.

"You showed him a piece of the rope from number one and got no reaction . . ."

"Nah, nothing. I wasn't thinking it could be him . . ." Donny said.

They thought about it for a few minutes and Q.P. sent him over to the store, where he was to go in the back and, as discreetly as possible, cut off a length from the spool so the lab in Raleigh could analyze that, too.

In the heat of the day he drove out to see Stick Niles in an effort to get more information about Red Bill Scowen, although they had checked him out pretty thoroughly in the beginning.

Stick and his brother Percy spent most of their time at the Nileses' dilapidated garage, where Percy worked and Stick based his various operations. Ellis came along but Q.P. wanted him to wait out at the car and maybe Stick might feel more ready to talk.

The sun was pounding down on the pavement when he got out of the Chevy. The air was still and he hadn't got much sleep and the heat was just knocking him right out. Percy had the doors up to give a little breeze to the place while he tested an engine he was rebuilding. The engine was revved up to one long howl; there was a great cloud of blue smoke wafting out of the garage by the time he got to the doorways.

Percy looked up at him and saw who it was, nodded, and then looked back down to his work. He had great wads of cotton stuck in his ears and was lean as an eel, Q.P. thought. Percy had an old hat on his head that said *Gilmour Racing* on it, and he was wearing a set of holey overalls that were two sizes too big.

He shut down the engine in a series of sharp crackerjack-sounding pops and a little black kid maybe ten years old who Q.P. hadn't seen when he first came into the darkness said, "Wooooo!" and skipped out the back door.

"That's the loudest goddamn thing I ever heard," Q.P. said.

"Yessir, we got to work on that one a little," Percy said. He just kept working.

Q.P. explained he wanted to talk to Stick and that Stick shouldn't worry because he wasn't in any trouble; he was there trying to find who killed Scowen and his girlfriend. Percy looked at him for a second and then put down his wrenches and took Q.P. back to the office, where Stick was busy on the phone, and he sat and waited, admiring the collection of calendars that the two men had assembled.

Both of the brothers were willing to talk and Percy went out to get them all Cokes out of the machine, while Stick leaned back, looked around at all the girls who papered the office, and told him what he knew about the dead man.

"Well, way back at the start, Billy was a kind of a *rival* to us," he said. "You know, Kewpie, my old man made his livin' from a variety of things . . ."

"Yeah, I know." Niles's father's career ended when he was paralyzed in a gunfight, and he eventually died in the N.C. State Penitentiary hospital.

"So the way we had it, whenever Scowen was dealin' with white folks, he was poaching on our sales area. We considered that our business, just like he has his business. You understand?"

"Yeah . . . like jurisdiction."

"That's right. But we got it all worked out and that's how I really got to know Billy. On account of there for a while he used to sell us things."

"What did he sell you?"

"C'mon now . . . Kewpie . . ." Stick and Percy both laughed.

He smiled along with them. "What sort of things could someone get off him, just supposing you were in the market?"

"Whatever you want."

"Dope?"

"Dope, liquor. He knew girls he could get for you. You like colored girls? No disrespect intended, Sheriff, but a colored girl's the best you could ever want."

"I'm sure," he said as Percy jabbed his Coke bottle at him; he was laughing so hard and then left to go tear down the engine.

"He could get you some great colored girls. He knew white girls, too, if that's what you wanted."

"And what did you sell him?"

"Well, the old man always had good liquor. Anytime he needed it he knew we had some. He wanted to haul for some people way out in the back of South Carolina and we fixed up a car for him so he could do that."

"And other kinds of merchandise?" Q.P. asked. He knew that Stick made most of his money by fencing and, if he saw an opportunity, by robbery.

"You might say we had a flea market every once in a while, yeah."
The way Stick said it made Q.P. laugh.

"You know anybody who'd want to kill him?"

"Nah. Maybe some of the Klan—" When Q.P. shook his head, Stick just shrugged.

There was a flutter of explosions in the garage that suddenly got ragged and there was a clanking sound.

"Well, there goes about two hundred bucks," Stick said.

"Okay, one more thing. Could you make me a list?"

"What kinda list?" Stick had started to frown.

"Make a list of people that you thought Scowen was selling to, or buying from, or who he let sleep with Cora."

"Kewpie, man, I don't know everybody, shit . . ."

"Yeah, but I want you to do it for me, okay?"

Stick thought for a second and then nodded. "I don't want to sign nothin', you understand?"

"Sure."

"Just a second then." He turned on his light and made up the list.

And it was from this list Q.P. learned that Scowen had provided services, women, substances, et cetera to several prominent Wilmingtonians and one white customer in particular: Henry Houldings, owner of Houldings Hardware.

Now he had the locks changed on the door of the Case Room, thinking that if Henry Houldings was involved, perhaps together with the dentist, he didn't want any of their courthouse friends rummaging through the room where he was trying to develop the case. He and Keating had the only keys. Nina would come by sometimes and find him back there and they would have sandwiches and talk. About the rebuilding of her father's house, started the moment when Keating was done. "He loves that," she said. "He watches, he yells out the window suggestions to them . . ." The whole thing was, she said, "giving him new life," but always the pictures pulled them back.

On the next Monday Keating finally got his news from the SBI lab about the fragments of the burned cross they had recovered.

"Okay, so we have some more evidence for your hardware man, but here is something that really is strange . . ."

He passed the report across the desk. "Everything could have been bought there. The scrap lumber, which was brand-new, the wire, which was brand-new, all right?"

"All right, okay. He goes shopping . . ." said Nina, who had made herself a corner by the stacks of ledgers where she could kibitz on their discussions.

"All of it's brand-new and obviously Houldings Hardware is a possible source, except"—he pointed to a paragraph at the bottom of the SBI report—"except the burlap that they tied on there and soaked with gas."

"It says it's from *1909?*" He frowned up at Keating.

"*Before* 1909," Keating corrected him. "That's when they made burlap on looms with a different weave or something. They don't know the exact date." He shook his head. "When I found it I didn't think it looked that old. Sounds like a mistake . . ."

"An antique flour bag?" Nina was poised in the middle of her sandwich.

"It's probably a mistake . . . they're sending a piece of it over to some professor at Duke. On the other hand, if you go out and find some more 1909 burlap bags, you'll probably have the source."

"Great . . ." Q.P. was trying to digest that. He wrote "Bag" on a blue file card and pinned it up to a bulletin board they had set up along one wall.

Nina watched him arranging things. Letting her head lean back against the musty ledgers, thinking it through. The arson wasn't really connected to the stranglings. There were all these little pieces that were missing . . .

They needed to link Allison in, and without a thorough search, they couldn't. It was entirely plausible that Allison and Houldings knew each other, but they hadn't established any real association between the two men. Q.P. had decided not to go talking to all their friends and associates because so far there was no case. No one knew that they were looking at Henry Houldings a little more closely, and Q.P. didn't want it getting back to either man, afraid that if there was any evidence anywhere it would get destroyed pretty quickly.

On Tuesday he was in court for most of the day, losing votes the whole time, he figured. He could feel people shaking their heads as they saw him sitting there, looking about fifteen, wearing his brand-new uniform shirt that itched and made him sweaty and uncomfortable when he was on the stand. When they recessed he went downstairs for a break and to check up on things and Mary Helen gave him the SBI's background report on Houldings.

In it he learned for the first time about the suspicions surrounding the death of Houldings's wife, Lavinia Buell.

Lavinia had died while the two of them were on a yachting trip down in the Florida Keys. Fallen from the rigging in bad weather and hit her head and drowned before Houldings himself could pull her out. He finally hauled her on board and piloted the broken boat alone for two days until he could get back into port, where he collapsed and was put in the hospital with what the doctors thought was a heart attack.

Houldings had refused to allow an autopsy and the doctor at the little hospital on Andros Island hadn't put up a fight. He had gone a little crazy, he admitted; sitting below while the boat pitched around in the Florida Straits and having conversations with Lavinia's spirit. In these she had communicated to him explicit instructions that she wanted to be interred right away as soon as they hit dry land.

Which is why she was buried in a cemetery somewhere way down in the Bahamas, only about a thousand miles away from the rest of the Buell family plots.

Milton and Nina filled him in on the rest of it. Houldings had come into the family like some kind of night raider, scooped up the beautiful Lavinia, and sneaked her off to Charleston.

It wasn't a tragedy, not yet. All the business was going to descend to Teddy Buell, who was the last of the boys, the only one who hadn't been killed in the war. The family had been furious about Houldings absconding with Lavinia, and although they welcomed *her* back anytime, Houldings was banished from Wilmington.

Then he got lucky. Only a year of exile and Teddy called him back, desperate for a reconciliation after his first big heart attack, and it became clear that someone would eventually have to take over the business.

Then only another year or so when Lavinia was drowned. By then Houldings had control, and when Teddy finally passed, Q.P. remembered Thelma saying, it all came down to Henry.

According to Milton, Houldings had come back to town and managed to get in good with everybody. Now he had money. And things had changed around by that time anyway. The people who had got through the thirties in good shape weren't necessarily the people who got through the forties in good shape. Old money and family wasn't so important. But getting the job done was, and Houldings had connections. In only a few months he'd expanded and sold off properties that various Buells had acquired over two centuries. He put out bids on government contracts. Together with Lamont Sanders he cleared a few stands of pine trees and put up some quality homes for veterans. He spent his time golfing and drinking with the more important people in town. But he lived high and he'd eaten up a lot of bucks on frills and now the family fortune was not nearly as great as the gigantic Buell house and Forest Hills estate would indicate.

"I never have liked him, you know," Milton said, while they were watching Edward R. Murrow slowly and surely destroy "Tailgunner Joe" McCarthy. It was like watching a boa constrictor fighting a noisy rabbit.

"How come?"

"He's just *cheap.* You know?" Milton looked over and nodded his head. "Fundamentally Henry's a cheapskate. He has a ton of money and he's always takin' the cheap way out. Squeeze a nickel till the buffalo shit . . ."

"Pop . . ." Nina said, rolling her eyes.

"It's true, goddamn it."

"Okay, but you don't have to—"

"Leave me alone," Milton said, and Q.P. was aware that the old man was deeply angry at something that must have flown right by him and he hadn't seen it at all.

"Just leave me alone," Milton said again. Nina looked over and he thought she had tears in her eyes.

"You want me to take you back, Milt?" he asked, and the old man nodded. He took the blanket off and lifted Milton up and he could smell the old man in his arms. A kind of rotten smell; the smell of cancer winning a big victory somewhere inside him. He groaned when Q.P. got him up, light as a feather, and helped him down the hall to his room, set him on the bed, pulled back the covers and tucked him in.

"You want to take anything?" Q.P. said, looking for his pills.

"Nah. It doesn't do any goddamn good anyway."

"You don't need to go, do you?" he said, looking for the bedpan. The old man shook his head.

"Okay, then. Night, Milt," he said, trying to keep his voice light and reassuring, not afraid of death in the night.

"Night, Kewpie . . ." whispered Milton, his voice like a dried leaf skittering along the sidewalk, thin as tissue.

They parked themselves in front of the television and he pulled out the list of names he'd got from Stick, handwritten on two sheets of greasy Perfect Circle Piston Ring scratch paper. She took the paper and fished in her purse for her glasses and for a while they started classifying names using Nina and Conrad's system.

"You know, the more I look at this, the more I think it's just about impossible." She shrugged and looked up from the papers.

"You can't draw all these people out in boxes like that other stuff?"

"Sure, yeah, but it'd take forever. This is a major grant project to graph all these people out. Besides, there are lots of names in the sample that we don't know, ones that we have no idea who they are, or how to find them—"

"Yeah?"

"Even taking them out, that leaves us with more than a dozen different family names. And then you're talking about some of the first families of Wilmington here, Kewpie. Some of these people go back way before the Revolutionary War."

"Well . . ."

"Luola Vestry's family has been published. The *Vestry Papers*. It's only about a seven-hundred-page *book*."

"Damn . . ."

"Crazy list," she said.

"These are all connected in one way or another to Allison and Henry. You know, they go to the same restaurants, give to the same charities." Nina had grown serious, staring at him like he'd turned to wax, her eyes deep and sad. Then something flickered across her face and then she'd made up her mind. She smiled at him for a second.

"Okay, so now that I'm your undercover research deputy, I guess this is business, huh?"

"Well, I was hoping to turn the lights down low and tell you all the reasons why I'm in love with you." She almost didn't blush, but she couldn't help smiling.

"Yeah, I think so . . ." he said.

"Well, gee," she said in a little voice. "Undercover, huh?" She laughed and put away her glasses and, still laughing, reached up and turned off the lamp.

THIRTY-ONE

He was up before dawn, out the back way with Nina's keys, and he let the Buick roll down the hill before he started it and quietly drove out to Forest Hills.

He came in the gates and drove along under the heavy-limbed oaks and past the old Buell place and along until the street curved and he found a place where he could park in the shade and watch the front of Henry Houldings's house.

He just wanted to get a look at the man, but he had to wait until almost eight-thirty until Houldings came out; a big man, overweight but light on his feet, dark hair slicked back, dressed in white trousers with a yachting blazer over his arm. Opened one of the garage doors and rolled out for the city in his Packard. On the drive into town Q.P. got right up behind him at the light down on Front Street. Watched while Houldings aired out his arm along the wide seat back, cigarette burning between his fingers, fiddled with his radio.

Rolling on quietly through Wilmington on a hot summer morning, people walking along under the awnings, sheltering their eyes against the sun.

Houldings parked and went into the savings and loan for about ten minutes, moved a little money around, and then came out and headed out to his offices, driving at an easy pace; cruised into his personal parking spot behind the wing of his store. Q.P. breezed on by and to the end of the block, where he turned and saw Houldings slipping on the blazer just before he hit the big showroom doors.

She found his note about borrowing the car and took the opportunity to walk down to the library, where she started to work on Q.P.'s list of names. She was interrupted by a meeting with Kate Pullam over budget revisions for the new library and so she hadn't had much time to do any undercover research before she ran across the street to the courthouse.

"He's gone," Mary Helen said, shrugging, holding her hands up helplessly, and looking around the foyer for Q.P., who had just taken off somewhere.

"Well, that's great. He was supposed to meet me for lunch, the jerk," Nina said. "That cheeses me off, I must say."

"Lotta strange things goin' on round here, girl," Mary Helen said, shaking her head.

"You don't have any idea where?"

"Well, I've got *ideas,* if you know what I mean, but I don't *know* for certain-sure," the older woman said. Was she smiling? Nina thought she had a few conspiratorial glints shining out of her glasses.

"Spill," she said.

"Okay." Mary Helen looked around. Ellis was reading a copy of *Argosy* over on one of the benches and eating a thick roast beef sandwich at the same time. She was safe. "*This* is a *list.*"

"A list of what?"

"A list of *names.*"

"Okay."

"You wouldn't believe the people who are on this list, Nina. I mean, *everybody* is on this list. 'Cept me. I don't have enough money to get on it. Now, he's scratched some names off of it, and he wants me to look up their addresses and phone numbers and put those on it, too. It's only about a hundred people. It'll only take me most of the morning to do it. But then he says, 'One copy, no carbon,' to me. So it's very hush-hush for some reason."

Nina shook her head. She knew which list it was and knew why Mary Helen had got saddled with the retyping. "Well, his people did come from up North, we have to remember that," she said.

"It's that Yankee blood. That must be it." Mary Helen laughed.

"But let me tell you, you think things like this only happen some-where else, you know? Not in a little town like Wilmington, but . . ."

"What?"

"Well, you know what I think? I think it's got something to do with *communism* down at the railroad," she whispered as she leaned forward on the desk, clutching the folder across her breasts.

Nina put on her most conspiratorial expression. "Communists are everywhere these days," she whispered to Mary Helen. "I've got a list right here of a couple dozen people over at the library who are *library* card–carrying Reds," Nina said.

"I know, I *know*. You think I'm soft in the head, but I can't think of anything else. We can't *buy* a search warrant, we've got women bein' abducted all over town, the Ku Klux Klan is threatening to burn down City Hall, and he's out looking for Communists . . ."

They went to lunch after all. At Binky's for a chili dog and conver-sation. The talk led from Q.P.'s answer to a question about a Negro man who was found beaten in the gutter over on Grace Street (he was still unconscious, there were no suspects) and rapidly pro-gressed to the impossibility of New Hanover County complying with the Supreme Court *Brown vs. Board of Education* decision. She stared at her food and kept her mouth shut but she was thinking at light speed. It was one more thing she hated about Southerners, she thought; how they liked to get together in groups and get wound up about some issue. As usual it was Negroes. Everybody knew it by heart, instinctively. First Negroes invade our towns and cities, then Negroes invade our neighborhoods and shop floors. Negroes in-vade our restaurants and our washrooms. Negroes invade our schools, and not long after that, Negroes snatch our husbands from us and big buck Negroes invade our women. It went on and on. Like painting new paint over the same old paint. She concentrated on chewing, on counting each bite as she ate, but pretty soon she would be the only one not putting in a comment.

Some man she didn't know had half turned around from the counter and was making a long complaint. He had been working outside; his shirt was still wet down the center of the back with sweat. His voice was like a cow bawling.

"... yeah, but what the hell are yew gon' dew? I'm not talkin' 'bout all 'em others. I'm talkin' 'bout yew, Kewpie. Yew!" Christ, she thought, and longed for the chill and the smog of dank Chicago.

"Well, I'm gon' enforce the law, Danny . . ." Q.P. was explaining between bites of his okra. She marveled how his voice got more of a drawl depending on who he was talking to. Maybe it was some of the politician coming out in him.

"What are yew gon' dew, Binky? What about yew?" The man was challenging them all to admit they weren't ready to change, they didn't have the money to change or the plans developed for change. Challenging them to admit that they certainly didn't want to change. Hoping that they'd say they *wouldn't* change. That all together they'd go down in defiance of the United States Supreme Court and *never* change. God save us from Southerners and their lost causes, she thought.

"He's gonna obey the law, too, Danny," Q.P. said without even looking around.

"C'mon! Awww, Kewpie . . ." The man's voice reached full bellow. Southern Redneck Dies Whining, she saw on Pagett's front page.

"I don't mind eatin' with 'em," Binky said firmly. For a moment the situation was defused. Everybody looked at Binky and maybe for a second realized that neither did they. "I don't mind peein' in the same outhouse— Excuse me, Little Miss," Binky said to her, "but I ain't gonna let my girl go out with one, I ain't gonna have one for my *doctor*"—there was a chorus of negative groans from the customers—"and I ain't gonna have one *embalm* me!" The room erupted with appreciation. Q.P. looked over at her and smiled.

"What are yew gon' dew, Little Miss?" the man said to her. He had been looking her over since they came in. She started to say something but Danny just went ahead and did it for her.

"I tell yew! This right here's what yew're gon' dew! Yew're gon' be scared to death ever' time yew go *anywhere at all!*"

"Well, I'm scared already," she said, looking straight at Danny, who was momentarily taken aback but recovered nicely. Woman has voice!

"Yeah, yew see there—" he said to Binky, who was nodding.

"I'm *real* scared. I'm scared I'll be killed by an atomic attack. I'm scared I'll get run into by some drunk driver." Q.P. was looking up at her. He had stopped chewing. "I'm scared that if I lose my job I won't be able to afford to eat—"

The man called Danny was alternately nodding and frowning at her. Binky's jaw was open and he was starting to frown with concentration.

"I'm scared I'll get lung cancer and die because I started smoking these—" She pulled out her Pall Malls and dumped them on the table. A couple fell to the floor and she didn't make any move to pick them up.

"I'm scared to get pregnant and bring another child into this crazy mixed-up world—"

"You can say that again, Nina," Binky put in. He could tell when a woman was coming apart right in front of him. Great, she thought, I have to make some kind of a neurotic demonstration to get Binky to remember my name. Q.P. had reached over and was holding her hand. He probably thought she was going to cry, but she wasn't.

"I'm scared more than enough. I live in a perpetual atmosphere of fear," she said. Danny almost flinched as he grappled with the word "perpetual." She just kept on going. "I'm scared about what McCarthy will try and do next and what Eisenhower won't. So, yes, I am scared. I'm shaking in my boots. And, frankly, the thought of sharing the universe with colored people doesn't bother me at all next to that."

The room was silent. Q.P. was holding her hand and looking right at her. She smiled and raised her eyebrows at him and took another French fry off his plate. Your wild girlfriend, she thought.

"Well," the man called Danny said, "I think . . . that what *yew* jes' said proves . . . jes' what *I* said." She looked up at Q.P. Who *are* these people? Do they actually get to vote?

Q.P. laughed and shook his head. "Sounds like you oughta run in this election, Danny," he said.

"Now, that's what *I'm* scared of," said Binky as he went back to work, and the room laughed and relaxed again. Q.P. had turned back to his food, but he was still holding her hand.

THIRTY-TWO

"Okay? I gotta go now, okay?" He had the phone in one hand and was buttoning up his pants with the other.

"Well, my, my, if we aren't all het up today," Nina said on the other end of the line.

"Rollin' the dice a little here . . ."

"Sure, be a hero. Win the election. Stay in Wilmington forever and become your worst nightmare," she said dryly and hung up. He was in the basement at the courthouse five minutes later. Nokes was waiting.

"Okay," he said. "Go over and pick him up." And Nokes and Ellis Strickland went out to drive over and pick up Henry Houldings.

After they brought him down, Q.P. let him wait in the interrogation room for ten minutes while he watched him through the window.

Houldings was irritated at being there but determined not to lose his composure. Now Q.P. saw him closer: His hair was thick and dark, slicked back with something that didn't make it look greasy. Little eyes but they were clear and bright blue. A fine nose. All of his features were little and clustered in the center of his big smooth head.

Today he was wearing a dark suit. Not brown, not black, but something that looked like a deep plum color; when it caught the light, it had a little shine to it. Probably cost half a year's wages, Q.P. thought.

Houldings sat at the table and smoked a Chesterfield and flicked his ashes on the floor. There was no ashtray, but he was socially conscious enough to look around before he stubbed the butt out on the floor.

That was when Q.P. and Glen Petty came in. Petty took up his station leaning in the corner and Q.P. just looked over at Houldings and said, "We wanted to ask you some questions about some people who you'd employed in your business."

Houldings sighed and raised his eyebrows. One damn thing after another. "Certainly," he said.

"You remember a girl named Cora Snow, colored girl?"

Houldings's sigh turned into a frown. He turned his mouth down while he thought about it. "Cora Snow? No. No, I don't remember her. She worked for *me*?" he asked.

"That's right."

"Nope. Don't know her."

"She's a little woman. Pretty girl, they say."

"When did she work for me?"

"During the last couple of years for sure. We're trying to find out exactly."

"Is she in some kind of trouble?" Houldings said. Generous. Always interested in his employees, even the ones he didn't know.

"She's dead," Q.P. said, wondering if Houldings was going to pretend he hadn't heard anything about it, watching Houldings's little blue eyes.

But Houldings didn't blink. His look only narrowed and he lowered his chin and gave a glance over to where Petty was holding up the wall.

"All right . . ." he said.

"So you're sure you don't remember her?"

"Cora . . . Cora . . . I don't know, Sheriff. Maybe. I just don't remember," Houldings said. He was doing a good job at being convincing.

"Okay, I tell you what. I think we've got a picture of her someplace maybe that'll help." He went out to get one of Giddings's portraits.

When Houldings saw it, he frowned for a second and then took a deep breath when he realized that it was a picture of a dead person.

"You remember her?"

"I think so . . ."

"She cleaned up for you?"

"Ahh . . . I think . . . Yes!" He smiled at Q.P. "Yes . . . over in the gallery. Where we show the suites. I remember her now. She had another girl that worked with her—"

"So you do remember her, then."

"Yes, now that I've seen her—" He looked down at the eight-by-ten again and shook his head. "Poor kid . . . What happened to her?" Houldings said, as if he really didn't know, as if he not only wasn't involved, but as though he really *hadn't* heard anything about the killer who had the whole city locking their windows at night. Q.P. ignored the question.

"You ever run into a fella name of Red Bill at all?" Q.P. said and struck home.

Houldings sat up in his chair and his mouth opened for a second and he looked over at Glen Petty, who pointed his finger at him like a gun and pulled the trigger.

"I . . . I'm sorry?"

"You're sorry?"

"I mean . . . *who?*"

"Red Billy," Glen said. "Y'all know him, don't you?"

"You know him?" Q.P. asked.

Houldings was sitting back in his chair now, looking at each one of them in turn. His cheeks had gone pale with little splotches of pink showing through. He started frowning again and pulled his eyes away and down to the tabletop.

"I never heard of anybody of that name," he said flatly. Glen started laughing.

"You're sure about that?"

"What was it again?" he said. Houldings was thinking that he was very smooth, Q.P. thought.

"This is all just routine," he said to Houldings. "Okay? We're just trying to get a line on some of these folks." He smiled.

"Sure . . ." Houldings said and reached in his pocket for another Chesterfield.

"Could I—?" Q.P. asked and Houldings put the pack down. Glen went out and came back with a glass ashtray that had a blue New

Hanover County Sheriff's Department beehive decal glued to the bottom of it.

"So, you never heard of an associate of Cora Snow's name of Red Bill?"

"Husband? Maybe I saw him if he came to pick her up?"

"So she came to work and then got picked up."

"Ah . . . yes . . ." Houldings made a supreme effort to remember the details. "Yes, I seem to remember that. I remember her being picked up in the *rain* . . ." He smiled at the crazy things that sometimes came back to you. Q.P. couldn't quite manage a smile, maybe because he remembered pulling her out of the Cape Fear River in the rain. He put Houldings's cigarettes in his pocket.

He slid a mug shot of Scowen across the table. In the photo Scowen's expression was neutral, like a blank sheet of paper waiting for Spud Reid to write something on it.

"Uh-huh," Houldings said as he considered the photograph.

"And you think it was him that got her?"

"Maybe, could be. I think she did have a . . . boyfriend." He had to search for the word to describe Scowen's relationship to the dead girl.

"Yeah, she had a boyfriend, all right," Glen said and laughed again. Houldings straightened up; he was trying to figure out the strange deputy in the corner.

"But you never had any . . . dealings with him?" Q.P. asked.

"No. Absolutely not. I barely knew him."

"Okay."

"Cora and her sister and, sometimes, her aunt, I think, occasionally cleaned for us, but I think that's all I know," Houldings said and nodded. He was certain of that much.

"Okay, then. Let's just start all over again, Henry. When did Cora start working for you?"

They questioned Houldings for almost three hours without a break except once when he said he had to go to the bathroom and Petty took him.

Q.P. went out and washed up at the same time and let Houldings cool it in the Interrogation Room and washed his face and changed into a clean shirt and threw the Chesterfields away.

Houldings didn't know very much at all. Apparently his brain just didn't hold a lot of information. He barely remembered the Snow girl or her boyfriend. He eventually recalled he had bought fifty pounds of shrimp from the boyfriend for a party that he was throwing at the Elks club and that was how he remembered the boyfriend. As a fisherman.

When they tried to refresh his memory about Cora and Scowen's other life as prostitute and handler, he clammed up and asked if he was in any trouble.

"Trouble?" Q.P. said from his post in the corner. "Why would you think you were in any trouble? We've only got a couple of homicides to clean up here. It's just a couple of dead niggers, so who gives a shit, right?" Maybe he was getting tired. These things were always endurance contests. He got up and left the room and Glen went with him and they paced back and forth in the hall.

"You okay, Kewpie?" Glen asked him quietly.

"Yeah. Yeah, sure," he said.

"Take it easy, now."

"Yeah, okay. Sure," he said, wishing the State of North Carolina would legalize torture to extract a confession, angry that he was more ethical than Tommy Wills. Wondering if he should just defy Spud Reid and Judge Burke and break into Houldings's house or Allison's garage in the middle of the night. If he had to hang around guys like Houldings much longer, all that might change.

They waited another five minutes, and after he'd calmed down, Q.P. went in and showed Houldings the old portrait photograph of Mildred Garnet. Houldings went through his whole repertoire of not knowing and managed to stick to it this time. He took a photograph of Ruth Micheaux and slid it across the table. Houldings just stared at it for a second and then looked up and simply shook his head. "I read about *her* in the paper. That kind of thing's just awful," he said sincerely.

It was suppertime when they all got together up in his office. Through it all Houldings had not budged from his story, or not budged enough. It sounded phony as hell to all of them. Q.P. didn't want to show him the ropes, but Nokes said that it might shock him.

"He asked for his lawyer last time," Q.P. said.

"He said he wanted to know if he was a *suspect*."

"He said that *if* he *was* a suspect, he wanted to speak to his lawyer. We let him make a call we'll have Ed Nicholson all over us."

"The question is," Nokes said, "is if we have anything."

"No," Q.P. said, "we don't."

"We don't have anything?"

"We've got something but it's just not enough."

"We've got shit, then," Nokes said and kicked a filing cabinet.

"Shit on a stick," Q.P. said quietly.

So he sent Glen Petty down to let Houldings go with the warning that they might need to speak to him again soon. He was too infuriated to do it himself.

Everything broke the next morning.

Over at Wrightsville Beach there'd been some noise in the night coming from one of the big beach houses. The lights were still on. The doors were open. The woman staying there hadn't been seen all day.

The Wrightsville Beach police had gone up there and it was suspicious. It was a big house, it obviously cost a pretty penny to rent, so she might have been robbed in the night. Anyway, she didn't come to the door. There'd been noise all night, the people in the nearby houses said. Like a fight. Cars driving in and out in a hurry. Now *nobody* came to the door. Somebody remembered that Q. P. Waldeau was the specialist in missing women and Mookie Pritchard called him up.

He and Donny drove out and parked in front of the house. Mookie tucked in behind, and together they went up to the front door of the big beach house. The door swung open at the first touch of his knuckles. Everything was quiet.

"We left it just like it was, Kewpie. Nobody's been in there yet," Mookie whispered behind him.

"Okay, that's good, Mook," he said. He pulled out his revolver and Mookie moved down the stairs behind him and did the same. Nokes would be around at the back door by now.

Through the crack in the open front door he could see dim outlines of furniture in the front room.

"Hello?" he called. "Hello?" There was no answer, no creaking of bedsprings, no one walking to the door. He waited and listened. Nothing but the sound of the stiff wind off the Atlantic and the regular crash of the breakers. It smelled like autumn, he thought.

"This is the Sheriff's Department," he said and opened the door and walked into the front room. He heard Nokes come in the back door, saw the sunlight reflecting on the glass flash across the wall and then slip back again. He took a breath and stepped through the door into the living room.

"She don't keep house too good," Mookie said behind him.

The place was a mess. A chair was turned over and the rug pushed back like somebody had slipped on it and fallen. He moved through the room and off to the side where the bedroom ought to be.

"The people at the real-estate office said she was a 'Miss Alice Farmer,' single woman from Nashville, Tennessee. She had a friend staying here with her, another woman, but she was gone back 'bout a week ago."

The bed looked like somebody had had a lot of bad dreams and was too tired to change the sheets. The blankets were off on the floor. There were a few bottles around. It smelled like perfume in there. Sweet, like roses. A woman's room. Alice Farmer's clothes were on the floor and hanging over the edge of the chair. Lacy things that looked like they would be fun to take off.

There was blood on the floor, he saw. A trail of little drops.

"Big bloodstain back there," Nokes said.

"Watch your feet," Q.P. said, and they all froze and tried to find a safe place to step while they followed the little drops of blood around the house. There was another empty bedroom where the friend must have stayed, and in the bathroom they saw a white bathing suit hanging over the shower curtain rod. She was a little woman, he saw.

In the bedroom on the night table Nokes found her purse. There was a billfold inside and he fished it out.

Tennessee driver's license; "Alicia Farmer," an address in Nashville. Money still inside, seventy-five dollars in cash.

"And I think this here tells us a little something about Miss Farmer," Nokes said. He'd found an open box of Sheik rubbers in the drawer. There wasn't much else; two toothbrushes in a glass in the bathroom, she'd left her suitcase in the closet.

There was a third bedroom upstairs, but the door was jammed shut, and when Q.P. opened it, he could smell the mildew. No perfume anywhere. A double bed with no covers, just a stained mattress.

"Take a look around and see if there's any sash cord or old flour bags," he told Nokes and watched his eyebrows shoot up. For a second the deputy stood there and looked around.

"Okay, sure," he said and went outside.

But they didn't come up with anything. The house was sterile. Like a rental unit, he saw now. The kind of place you tried not to leave anything behind when you packed. There were some magazines strewn around, a chilled half bottle of rum and a little food in the refrigerator. But except for the appliances and their contents, everything else in the beach house was strictly temporary.

Outside the Wrightsville Beach P.D. was directing curious tourists down the opposite side of the street. Traffic had slowed, everybody cruising along so they could watch.

Then they noticed there was blood on the front steps that they hadn't seen when they came up to knock on the door, little drops of blood on the sand inside the breezeway carport. He told Mookie that he'd better seal the whole place off. It would require somebody staying there all the time to keep the tourists away from the place.

Back at the courthouse he got Keating right in the middle of his dinner. They talked for several minutes and Q.P. passed on everything he knew and both of them agreed that there was a remote chance at least that the cases were linked.

It was puzzling. On the surface there was no reason to think the Tennessee woman's abduction was related to the sash cord killings. In the other homicides the victims were local; the obvious connection between Cora Snow and William Scowen and the link to Allison and Houldings didn't seem to include some rich white party gal from Tennessee. But he mentioned it to Keating. "Just a hunch," he said.

"Hunches are good," said Keating.

"You think?"

"Oh, yeah. Hunches are good," he said again. Carruthers phoned up and wanted to know what he had, which wasn't very much, but Q.P. told him anyway and Carruthers just grunted and hung up. Then he had to do the same thing for Spud Reid. It went on like that for the rest of the day.

The phones didn't stop for the remainder of the day, and when he finally managed to get out of there, he passed Mary Helen looking equally distraught behind her desk.

"Lord God help us all," she said, "somebody's gone and kidnapped a tourist."

THIRTY-THREE

There was a slow line of Negroes walking across the front of City Hall. They carried handmade signs that said FREEDOM TO LEARN and SEPARATE BUT EQUAL IS DEAD. Every so often they would sing a long slow hymn that she recognized as the old ballad "We Shall Overcome."

Irate Wilmington city policemen stood around ready to escort anyone who needed to enter or exit the building through the picket line. Angry white civilians stood around spitting on the pavement and muttering threats just behind the uniformed officers. Every few minutes cars would drive by filled with angry white men who would scream at the pickets.

It had been like that all morning. So far at least there had been no violence; for the time being people were managing to hang on to their tempers.

Nina recognized several faces in the line and when she saw Miss Selma she steeled herself and slipped through the police and walked along beside her for a moment.

"You better not join in this here line unless you want some trouble come your way," Selma said to her.

"I just wanted to ask how you were doing."

"We're doin' the best we can, Nina. That's all we can do. These people that you work for said we can't come in and read books. Like us reading their books is going to get them dirty. Now, you know that's not right."

Margaret Duryea, Wilmington's sole Negro librarian, came over and walked along and chatted with them for a moment longer in a low voice. She had quit her job, she said. She didn't know what she was going to do. Maybe if the library integrated she'd be offered the job again.

They came to the end of the line and circled around. "You goddamn nigger-loving *cunt*," a little red-haired boy spat at her. He looked like he was all of twelve years old.

"Mind your goddamn mouth," said a man standing beside him. He gave the kid a cuff in the back of the head and shook his head in embarrassment.

"I swear . . ." said Selma as they walked back along the hot sidewalk.

"You better get out of here," Margaret said to her quietly. A car drove past full of screaming white teenagers and the police scurried away as a hail of eggs flew through the air toward the sidewalk. There was the loud roar of exhaust as the car sped down the street, some laughter up ahead as the police watched the pickets trying to clean themselves off.

"They see you here, it just makes it worse," Selma said.

"Okay." She squeezed Selma's hand and slipped past the angry white policemen. She tried to smile defiantly as she jaywalked across the street to the courthouse basement.

"Is he in?"

"He's upstairs talking to Hal Lutz and Ezzard, trying to work out some way to keep the entire city of Wilmington from being paralyzed by the United States Supreme Court."

"How are you doing?" she asked. Mary Helen looked frazzled.

"Oh, we're just about to fall apart. We're stretched to the breaking point. There's people bein' attacked all over town on account of this latest kidnapping. Phone is ringin' off the hook, the jail is full. Did you know that? *Full*."

"You're kidding?"

"Look around. Do you see any deputies?" She was right—the place was empty. "This is a crisis, Nina," Mary Helen said. "We're in a real true crisis. Next step is martial law, I guess . . ."

"I'll just wait, okay?" She made the effort to smile at Mary Helen, took the *Morning Star* in, and sat in Franklin's chair and swiveled from side to side a couple of times.

She tossed the paper on the desk. She'd refused to read it any-more except for the television schedules, since there was no un-biased news inside. Her gaze fell on all the old photographs of Franklin around the walls. Q.P. had left them up for some reason. Probably because he liked the man or maybe there was just nowhere else to put them.

While she waited for Q.P. to come and unlock the Case Room, she pulled a piece of notepaper off his pad and began to draw boxes. Then she'd write in "Alice Farmer," a big box with an *H* for Houldings. Scowen and Cora had their boxes next to each other. Millie Garnet and Ruth Micheaux were off by themselves. Beside Houldings was another box with an *A* in it. And she looked at it for a long time and started to doodle in little connections. Then she stopped, looked at the paper for a moment, balled it up, and started all over again, this time rearranging the boxes in a circle.

It all boiled down to community, she thought. Who you knew, who you owed, who you worked for. Who you were related to. Who you loved or hated. She stared at the paper for some moments. There were angry voices outside the door.

". . . and I am telling you that people are *good* and pissed off. Where do these niggers get off tellin' us what's fair and what isn't . . ." She quickly got up from the big chair and moved around to the front of the desk just as Q.P. came in. An angry man dressed in a business suit came in right behind him.

"Well, as long as I'm the sheriff, I'm gonna enforce the law, and that's all there is to it," Q.P. said and gave her a weary look.

"Excuse me," the man said. He was large and red-faced with anger and frustration.

"I was just going," she said, and went out as they closed the door.

"Who's that gorilla?" she asked Mary Helen.

"That is Mr. Ralph T. Hackett. He's one of the lawyers for the lo-cal Klan, and every now and then he comes down and complains about something and drives everybody crazy for nothin'."

"You're kidding."

"Nope."

"What's he want?"

Mary Helen looked at her like she was an infant. "Besides a vic-tory at Gettysburg, I don't know. I'd guess he wants all the niggers to get off the lawn over at City Hall. Probably he wants some kind of guarantee that the county won't integrate their schools next year. He probably wants Q.P. to say that he won't bother them if they feel like sending the Klavaliers out to do some kluxin' here and there. But I'd guess he's barkin' up the wrong tree on that, wouldn't you say?"

"Yeah, I would. The law's the law, right?"

For a second Mary Helen looked very sad. For a second she looked her age. Maybe she was coming down with something.

"Yes," she said. "I guess it is."

Nina sat over on the bench and looked through the magazines. There was an *Esquire* that had been thumbed through so many times that the paper had started to crumble. The remains of a *True Detective* that she ignored. She finally found a copy of *Life* that was over a year old. It had a long article about the new secretary of the treasury. He was a white-haired executive with a kind smile. There was a series of photos showing him in a vault surrounded by wrapped stacks of bills, rolls of change at his feet.

She saw that Mary Helen was on the phone. Standing at her desk and pacing back and forth.

"*What?*" Mary Helen was saying to someone on the other end of the line. "Are you sure?" There was something in the tone of her voice, Nina thought.

"Yes . . . Well, *when*, then?" she said with an edge of frustration. Mary Helen stood there with one hand on her hip. She was wearing a frilly white blouse and the world's tightest skirt. She pivoted in the door and looked over at Nina. Whatever it was, it was serious.

"Okay . . . okay . . . If you find out any more call me, okay? Call me right away." She hung up.

"What is it?" Nina called over to her.

"Nothing," she said. It hadn't sounded like nothing a couple of seconds ago. The phone rang again. She didn't even say hello.

"You're *sure*, then," she said. "No, no, I've got his address." And then she hung up, wrote out something on a scrap of paper, and tapped on Q.P.'s door. The two men were still arguing inside. The Klan attorney was talking so loud that Q.P. probably hadn't heard Mary Helen's knock.

"What *happened?*" said Nina.

Mary Helen shrugged and then turned to see if anyone was listening and stage-whispered across the foyer, "You know the dentist, the orthodontist, Dr. Allison?"

"Yeah." Nina was already starting to sit up on the bench.

"He killed himself this morning," she said.

THIRTY-FOUR

Allison had decided to do it in his Oldsmobile. By Wilmington city law, ambulance attendants or funeral home staff couldn't move a body that was an apparent suicide. The police had to check it out first and that had been how Mary Helen had got the news, from somebody over at City Hall. A couple of patrolmen had already driven out to Forest Hills, glanced at the scene, and let the courteous staff from Waddell's funeral parlor take over.

Q.P. got there just as they were getting ready to take off and they all stood there shuffling from one foot to another while he took his time looking over the garage. The big doors were open and the exhaust smell was just about gone. Allison had taken the hose from the vacuum cleaner and then, because it wouldn't reach, he had opened the trunk, knocked the backseat loose and brought it in that way.

Q.P. took his time checking out the car and used the opportunity to get a good look all around the garage. No sash cords anywhere that he could see. No burlap. In the trunk there was nothing but sand and a roll of masking tape he'd used to stick the hose on the tailpipe. Tossed there when he was finished.

The cops gave him the details. They'd found him slumped over in the front seat. The radio had been on when they got there. Maybe he'd wanted to catch the news; maybe he'd just wanted to listen to music.

"I've seen that before," one of Waddell's men put in. "Some people just want to lull away their last hours."

He borrowed one of the cop's flashlights and shone it across the wide front seat. Allison had urinated all over it while he was dying and Q.P. didn't notice until he put his hand on the damp fabric.

There was a lot of sand on the floor of the driver's side, he thought. None anywhere else. He noticed it right away. It was like Allison had gone to the beach, walked around and got a lot of sand on his shoes, and then it had come off in the car. He looked in the backseat. It was sprung forward on one side where Allison had managed to knock it loose. There was no sand on the floor.

He let the cops go and made the attendants open up the bag.

Allison looked terrible dead. The hair was scraggly and tangled. He hadn't shaved for a day or two it looked like, and there were circles under his eyes. He was still wearing pajamas. Silk with a little silver monogrammed *R A* on the pocket. He'd done it sometime in the early morning, the attendant said. Three or four in the morning, just before the dawn. "Seen that before, too," the attendant said. "You know, they make up their minds and they just don't want to face another day."

"Can we take him then, okay?" said Waddell's other attendant. He was younger, a little more impatient. Lots of work waiting back at the shop, Q.P. guessed.

"Yeah, sure. Is his wife here?"

"Yeah, she's the one that called us."

"Irene's upstairs," her friend said; one of her bridge pals, Mrs. Letta Shields was her name. She was a little woman with fine wrinkles around her eyes and accurate pink lipstick.

"You want some coffee, Sheriff?" she asked.

"Sure, thanks. How's she taking it?" he asked.

"Pretty well, I guess." Letta Shields turned away and led him back to the kitchen. "She's takin' it better than she ought to, I guess, but then Idy's a strong 'un."

"What did she tell you?"

"She said she'd woke up and heard the car runnin' in the garage. He'd gone in there and locked the door, the one that leads off the hallway from the laundry room. She could smell the exhaust, and so she ran outside and opened the garage from that way and found him in there."

"What time about was that? Did she say?"

"I'm not sure exactly. She called me just a little before eight," she said as she filled the percolator. "It's awful, something like this. Just awful," she said quietly, and he agreed.

"Well, ah . . . You think that I could maybe talk to her? Just for a second or two?

"Do you *have* to?"

"Yes ma'am, I do. Just for a second or two, then I'll go."

"Maybe it's best that you go on and do it now, then. People will be coming by soon." The phone rang somewhere and Mrs. Shields went off to take care of it, and after that she went upstairs to arrange things with Irene Allison.

A few minutes later she came down and shrugged and smiled.

"She said she'd be glad to talk with you. She seems to be taking this really well. But I think it's bound to be a shock, don't you know? Suicide? It's a very shocking thing."

"Yes, I guess it is," Q.P. said.

"It's just upstairs and then to the left," Mrs. Shields said and went off to answer another telephone call.

Irene Allison was sitting at her writing desk by the window of her bedroom. She had pulled the curtains back so she could see out to the yard. The room was huge and so was her bed, with a lace canopy and mosquito netting tied up above it so she could sleep in the heat with the windows open. She was still in her nightdress and she'd put on a robe that was made from ornate embroidered Chinese silk. Her hair was down and she tried to smile when she turned to see him standing there in the doorway.

She offered him some coffee, but he explained that Mrs. Shields had already taken care of that.

"She's my best friend, Letta is. Just about my only friend, really," Irene Allison said and looked out at the garden.

"I'm very sorry about your husband," Q.P. said, and she looked away from the garden and directly at him. Those blue eyes, he remembered.

"Are you?"

"I'm . . . sorry for you. It must be quite a shock." She turned her attention to the garden again.

"I'm surprised, actually." Her face cracked for a second and she looked further out into the yard, holding her breath for a moment, unwilling to break down again. "It's the last thing I would have expected of him," she eventually said. She didn't sound sad, he thought. Angry maybe, but not sad.

"I just need to ask a few questions . . ." he began, but she didn't say anything. She was just staring out at the rhododendrons. He looked to see if she was crying now, but she wasn't.

"I'm sorry, what did you say?" she asked when she realized she'd floated away.

"I just need to ask you a few questions, if that's okay?" He didn't know what he'd do if she said that it wasn't. Now she had turned so she was looking right at him again. She took a breath and her mouth hardened.

"And what is it exactly that you are trying to find out, Sheriff?" Now her voice had sharpened by a couple of notches.

"Well, I . . ."

"Are you trying to find out why he killed himself? That's what you'd like to know, right? You'd like to know why? *Why* he did it?"

He opened his mouth to say something but nothing came out.

"That's usually what people want to know when someone's killed themselves. Why they did it." She took a determined breath. "All right, then, just hold your horses," she said and got up and left the room. He heard the telephone ring again in the distance. It rang a second time before Letta picked it up.

Irene came back across the pink carpet. She was carrying a manila envelope straining with papers.

"This ought to be enough to get you started," she said and handed it to him. "It doesn't matter anymore, does it?" She looked at him and for a second he thought she was smiling. "After all, he's dead, so . . ."

She brushed her long hair aside. "Go ahead, skoal," she said.

Allison had wedged the papers into the envelope so tightly that it was difficult to get his fingers into the top. What he pulled out first was a photograph of two men having sex with a young Negro woman. Under that was another photograph of a woman tied up to a single bed. She was performing fellatio on one man while the other was waiting beside her with a dildo. The man with the dildo was smiling at the camera. Both men were wearing masks, but he recognized Allison immediately.

He looked up and saw that she was smiling at his reaction.

"Shocked? I'm afraid I'm *not*, not anymore. I'm not shocked by anything," she said and turned her gaze back to her yard.

He didn't know what to do for a moment, just looked at her and then he started to leaf through the papers. There were letters inside. Love notes. Receipts for hotel rooms. What Allison had figured would be some kind of evidence. Now he'd decided to take his case to a higher court. After looking at a few of the prints Q.P. recognized Cora Snow as one of the participants, and a few moments later, the sleek head of Henry Houldings.

"No. I'm not shocked," Irene Allison was saying quietly.

All of the photographs were eight-by-ten glossies. After looking through a few of them, he realized they had been taken without a flash. In what looked like a stage-set bedroom, a cozy little pad Allison had probably set up somewhere. Some of the action was a little blurry. There were bright slashes and he realized that curtains had been pulled and candles lit.

"He has his own darkroom," she said as he turned through the photographs. "They won't let you get these kind of pictures developed at Ripley's."

"Was someone trying to . . ."

"Blackmail? You think that's why he did it?" She turned from the window and this time, he was sure of it, she was smiling at him.

"Maybe, but I don't think so," she said. "He could have done the same things to others. It was more complicated, some kind of insurance. Maybe it was revenge. I don't know . . ." She fell silent for a moment. "It was some kind of . . . mutual protection society. They called themselves the Arabian Knights," she said, shaking her head back and forth. "That was their nickname. They thought it was *funny*."

He turned through another series of photographs. Posed this time, Allison's attempt at the art of pornography. Close-ups of genitalia. There were additional players in Allison's dramas, unidentifiable body parts of different races, both colored and white. He moved through the photographs as quickly as he could, wondering if what he was seeing was Millie Garnet or Ruth Micheaux. Some of the photographs were taken on a blanket spread on the floor and illuminated by sunlight that made undulating shadows from the window mullions over the intertwined bodies.

He must have taken it from a stepladder. On the floor were two colored women, both very young. They were having intercourse on a mattress. Wearing masks again; lingerie to make it look more inviting.

She had been watching him as he leafed through the papers, measuring his reaction. "It's fascinating, isn't it?" she said.

He couldn't think of what to say, so he nodded.

"Men find it fascinating, wouldn't you say? Men find it beautiful? All men? Do you find it fascinating, Sheriff?" She had reached out and taken a couple of photographs and was looking at them herself; she looked at one and turned it so that he could see it. It was a young black woman on her hands and knees, being used by two men simultaneously. Her eyes were closed tightly. Maybe in pain, maybe in ecstasy.

"Do men *like* this? Is this what they want?"

"I don't know . . . I . . . I guess that . . . I guess some of them do," he said to her. He tried to take a deep breath but his chest was tight. He was profoundly embarrassed, blushing. Trying not to stutter. He'd been around, he'd seen plenty. He remembered a few places he had been in Korea where you could get whatever you could imagine if you could put it into words, and when it was all over you'd still have change from a ten-spot. Irene Allison was peering at him intently, watching him squirm. Perplexed. Frowning at some eternal mystery.

"I'm only asking you because I never . . . knew very many men. Except for Ricky. I'm just curious. I'm curious, you see, because it's what *he* liked. You can tell he liked it." She waved at the envelope. "There's more, I think. There could be a lot more. It's not as if he always told me everything. I just wondered if all men were the same." She fell silent, took a sip of her coffee.

"Some of the people in these photographs are under investigation," he said.

"You mean Cora?" She seemed to sigh a little.

"People associated with Cora, yes. And Henry Houldings now, depending on some tests that the SBI is doing."

"Henry's gone. You won't catch him. He's in Cuba."

"Gone?" Q.P. said.

"Something happened the last night. I don't know what, exactly. Ricky was on the phone all through dinner. After that he drove off and didn't come back until I was in bed. I heard him screaming at someone, and when I went down to find out about it, I realized he was arguing with someone on the phone. I went into the den and he threw me out. He was completely out of control. Completely. He was drunk already and he kept on drinking after that."

"Who was he talking to?"

"Henry, probably," she said. "They *did* things together," she said dryly and looked over at him to see if he knew what she meant. "He sounded like he was scared," she said. "I liked the sound of it, the way his voice changed like that." Her voice was level. As clinical as a scientist. As if she were remembering something from a distant classroom instead of two nights before. "Yes, I liked to see him scared, I liked it very much. He must have made Henry scared too."

He gathered up the photographs and stood up. "Can I take this?"

"You must be joking."

"There's a woman missing who was staying out at a beach house that Houldings owned . . ."

"Ahh . . ."

"It's a woman visiting from Tennessee. She's gone missing since last night. Forcible abduction."

"Ahh . . ." she said. "Well . . ." She stood up and took the envelope from him. "To be honest I don't quite feel sorry for her. Do you think I *should* feel sorry for her?" she asked.

He thought for a minute. "Well, she might not have the greatest reputation in the world, but she's in trouble. She might be hurt. She might be dead . . ."

"So what? People die all the time. I don't give a damn about her. And I don't really give much of a damn about him either," she said. On the table was a picture of Allison being masturbated by someone who was out of the frame. "He got to me when I was young. I thought he was exciting. I had a lot of . . . illusions. I thought he was smart. I thought he was going to be the answer to my prayers." And now she finally had started to cry. "You wouldn't *believe* some of the things he made me do," she said. "You just wouldn't . . . believe it." She abruptly grabbed a tissue and blew her nose, pulled herself back together.

"So, no, Sheriff, you can't have this and you can't have my permission to search his darkroom. These'll be ashes within the hour, if you don't mind. I'm putting the house up for sale, and I wouldn't be surprised if someone makes me a good offer for it. It's a nice house."

"Do you know any more about these, where they had their . . . studio?"

She shook her head. "I thought he was going to work, going to the club. That's what he said and that's what I decided he was doing, all right?"

He gathered the papers back into a bundle and pushed them across the table to her.

"These are *evidence,* you know," he said. "I can take these. I can take them right now." Irene Allison looked away from him then, out into the garden. She brushed her hair back from her forehead, gave a little sniff and managed a little smile. "So what if everybody . . ." She pushed the bundle back at him. "I don't care what any of these phony bastards say . . . I'm going back to Wyoming, where there are a lot fewer people to mess things up, and I'm going to sit there and watch the mountains and the sky and raise horses like I did when I was a girl. That's the last time I was happy anyway." By then she was crying.

"I'll be as . . . discreet about it as I can, Mrs. Allison," he said quietly and took the bundle of papers from the table and headed out of her bedroom.

Downstairs Letta Shields was sitting with another woman and he thanked her and said something to the other woman that sounded sympathetic and then went out by the front door.

Another couple of women were coming up the walk. They had dishes covered with tinfoil in their hands.

The wives, he thought. The wives of the Arabian Knights.

THIRTY-FIVE

He walked into the office and Mary Helen was waiting for him, white-faced, almost shaking, he thought. "Why don't you sit down before you fall down," he said to her. She just waved him off, reached around the corner and held up the phone and said that Marly needed to talk to him.

"Hold on to your hat, Kewpie," Marly said to him.

It turned out the big beach house Alice Farmer had been renting was owned by Vidalia Real Estate, Inc., and according to Marly's records, Vidalia Real Estate was owned by Henry Houldings and kept separate from the rest of the rental properties for him to book for his friends.

"How 'bout them apples," said Marly.

"You could be a good cop," he said to her.

"Thanks, but I consider that a giant step down, Kewpie. Now let me talk to the Queen." Q.P. passed the phone to Mary Helen and went right out and told Glen Petty and Ellis to go pick up Houldings. At his office, house, out on the golf course, wherever they found him.

He telephoned Keating at the Carolina Inn and told him everything, and Keating said he'd have a shower and get right down to the courthouse.

Q.P. held his breath and called Spud Reid and told him that he wanted a search warrant for Houldings and that he was putting out a warrant on him for kidnapping.

"Okay, Kewpie," Spud said. "Who's he supposed to be kidnapping?"

"Woman named Alice Farmer from Nashville, Tennessee."

"And just how do you know this?"

"She's missing overnight."

"Missing?"

"There's signs of a struggle. Blood."

"Okay. What makes you think Henry Houldings is involved?"

"Let's just say I've got reasons."

"What reasons, for chrissake, Kewpie?" Reid was starting to crack, Q.P. thought.

"Houldings is linked to some of my other cases."

Spud thought about it for a few seconds.

"Where's Henry now?" he asked. Reid sounded like he was starting to get a little worried and wanted to make sure all the details were straight so he could cover his ass.

"We're trying to pick him up right now. We have reason to believe he is fleeing."

"You don't have enough to arrest him, though, do you?"

"Yeah, I think we might, Spud. Depends on what he says. Depends if he's got somebody tied up over at his house. That's why I want to *search* his place, Spud." There was a long pause. Q.P. just stood there and stared at one of Franklin's fishing portraits on the wall across from him. Franklin was almost sixty in the photograph, smiling as he strained to hold up his catch. Q.P. couldn't identify the fish. Huge. A salmon or something.

"Who is this woman again?"

"It's a woman from Nashville, staying with her friend—"

"Well, where's the friend?" Reid asked. Now he was looking for a way out.

"Went home early."

"Is this Farmer woman in any trouble? Is she a felon or avoiding a warrant?"

"No, not as far as we know." He wondered why Reid would think that.

"All right, well. You pick him up first and see what he says, then maybe we'll ask for a warrant," Reid said.

"Thanks, Spud, you're a big help," he said as he was hanging up and heading for the parking lot. Fuck Reid.

Houldings hadn't gotten out of bed yet, the housekeeper said. And then, when she went up to check, she found out that he wasn't even in. It was news to her.

"He must have left sometime in the night." But it wasn't all that unusual for him to do that, she said. "Sometimes he just up and *goes*. He doesn't have to tell us. It's his house an' he's the boss," the housekeeper said. Her name was Kitty. She was huge with a gigantic bosom and dressed sort of like Alice in Wonderland, with a dress that had puffy sleeves and an immaculate white apron. She had a little watch pinned on it in the old style.

"Can I look around?" He smiled at her.

"Yes, sir, you can look wherever you want, just wipe your shoes."

They walked outside to the garage. He'd taken the big Packard, the woman said. The little Packard was still there.

They got a description of the car and Nokes went to put that out on the wire.

He went up to the bedroom and looked around. There wasn't any blood. Besides Kitty there were two other live-in servants, an old man who occasionally drove Houldings around town and who was a handyman, and a young girl, Kitty's niece, not more than sixteen, who worked there as a maid. None of them had heard anything unusual in the night.

Houldings may have lived pretty good, but he didn't live much at home. The only trace of Lavinia Buell was a black-and-white portrait on the closed lid of the piano.

The basement of the house was nearly as big as the courthouse offices and was the domain of Mr. Cole, who tended the yard and occasionally did driving for Houldings. There was some window cord down there and he showed Q.P. where it was. It was too small and Mr. Cole could account for its purchase and its use. He'd only seen Mr. Houldings come down in the basement one time, he said.

"One time he come back from New York City with a whole bunch of *wine*," the old man said. "He wanted me to fix up a place for it back over there, a wine *cellar*." The old man pointed back into the shadows. Q.P. started to pick his way back over to the place.

There were cobwebs and he realized after a couple of steps that nobody had been back over there in years.

"Back over here?" he said to the old man.

"They drunk it all up long time ago."

There was a garden shed in the back of the property and Cole took him back there. There were fertilizer bags and some burlap but even he could see the difference between the modern bags and the samples Keating had collected.

He met Keating and they had food brought in and sat in his office and tried to puzzle it through. Keating made a few phone calls and assured them that any additional search warrants they needed would be approved within the hour.

"Looks like we're on to something big," he said to Q.P. and they both laughed and then got down to it again.

Without making a fuss about it, he took Keating back and locked the door of the Case Room behind them and showed him Allison's photographs.

"Oh, boy . . ." whispered Keating as he leafed through them one by one. "Oh brother . . . there you go, then," he said. They put all of Allison's documentation in a folder and locked it away in the cabinet and went back out front. Mary Helen was on the phone and he went into his office and it was Ellis, telling him they'd found Houldings's Packard parked out at Bluethenthal Field and that he had bought two tickets that morning, one to Raleigh-Durham and one to Atlanta. Both planes had left as scheduled. The airlines had no idea if he had actually flown on either plane.

"Maybe he put her in one and he took the other," Keating said and Q.P. told Ellis to see if anyone had noticed Alice Farmer getting on one of the flights.

"I reckon they'd notice a real good-lookin' woman like her right off, don't you, Kewpie?" said Ellis over the phone. Nobody had actually *seen* Alice Farmer or even a picture of her, but still everybody knew what a knockout she was supposed to be.

"Yeah, I guess they would, Ellis. Just ask around, okay?" he said and hung up marveling at Ellis's showing signs of becoming a detective.

Keating went right to work and gave Mary Helen a list of things to do. He got her to call Houldings's business and find out what banks they used and to get the managers on the line for him to talk to.

After a few calls they learned that Houldings had come in first thing that morning and transferred funds from the savings and loan to other accounts in two other banks, one in Charleston, South Carolina, and another business account in Atlanta. He had gone back to his safe-deposit box for a few minutes and then he had said good-bye and left.

Q.P. walked over to the savings and loan and talked to the girl who'd signed him in and out. No, Mr. Houldings hadn't seemed nervous, she said. He looked a little tired maybe. She didn't think he'd shaved, but he was dressed nicely. He was always dressed nicely, she said.

Ed Nicholson phoned and said that he wanted to know what was up regarding Houldings, who was his client. Was there a warrant for his arrest, and if not, why was he being harassed?

"He's not being harassed. We're just trying to find out where he is, Ed," Q.P. told him. Keating was watching from across the desk. "You wouldn't have any idea where he's gone to, would you? We want to question him in connection with a break-in." He looked over at Keating, who nodded.

"What break-in? What the hell are you talkin' about?"

"Why don't you come on down and we'll fill you in. We want to keep these phones clear right now, okay, Ed?" He figured that might give Keating a little more time.

They sat around biting their nails for another ten minutes until the phone rang. It was a connection that Keating had made through one of his SBI amigos at the Atlanta P.D.

Keating's face grew serious while he listened to the Atlanta cop. "Ah . . . shit then," he said quietly, glanced up, and shook his head.

Q.P. looked down and was surprised to see that he'd broken a pencil in his hand. He hadn't even noticed it.

"Okay, thanks," said Keating and hung up. The Atlanta FBI had just missed Houldings. He'd flown out of town aboard a TWA flight for Havana not more than forty-five minutes earlier. He wasn't traveling with anyone, they said.

"Well, hell," said Q.P., holding his hands over the waste can and trying to rub the graphite off. "That's it," he said.

Keating sighed. "Yeah, when they run off to Cuba, you gotta figure they're not coming back anytime soon."

"Shit . . . shit . . . shit . . ." he muttered and walked out of the department so that he wouldn't smash the furniture, he was so exasperated.

He jumped in the Chevy and drove out to Wrightsville and knocked on the doors of all the neighboring beach houses and talked to whatever people he could find. A woman hadn't been able to sleep because of her sunburn. She had already told what she knew to the Wrightsville Beach Police, she said.

"If you could just go through it once more," he said to her. She sighed and looked at the street behind him. "I couldn't sleep," she said. "I thought I heard something. Like somebody having a fight. I could hear her yelling at him."

"Him?"

"Whoever . . ." She sighed and looked out at the street. It was boiling hot out there and her energy was gone.

First it was loud voices, she said, and then some glass breaking and then something like a snapping sound, she said. Like Lash LaRue or like someone chopping wood. And in a while after that she heard a car pulling away. A loud car, she said, leaving in a hurry. Then another car came and went; she wasn't sure. It went on all night, she thought. "I went to sleep after that, I guess." The woman stood there in the shade of the doorway with Noxzema spread across her cheeks. She looked miserable.

Petty pulled him away and they walked over to the side of Houldings's beach house. Mookie had sawn up the steps and collected the bloodstains one by one. Around the corner one of the Wrightsville Beach cops was there. Beside him was a man with a mine detector strapped onto his back.

"Found this little item here for you, Kewpie," Petty said. "Left it right in the sand." It was a little nickel-plated automatic, maybe a .25 caliber. Tossed away in the dune beside the back steps. Maybe that was what had caused all the blood, he thought.

"That's a pretty hot gizmo you got there," he said, pointing to the man who was carrying the detector.

"Makes it easy to find your car keys. Hell, we use it all the time now . . ."

He pulled out his pocketknife and turned the gun over and saw that the safety was off. Petty handed him a manila envelope and he eased the gun into it. He could feel the heat of it through the paper. The rest of the house was sealed and waiting for Keating's lab people to get down there from Raleigh, so he didn't go inside. He made a mental note to tell them to look for a casing from the automatic, thanked the guy with the mine detector, and drove back to the courthouse to write up a charge of homicide against Henry Houldings.

THIRTY-SIX

The wind woke her up.

It had been rising through the night. She felt her way through to Q.P.'s kitchen and put the kettle on. Leaned against the cupboard and looked at the trees recoiling from the gusts, heard the creaking of the house, the rain pounding against the shingles.

Maybe Allison had built himself up to the point where he had decided he loved Alicia Farmer, she thought. Maybe he thought being tied up like that was some kind of love. She had looked through the file. Over and over. Longer than any of the men. Staring at the women, trying to identify their bodies. Is that you, Ruth? Eerily dismembered by the orthodontists' cropping. An arm, a thigh, an elbow. The hard-edged, almost clinical realism of their vulvas. The parts of bodies slotted together and examined. Maybe he was trying to understand it. Is that you?

The bony body of Allison, lubricated and masked, sliding into second base in hell.

Mad, she thought. You're going crazy yourself, she thought, and shook her head to try and clear the images away. She shuffled out and made herself a pot of tea and sat and turned on the radio.

Something quiet and classical. The swirl of the music matched the wrenching of the oaks outside the window. There was a long drumming of rain, a crescendo of wind whipping around the gables. Blurring the music was a lot of static and when she got the news the man said it was the first big hurricane of the season. Edna, the man said, and it had already missed them on its way up the edge of the Atlantic. Nags Head would be getting it in the morning.

It was the start of some stormy weather, the man said. And then everything would be back to normal.

The wind had died down some in the morning and then just hung there with the high gray clouds blowing over. And then it started to rain again. And it got heavier all morning. Freshening, the men would say and laugh.

She got into the Case Room late. Sat over in her corner clutching her coffee, shivering against the damp morning. It felt even colder after the summer heat. Q.P. had come in earlier. Now he was sitting, tight as a drum, in the corner. His bandage had come off and he had a little red scar there still. A little red place where the skin was trying to heal. She tried to get him to put oil on it, but of course he wouldn't. Now his eyes were dead, she thought. Defeated.

Grief, she thought. They were all grieving, she thought. Beaten by Allison and his well-tuned car, by Henry and his ability to slip the net. Q.P. was shaking his head. Just let it drop off your shoulders, she thought.

She went ahead and let it overtake her. Beautiful, blond Alice Farmer; a princess stolen away from her beach house. A little hideaway where Houldings kept his friends. Good friends. Friends who starred in home movies, friends who all of a sudden left an occasional bloodstain around. And everything was so friendly that as you went you just pitched your shiny little pistol out into the dunes. Maybe you didn't need a gun anymore. Maybe because you had friends who wouldn't let you pack before you left.

"I don't get it," Q.P. was saying. "I just don't get it . . ." He was looking up at the plywood board now.

"Don't look at that thing too long or you'll go crazy," Donny said quietly.

"Anyway . . . she's dead," Keating said with finality.

"You don't know that. Prove it," she said, a little angrier than she'd planned. She was tired, too.

"Well, let's try this on for size: Houldings and Allison are friends, we know that—"

"Special friends—"

"Very special friends," Donny said and made his wrist go limp.

"Maybe Allison has something special going on with Alice Farmer. Houldings gets jealous, abducts her, knocks her off, Allison kill himself out of sadness—" He didn't finish because Donny and Nina had started groaning.

"You mean he *falls in love* with her?" She aimed her most withering look at Keating, who almost flinched and looked away.

"It really doesn't matter what they did with her, she's gone," Q.P. said. "She's unaccounted for. She's kidnapped." Keating sighed; he didn't want to bounce the case up to the FBI needlessly.

"Allison is dead, Houldings is gone. Wherever they took her, or if they both did it, or if Houldings did it and Allison discovered it . . . all that is just *fantasy*."

"Whatever it is . . . something goes wrong," she said.

"Yeah," said Q.P. "And it goes wrong differently than it did for the others."

"Yes . . ." she said quietly. *Is that you?*

"It fits on Tuesday but it doesn't fit on Wednesday," Q.P. complained.

"Okay, okay, yeah, yeah, yeah . . ." Donny said.

She leaned forward and pushed her fingernail through the pictures again. She picked out Houldings's masked face.

"They broke up," I think. "They did this and they got caught up and they got scared and they broke up."

"Well," said Keating, thinking about it. "Maybe it starts when we begin looking at Allison over the connection to Cora Snow, and when he finds out that we're bringing in Henry and there's recrimination . . ."

"Something goes wrong and *she* phones. She phones Allison. She phones him at home. Maybe he phones Houldings, the special friend who has so thoughtfully provided the vine-covered cottage—" she said to herself, "—stuck out in the beach . . ."

"I told you never to phone me here!" Donny exclaimed and she just stared at him.

". . . it's important enough that Allison drives out there in the middle of the night and right into the teeth of . . . something, a big argument . . ." she said.

". . . confrontation," Q.P. mumbled.

"Please, please, Rhett, dahlin', take me away from awl this!" Donny said in a high voice.

"Will you just shut up?" she said to Donny, who nodded and blushed like a nine-year-old. "You said there was a struggle, right?" she asked.

"Yeah, the furniture was all over the place . . ."

"And there's the blood."

"Yeah," said Keating. "We're waiting on the blood."

One of the Hong kids brought them lunch, drenched in his passage from the parking lot to the double doors, the food steaming as he carted it through the office, causing heads to turn, giving Mary Helen a chance to chaperone him back to the Case Room and peek in.

They ate in silence. She pushed the Allison file into its big folder and started tidying up the table.

Q.P. ate quickly and went upstairs, where he had been called in for a meeting with the city to go over what they were planning to do this hurricane season.

Nina pecked away at her food and then began to putter around the room, gathering the oldest files she'd collected, about Cora Snow and her family. She was vaguely planning to box it all up, thinking that it might still be useful if there was ever an opportunity to extradite Henry Houldings. Thought for a while about what Q.P. had said about things fitting one day and not the next.

She put the files in the boxes in alphabetical order; Allison, Garnet, Houldings, Micheaux . . . Houldings's took by far the most space. Live fast, die young, and leave a big archive, she thought. Seeing Conrad before her, laughing, in some classroom. A million years ago, it seemed.

Most of the Houldings file was devoted to his business interests. Official documents that Keating had requested. Lists of real estate that he owned directly or via the old Buell family business. Another file of yellowed background information about Lavinia. Society-page clippings. Looking more and more like murder, she thought. And now Henry was back in Havana . . . Raining on him, too, she thought.

Q.P. came back shaking his head about the disorganization

threatening to overwhelm the city of Wilmington and was interrupted when Keating blew in, ignoring the food, to report on what
he'd learned about the blood work they'd done up in Raleigh.

"Okay," he said frowning. "The blood is *not* Alice Farmer's. The
blood type is wrong."

"Okay, okay, then. Whose blood?" Q.P. leaned forward; he was
getting angry already, she thought, watching murder evidence
against Houldings evaporate right in front of him.

"It's not Houldings's either," Keating said, "for the same reason."

"Allison?" Q.P. frowned.

"It's the same type."

"But he wasn't wounded, *right?*" Q.P. started looking around the
table for Sykes's report, but she'd cleaned everything into files. "I remember that . . ."

"That's right," she said.

"Yeah, so . . ."

"So it wasn't him that got shot . . ." Q.P. said.

"And there's no blood in his car. None. We went all over his car,"
Donny said. He spun a chopstick through the dirty container in
front of him, trying to lever a piece of broccoli over the edge.

"And because there's no blood in Houldings's car either, therefore . . ." Q. P. paused for a few moments, as if he'd forgotten what
he was going to say. Keating looked up at Nina and shook his head.

"Therefore *what?*" she said gently.

"Therefore . . . Because we haven't found Alice, and because the
blood just goes *nowhere* . . . we have to assume—" He was staring
directly across at the wall like he was trying to make it burst into
flame. "We have to assume that . . . somebody else was there," he
said.

"A *fourth* person?" she said.

"Yeah," Q.P. said, running his fingertips across the top surface of
the stack of file folders.

"Well, pardner . . . it fits on Wednesday . . ."

He turned and looked at her. "Yeah . . ."

They fell on the photographs again because everyone who had
seen them had been unsure about exactly how many people were in
them. Nina had already begun to do the sorting in her head.

"We go back to basics . . ." Keating was saying.

They worked through the night until it ended in the rainy dawn, all leafing through the photographs. There were exactly 503 of them.

Q.P. thought he could identify Cora and another Negro woman. But it wasn't Ruth. They couldn't find Ruth Micheaux anywhere. Allison was behind the camera most of the time. Q.P. thought he could recognize him a total of seven times. Houldings was in more than eighty pictures. There was a series with a woman he thought was Millie Garnet. There weren't many faces to use for identification, they'd all been covered with masks or blindfolds.

But there were images of two unknown white men and as many as four Negro men performing various sexual acts.

"Our fourth person is one of them," he said.

"And . . . he's wounded, and he's still got her . . ." she said breathlessly from her corner. "She's still alive."

"Ay, caramba!" Donny said but nobody laughed.

THIRTY-SEVEN

It was somewhere between midnight and dawn. Nina sat drinking her first coffee and watching the basement walls of the courthouse slowly start seeping.

Okay, she decided, if Alice Farmer wasn't dead already, she was going to be dead soon, and the killer was going to get away. Mister Four, if he had any sense at all, would have already dumped her body and left town, but if he hadn't, it looked like his best opportunity was coming up.

Waltzing in behind Edna was the next hurricane. Her name was Hazel and at the moment she was smashing into Carriacou with ninety-five-mile-an-hour winds. Heading toward the Carolinas, people said.

If his wound wasn't incapacitating, he'd wait and see how strong the storm got and then, if he could travel, when the traffic out of town was increasing, he'd kill her and run, she thought.

And then how long would it take? A few weeks, a month or two? Soon people would forget about the murders that had sparked all the tension in town. They'd be free to concentrate on hating the politicians and the Supreme Court.

Alice would be dead along with all the others and Mister Four could take his disease to someplace new; the killings would remain unsolved and everybody could pretend it had never happened.

Q.P.'s attention was already being pulled off the case by the weather. He was spending more and more time in the Chevy driving around the county helping get people ready for Hazel. He drove up to the near limit of Pender County on the road where they'd cut Scowen down out of the pines, and later that day he drove along the winding River Road down all the way past Davis Beach Road and into the huge hummocks of Fort Fisher itself.

Still, the whole time he thought obsessively about the case, thought about the victims. When there weren't any other cops in the car, he tried to let his mind get back to the basics of the case. What he ended up doing was just dwelling on his memories of the pictures, now taking on a life of their own in his tired brain.

There was nothing new about hurricanes, of course. Most Wilmingtonians took these disturbances in stride. Usually the storms blew past or made a turn away. Homeowners walked around their yards checking the oldest trees to see if any looked like they'd blow down this time. It was the fishermen who were busiest, doubling up on their moorings. Those who were really worried lined up to have their boats hauled out of the water and set on blocks.

That evening there was a planning meeting on the stage of Thalian Hall and the location of the various shelters was announced. If it was necessary people would be able to be housed in the school gymnasiums. There was the capacity for over a thousand mattresses and this was thought to be more than enough.

Q.P. had already been in touch with all the other county police forces. The police at the beach towns were the ones who always had it tough. On occasions the breakers might push right through the barrier dunes and a beach road might wash out; often there was a loss of electricity. That made it difficult if there was a medical emergency, and an ambulance had to go pick someone up. So they'd developed a system where the police would go door-to-door following any lengthy power outage and check up on people.

If they could figure out a description for Mister Four, they could put it out and maybe something might click, but what do you tell Mookie Pritchard? "We're looking for a naked colored man, or maybe he's white and, oh yeah, he's wearing a blindfold . . ."

He drove on, splashing through the puddles from beach town to beach town.

Maybe they'd be lucky and the biggest problem would be teenagers who wanted to have hurricane parties out on the fishing piers. There were several piers that were famous for this sort of activity. Wrightsville had its "Steel Pier," constructed to last a good long time, pushing out further into the Atlantic than any of its competitors. All year, morning, noon, and night, men and women would gather there to fish. Lovers would walk out there at night arm in arm. Teenagers would go out there to smoke and sneak beers. But when a big storm came, it tempted the kids out to the end, where they'd sit and get soaked and try and ride it out. It was thrilling to be out there and feel the pier trembling as each of the big waves smashed into the pilings and to have the wind nearly upset you as you leaned into the warm salty rain and tried to walk along, soaked to the bone.

And, of course, it was terribly dangerous. Every big storm claimed at least part of a pier when it struck. Maybe that was part of the thrill, too, Q.P. thought, the thrill of doing something dangerous and forcing some poor cop to go out there and haul you back in before you drowned. When he complained, Nina said that she and all her friends had always gone out during the hurricanes when she was a girl, wading through the flooded streets, marveling at the power of the weather. He just shook his head.

By evening they learned that Hazel had crushed Haiti. What news was coming out of the island was all bad. There were floods and mud slides. Villages had disappeared completely. Right off the bat more than two hundred people were dead or missing. They had managed to measure the wind at over a hundred and twenty-five miles per hour.

Wilmington's planning was as complete as it was ever going to be. They had moved cots into the department and Q.P. pulled rank and went home sometime during the night and got a few hours' sleep.

During the next day they went about their preparations, but there seemed to be a hopeful, almost giddy feeling. Maybe this would be just another false alarm. All along Front Street the merchants had nailed plywood up over their show windows. Most businesses were closed. The food stores had sold out of most of their canned goods.

He had grabbed a quick supper off the department hot plate and had just fallen asleep in Franklin's big chair when Glen Petty came in and reported that the airport had said the storm had hit the Bahamas hard and the wind speed was back up again.

"More 'n a hundred mile 'n hour, the weather man said," Glen told him.

Glen was worried about the tides. He'd got out his book of tide tables and then called up Bluethenthal Field to talk to the weather people again. They gave him their best estimate of when the storm would make landfall, and he held the receiver between his shoulder and his ear while he got out a pencil and did some figuring. Q.P. rubbed his eyes and stared at him across the table for a few seconds.

"Well, that right there is right at the peak of the tide, then," Petty said to the weather people on the phone, and then he waited while the weather people talked to him about it.

"Hell, *evacuation*, I guess," he said after that, and then he looked up at Q.P. and slowly shook his head no.

Q.P. sat up in his chair and drank the remains of a cold cup of coffee. The weather people were taking their time explaining about the tides and the storm surge and Glen kept shaking his head. "Okay," he said. "Hell, if that's the only goddamn plan we've got, that's the only goddamn plan we can put into effect, I reckon," he said and hung up.

They called everyone together in Thalian Hall again and explained that the timing of the storm could not have been more unlucky. It was set to make landfall at what was called a "Marsh-Hen Tide." It was the full moon in October when the tide was so high that it drove the birds out of their nests in the marshes. Now with the added storm surge it meant that there was going to be certain flooding.

He sat with Nina in one of the new seats and listened. He had been around relatively few *big* hurricanes. There had been a scare the year before when Barbara came through, but the eye of the storm hit up at Nags Head. He'd learned that the windows at the back of his apartment didn't shut all the way. A little mopping was all it amounted to.

"This is not sounding so good," she whispered to him as various officials from State Ports, the Highways, and the Red Cross all explained what they'd be doing to react to the flooding. "This is not sounding very good, at all." He looked over and saw that she was worried. A change had come over all the longtime Wilmingtonians, he noticed. There weren't as many jokes. People had started to prepare for the storm *seriously.*

His deputies went out with the fire department and various police forces to evacuate people into the nearest shelters. This always took time. In an emergency all of a sudden everybody remembered their civil rights. Everything had to be explained to each household. Objections had to be dealt with. There were always people who refused to go, who wanted to stay and protect their dwellings, or people who'd pretend to evacuate and then sneak right back again.

They were getting the message out on the radio, but by now the winds had increased, and all over the county there were power failures from tree falls. Down in the basement they put on more coffee and did as best as they could.

It was after he had returned from a long rainy shift, tired and edgy from having to deal with all the amateur constitutional lawyers who lived in the lower parts of town, that he staggered back to the Case Room. He'd gone back there more to get away from everyone than to actually work on trying to solve the case, but he got entranced when he looked at the new configuration of *data* that Keating and Nina had arranged on the table.

"Have you eaten anything?" Nina stuck her head in to check on him, but he just shook his head.

"In this Allison file here . . . you've got a list of all of his assets, right?"

"Umm-hmm." She was leaning against the door picking at a cheese sandwich and staring down at the linoleum. Her eyes were red rimmed and she looked like she was coming down with a cold.

"Have *you* eaten anything?" he asked her.

"I think she's dead now," Nina said quietly, and he saw that she'd been crying. She came in the room and they held on to each other and leaned there together against the wall.

"Okay," she said after a minute or two, "I'm okay . . . now," and touched him on the cheek and slipped out of his arms. She showed him where Allison's property tax records were, and a much bigger folder for Houldings's.

"I was just thinking . . . after dealing with all these people who've been so concerned about their beach houses . . ."

"What?" she said. He was flipping through the records.

"I was just thinking that we should be looking for the *place* . . ."

"The darkroom?"

"Allison had his darkroom at his house, but, I mean . . . where is *this*? He had left the tax lists and gone over to the file cabinet where they kept the photographs.

"Where is *this*?" The photograph showed a bloated white male torso, probably Henry Houldings, being masturbated by a black woman whose face was out of the frame.

"Oh . . . God, it could be anywhere." She pushed aside the photograph to expose another beneath it.

"It's the same place, though, I think . . ." she said. "They've hung curtains up . . ."

"But . . . one of them rented it, probably, right?"

"No . . ." she said after a second, her voice in a daze. "No, when you rent, the landlord comes around, you know?" The studio would have to be more secure.

She had started to riffle compulsively through the folders. Allison's was slim. He owned his house, leased his office, and had a cabin in the mountains. But Houldings, through his own businesses and those he'd inherited through his wife, controlled much, much more real estate.

"This is going to take some time," she said.

He stood there and watched her go to work and then walked down the hall and washed his face and tried to wake up and when he got back Mary Helen was there at her desk.

"I wish I had the plywood concession in this city," she said, and he tried to laugh. "Now, listen," she said seriously. "If you were smart, you'd juggle this so that you got most of your sleep tonight, Kewpie, 'cause after this thing hits nobody is going to get any rest."

"Yeah, I thought about that."

"Take Nina home and y'all be good and get some rest, because it's all going to start tomorrow, I'm telling you," she said.

He decided to take her advice once he'd gotten a list of properties from Nina. "Okay, consider me fast asleep," he said.

"Smart man," she said just as the phone rang.

He went into the office and told Glen that he was going home for the remainder of the night and that he'd be back on duty at dawn. Glen was reasonably fresh. He'd managed to get his boat out of the water earlier in the day and his house was all boarded up. That was as much as he could do.

"It's all over but the waitin' now," he said.

He took a few minutes and went over all their plans one more time and made sure everything was in order, then walked back where he found a manila folder with a penciled list of addresses that Nina had left for him, folded it into his raincoat, and jaywalked over to Thalian Hall.

He found Nina dividing up boxes of K rations that had been trucked over from the National Guard. Great gusts of wind were swirling through the hall as a steady stream of volunteers loaded boxes into the backs of pickup trucks for delivery to churches around the county. Winky Peters was there wearing his Shriners fez, sitting at a table on the stage and making each driver sign his load of food.

"You got your shopping list?" She frowned at him. "You really look beat," she said to Q.P.

"I'm going home," he said.

"Well, you *might* get some sleep, but when this thing hits town, you're gonna wake up, for sure, Sheriff. You're gonna think you're Judy Garland flying up to Oz . . ."

"You ought to go home, get some sleep yourself, maybe see about your father?"

"I did that already. Mrs. Stasik came over to be there with him. They've got candles and she made food up ahead of time. He's all excited, he always gets like that." She smiled.

"You're beautiful when you're tired," he said.

"I know," she said and gave him a little peck, and he headed home.

THIRTY-EIGHT

But he didn't go home. Instead he started driving around, checking Nina's addresses, one by one. He told himself he'd just do one side of town, thinking really that it was just about their last chance.

He ignored Allison's list. The dentist's office wasn't big enough and the pictures obviously weren't taken in a vacation cabin up in the mountains.

He cruised out Oleander, which was not as busy as he thought it would be. There was debris that had blown across the road and he drove slowly, out to Houldings's showroom. It was closed up tight; they had taken the precaution of putting plywood up over the big showroom windows. There was a searchlight that he could work with a lever attached to the passenger side of the car and he shone it around the upper windows of the building. Then he drove around the corner and thought for a moment he had actually found the place when he saw the big loading doors, but they weren't right.

He realized that what he had been thinking of was the shadows on the floor. They were in almost all of Allison's photographs that had been taken in natural light. They came from the sun shining through a great window made of many panes of glass. The lines of the mullions rippled across the skin of the two women on the floor.

When he'd seen the big loading doors, he thought for a second he'd found the place.

He stepped on the gas now and went around the back of the building. There were several delivery vans and a pair of panel trucks parked back in a little pen. There was a little pad there with a hose and a drain so they could keep them looking good as they rolled around town advertising Houldings' Furniture. Appearance was everything for a guy like that, Q.P. figured. The appearance of money, of strength. Of power. Of a heart attack after a yachting accident. He thought about what he'd learned about Houldings, the one he'd decided was the "man" in the Allison/Houldings family. The one who stayed in control. Ricky got hysterical when things went wrong. But Henry was the one who'd had the sense to blow town. He might die of syphilis down in Havana, but you'd never find him with a hose pipe in his mouth.

Allison was the crazy one. They had found wire in his garden shed like the kind that was used to tie the burlap on the cross that the "Klan" had burned in front of Nina's. When Q.P.'s investigation had got too close, he'd tried bribery. And because he was always the kind of guy who got scared, he tried to scare him off. Because he was so ashamed about his secret life, he'd invested a little time digging up something to blackmail Nina with. Thinking Q.P. would just go along with it, like Irene Allison had just gone along with it.

He braked to a stop and flicked on the lights inside the Chevy and riffled through Nina's list. There were several houses that Houldings controlled through his real-estate interests, properties out in the new suburbs where he and Lamont Sanders had scraped away all the topsoil and sold it before they gridded out their streets. Some of these were demonstration homes built out in the middle of the development; they'd be isolated enough for the scenarios that Allison and Henry seemed to like.

He let his finger run down the list and was just about to start out for Emerald Acres, their newest scheme, bulldozed out of the pines down close to Carolina Beach. But then his eye fell on the last entry on Nina's sheet, *190–280 Colfax.* Where the hell was that?

He tried calling in for the location, but the radio only sent out a long burst of static. He flicked off the light and drove around the corner and tried the radio again and this time it came in loudly. *"Hold on for that location, Kewpie . . ."* he heard George Fosters's voice saying.

Q.P. pulled out of the large parking lot that surrounded the showroom building and out on Oleander and started heading south so he could run by the new housing development, when the radio erupted with a burst of static. George Foster calling for him again.

"*. . . and we did get that location for y'all. Colfax is a disused street out at State Ports, Kewpie . . .*"

"Say again? A disused street?"

"*. . . hello, One?*" George said more firmly and then when he didn't hear anything he repeated his message, "*. . . a disused address. Colfax is the name of an old address out there on River Road . . .*"

And then Q.P. didn't hear any more because he was driving fast now, the gas pedal pressed to the floor, barreling along the streets heading for River Road.

Because now he knew where Ricky Allison had his studio.

The rain had strengthened and his wipers could barely keep up with it. He swerved to avoid a tree that was down and its branches partially blocking the road. The wind was stronger here and it shook the Chevy from side to side so that his steering was always unsure. He tried the radio again and got nothing. He called it in anyway, hoping they might be able to hear him, and then jammed on the brakes and turned onto a narrow street, hoping that it was clear and he'd be able to make it across to River Road.

He was heading for a strip of land south of the junkyard where they'd found Millie Garnet. Altogether the place he was thinking of was a tract of land maybe thirty or forty acres. There was a long brick wall along one side of it, and the rest was surrounded by chain-link fence. It was a series of old masonry warehouses.

He saw in front of him all Nina's charts, all the lists and dotted lines and connections they'd made, remembered sitting on the porch with Thelma as she told the history of the Snows and the Rowells in her steady refrain.

Saw the old buildings, all of them constructed along the east bank of the Cape Fear. The oldest building there had been built cheaply, right after the Civil War when carpetbag fortunes were made in Wilmington. It was choice real estate because in those years having good access to river transportation still meant money. For a while there, when mass production merged with King Cotton, real serious money was made down in those buildings. It was a particular kind of Southern Gilded Age.

And he remembered that the warehouses, the old mill, the docks, all of it had once been part of the *Vestry-Buell* textile fortune. That after the Civil War the Buells had emerged as *the* preeminent Wilmington family. Become aristocrats by the turn of the century, royalty by the end of the First World War, history by the end of the Second.

Now the mill buildings were just crumbling brick monsters, built right on the edge of the river so they could load easily. They'd been condemned for decades, and if V-J Day hadn't arrived when it did, they almost certainly would have been razed and put to some other use. He'd driven right past them a hundred times. He'd *fished* along the abandoned piers, quietly floating beneath the strange orange brickwork. Found himself floating through strange designs and patterns on the water; glancing up, momentarily dazzled in the reflections from the great looming windows that looked over the Cape Fear. Now with the high October tide and the storm surge, the water would be steadily lapping against their foundations.

And *all* of it, every doorknob, every broken window, every corn husk and brick and cockroach in every abandoned building on every forgotten tract of Buell land, had all come down to Henry Houldings.

The wind was buffeting his car as he reached the intersection of River Road and skidded the Chevy around the corner.

He lost control of the Chevy for a second, the back end of the car swerving first one way and then back again as he went through a low spot near the Sunset Park community, a grid of mostly identical bungalows put up in a few weeks at the beginning of the war for all the defense workers.

There were no lights on, he noticed. The power had already gone out through the project.

The road straightened as it passed the State Ports, and he sped by the yard where they'd found Mildred Garnet. Up ahead he saw the dark hulks of the warehouses rising up on the flat land below him.

He pulled over at the entrance and rolled down the side window and held his hand up against the rain. He heard a horn honking, and a car drove past him, dangerously close, and then vanished in the rain.

He squinted into the rain and thought for a second he could see some kind of light on down there. Spilling out at the entrance to the last of the buildings. He looked harder and it seemed to go out. Squinting, he looked harder and thought he saw the light come on again.

"Headquarters . . ." he said into the radio and waited for a second, watching for the light. There was too much rain to be sure; he might have been just wishing it into being. He stared into the rain for another few seconds until he was good and soaked. "Headquarters?" Nothing. He held the key open and called it in anyway. That's what you were supposed to do.

He put the Chevy in gear and fishtailed through the open chain-link fence that surrounded the property, turned on his searchlight, which just produced a blinding fog in front of him, turned it off again, and slowly negotiated his way down the steep road to the yard. The road had deteriorated, hunks of the blacktop had broken out of it. The Chevy bounced hard on its suspension and then bumped again as it made it to the bottom, past the darkened warehouses and across a set of abandoned railroad tracks. There were outbuildings, the honeysuckle-covered remains of a substation put in when the complex had converted to electricity after the turn of the century, a stack of mossy railroad ties.

He finally turned around the corner of a collapsed storage shed to where he could see. From an office door there was a long blurry triangle of light spilling out. There was a panel truck parked there. Maybe Mister Four was packing up, he thought and switched off his lights and rolled to a stop a few yards away. The river would breach the banks if the hurricane came any nearer to the city, he thought. If they'd heard his radio call, Donny or Glen or whoever was available would have to come soon. He looked for lights up in the windows on the second floor. There was nothing up there now.

He opened the door and was immediately knocked back a step by the wind. It sounded like a long howling, like a boxcar with a seized truck being dragged along the tracks. Like something being pulverized all around him. There was a second where the wind seemed to stop altogether and he rocked forward, thrown off balance, recovered and managed to get the door of the car shut, and then threw himself forward when the wind hit him again.

He braced himself along the fender and headed toward the yellow glow of the open door. The wind pulled another of its tricks and he straightened up and made for the wildly swinging door. It was slamming back and forth with each change in gusts.

Now it slammed open and he leaned for it and tried to keep from slipping and going down in the water that had flooded ankle deep across the parking lot.

The door slammed open again as he made it to the last few sheltered feet before the offices. He could see that the light was coming from a storm lantern set out on a counter there in an office, a kind of foyer that opened into a large stairwell that led up to the big shop floors.

Okay, now, he thought as he reached down and slipped his revolver out of its holster. Okay . . . okay . . .

And the next time the wind blew it open, he stepped through the door.

THIRTY-NINE

It used to be an office. The kind of place where you brought in bills of lading, signed the papers, asked the price. If it was important they took you somewhere else to see the foreman or the supervisor. There was a counter there with rotten linoleum, and a little wooden swinging door that was broken off. The roof had been leaking, and there were berries that had grown up around a hole at the far end of the room. All kinds of broken furniture piled up back there, the kind of place you might get bit by a snake.

It was a little wood-framed building and it was attached to the old masonry structure at the corner. Every time the wind blew the whole place creaked. He got out of the silhouette and waited for a second. There was so much noise that he didn't have to worry about being heard.

The light was coming from a kerosene storm lantern that was on the steps around the corner. He looked deep into the shadows. Nothing. As quickly as he could, he slipped across the bottom of the stairwell and stole a look out onto the darkened first floor of the mill.

There was a leak somewhere above and water was steadily running down the wall. Already there was about an inch of water on the thick planked floor of the warehouse. He felt the breathing of the river as it pushed against the pilings. The Cape Fear was seeping out as quickly as it came in off the parking lot, then it would well up again from below, pushed higher by a swell in the river.

He didn't want to go out there, walk around in the dark and

probably fall through a rotten hole where they'd ripped out some machinery. He moved back to the thick post that held up the wide staircase and then went up the stairs so that he could look over onto the second floor of the mill.

As soon as he looked over, he could see a light way down there, somewhere out in the middle of the shop floor.

Okay, he thought again and started out onto the floor.

The floor quivered more now. Sometimes it seemed to heave up and he thought he was rising into the air. He could see the shadow of someone moving ahead of him. There were old packing cases up there, a tangle of obsolete machinery that blocked the light.

He could recognize the studio now, see the curtains they'd hung. The place where the photographs had been taken. From the high ceilings, tarpaulins had been hung down to make curtains, effectively masking light from spilling out where it could be observed by anybody who might be cruising down the Cape Fear. It was like an apartment in the center of the abandoned mill, a kind of a parody of a living room from somebody's modern home. Old surplus tarps and packing cases blocked off the River Road side from view. In the day nobody ever came down there; you could make all the noise you wanted; the perfect place to do whatever you'd always wanted to do.

He began to edge around to the doubled entrance . . . like a darkroom, Q.P. thought. Pictures and photographs had been hung up on the walls. The shadow-man was working hard under the swaying lightbulb, breathing heavily, struggling to wrap something up. Q.P. moved then to the entrance.

"Put your hands up!" he screamed and then stepped sideways and crouched with the gun held out where the man would see it when he whirled.

It was Otha Snow, his hands flying up and backing away now from the couch they had set up there. Like a bed but raised on one end like a lawn chair. It had a French name, he remembered; a *chaise*. It had been raised up on boxes until it was about belt height and covered with a rubber sheet. It reminded him of a table in an operating room. Something that Sykes might have to use.

Alice Farmer was tied to the chaise with lengths of sash cord.

She was naked and she was dead.

"I found this woman," Otha said, holding his hands up and moving away. "I found her!" he yelled. He was going to run, Q.P. thought and pointed the gun at him now.

"Don't move—" he yelled.

"*That,* right yonder, is what they done," Otha said, and for a second his face was terrible. He pointed at the chaise. "*That* right there is only just *part* of what they done!"

There was no blood. She was tied to the legs of the little couch and her arms and legs had been bent back. There were other appliances in the "room," Q.P. saw. Chairs and slings, sawhorses and pulleys that could be arranged for different purposes.

"We have to get her to the *hospital!*" Otha was yelling and looking around.

And then he did run, and Q.P. pulled the trigger.

He thought he heard Otha cry out, and he shot through the curtains a second time, aiming where he thought he might have moved, and ran toward the corner himself, pulling the trigger again just as he got there, not thinking anymore, just running into the darkness.

And then something crashed into the side of his head and his feet went out from under him and he was down to his knees and then Otha hit him again. Something long and heavy, something like an oar, or a small tree, he thought dreamily. And then Q.P. was falling to the floor with the wind knocked out of him.

This is it, he thought, as he went down, this is the last stupid thing you ever do.

He looked up into the night that seemed to be roiling with fireworks, his eyes seeing patterns in the darkness . . . tried to point the revolver at the shape in front of him. Managed to actually cock the hammer back and pull the trigger—a bright flash illuminating the old factory floor around him.

And Otha gone.

The floor was waving under him and he staggered to one side. From somewhere down at the end of the huge floor there was a shattering of glass. He moved ahead, banging his knees sharply against a stack of pallets, nearly slipping to the floor with the fresh pain. There were voices, he thought, people calling out in terror. Maybe it was angels coming to get him, he thought. He tried to take a step but he couldn't and then managed to back away further out of the light, not surrendering to Otha yet, thinking that he would try to get away now, get out of the building.

The man came silently, like a shadow. A big man, very strong. Pinning his hand back and twisting the revolver out of his grip as easily as taking a rattle away from a child. It didn't keep Q.P. from trying something desperate now, but the guy turned with him, cornering him and twisting him around.

"Turn round, Officer, 'cause I don't want to hurt you," the man hissed, and now that they were nose to nose, Q.P. could see that his attacker was another Negro and that he had his gun. He knew that because there was something cold and hard pressed up under his chin that felt a lot like a gun. Yeah. He was sure of it.

Maybe he was acting purely on reflex, or maybe he was falling down, but he made a little swipe at the man's gun hand and tried to knee him. It was dumb and awkward, but it was enough to make the man step back, and Q.P. heard him say "Shit . . ." under his breath.

And then he was flying through the air and into one of the thick posts that held up the top floor. There was a little moment where he went away for a second and then he felt someone turning him over.

"Please don't move, Officer, *please* don't," the big man was saying. Q.P. turned his head and saw the barrel of the pistol pointed at his face. It was shaking and the big man was crying. It was the absurdity of the situation that was keeping him conscious, Q.P. thought, and he tried to sit up a little and look around so he could figure out what was going on.

The guy wasn't going to kill him, Q.P. knew. He wouldn't be talking like that if he was, he was talking like someone who was scared. He was *pleading*.

"You're . . . under . . . arrest," Q.P. said, a word at a time, still trying to get his breath.

"Don't you *move*, I tol' you!" The big man was crouched down, as if he was going to have to fight a tiger. Q.P. twisted himself over and tried to push himself up to his knees. "You're in a lotta trouble . . ." he said to the man.

And just at that moment he heard a series of gunshots coming from the opposite stairway, echoing above the storm through the big warehouse. Great huge booms. Both of them flinched and the big man glanced around. Q.P. thought for a second that he looked familiar. He staggered to his feet, stood there with his knees buckling, trying to breathe, and working on the problems of where he'd seen the man before, and who Otha was shooting at.

Now Q.P. saw that the man was wearing a fisherman's rubber overalls and a long underwear shirt. He was soaking wet. He couldn't have broken into the building by himself. When he'd driven down to the mill, he hadn't seen any cars. The big man must have followed him in.

There was another series of shots. The shots were all alike. It was like they all came from one gun. One person was shooting at something in a panic, the shots coming in these little series of three or four. Too scared to aim.

Q.P. tried to walk forward a step. He might have had to do it anyway to keep from falling. He stood there like an Egyptian for a second before he got the other leg to work. His legs were all rubbery. He felt for his revolver before he remembered the big guy had it.

"*Please*, now . . . Don't *move*," the big man said. He looked as if he'd just lost his favorite puppy.

Q.P. finally took another step and the big man gave a painful sigh and shook his head. It was like he was going to cry again. He tucked the gun in his pocket and started toward Q.P.

"It don't matter, Matthew!" It was another man coming out of the darkness, a little guy with a long coil of rope in his hand. The big man hung his head and nodded.

"Good," he said, tired of fussing with the sheriff, who was too stupid to know when to quit.

"This whole building's gon' float away, boys," he said to the men who were tying him up. "If I drown, that's murder, y'all know that? *Murder*, you hear me?" The big man just sighed behind him.

"Don't you talk no more," said the smaller man as he tied Q.P.'s hand behind him and pulled the knots tight.

"All right," said a smoky voice, and Q.P. looked around to see Reverend Gaylord Chaffee standing there with a revolver in his hand. The old man wasn't happy either.

"Are you okay, Sheriff Waldeau?" he asked. Q.P. wondered if he meant spiritually or physically. Chaffee was looking deeply into his eyes, working on some big decision.

"I'm . . ." Q.P. started to say. His head felt very heavy and he thought he was really going to fall asleep. Another gunshot from down at the stairs woke him up. A leak had opened up in the roof and there was more water spilling out onto the floor.

"If you try to escape, we'll have to stop you, Sheriff," Chaffee said. From the tone of his voice he felt genuinely sorry about it.

"You're under . . . arrest, too," Q.P. said. It came out like a whisper, as if being arrested would be all right. Chaffee leaned closer to hear what he was saying. ". . . under arrest for breaking in here, for . . . assault on a . . . officer of the law . . ." He was droning on and on, like Spud Reid reading the docket.

There were another series of gunshots and Chaffee looked down to the end of the warehouse. "He's almost out of bullets . . ." There was a single shot; a flurry of footsteps.

The big man came back out of the darkness, his voice edged with panic. "They got him turned round!" he said, and then there was another spray of shooting. Loud, right up above them in the stairwell this time.

Someone screamed and then there were footsteps racing higher up to the third floor. The big man ran away just as fast as he had appeared.

"Come on," Chaffee said urgently.

"Otha Snow is under arrest, too," Q.P. muttered as they began to move back to the safety of the staircase.

"Sheriff," Chaffee said quietly, "you're not in charge right now."

Over the storm and the gunfight he recognized the voice of Otha Snow. Some of what he was screaming was portions of prayers and psalms, but about half the time he was speaking in tongues. Then he'd switch to cursing—a string of profanity with no logic, just a list of bad words. Then he'd go back to the psalms. He'd get quiet and then he'd start it up again, over and over.

There was a burst of yelling from the men who were chasing Otha, and then Q.P. smelled smoke begin to gust through the stairwell. They got to the wide arched doorway that led to the landing.

"No . . . back . . . *back!*" Chaffee said, and they retreated onto the shop floor, almost running now. Down one side of the warehouse along a row of crates, passing under the mechanism for a huge crane that occupied the center of the second floor. There were twin loading doors that opened onto the river. Held shut by beams wedged between three cleats, like the gates in a medieval castle. The doors were breathing with each gust of the hurricane.

"We might have to get out of here real fast maybe," the small man said behind him as they waited there. Chaffee had gone on ahead.

Soon the whole building would want to float off its foundations. The next thing that would happen would be that the mortar would go and then the walls would collapse. Smoke was starting to fill the warehouse. Two of Chaffee's men ran past them, racing toward the stairs. Then there was a big wave that crossed the floor, and he figured the river had broken over the pilings. The floor was vibrating, humming against the force of the river. It wouldn't be long now.

"C'mon," he said to the little man.

"Okay." They started ahead into the gloom. The room was getting smoky now, and from the floor above he could hear the high, terrible squealing as they finally cornered Otha.

Now he and the little man ran through the smoke, crashing into boxes and pallets that had been stacked around the floor, through the smoke, trying to get to the glow that was coming out of the corner stairway. The building was starting to heave in a kind of rhythm, leaning and recoiling, like a tree getting ready to be uprooted.

They got to the stairs and leaned back into the doorway as a group of Negro men came stumbling through the smoke, coughing and wiping the tears out of their eyes. They had Otha Snow tied in a blanket, and they were carrying him down as fast as they could go.

Q.P. saw his face as they carried him past. His skin was burned, smoke was coming off his hair. It smelled like somebody had tried to use too much starter on their barbecue. His eyes were red and bloody; his mouth was open wide, and it looked as if he was smiling. Otha was moaning, delirious. Whatever he was trying to say, it only came out just as little chains of whimpering noises. It sounded like a chant or like he was trying to sing something.

"He was scared, so he set himself on *fire*," one of the men from the choir said as they rushed to carry Otha outside to meet the storm.

FORTY

Chaffee stayed behind him, one hand on the back of his belt as they struggled through the wind toward the patrol car. They walked right beside the wall of the building, feeling their way with their feet through the water. There was another man from the choir holding a flashlight. It was just a blur moving around in front of them. Q.P. put his arm out to feel along the wall. He couldn't see anything until it was too late. Behind them was the orange light of the growing fire. He thought it might be an illusion but some of the water felt hot as it blasted onto him.

He kept going and then put his hands up just in time to stop from running into the side of a panel truck. He could hear Chaffee calling to him, and they felt their way around the truck and kept on walking into the darkness. Then he realized it was Otha's truck, the delivery truck he drove for Houldings Hardware, and it was way too late to look inside.

The water in the parking lot was flowing with the same current as the Cape Fear, a steady slow pull of water up to his calves. The ground was groaning with the force of the river. He slammed his knees into the bumper of the squad car and Chaffee pushed him around to the driver's side and got in ahead of him and then pulled him inside.

"See if it'll start," Chaffee said, panting. In the glow from the other man's flashlight he saw Chaffee's gun pointed at his stomach.

He felt for his keys and found the ignition. They all waited while the engine coughed itself to life.

"Don't flood it!" the man with the light called, and then the

Chevy turned over and Q.P. put his foot down to keep it from stalling.

"Okay." The man shut the door and walked ahead of them with the flashlight. "Just follow the man ahead of you and we'll get ourselves out of here," Chaffee said. He was breathing heavily and sounded tired.

Q.P. felt the flood dragging on the tires as he turned the steering wheel and tried to follow the man's light back toward the high ground.

"Man . . ." Q.P. said. His eyes were locked on the blur of the flashlight ahead of them. He tried turning on the headlights, but it just produced a whiteout and he snapped them off again.

The man stopped them and came back to the door.

"We're at the bottom of the ramp up to the road," he yelled into the window. "I'll just go up here and look at it real good. You won't be able to stop on the way up."

"Okay," he yelled back, and he rolled the window up and he and Chaffee waited. Out the back window they could see the warehouse burning, the winds fanning it into an inferno just as fast as the rain could put it out.

"What are you going to do with him?" he asked Chaffee. Chaffee had reached around and wiped the condensation off the side window so he could see the fire. The gun was just tucked in Chaffee's belt; he could just reach over, take it and arrest the old man, he thought. It would be all over in a second or two. He'd still have to get up to the road, though.

"We'll have a . . . kind of a trial," Chaffee said.

"A trial?"

"It'll be like a hearing. He'll get a chance to testify."

"If he lives."

"Umm-hmm," Chaffee said quietly. He hadn't taken his eyes off the burning building.

"He'd been watching her, I guess," Q.P. said.

"I don't know anything about that poor woman he had in there." Chaffee pulled his gaze away. "But we've been watching him for some time now. He had started to act . . . different. And we started watching him regularly. Then he ran and we started watching *you* . . ." The old man trailed off, eased himself back against the corner of the door.

"We should have guessed, you know? He worked for Houldings, he did his errands for him, drove his truck around for him, did yard work for him," Chaffee said. "Otha worked hard. A good worker. A good *boy*." Chaffee sounded tired.

Otha Snow was reliable, he said. He'd been quiet, well mannered, as diligent a worker as he was a preacher. He had served Houldings for some years at low wages and without any obvious problems, on the sole condition that he have Sundays free for church. Then he'd even come back and work again in the afternoon, bringing ice for Houldings's parties, raking his leaves.

"And then he killed Cora . . ." Q.P. said quietly, and Chaffee nodded and sighed.

"She was his *sister*, his half sister really," Chaffee said. "He had always known her, but all his life he'd been taught that she was just his cousin. His father was gone. They were raised up apart about half the time." Q.P. remembered Nina's grids, the dotted lines not quite connecting Otha into the Snow family tree. A problem with paternity, Nina had said.

"He must have found out."

"Yes, and it was a shock I guess. He knew what she was gettin' up to." Chaffee sighed. "I guess he just couldn't take it."

"Her being Bill Scowen's girl?"

"Yeah, all that kind of thing." Chaffee turned to him. Q.P. could see the orange light flickering over his craggy face.

"I was trying, you know, to put myself in his shoes," Chaffee said. "But I don't know if it's possible or not." The old man sighed again. "I think he thought that he *loved* her. I think he went and killed her on account of he loved her. Because he wasn't supposed to love her. Not love her in the way that he felt about it. He couldn't do that. She was his sister and she was a harlot both."

A *harlot*. That was where it had started, Q.P. thought.

Maybe Otha *had* loved his sister. Maybe he just wanted to do the kinds of things that everybody else was doing with her. But the way he'd come up, all his life that was always wrong. Wrong to even think about.

"All along he was the good one," Chaffee said. "He was tryin' to pay off her debt, see? Makin' up to God for all of her bad deeds."

But no matter how hard Otha had tried, or what he said to her, she kept on going bad. And he kept having to pray more and more often for her soul. And then she'd tease him, act wild around him because she knew how he felt.

"Yeah," said Chaffee, "she'd egg him on. Maybe she wanted him to be bad with her, maybe she wanted him to rescue her from Red Bill. Nobody knows about the personal part of it really, I suppose," he said quietly. Q.P. thought about the pictures of the masked men back in his Case Room. Is that you? he wondered.

"So even if he just thought about it, he was sinning all the time," Q.P. said.

"Yes, that's probably how he felt about it. He was living in sin all the time, in his mind. In his heart. That's right. He was telling a lie to God every time he raised his voice up to heaven."

"When did it all start?"

"I guess around the time when Cora went missing, but looking back, I realize that it had been building up, building up slowly."

"How did you notice?"

"He was . . . It was like he was a different person. He wasn't preaching from his joy or his love or his need to be saved. He'd changed to where there wasn't any love in him. He had got angry. He was becoming a dark angel, consumed with righteous anger, and you know—" Chaffee stopped.

"What?"

"That was what I had always *admired* about him. He was a strong young man. He was a fighter, and he was angry. He was an avenging angel." Chaffee took a deep breath and for a moment seemed to break down. He reached out and braced himself against the dashboard. "That was *my* fault. That was the devil blinding *me*. I thought that Otha was the one who had come to save us . . ."

When Cora had become Scowen's whore, like a seed, Otha's obsessions and his plans started to grow. Somehow he'd found out what she was up to with Allison and Houldings. Maybe he'd been recruited into it himself, Q.P. thought. To have gone that far would have made everything more complicated. Whatever justifications Otha told himself, the logic would have had to get more elaborate, like a spider's web or a work of art, something intricate and magical and inspired from the heavens.

Chaffee had his own version. "Brother William had let all these white men go with her. Otha had always been proud, and so that's what he hated, too. And I tell you," Chaffee said, looking at him, "I admired that part of him, too. I wanted him to go out there and carry the banner. I looked at him and I saw myself in the bad days. Back before I found God. I had wasted so much time that I coveted all the years that he had ahead of him, see?" Chaffee's face was etched with regret.

"But an angel can't just go out and *kill*," Chaffee said, looking at him. "He couldn't kill *all* of the white people. Even if it was the right thing to do, to kill all of them would be . . ."

"Impossible."

"There's a whole ocean of white people, so—"

"So then he kidnapped her?"

"He stole her away. Took her away so that she'd be free of temptation. Took her off so he could keep her from havin' to be degraded, make her safe."

"And then?"

"And then, I think, see, that he thought that he had to punish her."

There was a sudden glow in front of the Chevy, and the man with the flashlight groped his way down the fenders and Q.P. wound down the window. "How's it up there?" Chaffee shouted.

"It's fallin' apart but we can get out," the man said. He was almost laughing. And Q.P. actually did laugh, but he didn't know why.

"Just follow me, I'm gon' run on up ahead. Whatever you do, stay on the right of me, okay, Sheriff?"

"Okay," he said.

"Don't run me over, but don't stall it, now."

"Yeah," Q.P. said, getting a little irritated with the man, as if he'd stall the Chevy on purpose while they were trying to flee a hurricane. He gave the car more gas and eased out the clutch and tried to follow the man's light up the ramp. He was in first gear all the time, but the Chevy slewed from side to side on the crumbling shoulders of the ramp, the wheels spinning, kicking up hunks of old blacktop. He was driving blind, by feel more than anything else, and when the tires finally got some grip, he blew right past the man with the flashlight, the Chevy roaring up to the top of the ramp, scraping through the gate and skidding around out onto River Road.

"Praise God," Chaffee breathed beside him. The old preacher was smiling. "That's a good job of drivin', Sheriff. I guess I'll be getting out here," he said.

"Whoa, just hold on here a second," Q.P. said to him. "Tell me what the hell I'm supposed to do about all this?"

Chaffee's eyes narrowed. "What do you think you have to do?" He held his hand lightly against his belt. Not all that far away from the gun. Looking at him made Q.P. wonder about Chaffee's bad old days before he'd found the true path.

Q.P. looked back at the warehouses. There was an orange glow from the fire, but it was all he could see. "Otha Snow is under *arrest*, I already told you that, right? He's under arrest for all these god-damn murders—" Chaffee stopped him by simply holding up his hand; he shook his head slowly.

"You know that you'll not ever get to him now, don't you, Sheriff? He's my prisoner now."

"Hey, now, look—" he started but Chaffee cut him off.

"It's too late anyway. He's gone." And when Chaffee said that Q.P. knew he could argue with the old man all night long, but that it was true. He'd never be seeing Otha again.

"It is justice that you want, right, Sheriff?"

"Yes . . ."

"All right, then, I can promise you justice. You don't have to worry about that. Render unto Caesar what's Caesar's, and render unto God what belongs to Him, Sheriff. Right now you're free. You don't *have* to do anything at all." The fire was burning brightly down on the flooded bank of the river; Chaffee's face glowed with the orange light. He looked at Q.P. for a long moment; it was as if he was trying to read his mind.

"Do you think you can get back into town by yourself?"

"I guess," Q.P. said, his voice so quiet he could barely hear it over the storm.

"All right." Chaffee pushed the door open. "God bless you, then, Sheriff," he said, and then he turned and vanished into the storm.

Q.P. sat there for a minute, the wind roaring all around him, rocking the Chevy from side to side on its springs. Then, finally, be-cause he was afraid he might pass out, he put the car in gear and be-gan to drive along the center line of River Road until it angled away from the river and became more sheltered. Now he could see, between the gusts, the street ahead of him. He tried calling in, but the radio was just one long blur of crackling static.

So he just idled along into Wilmington, trying to avoid the low places where he was sure the Chevy would be flooded, and thought about it all.

Otha, then, had been the one who'd taken Cora sometime after Allison had dropped her off. Maybe he was sitting outside watching from his truck. Maybe he was waiting inside the house with all the empty liquor bottles. He'd met her, talked her into going with him. Took her off somewhere. That part didn't matter.

But he'd seen that she'd gone back to Scowen again. He knew why and he knew she'd never clean up her act and that meant that she probably enjoyed it.

And so, like Chaffee had said, it meant that he had to punish her.

And so after he tricked her out of the house, he restrained her. Tied her up as best he could.

And then because he was just as hungry for her as all the rest, he raped her. And afterward to make sure that there would be no possibility of her ever sinning again, he strangled her.

That was how he'd cleansed her, how he'd "purified" her.

He did it for her own good, he probably thought. He did it as a sacrifice.

Ahead of him power lines snapped across the pavement like snakes. They slapped against the Chevy's fenders as he drove over them. He came to a place where an oak tree had fallen across the road, flattening a car parked on the other side, and so he backed up Market Street to a corner and began to try to zigzag his way back downtown. Another tangle of trees blocked the road and he backed up again and tried to cut downhill through the streets a different way.

It was a maze now. He wasn't even sure what street he was on until he got to the corner. The street sign was twisting in the wind, but he realized he was up around Twelfth. If he could just follow the ground as it sloped toward the river, he'd eventually find the downtown.

He kept stumbling his way lower into the city.

Otha must have been miserable after he'd sent Cora to a better life, and because he couldn't live with his own self-hatred, he must have had to rationalize it all, to make himself *believe*. Belief that it had all been for some reason, that he had been chosen for some big mission by God. It was no wonder the congregation had felt the change. All of a sudden he was a direct pipeline to God's holy wrath. It must have been electrifying for them to watch him week after week as he metamorphosed into a crusading angel. Q.P. could almost visualize him now. Patrolling Brooklyn in his panel truck, making the deliveries and judging people.

Sitting in judgment. That's what had probably happened to Ruth Micheaux. A much more violent killing. He'd probably rushed through that one. That's why she wasn't in any photographs. It was something that just happened, an afternoon gone wrong. He had snapped. Maybe all she'd done was smile at him, or say something he took the wrong way. And when it was done he bundled her in a remnant from his boss's warehouse.

He might have tried to stop after that. He probably thought that his own temptations were why he was so uniquely qualified to purge the harlots on behalf of God.

So as he refined his hate he looked around and only saw what he wanted to see. Everything was sin, everything was corruption. He couldn't help but see Millie Garnet. If it wasn't Otha in the pictures with her, he'd almost certainly seen her on the streets every day of his life. And if Cora was bad, if *she* deserved to be punished, why not someone like Mildred? How long had it taken him to get up the courage to steal her away? And then he'd dumped her in the yard when he was done.

Like garbage.

And after that, why not the guy who had started it all? Why not Scowen, whom he loathed? And he was miserable now, too. Cora was gone and somehow it was all Scowen's fault.

Scowen. Who was everything he wasn't—strong, daring, a lady's man, the kind of man who had no respect for the law and the commandments. And Scowen had been proud, undefeated and popular. The kind of man people respected. That must have been agonizing for Otha. And so he began dreaming of how he'd bring Scowen down, the real villain, the man who'd corrupted his sister and led her to Allison and Houldings.

And then, probably while he was planning some vengeance against his masters, as he was running errands for Houldings and his buddies, he'd run up against Alice Farmer. Probably when he had delivered supplies to the beach house.

And how could he not notice her?

And Q.P. could see Otha now, see into his mind.

He could see him as he stole the sash cord. See him as he copied his boss's keys. See him afraid, waiting to be caught. See him awake and uncoiling, unable to resist doing it again. See him as he watched Alice Farmer, the white harlot from Nashville, a creature perfectly designed to send a man sliding down to hellfire. Surely she deserved to be redeemed.

So he'd stolen Alice out of Houldings's cottage. Allison only found out about it when Henry went out to the beach and discovered she was missing. Neither man knew what had happened and each probably blamed the other. Then came the panic, the midnight calls, the screeching tires, their lives unraveled . . . By then Otha had taken her back to the studio, the silent, perfect torture chamber.

A large sheet of metal roofing sailed across the hood of the Chevy so quickly that he jerked his hand up to protect his face, much too late. He thought he might have to get out and find some kind of shelter in somebody's house if it got worse. He was going dead slow, winding his way downhill, like a pinball slowly bouncing closer to the bottom of the game.

As far as doing anything about Chaffee making Otha his "prisoner," his hands were tied, Q.P. was thinking. If he actually arrested Chaffee, it would only confirm everything the Klan had been saying: there *had* been a crazed nigger going around killing women, the Sheriff's Department *was* so incompetent they couldn't hold on to a murderer when they'd found him.

Pagett would love it. It would sell thousands of *Morning Star*s to thousands of rednecks who'd all be talking about how they'd known it was a nigger all along. They'd enjoy their revenge and it wouldn't stop with just some motorcade. If Chaffee wasn't lynched himself, Spud Reid and the FBI would throw the book at him for kidnapping, for harboring, and for assaulting an officer. If Otha was dead, they'd even try to pin that on the old man and his choir. The big guy, Matthew, would be easy to recognize and pick up. Tommy Wills would probably enjoy the challenge personally and

Mr. and Mrs. Baker would stay in their cubbyhole. He'd have to sit up there with a shotgun just to protect his prisoners from the P.D.

He'd be fired by Doc Sykes and Burton Pardee would be appointed to office a few months early. About half of Ezzard Carruthers's men would look the other way and the other half would join in. The next building to burn would be Chaffee's church. There would be a massacre. No Negro in Wilmington would be safe if the news got out.

The Chevy had come to another dead end. He tried backing out, but other trees had fallen behind him while he was driving along the street and he was locked there.

He pushed the door open. It felt like it weighed a couple of hundred pounds. He was immediately blown backwards, and he grabbed the rear door handle to steady himself. He pulled himself along the fallen tree until he got to the sidewalk, and then he let the wind carry him up to somebody's front porch, where he banged on the door until he saw candlelight shining through the little windows in the door.

The door blew open but the chain held. An old man was peering out; he held a big flashlight in his hand. Q.P. yelled out who he was and tried to show the man his badge, but it had blown right off his shirt. For a second when the old guy closed the door he thought he was too afraid to let him inside, but then the door whipped itself open and he slipped in and together they pushed against the door until they got it locked.

The old man had plenty of time to get ready for the hurricane, but this was a little more than he'd expected. He shuffled off into the darkness and came back with some towels and persuaded Q.P. that he wasn't going anywhere else that night. The house creaked and shuddered with each gust. It sounded like a combination of a train wreck and a chorus of wild animals outside, an unending cry of rage.

"Son, if in your life y'all ever did somethin' *wrong*," the old man said as he emerged from the dark and handed him a bathrobe, "this, right now, is the time to repent and say you're sorry for it."

"Oh, I'm sorry," Q.P. said as he was starting to peel off his soaking uniform.

"I'm definitely sorry . . ."

FORTY-ONE

Hazel hit the Carolina coast right in time for breakfast. She tracked herself right over Southport at the mouth of the Cape Fear in Brunswick County. And then she headed straight up the river doing a forward speed of about sixty miles an hour.

Waters broke across the dunes that protected the southern beach towns with a flood surge more than eighteen feet above average. Winds at Wrightsville Beach were measured up to a hundred and twenty-five miles per hour and then the anemometer blew away.

The thing about Hazel was that she didn't bounce off the coast, or slow down, or lose any intensity as she went along. She just blazed a trail right into Carolina, blowing away anything that wasn't tied down and drowning anything that couldn't get to high ground.

Thousands of trees were blown down, across power lines, across roads, onto houses. Rains reached record levels all through the state. The wind would blow the trees right out of the ground, roots and all. And right beside that would be another place where the wind had just snapped the trees off at ten or fifteen feet above the ground.

Behind the storm came little tornadoes, skipping from hill to hill, tossing the broken trees around every which way, ripping buildings apart, shredding roofs, lifting cars over on their sides. People thought it was God's judgment, retribution for all their sins and all the sins of their politicians.

They got a full seven inches of rain up in the Piedmont, in

Burlington and High Point. Winds of more than a hundred miles an hour were recorded at the airport at Raleigh-Durham.

Wearing a borrowed slicker, Q.P. was able to leave the old man's house a little after two o'clock. He still had to lean forward against the wind and climb through the maze of fallen trees that had blocked the street. He counted more than twenty-five trees fallen across the street in the dozen blocks he had to walk to get down to the courthouse.

"We wondered where you'd got to," Mary Helen said as soon as he got through the double doors.

"My car's up somewhere on Church Street stuck between two trees," he said. It sounded dumb. Maybe he was still in shock or maybe Otha or Matthew had hurt him worse than he realized.

"Glen lost his house," she said.

"Good Lord." Glen didn't have much to begin with, he thought. Now he'd lost that. "I haven't been home. I don't have anything there anyway . . ." he said. He was babbling, just running off at the mouth.

Mary Helen gave him a long look. "We've got some coffee back there. You want some? You look like you could use it."

The coffee helped, and after he'd dealt with the immediate crises, he walked over to Thalian Hall to see Nina, but she was asleep. Curled up on one of the cots they'd arranged over behind the tall rack where they stored the canvas flats they used for scenery. They had given out all of their food that morning and were telling people they'd have to wait for more to come.

Nobody knew very much. Telephones were out and there was no radio or television because most of the towers had blown down and nobody had any electricity to pick up what signals might be floating around out there. Hal Lutz was exhausted. He stared into the distance, and sometimes he would just fade out while he was talking. He still wore his Shriners fez and was chain-smoking the whole time.

Hazel destroyed the town of Long Beach. The storm surge had blown all but five of the beach houses back across the street and into the sound behind the island. There was nothing afterward; the road was gone and so was the bridge. Southport, where Woody Forbes had his office over in Brunswick County, was completely flooded. Shrimp boats had been blown right up into the middle of Main Street.

Up and down the beaches Q.P. and his men worked nonstop to catch looters. They'd brought out the dogs to look for bodies, but the only corpses they'd found so far were animals. Dogs and cats that had gotten caught out in the storm and drowned. It looked as though most people had the good sense to evacuate when they heard the big storm was on its way.

The looters were working with boats because the roads were blocked and it was too hard to make a clean getaway using a car. In the early hours of the second morning Q.P. and Ellis Strickland were in a boat that the Naval Reserve was letting them use, and they saw the whole thing. They hid around behind the remains of a fishing pier and waited while the men beached their boat in front of one of the evacuated houses at Wrightsville. They saw them look around, saw them go in, saw them come out, and finally saw them begin packing a motorboat full of silverware.

Q.P. got out and went around the dunes to the front of the house, and Ellis just waited until he saw the men come running toward their boat and then he motored out and pointed his shotgun their direction.

And when they had locked them up on the Fifth Floor and checked their identification, they turned out to be the Exalted Cyclops, the Klaliff, and two Klexters of the East Carolina region. One of the Klexters had been arrested over on Rankin Street after the shoot-out. As it happened, they weren't friends of Spud Reid's, and none of them was a cop, so he agreed to throw the book at them just as an example. And so if there were any more plans for motorcades, cross burnings, or lynchings to protest the *Brown* decision, they were delayed indefinitely by the demise of the local branch of the Invisible Empire.

A week later Jimmy Satterwhite got a picture in *Life* magazine just like he'd always hoped. It was of George Foster, exhausted after twenty-four hours of emergency work. His prowl car was in water up to its hubcaps, and he was sitting on the seat with his pants rolled up and his bare feet out in the water, leaning on the open window of the car, a big New Hanover County Sheriff's Department shield painted on the door just below his chin. "We'll have to frame *that*," Mary Helen said to him proudly.

But Hazel didn't stop in North Carolina. She sank ships moored in the James River and killed thirteen people in Virginia. Baltimore was flooded with a tide as deep as six feet in places. Not quite high enough to get Q.P.'s aunt Yvonne up on the second floor. Winds on the Delaware coast reached a hundred miles an hour, and they weren't ready for the big storm up there. In Pennsylvania she killed twenty-six people and then in New York another twenty.

Hazel picked up a lot of water crossing Lake Ontario. When seven inches of rain fell on the city of Toronto, the Humber River flooded its banks. People were trapped in their cars, washed away in flash floods throughout the city. More than seventy Canadians died before Hazel turned east and got lost one night on her way to Iceland.

Besides the obvious, it seemed that in New Hanover County the storm blew a lot of other things away. At least for the moment a lot of problems had just seemed to vanish in the wind, get knocked over with the trees, or be washed clean by the rains. Maybe it was a message from above. If it was, North Carolina heard it loud and clear.

"There might be something in all that," Keating said. "Hell, it never hurts to play it safe, is what my daddy always told me . . ."

Q.P. and Keating drove out to the site of the Vestry-Buell mill and stood up on the bluff and shook their heads at the destruction. The river had claimed back the burned building, and part of a second warehouse had collapsed; now it was a pile of charred bricks cascading into the Cape Fear. There was a fresh new bluff where the fire had raged until the pilings had collapsed. The dirt was all eaten away from under the asphalt, and the site would have to be condemned before kids came down there and got hurt. The old railroad tracks were broken off and hung out over the abyss.

"Well, we can't recover anything from that." Keating shrugged. The Cape Fear had fallen by nearly twenty-five feet. Keating leaned out over the cracking asphalt as far as he dared and then walked back to where it was safe.

"She's gone, I guess." Keating gave him a little pat on the back.

"Yeah, I guess," he said. Case closed.

"Well, you were goddamn lucky, Kewpie," Keating said quietly.

"Yeah."

"And you say whoever this man was, he died in the fire while you were chasing him?" Keating sounded as if he didn't believe it.

"Yeah . . ."

"You didn't see him enough so you could identify him or—"

"It was just a shadow, that's all."

"A shadow?" Keating said to him in disbelief.

"Yeah."

"And he just *fell into the fire?*"

"Yeah. The planks were weak there, I guess. You know, it was an old building. He just . . . fell through."

"You're *sure,* Kewpie?" Keating was looking at him doubtfully.

"Umm-hmm," Q.P. said. "Saw it with my own eyes."

"Well, damn . . ." Keating said. "Be nice to wrap up a big case like that." Keating shook his head and walked over to where the asphalt was cracked and he could look back under the scorched pilings. "But, honest, Kewpie, you're doing the right thing to keep it quiet, I think." Gulls were swooping in on them, trying to scare them away from the brown water that swirled around the wreckage. ". . . something like this could . . . *ignite* a race war for sure down here, I expect."

And Q.P. nodded, let his gaze widen out to follow the Cape Fear back up toward the city. "Yep," he said.

"Bunch of innocent people get hurt . . ."

"That's what I was thinking, too," he said.

"Yeah . . . never get anything out of there," Keating said and turned and started walking back to their car.

FORTY-TWO

He woke up early on the morning of the big day. He hadn't slept well, tormented with dreams of Korea and ice in the pathways so slippery that he couldn't find his feet in the dreams. He was always sliding down. Into the stinking backstreets in Baltimore, into the fire with Otha Snow and the trussed-up corpse of a redhead from Tennessee.

So when he woke up he was sore and stiff and kind of stupid, and every now and then his mind would wander.

The Big Day, he thought as he stared out into the hot morning light that was frying what was left of Milton's front yard. Big Day.

After lunch Q.P. walked up to the high school, shook a few hands going in and going out. A lot of people slapped him on the back who he knew wouldn't be voting for him.

Went in and checked himself off the list and waited in line there for a few minutes like everyone else. Every time he got a second for himself, somebody else was smiling or nodding to him. Maybe a lot of them really were friends. It was hard to tell. Some people were looking at him with bitter faces, and he knew the talk was all about his shortcomings.

Pretty dismal record; the unsolved killing of Millie Garnet, the mob violence over at the Terry house, the rumors that were starting to swirl around town about Henry Houldings and Ricky Allison.

Somehow it was all his fault. Racial friction in town was the result of police incompetence, people were saying. Okay, great. He agreed. But they never seemed to bring Carruthers's boys into the discussion. A million dollars could fall off the boxcars under the noses of the ACL cops, but now it had become something the sheriff's department was doing wrong.

So let them do better, he was thinking.

He went in and checked out the machine. It was the first time he'd used one like it. To make any choice other than an incumbent Democrat required a few moments to flick toggles either up or down. He stood there figuring it out, marveling at his name in print:

Sheriff
Waldeau, Quentin Payne
Pardee, Warburton Royce II

"Warburton" or "Quentin"; vote for the guy with the stupidest name, he thought. Then he looked at the Roman numeral stuck behind Pardee's name and realized that it must have been dogging him all his life. He sure never used it in public.

He flicked a couple of toggles, voted for himself, and pushed his way through the curtain and started saying hello to people again.

By the time Nina had parked down past the Democratic Party's headquarters on Chestnut Street, the polls were closing and the long night's party was just starting. There was a warm wind blowing up and it felt like it would be bad weather coming for another couple of days. The wind kicked her hair back and lashed it into her face, and she ran along with one hand shielding her eyes.

The street in front of the Cape Fear Hall had been cleared for the huge bus that was Alton Lennox's campaign vehicle. It was streamlined so that the back tapered almost to a point, designed to look like it could swim quickly through water. It had a nickname, "Big Boy," and was garishly painted with LENNOX FOR SENATE! banners down each side. LENNOX FOR SENATE! had been painted across the prow of the bus in backwards script for the benefit of any motorists who they might come up behind as they blew along the highways of North Carolina.

When she made the steps, she could hear Lennox speaking to the faithful assembled inside. Every phrase he uttered brought cheering. She stood behind burly men who clogged the entrance. Standing on tiptoes she could just see Lennox's face smiling at the volunteers.

". . . not gonna let them take away our God-given rights. We're not gonna knuckle under just because of a bunch of misguided legal gobbledygook generated by the Supreme Court—" The rest of what he said was smothered in applause and laughter.

She stood there at the edge of the seats and looked around and decided to just wait until she saw him, just to relax and let her mind go and observe for a while.

He had told her all about the mill and the fire and Alice Farmer. It left her feeling drained and curiously numb. Like she'd never be able to recover because deep down she was afraid it was all going to come back again.

Was that the cost of loving a cop?

That's what had been bothering her from the start, and she'd started to realize how much it scared her. Could she do it?

And because she had gotten so afraid, she was making herself numb again, she thought. Part of it was accumulated tension and fatigue. Like her brain was floating off somewhere, off in some kind of a dream without any story to it. On her way toward a nervous breakdown probably.

She hated elections. What they did to her, how they changed her from a scientist into a Joan of Arc. How they made her care. And how it hurt when she saw the corruption of the process, the heroes with feet of clay, the bosses and their crimes, so that now it just looked like the worst coming out in people.

Maybe it was just fear, she thought as she looked around at the mob of Democrats. Maybe this is what happens when I get scared? Terror had immobilized her, she thought. They've won. I'm no good anymore.

Otha, if he was still alive, being tried by his own people? Was that going to change anything? What about Houldings and Allison; what about the men who made it possible for Red Bill Scowen to sell the woman he said he loved? What about them? Was it all just going to slip away?

And here we were in the cesspool of democracy, watching a good man like Q.P. Waldeau crash and burn.

She took a deep breath to gain back her self-control and found herself beginning to study the women. Watch them flirt and defend and control. Watch them aspire, and fail, and struggle, and make fools of themselves.

At night Q.P. kept telling her it was over. But it wasn't.

Soon another woman was going to end up dead. Soon another woman was going to disappear. Murdered, strangled, bludgeoned to death, poisoned. Her smiles, her hair, the way she wore her clothes—all that would be erased. Gone. One chart ended. One more life torn up and thrown away.

It wasn't over.

Q.P. was expected to make a speech of some kind, either a victory speech or a concession speech. It would be, he thought, his first speech of the entire campaign unless you counted the one he tried out on Mary Helen and some of the deputies in the basement of the courthouse.

He had written the two speeches on a large orange five-by-seven file card and folded it into his wallet. He watched the returns coming in. There were two scoreboards, one for the county and one for the state.

Lennox was losing and everybody knew it. The great man himself had been hiding in "Big Boy" out front. Southern Bell had wired him up into the telephone line there on Chestnut Street so he could jaw with the other candidates around the state while they waited for the inevitable.

But Q.P. was losing, too. He'd thought about it honestly and tried to prepare himself a little. He figured he had gotten over any disappointment he had about the election and come to think that mostly it didn't matter. At some point Pardee had come over and put a huge arm around him and they had both smiled like they meant it. He could tell that Pardee was already a little nervous. He had heard the story about the bullet through the collar and his eyes kept traveling up to the fresh square bandage that Nina had taped over his stitches. Now Pardee was beginning to realize what he'd signed up for.

Pardee had won the precinct that included Forest Hills by a huge percentage. Cammie must have gotten out all of their friends. The number was 159 to 14 in Pardee's favor. The one precinct that was going his way was the Third, the region that spread out on the north of town and that included most of the factory houses at the edge of the old "Brooklyn" neighborhood. He beat Pardee there, but everyone knew there were a lot more votes there. There was no big reason for Q.P. to get any more of that vote than any other white man. If they hadn't been scared away by the Klan, most of the black voters didn't even bother to go to the Democratic primary.

The polls were all in, most of the results from around the state had been posted, but Lennox still hadn't made it out of his bus. Q.P. looked around and finally saw Nina, sitting alone at the head of the balcony. She had a shawl wrapped around her shoulders, and her hair was blown wild from the wind outside.

"Okay, Kewpie, you're just postponin' the inevitable," said Winky Peters at his side.

He mounted the steps and headed for the microphone. The lights on the stage brightened. Jimmy Satterwhite fired off a flash-bulb at his feet. There was the sound of applause. Not cheering, just polite applause, he thought. He waited for it and unfolded his or-ange card.

"I'd like to congratulate Burton on being chosen to be the next candidate for sheriff," he said, and there was a cheer. Now they were happy, he thought.

"I'd like him to know that in the staff of the sheriff's department and in the deputies, he's going to be working with some of the best people in police work . . ." There was more applause, respectful. Most of them never noticed the deputies. He saw Nokes at the back of the room with Kay, and they both smiled and clapped their hands.

"I've been very happy to be your 'Acting Sheriff,'" he said sponta-neously. "I've been very happy to try and do the best that I could—" He realized that the room had started to go quiet and that he was starting to choke up all at the same time. Everything was turning uncomfortable.

"When you are a cop . . ." he said and looked down, trying to read something he'd written on the card, trying to pick up his place.

"—then you see the best in people, and you see the worst . . ." The lights were blinding him and it was enormously painful to look out at the crowd. He looked up to where he'd seen Nina sitting but it was just a glare. In the silence someone let out a long, high whistle. It was like a screaming firecracker. There was a little smattering of applause somewhere, some friends letting him know that it was all right if he simply wanted to stagger offstage screaming.

"When you just . . . ah . . . see the *worst,* when you just see that all the time—" He shook his head and there was some laughter. "When that happens, you get a little . . ." He had come to the place where he didn't know what he was going to say. He thought for a moment he was going to do something embarrassing; break down and actually start crying.

"I just . . . I just want everyone to help the next sheriff see nothing but the *best . . .*" And there was sudden applause now. It pounded him like a great wave of relief. He supposed that his speech had come to an end. He stood there for a second watching the Democrats applaud. There was movement out of the corner of his eye, and he saw Pardee walking across the stage toward him with his arm outstretched.

Q.P. put his hand out and it was engulfed. Pardee was squeezing his bicep with his other hand and smiling broadly. He had a great toothy grin, like Teddy Roosevelt, or a big beaver, Q.P. thought. Pardee was screaming something at him about coming by and getting a few lessons. He slipped past to the microphone. "Let's hear it for Kewpie, folks!" Pardee called out, and there was applause again as he made it to the steps. Somewhere they were playing "For He's a Jolly Good Fellow," and he looked up to see Pardee clapping to the beat and leading the tribute.

He smiled; he nodded. He shook hands and people slapped him on the back. He would be out of work in four months, and right then he found that he really didn't mind.

He stepped out into the night. The wind had come up and the men were standing around passing bottles in paper bags around. Lamont Sanders motioned him over and he shook everyone's hand

again and shared a nip of bourbon and turned to discover Nina
walking around from the front of the hall.

There was something in her look. She looked as if she was sunburned and her hair was blown out around her head in a great
black wreath. She was wearing her sundress and sandals. He
shrugged and she came up to him and held him close and kissed
him and looked into his eyes.

"Do you really care about all this?" she said.

He shrugged again. He didn't know, not really.

"Because if you do . . ."

"No. Not really. I don't know. It's a terrible job. Burton's welcome
to it, far as I'm concerned."

"Right."

"Really."

"So you don't care? About law and order. Or justice . . . or . . ."

"Catching the crooks?"

"Or catching the crooks. Or the whole city exploding, you don't
care about any of that?"

"Well, yeah I care about *that* . . . I don't want anybody to get
hurt." He looked around at all the Democrats celebrating. "I wanted
to do a good job."

"You did a good job. You're doing a good job."

"Yeah." He shrugged again.

"You could always run as a Republican," she said, and he laughed.
She looked around at the volunteers standing around drinking,
their backs turned to the wind. "This is . . . some gigantic parody,"
she said quietly, shaking her head. Way off in the distance there
were sirens, some trouble across town, she supposed.

"Do you want to maybe get out of here soon, because I'm . . ." he
started. She turned to look at him.

"Yeah, I do."

"Okay." And they started off down the sidewalk together. They
had to pass Pardee, who was standing on the steps talking to a couple of his supporters about the Supreme Court and how the problem was the new Chief Justice, the ex-governor of California, Earl
Warren. "Now, what *he's* doin' is *he's* taking a completely different
approach to the *law*," Pardee was saying. "He's not just interpreting
it anymore—"

"He's *writing* it," one of the men said.

"That's *right*," said Pardee.

"He sure is," said the other man.

"And he wasn't elected to do that," said Pardee, looking up and managing to wave at Q.P. as he talked. *It's over! The election's over!* Nina felt like screaming into Pardee's sweating face.

"You stick with me, kid," she said to Q.P., "and I'll take you away from all this," and she held him tightly against the gusts as they crossed to Milton's car parked up the block.

No one seemed to be paying any attention to the sirens.

She held him to her with all the strength in her soul, dug her fingers into his shoulders, and groaned in exquisite happiness that she had found him. And he made love to her like a man who had been drowning and was breaking the surface to gulp down all the oxygen in the world. A man delivered back to the living, reprieved at the last moment. I'll be your balm, she was thinking, I'll pour myself all over you and make you back the way you were.

Afterward they sat in the soapy tub, a kerosene lantern, kept for the hurricanes, lighting them while they drank bourbon and railed against Pardee and the others. She got broad and angry, and they laughed and prodded each other with their toes.

And she tried to straddle him right there in the tub, but only succeeded in wedging herself in on top of him and they laughed. And very gently she touched his stitches, bent over to kiss him there.

"You're healing nicely," she told him.

And then again when she toweled him off they luxuriated in the tastes of themselves, and she was so happy. So deliriously happy with this man in her arms. It was beyond belief. It was a phenomenon. Something like an accidental collision in the universe. The discovery of something so new and small that it was invisible, so elementary it was indestructible. Atomic love, she thought.

"And I'm *glad* you lost!" she had said to him, slurring her words across the soapy tub. "I'm *glad* . . . *I'm GLAD!*" she was yelling out. Wake every damn body up.

And he shrugged and said that, yes, he thought that he was, too.

Making love in the ashes was what it was like. The two last people on earth. Yes! she thought. Yes, she'd have their babies; she'd shoot them out like fireworks, little Ninas and Quentins ratting around and using their amazing intelligence to repair everything that was wrong with the world. She writhed against him, tucked a knee around his, pushed her face into the curve of his shoulder.

Really, she thought, remembering Pardee standing on the steps, all they had was each other. There was no trust, no alliances in Wilmington anymore. There was no loyalty, no matter how many oaths you signed. Nothing was permanent. And all those old certainties about getting out and leaving the South came crowding in on her and she curled around him more tightly, as tightly as a snail's shell.

And when he had fallen asleep and she was there curled around him, sheltering him from any mosquitoes that had solved the holey screens, guarding him from the blasts of the storm, she thought about the dead women, Cora and Ruth. Alice Farmer and Millie Garnet. And Red Bill, too.

Yes, don't forget Red Bill, too.

Here he was, sleeping in her embrace—her *cop*. Her white knight. Her lover. Her husband? Her atomic superman.

She got out and grabbed another blanket and covered them both over and then slipped back into the warmth beside him again, quiet as a prayer.

FORTY-THREE

It so happened that when Milton died, he went quietly. In his sleep. Mrs. Stasik had said it was coming and she and Nina had waited there together. As it turned out Nina was the one who found him. He had talked for a little while, little whispers nobody could interpret, then his breathing kept on; so lightly that she would watch and think that he was gone, put out her hand to hold his wrist. Then he'd take another little breath. A little sigh. A teaspoon of air to keep life going on inside of him. It had gone on like that all night. They had started to watch him in shifts. To be there when it came. In case he came back and wanted to say something. In case he wanted someone to hold his hand.

And then, finally when death did come, she was denied by him.

She'd gone out to make tea; it only took a moment to put the kettle on while the older woman catnapped in the rocking chair, and then, while the water boiled, she came back to lean against the doorjamb and watch him. And it was a few minutes more before she realized he'd stopped breathing. He'd managed to go in private, with his eyes half open, a little smile on his face. Slipping away while her back was turned. Gone so neatly, with no quarreling and no dramatics. Invisibly. Maybe he was determined to save her the trouble. Show her that he'd changed into more of a gentleman in death than he ever was in life. She heard a little sound and when she turned Mrs. Stasik was awake, looking up at her. And then the older woman just nodded, because she already knew somehow.

And what Nina thought so surprising was how little either of them cried.

The new Democratic machine took over from the old Democratic machine, thus ensuring that nothing much would change, unless something went terribly wrong. There was another fish fry at Democratic headquarters, which Q.P. and Nina walked into and right back out of. The next morning Pardee came down to the basement. He was a little hung over, giddy from political success, and he laughed his way through a tour of the basement with Mary Helen as his guide, shaking everyone's hand and letting them know that he'd need their help if the department was going to "turn itself around" and promising not to meddle as long as everyone did their job.

Q.P. and Pardee sat together in the office for a while and basically just bullshitted. Pardee alternated between loud jokes and nervous glances around at the file cabinets that he feared were overflowing with violent unsolved crimes. He'd tagged along and watched while Q.P. and the deputies put in three straight twenty-four-hour days pulling dead cattle out of culverts and arresting the looters crawling out of the blasted beach houses. Suddenly being county sheriff didn't look quite as romantic as he and Cammie had planned.

And while Q.P. could have told the sheriff-elect a lot of valuable things, instead he just congratulated him on his victory, assured him there were no hard feelings, pasted on a smile, and decided to give him as little help as possible. Let him see how easy it is to push the rock up the mountain, as Nina had said just that morning when he brought her coffee in bed.

The two of them ran into Reverend Chaffee on Front Street one sunny December morning. It was the first time he had seen the reverend since the night in the mill. News about the local Klan leaders going on trial for looting had made the *Morning Star,* and Q.P.'s reputation was at an all-time high, at least in Brooklyn. Chaffee was smiling and Q.P. thought it was a good sight to see.

He put out a large warm hand that surrounded Q.P.'s, then with his other shook it over and over again as he thanked Q.P. for everything he'd done during his term.

"—and if we'd known what a gentleman you were, Sheriff, we would have made sure you got the black vote in the primary. Always good to have a friend in law enforcement." And Nina said she agreed with that and they stood there on Front Street laughing.

"Things have settled down now for a while," Chaffee said, looking straight into Q.P.'s eyes, and all three of them knew what he was talking about. For a second they all measured each other and then Chaffee turned and looked around at the street. "As for everything else, we'll have to wait and see what this new bunch of Democrats decides to do, I guess."

"These are *dixiecrats,*" Nina said. "And you know they'll just drag their feet as long as they can. You know that," she said to the old man.

"Yes, I don't doubt it and I reckon they will, but the tide is flowin' our way, Miss Nina. That ought to be apparent to everyone now. You know it, and way down deep they do, too." And looking at Chaffee's eyes, so calm and so deep, Q.P. decided that he was probably right in the long run.

"So we're in for a better world?" Q.P. said.

"A *much* better world eventually," the reverend laughed. Chaffee asked what Q.P. was going to do now, and Q.P. tucked his hands in his back pockets and turned to look at the citizenry of Wilmington going about their business on Front Street. "I guess I'm gonna go back to school." He smiled at Chaffee.

"Gon' do your homework and try to get it right this time?" Chaffee asked, smiling.

"Yeah, Reverend, that's right. Get some more training. Soon as I serve out Sheriff Franklin's term, then in January head up to Chapel Hill."

"Or maybe up North to school in Chicago, if we can get him in." Nina was giggling. He shook his head it was such a crazy idea still.

"My, my," Chaffee said with his eyebrows raised.

"Yeah, but that's a long shot. Take a few courses at UNC, criminology and accounting. Get in the SBI if they'll have me. Goin' after all the white-collar criminals."

"Well, there's no shortage of them." Chaffee laughed and tapped the pavement with his toe. It was the happiest either of them had ever seen him.

"And I've got a job maybe," Nina said with a wide grin.

"My, my, *my!*" said Chaffee

"If we go to Chapel Hill, she's going to work at the library—"

"At the Southern Historical Collections," Nina said. "I got an assistanceship as an archivist."

"Well, you folks have got it *all* figured out. You folks are doing just *fine,*" Chaffee said.

"And what else . . ." She nudged Q.P.

"Oh, yeah." And she thought later that it was wonderful; surprising and charming how bashful he was about it. He had actually started to blush.

"We're going to be getting married," he said quietly.

"Ho! Ho!" the very Reverend Gaylord Chaffee laughed, and then gave them his blessing. "Well, if y'all ever have need of a good preacher, Miss Nina, you know where to find one. And I'll be sure to give a special rate for our friends in law enforcement."

And Chaffee congratulated them once again, gave Nina's hand a squeeze, and they parted.

And she and Q.P. strolled home, heading back to her place via Front Street, walking along beneath all the Christmas decorations that rustled in the breeze above them. Banners of shining foil and sparkling coils of glitter. Promises of snow and candy canes; of unending bags of toys and eternal Peace on Earth, that the merchants were already putting up so early that year.

And much later, when she thought about all of it, it seemed to her that everything had occurred like a fairy tale, a fable of how they'd had to go through the danger and the fear in order to find what they needed. How the old had to pass clean away so that the new could be revealed into its season; of how her life had come round so that she'd met and fallen in love with "Acting Sheriff" Q. P. Waldeau. A special man, a very special man indeed, that she had decided to let marry her.

And how, out of darkness and in the midst of some truly horrible events, the two of them had joined themselves, and helped the world put itself right again.

At least for some little time.

And it was the story of her return. From up North, where she'd fled, only to be pulled back to her home in the South. Seeking, and then finding, a place where she could make herself anew.

FORTY-FOUR

They came for him in the morning.

Perhaps they were going to take him to church, he thought. Or perhaps they were only going to move him again.

He did not know how many days had passed since the fire. Everything was all blown together, mixed up. Blended like cutouts on the floor, like newspapers pasted up on the walls to keep out the drafts. All twisted and turned around like a vision. He would see faces of friends above him, hear the concern in their voices.

Then he would move or they would move him and the fire would begin again. Testing him.

Angels came to anoint his wounds and he was better. In the coolness of the garden there was music and he thought he could hear, somewhere lost in the distance, the voice of God in quiet prayer.

To enter into the kingdom of heaven he had to answer questions from the angels, and they examined his life in detail, making him review everything. They were the voices of people from his past, the voices of friends and family, and they wanted to know why he'd done the things he did.

How could he explain?

Above him the angels circled, waiting for him to form his answers. He had sinned. He knew that. He admitted that he had sinned. No one, he said, was without sin. Everyone had at least thought about committing a sin. No one had the right to cast the first stone.

And knowing that he had sinned, knowing that the devil had found a comfortable place in his heart, he wept. And when he cried the tears hurt his cheeks, and the angels would leave him, still burning and frightened, still trying to force the words from his cracked lips. Still trying to explain even after they had gone away.

Maybe this was hell, he thought.

And then he was overtaken by nightmarish visions of shame. He saw the devils all around him, laughing triumphantly. Heard their groans of ecstasy as they watched another pure soul fall into corruption.

And then, when he was in the darkness, when he had abandoned all hope, when he was burned into purest carbon, reduced to something lower than dust, they came for him.

He could not believe it, at first, so far into nothingness he had fallen. But undeniably they had come for him. And he knew it was the morning that he would finally be set free. He could tell by the sounds the angels made, by the seriousness of their conversation. By the resolute way they lifted him up.

Miraculously he could see. Only a blur, like looking through the bottom of a Coke bottle, rings of confusion all around except for one clear spot right in the center. And it was in that still clear spot that he saw the people from his past life.

He had never felt so much love, he thought.

They put him in a chariot and three of the archangels went with him. They had faces that he knew. The kind faces of friends from his life before. And they opened the windows and he felt the cool rush of healing air across his burned face.

And wondrously, as in a miracle, he could walk. And the archangels were beside him, and he heard singing as they moved in rapture toward the garden, not so far ahead that he couldn't see it, glowing there where the road gave way onto a field.

And it was so overwhelming that he had to kneel and pray for his deliverance. And although his knees were burning, although it felt as if the skin on his legs was about to burst, he fell to the earth and turned his nearly blind eye to the sky.

An angel with the face of Reverend Gaylord was there and he extended his hand down to bless him. He was saying that the Lord God gave and that the Lord thy God took away and that the name of the Lord was forever blessed, and then the Reverend put his face close to him and whispered in his ear: "Are you ready, now, Otha?" he asked.

And Otha said yes he was.

And then, gliding as softly as smoke, the reverend moved around behind him, and he used that moment that had been given to him to raise his head.

And trembling, weak, and frightened, once again he tried. He tried until the tears burned along his cheeks, tried with all of his might and his last bit of strength.

Tried as hard as he could to remember how to pray.

SOURCES AND ACKNOWLEDGMENTS

This book would not have been possible without the contributions of several persons:

First, a big thank-you to Helen Heller, who suggested and helped me mold this book. Also to Charles Spicer at St. Martin's Press for his very effective editorial suggestions. In Vancouver both Pearl L. A. Hunt and Suzie Payne gave valuable feedback in the early stages. I also owe a particular debt to Mrs. Julia Davidson, an old friend, for her story of the monstrosity collection she visited on the first date with her future husband.

In Wilmington everyone was most helpful, particularly:

Ms. Beverly Tetterton and the staff of the North Carolina Room of the New Hanover County Public Library, who provided me with much information on New Hanover County during the fifties.

The staff of Thalian Hall for allowing me access to their archives, and to tour both the theater and, on the top floor, the site of the old Wilmington Public Library, now the chambers of the Wilmington City Council.

The staff of the Atlantic Coast Line Railroad Museum, particularly Mr. John Birmingham.

The City of Wilmington Tourist Information staff and Mr. Richard Williams, and the staff of the Cape Fear Museum.

Ms. Judy Thompson of the New Hanover County Sheriff's Department for her unpublished history of the department; the Wilmington City Police Department, who allowed me to dig around in their basement for old photographs of the department and its members.

Retired agent Bill Melvin for his reminiscences of the North Carolina SBI in the fifties.

Ms. Brenda Tucker, Clerk of Court, New Hanover County Superior Court, for allowing me access to the Fifth Floor Annex, now a very secure depository for vintage city files.

The park staff at Fort Fisher and at the radar station down by Davis Beach Road.

As far as truth goes, the Klan motorcade episode was inspired by events that took place in Monroe, North Carolina, in 1957. An invaluable portrait of Wilmington during the civil rights era is contained in the hard-to-find *Every Man Should Try* by Dr. Hubert A. Eaton (Wilmington, North Carolina: Bonaparte Press, 1984). The best history of Hurricane Hazel can be found in Jay Barnes's excellent *North Carolina's Hurricane History* (Chapel Hill: University of North Carolina Press, 1995).

None of those mentioned above should be held responsible for any errors or opinions expressed in *The Woman in the Yard*. *The Woman in the Yard* is a work of fiction; all of its characters, locations, and events are imaginary constructs. While there is a real *Morning Star*, readers should be careful not to confuse it or its editorial policies with my wholly fictional creation.